THE ONIS CHRONICLES

THE DRAGONS

From the Series:
REIGN OF THE ANCIENTS
PART 2

By: R.E. DAVIES

THE ONIS CHRONICLES

R.E. DAVIES

REIGN OF THE ANCIENTS:

Part 1: The Prophecy
Part 2: The Dragons
Part 3: The Rising

A NEW ERA:

Veiled In Grace
Raised In Ruins

TABLE OF CONTENTS

This book is once again dedicated to my supportive family, and also, to all of those who have encouraged me along the way. Your love and belief in me keep me moving forward on this incredible journey!

"Believe in yourself and all that you are. Know that there is something inside you that is greater than any obstacle."
~ Christian Larson

NOTE TO READER

I am so excited to have you continuing this journey with me!

Eight illustrations have been added to each book, but if you missed any, you can find them (and others) on my website listed below, under the gallery tab. The newest FULL-COLOR Illustrations can also be found there.

I'd love for you to connect with me, R.E. Davies (@REDaviesAuthor), on Facebook, or you can sign up to my Readers List via my website for news about giveaways, upcoming books, links to songs, maps, and other great information! Be sure to check your inbox and spam folder for your confirmation email. You will not be subscribed until you confirm your email address.

As a new author, I humbly request that you remember to leave a review or rating for the "Reign of the Ancients" novels in order to help others discover Onis for themselves. Your feedback is very important to me and greatly appreciated.

Enjoy!
RE Davies
www.redaviesauthor.com

PROLOGUE

DIVIDED

atching in horror as the young elf, the Omi Méa, propelled out past the ledge of the mountaintop into the empty sky beyond, Turathyl's jaw dropped low in disbelief. *How can this be happening?!* she questioned the gods above. But it *was* happening, and fast.

Struggling, the great Silver Dragon lifted her substantial mass, nearly at the end of her capacity of what her body could endure, but she managed to get to her feet. She fought her body and the stones underneath her, slick from the rain which had ceased the moment Aeris struck the elf with her tail. Turathyl's torn flesh and ripped wings spilled deep-blue blood, dripping all around her, as she forced her body to move against all of its inclinations. Although staggering, she made her way as quickly as physically possible toward the ledge, prepared to dive over the side, although unsure of whether she would even be able to fly in her condition.

'*Laila, I am coming!*' the great Silver Dragon attempted to mind-send to the falling elf, but she could not break through to her mind, sensing that it was shutting down.

Still damp from the storm, the dragon's beautiful silver scales glistened along with her oozing blood as she hobbled toward the edge, partially dragging her white armored abdomen, scraping it against the mountain rock beneath. The quills along her spine flared aggressively, and her white wing membranes flapped in the wind, displaying numerous slashes showing through to the other side.

'*What are you doing?!*' blared the monarch Silver into her mind.

Aeris stomped toward Turathyl, snarling and growling threateningly, the mountaintop stone rumbling with each angry step. But, by the time the old Silver monarch had realized what Turathyl was doing, she could not achieve enough haste to stop her.

'*Don't you dare!*' the monarch roared.

Turathyl didn't care and didn't listen to the threats of her leader. Instead, she leaped over the edge, summoning what will she had left. The traitorous Silver called upon the air spirit to assist in her descent toward the elf girl falling from the lofty height of the mountain.

'*You do this, and you can never come back!*' Aeris bellowed after her.

Turathyl shut the monarch from her mind, blocking any further communication or threats. After this, she had no intention of coming back. She could not fathom remaining loyal to a monarch so full of hate that she would refuse to listen to reason and would disobey the gods' will of the prophecy, denying evidence proving Lailalanthelus Dula'Quoy was the Omi Méa sent to Onis to end the war.

Fighting through the pain surging through her body, Turathyl dove, pulling her wings tight against her sides, the wind whipping wildly past her, and descended toward the elf plummeting to the ground. Using what meager strength she could muster, she pulled at the winds below the elf girl, utilizing her connection to the air spirit. She could sense it rushing around the Omi Méa, trying to slow her fall, but unfortunately, her efforts weren't enough in her weakened state. If she didn't get to her now, the girl would not survive the impact.

'Laila! I am here!' Turathyl called out to the young elf, but there was still no response, and she could not penetrate the girl's mind at all.

The great dragon sensed that Laila was now unconscious, but that a faint shimmer of life remained. The ground was rapidly approaching them both as the Silver finally neared her. Reaching out with her talons, the dragon snatched the elf damsel up safely within her paw. *'I have you. I am here.'*

Turathyl spread her wings swiftly before hitting the rocky ground beneath, and the wind caught on her just in time. She took on altitude back up into the safety of the open skies, ignoring the ripping pain shooting throughout her body. There was no time or allowance for her own ailments. All that mattered was the girl.

As she was about to head away from the mountains, she faintly heard yelling and screaming from high on the mountainside and realized that the other two-leggeds were still being held captive there.

'Dailan! Coryln!' she called out to the dragons guarding Laila's friends.

'We are with you, Elder. What do you need?' Dailan responded subserviently.

Turathyl thanked the gods. She had chosen Dailan and Coryln to guard the elf's companions because she did not sense the blinding hatred in them toward the other races as she had with Griton. Luckily for them, she was right. The dragons were still young to this world, not quite two hundred years old, and more open to change, to the idea that the land does not have to be divided, that there does not have to be endless killing and war.

She quickly commanded them to take the two-leggeds far from the mountain and head west, telling them that the Omi Méa believes she will need them to fulfill the prophecy. Whether Turathyl believed it or not was yet to be determined, but that was not relevant now.

As Turathyl veered west herself, she heard the dragons in a frenzy up at the top of the mountain. She knew she had infuriated their monarch, but it sounded more like a battle raging between all of her brethren. Reaching out her mind to the mountaintop, it became apparent why no one had chased after her to thwart her rescue attempt of the elf; a riot had broken out among the Silvers, a mutiny caused by herself and Laila. Several dragons were backing Turathyl and a chance for peace, tired of the war, tired of the tyranny. They were protecting her, she realized proudly.

Her heart pounding in exhilaration, she cawed out excitedly as she summoned Coryln and Dailan to follow her with the fugitives that were dangling screaming from their clutches. She was astonished to see that several others were answering her call as well.

'The dwarf!' she called out to them. 'We need to get all the two-leggeds and their mounts back to Lochlann!'

Three Silvers followed her guidance to where Glondora was hidden at the base with the mounts, swiftly collecting them before joining the others as they headed for the dwarven city in the mountain.

Turathyl was in shock from the support she was receiving and that they were willing to go against Aeris to stand up for what they believed. She tallied an astonishing total of fourteen Silvers by her side. Coming up behind the group were several more, advancing on them rapidly, and Turathyl was eager to see who else had decided to join her cause.

As the other Silvers approached, she quickly became aware that they were not coming to join her at all. They were being led by the irate monarch, Aeris. Her heart sank, and her body filled with adrenaline as she beat her wings in terror at the sight of her, her great heart pounding fiercely. The heated dragons were gaining on Turathyl and her followers with their roars of fury. The pursuers flapped their wings viciously, summoning the air spirit to bolster them forward through the skies at an alarming rate. Turathyl recognized Griton as he dove for one of the stragglers from Turathyl's group, gripping on to the dragon with his jaws and talons, tearing at her wings.

Infuriated with their pursuit and attack, Turathyl shrieked back at them, torn between defending those who chose to join her or getting the elf girl somewhere far away and safe from here.

Sensing her concern, the dragons that weren't carrying passengers in their clutches swarmed at the oncoming Silvers, colliding with them to hold them back so that Turathyl and the others could escape. The cries were horrific as dragon attacked dragon, crashing through the skies with their roars, shrieks, and bellows. Four of Turathyl's rebels went straight for Aeris, clamping on to her hide and causing her to freefall as she thrashed and snapped back at them. As claws dug into the thick armored hides, sprays of blue dragon blood rained to the ground below.

It broke her heart to see the Great Aeris attacked so. This was not at all how she envisioned the confrontation with the monarch, but there was no going back now. Frightened for her followers, Turathyl was afraid of leaving them behind and hesitated along with the other dragons that were carrying the elf's comrades.

'LET'S GO!' Dailan bellowed in her mind. 'WE NEED TO GO NOW!'

Turathyl knew he was right, and as she saw Aeris breaking free from the grasp of the dragons just shy of hitting the ground, she knew they needed to take advantage of the distraction while they could. Regardless, before she was able to get away, a Silver had snuck up from below and chomped down on her hind leg, pulling her backward through the air. Turathyl let out a screech, glaring below her at the culprit, and thrashed her wings fiercely to pull away. As the Silver yanked on her ankle, she could feel the flesh tear with searing pain and tried to kick him off while whipping her long-spiked tail at him aggressively.

Coming to her aid, one of her followers tackled the dragon below, snapping at his neck to release his hold on her— and it worked. As soon as Turathyl could pull her ankle free, she rapidly beat her wings to gain altitude while evading another oncoming dragon. Aeris and her clan began falling away, thanks to the distraction of Turathyl's followers, and the defecting Silver continued soaring westward through the sky with all of her might.

Leading the rebels with the two-leggeds and mounts, Turathyl speedily headed for Lochlann, praying to Kyrash to protect the others against Aeris and those still loyal to her—which was most of the clan.

It suddenly dawned on Turathyl that Aeris's clan no longer included herself. She couldn't believe what she had just done, throwing away her title, her brethren, and bonds to rescue an elf of all things. Even though Laila was obviously not just any elf, it still left her stunned by her actions. Never would she have thought she would be capable of such treason against her own kind, even though she knew it was for the right reasons. At least, she hoped it was.

As Turathyl glanced back, she was relieved to see that the battling dragons were falling farther behind them now and that her rebels were putting up a fighting chance. She and the five other dragons carrying their "cargo" linked telepathically, and she could sense their commitment to her and her cause to end the war between the dragons and the other races. Of course, they each were nervous with doubts and concerns, but connecting with Turathyl, they could sense her confidence, and she tried her best to quell any of their misgivings about Laila. Between that and witnessing the elf's gifts for themselves, they were not overly hard to convince.

Unified in thought, the six dragons all pulled simultaneously at the air spirit, thrusting themselves forward with astounding speed through the sky. They flew along the mountain ridge toward the dwarven city, the winds howling across their backs. Turathyl did her best to ignore the agony from the gashes in her wings and flesh, refusing to let it slow her down.

After a while of clear flying, Turathyl detected the bridge over the river and the tall parapets chiseled into the mountainside where the dwarven mining city of Lochlann lay.

'This is it,' she mind-sent to her cohorts.

The dragons destined toward the far side of the river for their landing, giving plenty of space away from the guards who were most certainly alarmed. The dwarven guards expeditiously began preparing for battle upon seeing the monstrous dragons approaching.

Turathyl landed heavily while still being as delicate as possible with her precious cargo. The injuries and blood loss were weighing on the dragon as her adrenaline wore off and her ailments caught up with her.

When the other dragons released the tiny passengers from their grasps, the dwarves—Hort and Glondora—ran ahead, shouting and waving their arms frantically in the air at the guards who were preparing to attack, the male's helmet wobbling with each hurried step. The other three all ran toward Turathyl, not hesitant of her as before but eager to see the elf girl she held tightly and safely in her grasp. Slowly, and ever-so-carefully, Turathyl brought her paw forward before her, opening it to reveal the prophesied elf, Lady Lailalanthelus Dula'Quoy, the Omi Méa, lying motionless in her palm.

Pushing the others aside, the tall male elf made his way to Laila and instantly began checking her for a pulse, staring at her in disbelief with his bright orange eyes. Turathyl could sense the girl's heartbeat, but it was very faint. She feared the damage too great, seeing the broken and limp body before her. Her beautiful golden hair was soaked with crimson blood, and her skin sliced multiple times over her entire body from talons and the quills of Aeris's tail. Several bones were shattered or broken, and Turathyl cringed at the state of her. All of that was merely what the dragon could observe from the outside. The elf was bleeding internally, and many of her organs were damaged and lacerated. It was a miracle she was alive at all. Turathyl lowered her paw farther for the male elf to get a clearer view of the girl; Salyaman Dula'Sintos—she believed his name was—a royal and a ranger with earth magic from the elven city of Má Lyndor.

"Laila!" the human pyromancer, Davion Collins, called out as he ran over to them, staff in hand. The drow rogue, Nikolean Den Faolin, was following closely behind, clad in his black and maroon armor.

"Is she alive? Will she be okay?" Davion hollered.

"She lives!" Salyaman stated, "but I cannot answer to the other. Please, get back! I will need space!"

"Laila! I'm here!" Davion called out frantically. "We're all here! You need to fight, Laila! FIGHT! Don't give up!"

Tears welled in the human's eyes, horror-struck at the thought of her dying, and Nikolean helped hold him back, gripping his brown mage robe tightly, but was just as eager to see her, to hold her, to know that she would be alright. He needed to be with her, even if only to take her hand in his. He needed to see her for himself.

Fighting against his instincts while Davion muttered prayers to the gods nearly pulling his hair out in distress, Nikolean let go of the human, unable to resist any further. Then, both of them stepped fervently towards the still-laying elf. Turathyl growled warningly at the human and drow to not interfere in Laila's healing, and they both stopped in their tracks, trying hard to get a look at what was going on, torn inside at the sight of her.

Salyaman waved his hands over Laila, mumbling incantations, unsure of where to start, and a blue light glowed from beneath his palms as he tried focusing on the damage to her head and her heart first. He was struggling, the damage too significant for his limited healing abilities. Panicked, he called out to the female dwarf hydromancer requesting her assistance, knowing she possessed superior healing abilities than he, and she ran to him as quick as her little legs could carry her.

Turathyl was relieved to see that the dwarven guards were standing down in light of seeing their own kind amongst the dragons and being assured that the ancient beings were on their side. Then, she kept her eye on Nikolean and Davion to make sure they kept out of the way as they watched in torment while the healers tried to work their magic on the elven girl. She could sense their affections for Laila and knew how hard it must be for them to watch from afar, knowing she probably wouldn't have the same willpower herself.

Mumbling their incantations repeatedly, Salyaman focused on healing Laila's head while Glondora cast spells over her heart in an attempt to strengthen its faint beating. Neither healer had ever witnessed such vast damage to a single being that was still alive, but they refused to believe she was done for, tackling one wound at a time. The young elf girl's heart began to beat somewhat steadier, and Glondora moved her focus on to the broken bones. At the same time, Salyaman attempted to tackle the internal damage to her organs and gaping wounds. They were grateful that Laila remained unconscious the entire time, terrified of her waking, knowing the excruciating pain she would most certainly be in while her bones and flesh mended. Their energy and strength quickly began to drain from the power needed to heal the extensive injuries suffered by the young elf.

Turathyl heaved sadly as Laila continued to lay there motionless, with little indication of outward improvement, and the healing lights began to flicker one after the other until they were both burnt out. For the first time ever, she wished she could speak with these beings to find out if the girl was going to be alright. Then the high elf man lifted Laila into his arms and was about to carry her off when Turathyl let out a low growl.

Startled, Salyaman said to her, "Great dragon, if she stands any chance of survival, we must take her inside. There we will have access to medicines and healing that we cannot provide her out here. She is badly wounded beyond my abilities, or Glondora's. But, hopefully, with time..."

Tucking her head in a slight nod, she allowed the tiny creatures to depart with Laila toward the gates of Lochlann. Turathyl hated that she could not go with them but decided she would stay close. After all, where else could she go now?

The human and drow quickly rushed to Laila, following Salyaman and the dwarves into the mountain.

'Elder,' interrupted Dailan, '*we are awaiting your orders.*'

Looking at her group of renegades, she really wasn't sure what to do with them. Every one of them was staring back at her, waiting for her command. She had not planned or intended any of this and didn't know what would happen next. After their betrayal, she presumed her followers couldn't simply return to the Silvers' Mountain with Aeris, just as she could never go back herself. However, many were still missing after having been left behind to fight so Turathyl and the others could escape with the two-legged companions.

Standing grandly before them, masking her pain from her injuries, she said, '*You all have honored me by choosing to follow me despite the Great Aeris's command. I had spoken with the wolf-god, Lupé Caelis, who told me the elf girl was the one prophesied to bring an end to this war that has raged on for far too long, how she would unite the land and bring peace between our kinds. I gave my word to Lupé Caelis, pledging my life to defend and protect the Omi Méa so that she can accomplish that task. I had hoped that Aeris would have seen for herself that the Omi Méa was sent to us by the gods to heal this land, but she has become too darkened from her hate to see light in anything else.*

'*It is now time to choose a side. For those who wish to help on this quest, I will need your aid against Aeris's hatred and attacks. I will stay on Lochlann Mountain until the Omi Méa is healed and ready to leave. I will need the rest of you to go back and find the others that were brave enough to help us escape. We must help any who survived the battle to get here safely. Aeris will likely order attacks against the dwarven city to get rid of the girl. It is up to us to defend Lochlann so that she will not be harmed while recovering.*

'*If, however, any of you have changed your mind, and wish to return to Aeris, now would be that time. It is possible that if you plead with her, claim you made a mistake, and appeal to her merciful side, she would consider your request to come back. I will hold no hatred nor judgment toward any of you and understand and accept your decision. To betray our monarch is more than I can ask of any dragon.'*

Dailan stepped forward and bowed his head before her. *'We are with you, Elder, until the end.'*

As all the dragons roared wildly in agreement, declaring Turathyl as their new monarch, the great Silver Dragon's heart swelled with pride and gratefulness. She really didn't know what would happen next, or if this was going to be enough, but it was at least a start, she decided, something that they could build on. Perhaps if they could just get enough followers, then that's all it would take to turn the tides and put a stop to this war.

Raising her head high and spreading her wings wide, Turathyl roared fiercely towards the gods, accepting her new role as the Silver rebels' monarch.

CHAPTER ONE

HELPLESS

*S*taring at his plate, looking past its contents and metal, Davion poked aimlessly at the pie that Glondora had insisted he eat, with the memory of the Silvers' Mountain plaguing his mind. Hort's modest home within Lochlann Mountain was eerily quiet for being so packed with people, but everyone was alone in their thoughts and fears, the silence distressing.

They had all been on edge since they returned, no one knowing quite what to do or say. While the men sat, quietly finishing their meals, Glondora softly shuffled pots in the kitchen. Her dark copper hair was pulled back out of the way in a long braid down to the backs of her knees as she cleaned up from preparing dinner, trying not to disturb the others. Salyaman slowly chewed each bite, a sound that was heard throughout the quiet room, and Hort painfully stifled a burp, afraid of disturbing everyone. Under normal circumstances, he'd release it loud and proud, but looking around, it was clearly not the time for that. Those were the only sounds in the tiny house for what seemed like an eternity. That is, until Davion started tapping his foot frustratedly on the stone floors under the table, his brown mage robe jostling with the motion.

"Two weeks," Davion said, breaking the long silence. "It's been two weeks." He looked up from his pie, his light-brown eyes focusing on Salyaman as he dropped the fork, it noisily clanging against his metal plate. "Why hasn't she woken up yet? Why hasn't she moved at all?!"

Sighing, Salyaman met his gaze and shook his head slowly without giving him an answer. Glondora continued to clean up the dinner mess, constantly keeping herself busy since they returned to Lochlann with the unconscious elf, trying her best to keep out of the way. She had been too afraid to return to her work on the farms in case Laila needed her.

Hort looked solemnly at Davion, scratching a distinctive scar that ran from his temple to his cheek. He wished he had an answer for him and could do something besides sit around helplessly. Instead, the dwarf folded his arms over his broad chest and leaned back in the chair, stretching his torso from the large meal he had just ingested. His thick brows were furrowed with grief for the boy, while his long brown beard with straggling gray hairs twitched as he used his tongue to pry a fatty remnant from his molars.

Davion stood, noisily scooting his chair back from the table, and then began pacing the room.

"We should have been there for her! We shouldn't have let the dragons take her! And now we don't even know whether she'll live or die! Why hasn't anything you've done worked for her?" He stopped pacing and glared back and forth between Glondora and Salyaman, commanding everyone's attention. "I thought you two were healers! But you can't even tell me when or *if* she'll ever wake up!" He felt his fear boiling over into anger,

"*Diascing énim!*" she cast, and Hort stepped back as a bucket-sized amount of water splashed down over Davion's head, drenching him.

"Glondora!"

"Dunna' ye Glondora me! Methinks tis time fer ye ta take a walk and finish coolin' off!" The dwarf placed her fists firmly on her hips, staring at the young pyromancer, ready to retaliate if needed.

While wiping the water from his eyes and combing the wet hair back from his face with his fingers, Davion looked around at the room that was staring back at him with concern and pity, then glanced over at his beloved in the bed. Everyone stood firm, waiting for Davion to make his next move, and he could feel them all judging him. However, what bothered him the most was how they had positioned themselves in the room as he realized they were all guarding Laila... from him.

"Yes," he finally replied, collecting himself. "Perhaps I should." Then, dripping wet, Davion grabbed his staff and left for the Stone Stein.

Standing alone in a clearing of tall grass and wildflowers, Laila listened for any familiar sounds as she tried to figure out where she was, but there was no sound at all. It was unnervingly quiet as she strained to hear anything. She couldn't hear the birds chirping in the trees nearby, nor the river water flowing in the distance. It also seemed unusually cold for such a bright, sunny day.

Suddenly, she had a feeling she was being watched and turned quickly, searching around her. She espied a group of trees parting at the edge of the clearing and anxiously watched as a colossal dragon slowly emerged from the vast forest. She could feel the vibrations through the ground with each hulking step of the ancient being. It was larger than

CHAPTER 1

any dragon she had ever seen, more colossal even than the Red Dragon from her previous dreams. However, this dragon was green, a bright emerald green that sparkled as the sun's rays reflected off its immaculate scales. But, as far as Laila was aware, there were no green dragons in Onis, and she wondered what it was doing there.

After emerging from the trees, the beautiful creature stopped and poised itself regally, watching her for a moment. It stood solid, its wings tucked, spiked tail curled by its side. Laila began taking steps toward it, but the more steps she took, the farther away the dragon appeared to be. She tried running, but the ancient being continued to grow farther away, although unmoving. She was about to call out for the dragon, but as soon as she opened her mouth to speak, the breathtaking green dragon was gone.

Laila whipped around, looking for where it went, but instead found herself in what appeared to be a cave. No, not a cave. A stone building of some sort, but old and falling apart.

Sunlight was piercing in from wide cracks, highlighting a strange, very-large stone table shaped like a cross sitting in the middle of the room. The table was buried in dust, but she could see it exhibited elaborate and peculiar markings engraved around its perimeter, which Laila determined to be some sort of written language. Unfortunately, Laila was unable to read any languages at all. At each point of the cross was a small circle carved into the stone. Then, five lines extended from each circle towards the middle of the table, swirling around a fifth carved circle at the center.

Laila reached out her hand to touch the table, and the light in the room suddenly shifted, forcing her attention toward the stone walls surrounding her, where something was painted and etched over them; dragons. Lots and lots of dragons. The remarkable depictions veiled the walls all the way around the room. Some were flying, some were fighting, some were standing peacefully. As she looked upon the final wall, she found herself gazing into a mirror, cracked and worn, clouded over time, but her reflection was definitely there, staring back at her, motionless.

With an uneasy feeling that something was off, she studied the reflection and was startled when she looked into the eyes and found black gaping holes staring back at her. Her heart skipped a beat as she jumped back from the mirror, screaming at the deathly hollows in her reflection. She clenched her eyes while crossing her arms frightfully in front of her, and the mirror instantly shattered outward. Time then slowed down as glass shards flew away from her like reflective icicles floating through the air.

She blinked. While lowering her arms, Laila felt herself falling, falling in blackness, a surge of panic overtaking her as she tried desperately to flail about, afraid of hitting the ground, but she could not move. The mountain, she remembered. I failed. I failed them all.

Blinking again, she opened her eyes and was no longer falling in blackness but was standing in pure, bright light—a white light all around as far as the eye could see; no ground, no sky, just light. When she blinked again, her adoptive mother, the great white Wolf God Lupé Caelis, appeared, standing before her in the vast light, staring intently at her.

The Wolf God was just as grand as she remembered, taller even than the high elves at her shoulder with a brilliant-white coat and thick mane.

"Mother!" she called out, ecstatic to see her. The Great Wolf simply continued to stare upon her with ice-blue eyes. "Where am I, Mother? I failed my quest. Am I dead?"

The Great Wolf slowly turned from the young elf and began trotting away.

"Wait, Mother! Don't go!" she cried, but the light grew brighter, blinding her from the Wolf God, causing her to cover her eyes.

The light then vanished, leaving Laila in darkness once again. Blinking around, she could make out nothing of her surroundings. The elf maiden began fumbling around, tripping over unseen objects on the ground, trying to find her way out of the dark.

"HELLO?!" she called out into the nothingness. "IS ANYONE THERE?!"

CHAPTER 1

Almost as though in response, a tiny light started flickering only a few paces away from her. The light was like a red, ghostly flame, dancing and hopping around her, making a high-pitched whirring sound as though it were trying to talk to her. Laila had never seen a will-o'-the-wisp before and was enchanted by it. She raised her hand to touch the light with her finger, and when she did, the light sparked brilliantly, and flaming walls shot up around her, illuminating the area. She recognized the walls of fire from her other dreams, but not the place. The ground was dry and cracked, with no vegetation in sight.

"HELLO?!" she called out again, searching for anyone or anything.

"Halvah, Omi Méa," Hello, Great Spirit, an intense and familiar voice answered in the Ancient tongue.

The earth rumbled below her as the mighty Red Dragon came into focus before her. He held his head high, gazing down upon her, and his beautiful scarlet scales gleamed with reflections of the flames, his black onyx eyes appearing bright orange from the fire's glare.

"I am not the Omi Méa," Laila said, hanging her head low. "I did not end the war. I failed everyone."

The Red Dragon continued to stare at the elf without responding.

After a moment, she hesitantly asked, "Am I dead?"

The great dragon heaved a long sigh and dolefully lowered his head. "Now, that is a tricky question with a complicated answer."

Laila didn't see how such a simple question could be tricky; either she was dead, or she wasn't, but she knew getting a straight answer from her dream-dragon was an unlikely feat.

"Well..." she began again, trying to think of something he might actually answer. "If I'm not dead, then what am I supposed to do now?"

The mighty Red Dragon beamed a smile at her, revealing his large pointy teeth. "Now, that is a simple question with an uncomplicated answer." The Ancient raised his head back up high and replied, "Wake up."

CHAPTER TWO

DESPONDENT

Blinking her eyes slowly open, Laila tried to see what was before her, but everything was blurry beyond recognition. She raised her hand to rub her eyes, but the motion made her overly aware of the pain shooting throughout her entire body. So, instead, she moaned as she brought her palm to her temple. It was as though someone had stuck a dagger into her skull, and was twisting it back and forth, paining her even behind the eyes.

"Laila?" she heard someone say, but it came muffled, as though hearing it from underwater. While attempting to look around again, she vaguely discerned that she was looking up at a ceiling in some type of structure. It appeared strangely familiar, but it was extremely blurry. Suddenly, she began to feel like the whole room was spinning and quickly shut her eyes again to make it stop.

"Sal! Glondy!" the voice yelled, causing more shooting pain throughout her skull. "Come quick!"

Wincing, she could hear the muffled scuffling of others approaching, but it simply hurt too much to acknowledge them. As she tried to move some more, she found her body resisting her every attempt, rebelling against her commands, leaving her powerless. Then, her whole body tightened up, and her head pulled back as she lost sight of everything once again.

Laila began to convulse and quiver on the bed, her eyes rolling back into her head.

Nikolean went into a panic. "What's happening to her?!" he yelled at the healers, who were promptly running to her side. The young elf maiden shook violently while Nikolean stepped aside, out of the way.

"Blastit!" Glondora yelled. "She be havin' a seizure! Quick! 'Elp me turn 'er ta 'er side!"

Salyaman and Nikolean sprung to her aid, grabbing hold of Laila. They rolled her onto her side while Glondora began mumbling incantations, waving her hands over her head and down to her chest. Nikolean stopped breathing, holding Laila tight against him, afraid of letting her go, while Glondora worked her magic. He clenched his eyes, feeling her body quake in his embrace while he prayed desperately for it to stop and for her to be out of harm's way.

After a few painfully long minutes had passed, Laila's body eased and stopped jerking. She became limp in the drow's arms, and Nikolean gasped for breath, fearing the worst.

"Is she...?"

"Nay," Glondora told him. "The seizure's jus' passed. Hush now, and lemme finish." The female dwarf continued casting her blue healing magic over the still-laying elf while Nikolean and Salyaman moved away, watching on frightfully.

"Can I help?" Salyaman asked, unable to keep silent.

The dwarf briskly shook her head without taking her attention away from Laila nor stopping her mumbled casting.

"Ahh, there ye be, ya lil' tardub," said Glondora with a smirk. She placed her hands against Laila's forehead and began mumbling a different set of spells in a deep, throaty tone.

Several moments later, the blue glow began to fade from the dwarf's palms, and she fell silent. Opening her eyes, she gazed upon the young elf.

"Lady Laila?" Glondora said softly. "M'lady, can ye 'ear me? Tis time ta wake up, me dear."

Laila moaned in response to the voice in her ear, and Nikolean dashed back over to her, swiftly grabbing her hand. As he held it tightly, his heart pounded hard in his chest, anxious for her to be okay.

"My lady."

The tips of Laila's lips twitched up into a slight smile as she heard Nikolean's familiar and welcomed voice beside her, causing the drow to chuckle and gasp with relief. She desperately tried again to blink her eyes open. To her relief, everything came into more focus than when she first looked upon the ceiling above. Able to manage a little more control over her body as well, she turned her head to the side and beheld her friends staring back at her with worry in their eyes.

"Where am I?" Laila asked, still trying to gather her bearings. "What happened?"

"M'lady," Glondora responded, "Ye've been unconscious fer a whiles now. We was all so scared ye wasna' ever gunna' wake up. Then, when ye finally did, ye gave us all a right fright, ye did— a blastit seizure from a blood clot in yer brain. Dunna' worry. I found that lil' tardub, and it be gone now, praise Jayenne."

As the dwarf continued on, the memories of the Silvers' Mountain started flooding back to Laila. She didn't hear nor comprehend much of what Glondora was telling her, but she finally realized that she was back in Lochlann in Davion's bed.

"Where's Davion?" she asked, interrupting Glondora while dazedly looking around the room.

Nikolean clenched his teeth at the mention of the human's name. "In the tavern, I would presume," he replied.

"Dunna' worry 'bout 'im right now, m'lady. The lad'll be tickled ta knows yer finally awake! And me Hort be wit' 'im too. I'm sure they be comin' back any time now."

Time... "How long has it been?"

"Forty-three days," Nikolean said without hesitation, his voice cracking slightly. "You have been asleep for forty-three days, my lady."

Speechless, Laila's eyes bulged in disbelief.

The drow looked up to Salyaman with a hardened expression and added, "Maybe it would be best if you went to retrieve Davion before it becomes any later in the night."

Salyaman and Nikolean exchanged a strange look as though they were the ones communicating to each other telepathically, leaving Laila feeling annoyed and left in the dark. Then Salyaman disappeared without another word.

"What's wrong?" Laila asked.

"Nothin' fer ye ta worry 'bout, m'lady," Glondora said with a half-smile.

"You're awake," Nikolean added. "That's all that matters now."

Laila looked away from them both, sadness in her eyes. "But... I failed," she said, remembering the battle with Aeris and the Silvers.

"No," the drow insisted. "You haven't failed anything. You live to see another day—we all do—and we are all here for you."

Although touched by his words, Laila turned her head away from Nikolean, feeling no better about herself as she fought to hold back tears.

"We'll let ye rest, m'lady," Glondora said, understanding. "Come now, Niko, she still be needin' ta recover. Let's give 'er some privacy."

Hesitantly, Nikolean stood while gazing upon Laila, who continued to look away at the wall, and then he departed with Glondora to the main room.

After everyone had left and the door was closed, Laila held a pillow tightly against her chest as her eyes filled with tears, and she wept. Her tears flowed into the pillow, which only slightly muffled the sound of her cries, and she wept for ever having left her home. She wept for ever thinking she could take on such a monumental task, for ever thinking she was the prophesied elf to end the war. She wept, remorseful to all the people who had supported her and believed in her. She wept for all of her friends and all the citizens of Onis who would continue in their suffering due to her disastrous confrontation with Aeris. She wept for her complete and utter failure in her quest... and in herself.

She wished desperately that it could all just be a bad dream she would wake up from and find herself back at home in her cozy little den with her mother, and her brother and sister wolves. She missed the cool waters of her river and the familiarity of her trees and safe boundaries. She missed frolicking with her sister pup and lounging blissfully under the great oak.

The walls weren't so thick as to drown out her sobs, but her friends respected her privacy nonetheless and tried their best not to disturb her. Nikolean wished he could comfort her, but Glondora stopped him more than once when he took a step toward the bedroom door. The dwarf insisted that the young elf needed a moment to let it all out.

CHAPTER 2

After several minutes of anxious anticipation, the front door flew open, and Davion came stumbling in with Salyaman's assistance and Hort hobbling close behind them.

"Sit 'im at the table, Sal. I've made 'im some tea," Glondora said, heading to the kitchen counter. She poured the hot water from the stove into a mug with herbs for quelling the effects of too much dwarven mead.

"No!" Davion shouted. "I need to see her! Where is she? LAILA?!"

Hort helped Salyaman force Davion to a chair. "Not like this, me boy," he said. "Ye need ta get yer wits 'bout ye."

"I will check on Lady Laila," Glondora said, buying them time. "I need ta make sure she be decent first."

After a soft rattle, Glondora creaked the door open just a crack and stuck her nose in. Laila, hearing the commotion, wiped her eyes and sat up in the bed, trying to collect herself. She didn't want to face Davion. He had believed in her wholeheartedly, and she let him down. Regardless, she knew that she would have no choice; she would have to face him and say how sorry she was that he had put his faith in the wrong elf.

"Davion can see me now," she told the dwarf while she straightened the plain white gown Glondora had dressed her in after healing her wounds and bathing her.

With all the grace of an elkan stampede, the door was thrust open as Davion clambered his way into the room, shouting, "You're awake! I can't believe you're actually awake!"

After staggering across the small room in a few long strides, he fell to his knees before her and buried his head in her lap, crying hysterically as he clung to her, relieved beyond words that his angel was alive and well.

Startled, Laila was unsure of how to respond, but she brushed her fingers soothingly through his brown wavy locks and said, "I'm so sorry I failed you, Davion. I'm so sorry I worried you."

Confused, he looked up into her eyes, wiping his face with the back of his sleeve, "You have nothing to be sorry for, Lady Laila. We are all so proud of you. But, I thought I had lost you forever..." He grasped on to her tighter, burying his face in her dress, breathing her in.

The others soon joined the pair in the room, and each of them gave Laila a gentle embrace, telling her how happy they were that she was well, how relieved they were. Then, in their over-excitement, they began telling her about everything that had happened while she was recovering. They told of how her dragon gathered others to help save them all and that they were still outside of Lochlann, guarding the mountain against any Silvers that might come looking for her or her dragon, Turathyl.

Laila became saddened again as she recalled her battle with the dragons and what Aeris, the monarch dragon, revealed about Turathyl. She finally knew the truth that the precious dragon that guided and guarded her on her journey, and the vicious Silver that savagely killed her elven mother when she was just a baby, were one-and-the-same dragon. She had trusted Turathyl, had believed that she was good, and that she was being truthful when she told her that she, Lady Lailalanthelus Dula'Quoy, was the prophesied elf, the Omi Méa, that was meant to stop the war. Obviously, she had been mistaken. Laila couldn't even convince one dragon to put aside her hatred and anger; how was she expected to convince them all? And how could she trust any of them again after learning what Turathyl had done and how vicious and hateful the dragons were?

As everyone jested and chuckled around her, rejoicing her lucidity, she found herself quickly wanting to be alone again, and so she told them that she was quite tired. They all hesitantly agreed to leave so she could get some more rest. Although fearful of leaving her side, Davion was escorted by the others and convinced to get some rest himself. Before departing, they all hugged her, then left her in peace. That is, all except for Nikolean, who no one had noticed lingering in a darkened corner as he remained behind.

"My lady," he said, stepping out of the shadows when they were alone. "Are you really alright?"

Having sensed him there, she was not at all surprised by him. "I am... not," she replied. She knew she couldn't hide anything from him, so there was no point in trying.

"What is it?" he prompted.

With a sigh, Laila laid back down on her side, her arm resting under her head as she gazed at him. He pulled up a chair nearer the bed and took a seat.

"This was all a big mistake," she said despondently as she focused on his blood-red irises and the two scars streaming from his right eye like tears. "If I truly was the Omi Méa, then I don't understand what I could have possibly done wrong. I did everything I could think of, but Aeris just wouldn't even listen to me. The hatred I felt from her was so strong and unbreakable. I should never have gone there. I should never have gone anywhere."

Nikolean looked at her empathetically as he asked, "What do you mean?"

"I should have stayed home in my woods with my family, but it's all too late now." Laila paused for a moment, recalling their earlier conversation from before they reached the Silvers. "Do you remember telling me that you would go anywhere with me? That you would take me somewhere without hate or danger? Somewhere that would only bring a smile to my lips?"

Nikolean grinned and nodded to her. "Of course I do."

"Did you mean it?"

Taking her free hand in his, he kissed the back of it tenderly and said sincerely, "If that is what you wish, then that is what we shall do. I will accompany you anywhere, my lady. You know that."

Laila recalled that he had pledged himself to her as a life-debt from when she saved him from their now-comrades and healed his fatal wounds. She wondered if that was what he intended by his comment. However, regardless of his reasons, the elf maiden smiled back at him briefly, wondering if it was possible. She was tired and ready for somewhere nice where no one was trying to kill her or expect the impossible of her.

"Does your dragon know you're awake?" Nikolean asked, interrupting her daydreaming and instantly tearing the smile from her lips. "I hear she cries out for you often."

"I have not spoken with her," Laila responded curtly. "I am not ready to."

Nikolean looked at her, confused. "Why not? She went up against her monarch for you and saved your life; saved all our lives. What has she done to anger you?"

Bitterly, Laila replied, "She killed my real mother."

Not wanting to press, Nikolean somberly nodded his understanding.

"I think I need some rest now," Laila told the drow, not feeling very sociable.

Nikolean kissed her hand again before letting it go and said, "Yes, my lady. As you wish." Then he turned and headed out the door, leaving her in solitude.

Sighing, Laila stared at the wall aimlessly for a few minutes while she thought about her conversation with Nikolean. She was angry and hurt, feeling defeated beyond measure and betrayed by Turathyl. However, she couldn't deny that the dragon had saved her on more than one occasion. Was that supposed to make up for killing her elven mother? Who

CHAPTER 2

knows what her life would have become had she never lost her mother or father? But dwelling wasn't going to solve anything; she was where she was, and there was nothing to be done now. Laila had faced the dragons and failed in her quest. All that was left to do was to go home to her Wolf God mother and tell her the stories of her adventure.

While heaving out another sigh, Laila sensed someone poking at her mind like a knock on the door, and it was irritating her.

'Yes, *Tury, I am awake.*' Laila sent coarsely to the dragon that had been waiting anxiously for her to rouse.

The dragon conveyed a sense of great relief, and responded, '*Thank you for telling me. I have been worried. I shall thank the gods for answering my prayers.*'

Not in the mood to communicate with her further, Laila sent the dragon a feeling of exhaustion before putting up a mental block, keeping her from her thoughts before she could say anything else. She knew it was inevitable that she would have to confront the dragon about what she had learned on top of the Silvers' Mountain, but it would not be that day.

Curling into a fetal position, with every part of her still hurting, both physically and emotionally, Laila closed her eyes and prayed for sleep to come. A part of her wished that she had never woken up. It would have been easier had she just died on the mountain than to have to face everyone, humiliated, and run home with her tail between her legs in shame.

CHAPTER THREE

DECISIONS

*T*he clattering of pots and pans woke Laila from her slumber, and the smell of cooking meat made its way through the door cracks and into her senses. It was an inviting aroma to her while she rubbed the sleep from her eyes. She attempted to stretch out her limbs, but cracking bones and aching muscles quickly reminded her of her reality and the series of events that had befallen her. Despite that, she decided it was time to get out of bed and test her legs.

Hobbling over to the door, her white gown swayed only to her knees, and she realized it must have been one of Glondora's garments. When she managed to make it across the room, she slowly cracked open the door to peek through. Laila winced from the subtle squeak it made, nervous of the attention she would receive the moment that they discovered her awake. Peering through the crack to the main room, she descried Glondora cooking away in the kitchen while humming some dwarven ditty and Salyaman standing near the back door sharpening his swords. She squinted, pressing her face closer to the crack against the door's rough wood surface, but was unable to find Davion, Hort, or...

"My Lady?" Nikolean said softly from somewhere on the other side of the door.

Blushing, she opened it the rest of the way, and everyone in the room turned to look at her. They had all been in a much better humor now that she was well. Smiles and cheer had taken over their worried wrinkles and frowns, and they were all eager to help bring her to the table. Nikolean held out his forearm for her to grasp, and Salyaman pulled out a chair for her after hastily putting away his blades.

"M'lady, yer lunch tis jus' 'bout ready. I can only imagine how starved ye must be after havin' slept so long!" Glondora called while she finished up and started preparing a plate for her. Glancing over at the table, she hollered, "Niko, dunna' jus' stand there gawkin' like ye be seein' a ghost! Get the lass some water already! My oh my, these boys." The dwarf shook her head, tsking at Nikolean while carrying over a plate of food, and he headed for the kitchen to get her water.

"Here ye are, then. Come now, eat up, m'lady. Yer skin and bones, ye are!"

Laila smiled at her host and looked down at the plate before her. While she inhaled the fragrance of the cooked meat and vegetables, she forgot for a moment that the two-leggeds use utensils to eat their food and tore into it hungrily. Unable to remember when she had ever felt so famished, the wolf child ripped the flesh apart slovenly with her hands and teeth, swallowing large chunks at a time. Even though Glondora's cooking tended to leave much to be desired, in Laila's starvation frenzy, she was convinced it was the best meat she had ever tasted and couldn't stop ripping more bites off, gobbling up the succulent pieces.

"Thank you," she managed to get out between bites after she was nearly finished with her meal.

"Yer most welcome, m'lady," Glondora replied. "There be plenty more if yer interested. Ye need but say the word."

As she emptied the plate and sucked the remaining flavor remnants from her fingers, the front door to the little house swung open, and Laila turned to see Davion and Hort entering. The look on Davion's face even lifted Laila's spirits for a moment as he beamed at her like she was the most incredible vision he had ever seen.

"Laila!" he called out as he made his way over to her. "I see I'm just in time!"

Davion enthusiastically brought forth a sack that he laid on the table next to her, and Laila could smell its contents the moment he opened it. "I knew you'd be hungry, so I wanted to get you something special."

He placed a marbled loaf cake on the table, which she recognized instantly as the famous dwarf Barden Cake she had enjoyed before they left for the mountain. It was a real treat to her palate, holding true to Davion's promise of being the sweetest thing she'd ever taste, and she was thankful for the gesture.

Hort walked up beside the human and put his hand on Davion's shoulder as he addressed her. "Nice ta see ye up and 'bout, lass. Now, dunna' worry 'bout havin' ta eat all that cake there yerself. I be 'appy ta take whatever be left off yer plate." He gave her a wink, then headed over to his wife, Glondora, kissing her on the cheek.

"Thank you for the cake." Laila smiled at Davion as she ripped a piece off and began indulging in its deliciousness.

As she became less ravenous and started to fill up, she was eerily aware of everyone watching her intently and suddenly felt uncomfortable under their stares. Davion was seated across from her, and Nikolean close beside her, while Salyaman and Hort maintained a respectable distance. When they saw they had her attention, Glondora stepped forward to take her empty plate and asked, "'Ow ye feelin', m'lady? Better now?"

Laila smiled sheepishly and nodded. "Yes, thank you. Much better."

She sensed Turathyl tapping at her mind now as well, but she still wasn't ready to talk to her and continued to ignore the dragon.

Everyone was peering at her as though waiting for something; perhaps some great revelation or reiteration of what she faced on the Silvers' Mountain, or her tale of her closeness to the phantom realm as she nearly lost her life, but no one said anything.

Feeling awkward and discombobulated under their stares, Laila pushed her chair back from the table and began to stand. "Thank you all for your help." She politely gave them a forced smile. "I think I'll go change now. Thank you, Glondora, for the gown and the food."

"Of course, m'lady," Glondora replied, returning her smile, concerned for the young elf.

Before her discomfort could increase any further, Laila excused herself and went back to Davion's room. She closed the door quickly behind her, latching it delicately. There wasn't much she wanted to tell them. There was nothing that she was proud of, and she was just ready to go back home. She didn't want to wait any longer or put anyone out any further with their hospitality and pity.

Unable to locate her armor, she discovered one of the elven gowns folded nicely on top of a chest of drawers and decided that would have to do. When she grabbed hold of the coral gown and pulled it forward, something small fell and clinked on the ground at her feet. As she stared down at it, her eyes fixated on the reflective silver dragon scale attached to the chain Davion had bought for her in Má Lyndor. Laila bent and picked it up. Thumbing the scale in her palm for a moment, her heart hurt in her chest as she recalled when she obtained it following her first encounter with Turathyl. Although, her brow furrowed as she realized that it hadn't been her first encounter with the deceitful creature; she had only been a baby when she first met the dragon.

Heatedly planting the chain with Turathyl's scale back on the dresser, Laila turned away, then began to change into the gown. She kept expecting Glondora to barge in to assist her or check on her, but everyone seemed to be respecting her privacy. Even so, she could hear them all whispering on the other side of the door, undoubtedly about her, but too quiet to understand what was being said, and she had no desire to eavesdrop into their minds. She told herself it didn't matter, that she'd be out of the way soon enough, and they could all have their lives back.

As Laila dressed in the elaborate elven garment, she became easily flustered with all the pieces and straps. While struggling with the tie, she felt tears welling in her eyes again, making her angry, and she threw one of the clasps on the ground in frustration. Curling her fingers in her hair, Laila took a deep breath, blowing out through pursed lips as she tried to calm herself. She knew it wasn't the gown that was the problem, but her hands were shaking and her world spinning, making even the simple task of getting dressed overwhelming. After another deep breath, she shook out her hands and tried to fasten the gown again while blinking her eyes up at the ceiling in an attempt to reabsorb the pooled tears. With a little patience and a gentler effort, the elf royal at long last managed to conquer the dress.

While searching the room in her overly adorned gown for its current purpose, she gathered up anything she spotted

CHAPTER 3

belonging to her and put them in an old sack of Davion's she'd found, hoping that he wouldn't mind. Hesitantly, she even grabbed the scale necklace and tossed it in amongst her other possessions. She wasn't able to locate much, but it was still more than she had left her home with.

As she re-emerged from the room, she saw that no one had left their spots, and they all went back to watching her as intently as before. Except, this time, noticing the sack in her hand, Davion jumped up promptly.

"What's going on, Laila?" he asked.

Nikolean also jumped up, but instead of joining the others in gathering around her, he went over to the far corner and began loading his things into his own sack.

"It's time for me to go home," Laila said nervously, unsure of how they were going to react.

"What are you talking about?" Davion probed.

Salyaman and Hort were also drawing closer to her, and Glondora folded her arms over her chest, watching the young elf curiously.

"I failed. I am not the Omi Méa. It was a mistake, and now it's time for me to go home, back to the Sacred Forest."

Hort smacked his knees, letting out a loud belly laugh as he stared at her in disbelief. "Are ye crazy, lass? Does ye really think that? Could someone please talk some sense inta this 'ere elf?!"

"My uncle's right," Davion said. "You really believe you failed? Aeris is just one dragon! We have a whole score of dragons above our very heads protecting us as we speak, waiting for *you*!"

Salyaman, seeing the sorrow and pain in her eyes, stepped forward and took her hand. "Lady Laila, only you, the Omi Méa, could have possibly confronted an entire dragon clan and survived. You may not have won them all over, but I do not think any of us believed it would be that simple. It is my belief that this is only the beginning. What you have managed to do is a true miracle and not one to be disregarded. We need you if we are to see this through and put an end to the war."

Everyone nodded in agreement with Salyaman, except for Nikolean, who was flinging his sack over his shoulder and approaching them.

"And where does ye think ye be off ta?" Hort sneered at the drow.

"My life belongs to her." Nikolean nodded at Laila. "I go wherever my lady decides to go."

Rolling his eyes at the dark elf, Davion raised his hands in the air, exasperated. "This is insane. Laila, you aren't going anywhere. We need to come up with the next phase of the plan. If I hadn't seen it for myself, I wouldn't believe it possible, but Salyaman is right. You may not have turned their monarch, but you convinced several of them that we *can* have peace between us and end the war—so much so that they turned on their own kind to rescue you and the rest of us! They even saved our mounts!" Laila lovingly remembered her half-unicorn, half-elkah with its beautiful white fur and horns, Merimer, and was relieved to hear that she was safe. "We can do this, Lady Laila! I know we can, but not without you!"

Her sack dropped to the floor as Laila took a moment to consider what they were telling her. She had only seen her failure in convincing Aeris of peace. It hadn't occurred to her that there could be any other way of ending the war. *So, what now?* she wondered unknowingly to herself.

Nudging her way through the group, Glondora approached Laila and grabbed hold of the elf's arms, then tenderly lead her back to a seat at the table. "M'lady, ye've been through more than any one of us could possibly understand. Ye need ta take a moment and jus' let it all sink in." As Laila took her seat, the dwarf affectionately stroked her hair. "There be no need ta run off anywhere. Ye take yer time and let us know when yer ready, but ye need ta know that we all be 'ere fer ye when ye are. All of us be committed ta yer quest and endin' the blastit war. I 'ave been so honored ta see ye in action, but I think the rest o' this lot agrees that we ain't done yet."

Glondora ordered Hort to get the lady some more water and for everyone to give her some space and some time.

Laila stared blankly at the table, unsure of what to do or say next. Perhaps they were right; this was just the beginning. That, however, was not at all comforting to her. She had honestly believed that it would all be over after she confronted Aeris, that she would win her over and that the Silvers would convince the others to stop the massacres and hatred that was destroying the land of Onis. Sighing gravely, she realized that they would have to find another way.

"So, what now?" Hort said gruffly, echoing everyone's thoughts while biting noisily into a crunchy, drippy mrit fruit.

"What has yer dragon said ta ye, m'lady? Does Turathyl 'ave a plan?" Glondora inquired.

Laila tensed at the mention of the dragon's name, and Nikolean took a protective step closer to her, knowing the dragon was a sore subject. He wanted her to see he was there should she need him.

Slowly shaking her head, Laila looked away from them to the ground. "I do not know."

Still sloppily eating his fruit that was in large part dripping down his long beard, Hort chimed in, "Hmmm... Well, I been talkin' ta Lord Kilgar." He swallowed his bite of the fruit. "He was suggestin' again that we should go ta Gortax. Seemed ta think King Brakdrath would be 'appy ta give us some assistance." Taking another bite, he added between chews, "Jus' a suggestion, mind ye."

"That is surprisingly not such a terrible suggestion," Salyaman speculated.

"Oiy!" the dwarf hollered at the elf prince.

"It was meant as a compliment," Salyaman replied with a slight smirk.

"Hmmm... Well, alright then, I s'pose." Hort eyed the elf, scowling, before shrugging and taking another bite from his fruit.

Salyaman continued, "First, I suggest we come up with a plan, something that we can present to Lord Kilgar and King Brakdrath. I fear it will take every race of Onis working together to convince the dragons that the time for their war is over."

"Tis a good point," Hort said. "But we canna' exacitally be trapesin' all over Onis wit' a bunch o' armies."

"No," Nikolean added, getting engaged in their plan, "but we *can* recruit them and meet at a set location after we've had a chance to visit with them all and then confront the dragons with the rest of the land united. We could head south to the dark elves after we leave Gortax."

Davion huffed at the drow's idea. "You honestly think the drow are going to let us address them or agree to join us?" He then added sarcastically, "I suppose the orcs and trolls should come along as well."

"The drow elders may not, but the Drakka might. I think it's at least worth a try," Nikolean retorted. "Not all drow are monsters, and I take offense to being compared to an orc or troll." He took a step challengingly toward Davion, who was more than eager for another excuse to swing at the drow, but Laila stood and put her hand gently on Nikolean's arm for him to stand down.

Glondora stood between the drow and human while Hort took Davion's arm.

CHAPTER 3

"Ye boys need ta quit yer squabblin'," Glondora chastised. "Tis enough o' that. Methinks we got a long journey ahead, and I've a right mind ta use me staff on the both o' ye!"

Davion scoffed at the dark elf before turning away and heading to the couch to keep his distance, afraid he was about to get another bucket of water dumped on him. Nikolean also stood down and took a step back while staying near Laila's side.

With a stern look around the room, Salyaman said, "I suspect the plan could work, but if we are to convince each of the civilizations to work together, it would be more convincing if we were not divided ourselves."

Everyone nodded, a couple with shame, as they agreed to the plan.

"But what of the dragons?" Davion asked. "Do we go back to Aeris after we have troops to back us?"

"I propose that is something to be discussed with the dragons we already have. What do you think, Lady Laila?" Salyaman asked, and they all looked at her expectantly.

Disconcerted, Laila swallowed the hard lump feeling in her throat, then nodded at the group. "I will discuss the plan with Turathyl."

Laila wondered if her life would ever be about what she wanted, or even be given a chance to discover what that was. It appeared that she wouldn't be able to hold on to her grudge against the dragon much longer. As angry as she was about Turathyl's lies and betrayal, and her role in her elven mother's death, she knew they would need the dragon to help them with their plan. Sadly, once again, it didn't matter much what she desired; she would have to put her feelings aside for the greater good of all of Onis.

CHAPTER FOUR

STONES

*A*fter a long night of tossing and turning through nightmares of dragons and fire, mountains and falling, Laila finally gave up trying to sleep and instead readied herself for the day. She was only somewhat starting to feel better and more like herself, but she remained very uneasy about what challenges still awaited them. Everything she had experienced since leaving her cozy den in the Sacred Forest had all been so surreal, and she wasn't confident that it was in a good way.

As she quietly stepped out of her room, she saw that everyone was still asleep and stealthily tip-toed around the snoring mounds scattered across the floor on thin straw mattresses, hoping desperately not to wake them. She had no sense of what time it was; if it was late or early. The light in Lochlann was unnatural, lit only by torches, dimmed during the night hours, and rejuvenated during the day. Learning how to read the peculiar time-tracking contraptions had never become a priority for her. So, all she was certain of was that it was not yet day again.

To ease her mind from her dreams and anxiety, she decided to go for a walk and see if she could clear her head. Delicately opening the door so as not to make a sound, she stepped outside of the small dwarven home and into the dimly lit city of pathways and bridges that tied together the mountain-stone buildings that made up Lochlann. The heat lingered in the recycled air from the fires and forges of the mines, and it was surprisingly quiet at that moment, a considerable contrast to the daytime when the mines and foundries were in a full bustle.

While strolling down the walkway toward a stone path, Laila startled when she heard the door to Hort's dwelling open behind her, and she looked to see Davion emerging. He smiled delightedly when he saw her and joined her on the path.

"Can't sleep?" he asked casually.

She shook her head, giving him an uncomfortable smile. "I'm sorry I woke you, Davion."

Davion's smile faded as he told her, "Lady Laila, you really should stop apologizing for things when you have done nothing wrong." With a hopeful gaze, he added, "Can I join you?"

Laila smiled sweetly at him and nodded. She then tucked her hand comfortably in his elbow, and they began to traverse casually through the sleeping city.

"So, what's troubling you?" he asked. "Is there anything I can do?"

"I'm afraid not," she replied. "I'm just not convinced that I am the one to lead this quest. I don't know how or where to go."

"Lady Laila," Davion sighed, "we are all in this together. No one expects you to have all the answers or do this on your own. But if and when you do feel ready, we will all have your back. Until then, I think going to Gortax is a good start."

As they continued, they walked in silence while carefully crossing a long bridge. Laila wasn't quite sure where Davion was leading her, but Lochlann was his home, so she followed him trustingly.

"Have you spoken with Turathyl yet?" he asked when they reached the other side of the bridge.

Laila shook her head despondently. "I will. I just haven't been ready to."

Discerning his confusion, Laila told him how she found out that her "Great Dragon" was the same dragon that had killed her mother over sixteen years prior, which caused her father to die as well when he sought revenge, believing both Laila and her mother dead. Davion listened intently to her story, starting from what Annallee in Má Lyndor had revealed up to the Silver monarch's unveiling of her dragon's betrayal. He understood why she was so angry with the dragon, commiserating with her pain since he had lost his mother and father to orcs when he was young also and would do anything to have them back.

As he led her into an unlit hollow, Laila began to get nervous about where they were going, but then they stopped a short way inside the dark cavern. Davion took her hands fondly and held them before her, reassuring her that it was okay.

He then released his grip and raised his hands, stretching them out on either side, all the while keeping his gaze fixed on her silhouette, barely visible through the blackness. Softly, he uttered, "Illioso."

Four sconces ignited on the cave walls and illuminated their surroundings. Laila's jaw dropped as she marveled at the beauty before her. Covering the surface of each wall were thousands of radiant gems of purples, blues, and pinks. They sparkled brilliantly from the dancing flames and twinkled as though talking to each other, but more like a song—a harmonious melody of pure perfection and grace.

"This is incredible!" Laila gasped.

Davion smiled from ear to ear, cherishing her joy as she twirled to see all the gems shining back at her. "This is my favorite place in Lochlann," he divulged, getting her attention, and she turned around to face him. "The gems crumble when they try to mine them, so the dwarves left this place alone. They call it Muk Narda Cabi, which means *False Crystal Cave*. The crystals may not have value, but I thought you might like it."

"I really do," she assured him.

"Lady Laila, I understand your hesitation with your dragon. I'm not sure if I could forgive her either if she were the one that had killed my family, and I can empathize with the pain you must be feeling."

While taking her hands in his once again, he stepped toward her, bringing himself intimately close to her. It seemed like an eternity since they had been so near. His heart was pounding in his chest and his palms becoming sweaty. He had feared that he would never get the chance to be that close with her again, that he would lose her to the Beyond, just as he had lost his family. But there she was, standing before him. Her eyes sparkled in the sconces' light like the gems surrounding them, and he felt that closeness to her again, like they had shared once before.

Laila's heart was aflutter, being so near to Davion in such a mystical place, the two of them completely alone. She still wasn't sure how she felt about him or Nikolean, but when Davion suddenly leaned in closer to her, she did not stop him or pull away as he pressed his lips against hers. Instead, she closed her eyes, returning his kiss, letting his lips brush softly and tenderly over hers while she followed his lead, mirroring the gentleness of the touch. He wrapped his arms around her, pulling her pleasingly against him in a loving embrace. Laila sank into it, solaced by the feel of their forms meshing together perfectly as she was filled with a sense of comfort and ease. It was reminiscent of the many nights on the road where she had experienced a similar sensation with him whenever he would place his arm around her.

As he kissed her, she could feel his heart pounding against her chest, conveying his nervousness, which in turn made her nervous as well. So, Laila pulled back for a moment and smiled at him warmly. He gleamed back at her, then she laid her head comfortingly against his chest while they stood there holding each other intimately for several minutes. Relieved that she had accepted his advance, Davion couldn't stop smiling into her hair as he affectionately kissed the top of her head.

Laila pondered whether she was allowed to indulge in such things as romance on their journey. She was curious about her undeniable link with Davion that still remained, ever since her first vision of him in the Sacred Forest. Now that her confrontation with Aeris was over and the quest was to continue, she wondered if it would be so terrible to explore her feelings further along the way. After all, who knew how much time any of them had left together?

"We should probably head back," Davion said to her after some time had passed, hesitantly breaking their embrace. "It's nearly day, and everyone will be worried about where you've gone."

Laila acknowledged and agreed, then looked around the cavern one more time, memorizing its splendor, before joining him back toward his home.

CHAPTER 4

Throughout breakfast, everyone noticed that the chemistry between the human and the elf maiden had shifted. Still, Laila remained tactful and reserved, unsure of what her kiss with Davion meant for them or how she even felt about it. It was very different from the passionate kiss she had experienced with Nikolean after the party when they were in Lochlann last. She enjoyed both of them very much, but for dissimilar reasons, and she needed time to process it all.

Hort had received an invitation for the group to see Lord Kilgar at the town hall that afternoon, presumably to discuss their plans of seeking support from Gortax, the dwarf capital where most of the warriors were. Laila was quite nervous about the idea after having had very little luck when they had requested the elves' aid, who were at the very heart of the war. She believed that if anyone should have offered to aid them, it should have been the elves. It left her somewhat confused and doubting herself since they didn't have enough faith in her to offer their support other than the gifts they bestowed on her. She wondered if perhaps she should have agreed to marry Rathca Saelethil to obtain the one hundred men he had offered, even though her friends had assured her that she made the right decision to refuse him.

When they all reached the town hall, they were led into the room where they had first met with Lord Kilgar, except this time there was no elaborate spread of food before him; the table remained bare, and the lord was standing beside it with two female miners.

"Ah! Good good! Ye made it!" Lord Kilgar exclaimed as they entered. "Me 'erd ye be takin' me advice and goin' ta see King Brakdrath Lightsword fer some 'elp?" The dwarf lord made his way briskly to Laila and took her arms, holding them out to look at her. "Lady Laila! I canna' believe me eyes! The elf that took on a whole nest o' Silvers and lived ta tell the tale! Londla,

Orga, can ye believe yer eyes?" he bellowed ecstatically at the two miners, who smiled and shook their heads. "Nay, I bet ye can't. Although, I canna' say I be 'appy 'bout all the attention ye've brought me way from the dragons. But it seems yer clan be doin' a right job protectin' me 'ome and fer that, I be grateful! Now then..." Lord Kilgar looked over Laila incredulously as he took a breath. "I 'ear we nearly lost ye there fer a bit. I be told yer armor was quite shredded when me men got a hold of it. They couldna' believe that the bearer still lived!"

Laila had been wondering what had happened to her armor, and her eyes perked at the mention of it.

"Yes, I see I 'ave yer attention nows. Yer armor tis all, well, umm. I wouldna' say 'fixed' exacitally, improved really if ye ask me. Yes, I dare say tis much improved. I admit it did take us a bit ta get the right enchantments together fer ye, but I think ye'll be quite 'appy wit' them."

As he let out a loud whistle, that startled all but Glondora and Hort, the doors to the hall opened, and the dwarf that had led them in stepped inside.

"The armor, lad, where be the armor?!" he hollered impatiently, and the dwarf disappeared post haste. "Now, lemme see..." Lord kilgar tapped around the outside of his pockets, searching for something. "I knows I put it 'ere somewhere. Ah, yes! 'Ere we go!" he exclaimed, revealing a small leather pouch with something rattling within as he held it out before them. "Now, these 'ere be very special and very rare. We dunna' know what they mean, but they not been good fer polishin' nor craftin', though, there be tales o' them havin' great power. So, we been 'oldin' them 'til the right time." Lord Kilgar poured out five stones into his hand, removed one, and raised the other four for them all to see. "These four be Dragon Stones, one fer each o' the four dragon elements."

As Lord Kilgar displayed the first four, the group gathered close around to see the grape-sized stones in his hand. There was one that had white and silver swirling around each other like clouds. Laila knew it had to be the stone of the Silvers—the Air Dragons. The Gold, or Earth Dragon Stone, was golden with burnt-orange cracks over it. The third stone, the Blue Dragon Stone, had ripples in its texture and was covered in what resembled blue and green waves of water. Davion was immediately drawn to the last stone, the Red Dragon Stone, and picked it up for a closer inspection, admiring its blood-red hue with orange flames.

"Beautiful," Davion said softly, examining it closely.

The group looked at Laila as she carefully handled each of the other gems, which were all quite warm to her touch, then she held them out toward the group. Salyaman found himself quite fond of the Earth Stone, taking it to study further. Nikolean took the silver stone gently from Laila's hand while looking deep into her eyes, causing her heart to flutter when his fingers brushed against her palm, but she did her best not to react.

Hort watched the others but wasn't intrigued by any of the stones as they were.

"May I?" Glondora asked, pointing at the remaining Blue Water Stone.

Smiling, Laila held it out, and she took it giddily, holding it up to the light with wonderment.

"Oh, and this one 'ere," Lord Kilgar said, opening his hand with a fifth stone, "this 'ere is a spirit stone, Norn Mornder, or Black Death."

Instantly, Laila was drawn to it, unlike the Dragon Stones she held. It was solid black, slightly larger than the others, and a perfect sphere without flaws. It reminded her of looking into Turathyl's onyx eyes. She hastily grabbed it from Lord Kilgar and was shocked to find it very cold to the touch, like holding on to an ice cube. To Laila, looking at the stone was like looking into nothingness, and she began shivering from its frigidity. A great power emanated from the stone through her fingers, creating a tingling sensation up her arm. She felt as though it was reaching into her very being and drawing from her energy. Then, everything around her started to darken and haze over, her heart beating hard and fast in her chest. Before her world could go completely black, she quickly turned to the closest person.

"Feel this!" Laila said, shoving the stone forcedly at Salyaman. As the stone left her fingertips, her vision began to return, and she could detect her body already starting to warm, her heart beginning to slow.

Salyaman took the stone and rolled it around in his hand.

"What do you feel?" she pressed.

"I feel nothing, Lady Laila. It feels just as the others had."

Confused, Laila motioned for Salyaman to give it to Davion next, who took it and examined it in kind. "It appears just like the others," he confirmed.

"Is it cold?"

Davion shook his head.

Laila looked to Salyaman, feeling like she must be mad, and he also shook his head.

"Are ye alright, lass? Ye look as though ye seen a ghost," Hort inquired, concerned.

Laila looked around and saw them all staring strangely at her. Feeling very unsettled, she nodded and blushed with embarrassment, replying, "Yes, I'm fine." Turning back to Lord Kilgar, she bowed her head. "Thank you so much for the gifts. They are beautiful."

Upon descrying the pouch in the dwarf leader's hand, she pointed to it and asked if she could have it, afraid of touching the stone again until she knew more.

CHAPTER 4

"Of course, lass! I dunna' know if those rocks'll be o' any use ta ye, but ye can show them ta King Brakdrath, and he'll knows ye got the support o' Lochlann behind ye at least."

As the comrades said their thank yous to Lord Kilgar, Laila returned the stones to the pouch and tucked them away safely. She was very disconcerted about Norn Mornder, needing to know more, and wondered why no one else was affected by it. She realized she would finally have to have her talk with Turathyl and find out what she knew about the Dragon Stones, leaving her anxious.

Just then, the door opened again, and in came the same dwarf carrying a bundle of armor that he placed on the table before departing once more.

"Good good! 'Ave a look, lass! I knows ye'll be pleased!" The dwarf lord gestured to the armor.

Laila approached the pile on the table and began to look through it. The leather armor prepared for her by the elves of Má Lyndor had been replaced with a strong metal. Yet, it did not seem much heavier than the leather had, and she could even sense enchantments imbued into the new pieces as well. She was surprised to see a more complete set than she had before, with vambraces and rerebraces to cover her arms and a full set of leg armor from the sabatons to cover her feet up to the cuisse for her thighs. There were matching spaulders for her shoulders, and all the pieces were intricately decorated with patterned engravings.

As the lord explained all the pieces to her, she admired how delicate they seemed, yet strong, and liked the muted bronze color as opposed to some of the bright, flashy plate she had seen worn by the humans and elves.

"That looks like some o' the best work I've seen, me lord," Hort praised.

"The enchantments...?" Laila began to ask.

"Yes, lass. They be there, the same ones jus' as before. We figured the elves 'ad em there fer a reason. Twas a tricky thing figurin' them out, but I be pretty confident with our enchanter, and she says she was able ta replicate them all."

Next, he showed her the bronze chest plate and the beautiful deep-purple, leather buckled corset with a modest veil of violet cloth, which appeared very fashionable for armor.

"Now, I knows ye be a caster, lass. Tis likely why the elves gave ye that other armor, but if yer ta be battlin' dragons and whatnot, then ye be needin' somethin' for the front lines like this. This 'ere armor will 'old up much better against them nasty tails and talons o' theirs. Ye mark me word."

Laila, overwhelmed with gratitude, bowed her head to the lord. "This is all so wonderful, Lord Kilgar. I don't know how I can ever repay you."

"Now isna' that the dumbest thing ye ever 'ad tickle yer ears? Lass! Ye off confrontin' dragons ta end the greatest and longest war Onis 'as ever 'ad! I think ye can call us even!" He gave her a wink and touched the side of his nose at her before letting out a belly laugh.

Smiling sheepishly, she bowed again, replying, "Yes, of course."

"Now, we already took care o' yer companions while ye was restin' by updating their weapons ta pierce the dragons' 'ides better. Ye know, jus' in case yer attempts at peace go the same as the last time." He winked at her. "But, as fer yer Dragonsbane—as I be told ye callin' 'er—a mighty fine piece of weaponry that be. She be totally unscathed. Just polished 'er up, and she good as new. I'll be sure ta 'ave one o' these laidens bring 'er by Mister Hort Strongarm's this evenin', if that be agreeable. Until then," the dwarf lord raised his hands, smiling widely at them, "try ta enjoy yerselves 'fore ye depart for the mighty Gortax!"

They all thanked the lord for his hospitality and kindness again and for aiding them during Laila's recovery. After saying their respected farewells to Lord Kilgar, they headed out of the hall.

As they departed, Davion pressed, "I still think you should replace that old wobbly helmet before we depart again, Uncle. Or at least get it better fitted."

"Hmmm..." Hort grumbled.

"Besides, it makes you look ridiculous." He nudged his uncle playfully.

"Ye know twas me paw's, and if twas good 'nuff fer 'im, then tis good 'nuff fer me. I wouldna' change it fer nothin'."

"Stubborn dwarf," Davion smirked, shaking his head.

While sitting on the edge of Davion's bed, Laila palmed the leather pouch of stones in her hand, nervous about connecting with Turathyl. She had asked the others for some privacy while she reached out to her dragon; Davion and Nikolean being the only two that understood her hesitation. With a heavy sigh, she decided it best to just get it over with.

'Turathyl?' Laila sent out, sensing the dragon just above the mountain.

'I am here,' the Silver responded.

'We have decided to go to Gortax, the dwarf capital, and request their aid in confronting the dragons.' Laila took a deep breath, shaking nervously, unsure if she was ready to speak to her about her mother's death. 'We will be leaving in a few days as soon as we are ready. I thought you should know.'

'I understand,' Turathyl replied. 'I will notify my clan that I will be leaving for a while and have them remain here to protect Lochlann Mountain and the dwarves from more attacks.'

'*Attacks?*' Laila asked, unaware.

'Yes,' she replied. '*there have been a few, but we have been resilient. We have even managed to recruit more of my brethren for our cause. Do not let yourself be worried for us.*'

Even though Laila was reassured to hear the news, she felt no inclination to express it at the moment. '*There was... something else,*' she added. '*We received gifts of Dragon Stones from Lord Kilgar. Do you know of them?*'

'*I have seen them in the past,*' she replied, '*and heard myths of them holding power, but as far as I am familiar, they are mostly ornamental keepsakes.*'

Laila sighed, disappointed. '*And a spirit stone, Norn Mornder.*' She mind-sent a picture of the stone.

'*Black Death? Is that what they are calling it?*' Turathyl chuckled, amused. '*I suppose that makes sense as it resembles a dragon's entrancing eye. I've heard our glare called that before. However, to us, it is simply a Dragon's Eye.*' Turathyl perceived Laila cringe and tried not to laugh again, sensing the elf's lingering anger toward her. '*It isn't an actual dragon's eye, Great Spirit. However, it is a powerful stone; believed by us to contain spirits of dragons past. That is something truly rare, indeed. I have only ever seen one before.*'

Laila shuddered, remembering the effect it held over her, and Turathyl added, '*I sense something is troubling you. What is it?*'

'*The stone,*' Laila said, '*it seemed to have some sort of power over me that I can't explain, but when the others held it, it did nothing.*'

'*Well, that is troubling, certainly. I do not understand enough about the stone—or you—to speculate why this would be. Until we know more, please do not touch it again.*' Turathyl responded, concerned and intrigued. After a long pause, the dragon added tentatively, '*Was there... anything else?*'

While attempting not to share her thoughts too openly with the dragon as before, or as she used to with her mother,

Laila pondered on the subject that had been tearing her apart inside. After thinking long and hard, she simply sent, 'My mother...'

The dragon heaved a long sigh that was also relayed through her thoughts. '*I know, Great Spirit. There is nothing I can ever do to make up for my part in that, and I am aware there is nothing I could ever say to make it right.*' The dragon sent her affections, wishing she could let her hold her snout again, feeling so distant from her, and sensed tears filling the young elf's eyes. '*Many have died needlessly on both sides. All I can hope now is to be a part of making things right for the land of Onis and to atone for my part in it all. And I also hope, Great Spirit, that in time you will find it in your heart to forgive me.*'

Laila wiped the tears from her eyes in an attempt to be resilient, and said curtly, '*I wish you wouldn't call me that.*'

'Great Spirit?'

'Yes. I am just me.'

'*Of course,*' Turathyl responded respectfully. '*What shall I call you then?*'

The elf recalled all the names people referred to her as since her birth; Lupé Pavula, Lady Lailalanthelus Dula'Quoy, Omi Méa, young one, Lady Laila, my lady, Great Spirit. But, the only one that mattered to her at that moment was the one that her mother, Lady Leonallan Dula'Quoy, wished for her to have. '*Please, I am just Laila.*'

'Yes, Laila.' The dragon sent a mental bow of her head in respect before Laila severed the telepathic connection, happy to once again be alone in her own thoughts.

CHAPTER FIVE

ONWARD

*H*aving all agreed on the plan to go to Gortax, the group was anxious to get back on their expedition following a nearly two-month-long recovery in the aftermath of the encounter with the Silvers. After a few more days of preparation, they packed up Glondora's old cart once again—repaired after being snatched up hastily in a dragon's talons—with plenty of supplies for the long trip ahead of them. It would be the longest yet, with no outposts or towns along the way. Typically, it was a twenty-day trek to Gortax from Lochlann in conjunction with many anticipated dangers during the journey. Albeit, they presumed that the trouble would be significantly less accompanied by a dragon at their sides.

At the end of the long tunnel passage, the gates of Lochlann opened before them, and they were startled to hear sounds of dragons cawing above. They were even more startled to be greeted by Turathyl and another Silver immediately upon exiting, with the dwarf guards nearby, seemingly unafraid.

They proceeded beyond the gates toward the majestic creatures, and the companions looked up in awe, admiring the terrifying-yet-exquisite sight of several Silvers flying to and from the mountaintop. The reflection on their luminescent scales from the morning sun shone brilliantly, and they couldn't help but appreciate the glamor of the spine-chilling display from a multitude of dragons soaring above their heads.

Turathyl lowered her muzzle to the elf in salutations. She was anticipating her to jump down from Merimer, run over to her, and wrap her arms around her snout in an affectionate embrace. Instead, Laila halted Merimer before her, eying Turathyl and the other dragon, giving a slight nod. She recognized the accompanying dragon from the ledge on Silvers' Mountain and shuddered slightly from the recollection of that moment.

'Laila,' Turathyl mind-sent, raising her head back up, disappointed. 'This is Dailan, my second in command. He and Coryln helped bring your friends back to Lochlann safely.'

"Thank you, Dailan," Laila said earnestly while still maintaining a stern visage. Seeing all the dragons was bringing back too many memories, and none of them good. She suspected that staying strong was the only way she could retain control of herself and her emotions at that moment, putting up a barricade around her heart.

'It was our honor,' the Silver replied. 'Monarch, are you certain you do not wish for some of us to accompany you to Gortax?' he asked. 'We are nineteen now. It would not affect our ability to protect the dwarves were we to spare a few.'

'That is not necessary,' Turathyl told him. 'I need you here, but I will call on you should we need your help. Keep scouts watching for Aeris and her clan, and let me know if they make a move toward us. I am sure that we can handle any orcs between here and the dwarven *capital. Unless...'* The great Silver paused and looked at Laila. *'Would Lady Laila like more of my clan to accompany us?'*

Laila stared back and forth between Turathyl and Dailan. She honestly didn't want to look at any Silvers, let alone a horde of them. It was not a hard decision for her to make.

After taking a deep breath to maintain her demeanor, she said, "Turathyl can call on you if needed. I do not wish to alarm the dwarves of Gortax by arriving with an army of Silvers."

Dailan bowed before the Omi Méa and said, *'Very well. I wish you all well on your journey, and I will make certain that our scouts do not allow any of Aeris's clan to follow.'*

After their quick farewells and Glondora yelling "Borghyn!" *Goodbye!* back at the guards a dozen times, the group was on their way, trekking west along the base of the Gorén Mountains. With no longer having to keep going back to Aeris, as when she first joined the two-leggeds, Turathyl stayed with the group for much more extended periods of time. She left primarily to hunt and connect with her kin back at Lochlann, the altitude aiding in the telepathic link.

Laila was happy to be back with Merimer, her unicorn-elkah hybrid mix with its beautiful all-white elkan horns, fur, and long flowing tail. She had a calming connection with the creature, something comforting with no judgments, hidden agendas, or intentions. There was simply a quiet exchange of affection and understanding between them, similar to her wolfkin back at home in the Sacred Forest, but deeper. She enjoyed the peace of it, keeping mostly to herself, as they clip-clopped along the hard stone ground.

The complete lack of vegetation disturbed Laila with nothing but hard, cracked rock and dirt ever since they left Lochlann and stepped beyond the Ashwood Forest. Davion had told her before that the Ashwood Forest was the only surviving forest west of the Emerald River, but she had no idea how significant the absence of life there was.

Each time Davion approached Laila with his horse Helna, the elf maiden politely nodded and smiled at him. Preferring to ride in silence, she kept any responses short and direct, deterring further conversation, though he continued to try, nonetheless. Davion would act as he used to around her; playfully flirting and trying to make her laugh, but Laila simply didn't feel very moved to laugh as of late. She had even been keeping apart from Turathyl stomping along behind her.

Ever since the young elf maiden had awakened from her coma, she'd not been feeling like herself, just wishing to be alone most of the time, and she wasn't sure how to shake it off.

Salyaman rode primarily with Hort and Glondora, and Nikolean typically stayed toward the back.

It was their fifth day out, and only a quarter of the way to their destination.

When they broke for lunch, Laila took her rations off to the side, away from the group, sitting by Merimer on a large boulder while she ate. The others, apart from Nikolean, all gathered together, talking merrily and sharing tales. Laila didn't understand how they could all be so upbeat given their circumstance. Still feeling quite defeated, she couldn't fathom what there was to be so cheery about.

With a curious look around, Laila was surprised to discover Nikolean sitting unafraid near the dragon while Turathyl cleaned her paws. The two of them had been getting closer each day, sharing a strange and growing connection, and Laila found it rather aggravating. Even though their conversations were only one-sided, they appeared to be getting on rather well. Laila wouldn't admit to herself that it was so irksome simply because she was missing her own connection with the dragon. Despite that, she hadn't been able to forgive

Turathyl for her role in her parent's death and wasn't sure if she'd ever be able to.

Laila looked up and gave a polite smile to Glondora, who was approaching her with a water flask.

"I noticed ye didna' 'ave anythin' ta drink, so's me thought ye might want some." Glondora handed her the flask, and Laila took it gratefully. Then, the dwarf went and sat down on the ground near her and pulled out some dried meat to gnaw on.

After a few minutes eating in silence, Glondora said, "Not that it be any o' me business, but I was wonderin' what be goin' on between ye and me lad, Davion. The lad been in such high spirits since the two o' ye were off on that walk o' yers. I gotta say, tis been nice seein' 'im so 'appy, but ye dunna' seem so 'appy as he."

Laila sighed, unsure of how to answer her curiosity. It encouraged her to see Davion acting like himself again too, but she just wasn't there yet.

"He kissed me," she said quietly, not looking away from her food.

"Oh?" Glondora perked up excitedly. "And?"

"And..." Laila looked at her. "I'm not sure. It was nice, but I honestly don't know how I feel about anything right now."

"I see," the dwarf replied with a frown, looking back to her meat. "Well, I knows ye be goin' through a lot, m'lady. Tis understandable. But I also be worried 'bout 'im getting' 'urt again too."

Laila nodded to her, understanding. She had no desire to hurt him again.

"And what 'bout that drow who always be starin' at ye?" Glondora continued.

CHAPTER 5

"I don't know how I feel for him either," she replied. "We haven't talked about what happened between us. I'm not even sure how he feels about me."

With another heavy sigh, Laila began to pack up her things and get Merimer ready to continue on their way. "Besides," she told Glondora, "it seems we have much bigger things to worry about now. Don't you agree?"

"Nay, m'lady!" Glondora said firmly. "Matters o' the heart be important, too. Who knows, maybe twill be what saves us all." The dwarf winked at her. "As fer yer drow. There be no doubt in me mind, or anyone's mind how he feels fer ye; how either of them feels fer ye. The question be, how does ye feel fer them?" And with that, the dwarf picked up her things and started heading back over to her husband, giving him a big, wet kiss when she reached him, toppling him over playfully.

Laila thought about what Glondora said and knew she was right. She knew at some point she'd have to figure out the answer to that question, but she just couldn't seem to focus her mind. It was almost as though she were still trapped inside somewhere, fighting to get out.

While she buried her face into Merimer's soft mane, the hybrid sensed her melancholy, and she nuzzled her head over her shoulder in comfort. '*Thanks, girl,*' she sent to the mare, and Merimer nickered, letting out a gentle, loving sound.

As everyone readied to leave, Turathyl watched the young elf with Merimer and wished she could comfort her as well. She was worried about Laila, sensing that something still wasn't right, and that it went beyond her merely being angry with her about her mother. But, while she waited for the elf to speak with her again, all she could do was stay with and protect her from the outside forces. Until Laila was ready to open up, the young elf maiden would have to keep fighting the inside forces on her own.

"We either take that risk, or we may as well turn back now. I do not see how we could possibly pass through the gorge with so many orcs."

Laila's head began to pound; the arguing whispers of the others became muffled in her thoughts as she examined the orc town before her. Her heart beating hard, panic began to seep in. If they couldn't get through the gorge to Gortax, then what were they supposed to do? Where were they supposed to go? Is her mission to be thwarted by a horde of measly orcs? Lost in her thoughts, she barely heard her name being called. When she looked back, everyone was talking to her at once.

'Laila, we need to go back or wait for my kin to join us,' Turathyl suggested.

Glondora asked, "M'lady, what should we do?"

Hort scoffed, "If ye thinkin' 'bout goin' in there, well, that'd be the dumbest thing I 'ad tickle me ears."

"We need to go back," Davion pressed.

"We should go around through the desert," Salyaman repeated.

"My lady..." Nikolean said calmly, touching her hand.

Gaping at the drow's hand on hers, it seemed to ground her. Laila's eyes then followed along the drow, past his wrist, to his arm, and up until she locked eyes with him, caught in his blood-red gaze. Then all the noise, all the pounding in her head, stopped.

"My lady, what do you want to do? We are here for you," Nikolean said.

With all other sounds shut out from her head, Laila tried to think. There was a lack of confidence that still lingered over her, and she didn't feel ready to be challenged so soon, terrified of fighting again... and failing. But if she didn't move forward and get the group to Gortax, how would she complete her quest?

Perhaps they should try asking the elves again. Or the humans. Or...

As she mulled possible alternatives over in her mind, a loud scream came from the gorge, and they all looked in terror, realizing that it wasn't only orcs within. From one of the orc's mighty clutch, dangled a male dwarf in battle gear, swinging his fists futilely at the monster as it ripped the pieces of armor from him. Behind them was a rudimentary wooden cage that held four other dwarves, including one female.

Startled and panicked, Laila jumped up. Nikolean grabbed her firmly by the wrist, pulling her back down behind the hill before she could be seen, and maintained his grasp on her.

"What are they doing to them?" she asked, alarmed.

"Food," Nikolean whispered.

Laila looked at him, confused.

"They are likely preparing to eat him," Salyaman added, confirming.

Eyes wide, Laila stared back at the poor dwarf being dangled about and poked at by the orcs.

"Hmmm... Couldna' we jus' send in the dragon?" Hort said, distraught and sick to his stomach. "I canna' watch..." he added, looking away and over at Turathyl as she kept out of sight.

'There are too many for only me,' the dragon assured her, letting out a quiet snort at the dwarf.

But then, a horrific sound came from the dangling dwarf as one of the orcs brutally ripped off his arm, and that was all that it took. Laila forcefully jerked her hand free from the drow's grasp and flew over the hilltop without another thought, running at full speed towards the gorge.

Her friends called after her, aghast, pleading with her to stop, but she didn't care; her mind had been made up for her. She couldn't watch those monsters tear apart defenseless dwarves to have for their dinners. There would be no more debate about it and no turning back as, above the gorge, the orc guards spotted her, sounding their ominous horns of battle.

CHAPTER 5

CHAPTER SIX

GORGE

"*O*h, Goddess Mother, Jayenne, and Kyrash! Why canna' ye kids use yer blastit 'eads once in a whiles?!" Hort grumbled after Laila.

While raising herself from hiding, Turathyl spread her massive wings, puffing herself out. But, the orcs did not appear intimidated at the sight of her, as orcs tended to be, which she found rather disconcerting. Summoning the wind spirit, she thrust downward and lifted into the sky while assessing the orcs' positions.

Merimer galloped forward at lightning speed toward Laila, catching up with her promptly. The elf, sensing her, reached out and effortlessly grabbed hold of her mane right as the hybrid came within reach, swinging herself up over and onto her back as the two of them charged for the gorge.

Salyaman quickly cast his six-inch thorns to sprout over his body and snatched his bow and an arrow from the quiver while running after them, leaving his elkah, Friet, behind. He prayed to Goddess Jayenne for her protection and guidance; certain Laila had just made a grave mistake.

Meanwhile, Hort was mumbling prayers to the god of war, Kyrash, as he grabbed his axe and began unburdening his okullo from the cart to ride out after Laila. Glondora immediately grabbed her staff and started casting wards, protections, and tranquility spells over the group. The comrades were now stronger, faster, and more clear-headed. Davion began casting minor shields and protections around everyone, focusing primarily on Laila. They wouldn't last long but hopefully would at least absorb a few blows.

After Hort managed to free the okullo, he was climbing onto his back when Orbek began walking off. The dwarf fumbled to get the rest of the way up, one foot caught in the stirrup, cursing and sneering at his old friend.

Once he was able to swing his other leg over, Hort called out to Glondora, "Stay 'ere, me love!" He gave Orbek a quick kick and chased after the others.

"Ta Ignisar's Lair wi' that!" Glondora called back at Hort. "Best be goin', lad," she said hurriedly to Davion while grabbing Helna for them both, upset with her husband for not taking her with him. "Ye'll not be leavin' me behind."

After Davion hastily mounted Helna, he helped pull Glondora up onto the horse's back, the dwarf surprisingly not afraid of the height like his Uncle Hort was. Then, they both rode after the others, staffs in hands at the ready.

As Laila dashed into the open atop Merimer toward the hulking monsters, two of which were riding hideous sorechons, her memories of her battle with the dragons suddenly hit her. It dawned on her that her powers would once again be limited since she would not be able to pull energy from the lifeless earth of the dried and rocky surface. She realized that she would have to act more sensibly than in her last battle, would have to space out her powers and not rely on them so heavily, reserving them for when she needed them most.

Grabbing her Dragonsbane spear from behind her, she gripped it firmly, feeling the balance in her clutch, the strength of its metal, and positioned it readily. Out of the corner of her eye, she saw Turathyl fly past her toward the north-ledge of the gorge where four orcs, half of whom were on sorechons, stood guard. She could hear the others approaching as they followed her lead.

Feeling a bit of confidence stirring—after all, it was just a bunch of measly orcs; not at all like fighting a lair of dragons— she raised her spear and launched it at an oncoming orc. Unfortunately, the orc was prepared and slammed the spear with its large metal shield, casting it aside. What the orc hadn't been prepared for was that the spear went flying back to Laila, replanting itself squarely in her palm as she used her telekinesis to summon it back to her before it could even hit the ground. The orc was confused, but its mount continued thundering forward until it slammed into Merimer's forcefield. Both orc and sorechon went catapulting backwards, crashing hard against the rocky ground. They were only down for a second, then they jumped back to their feet, ready for more.

The second mounted orc was closing in, and Laila heard from behind her, "*Ominus lacarté!*" Then a firebolt shot past her and headed for the closest beast, exploding in flames against it, knocking it from atop the startled sorechon. "*Lacarté!*" he shouted again, and a second shot erupted from his staff and blasted into the other orc, exploding against its chest just as Davion rode up beside Laila, Glondora holding him tightly from behind.

With the orcs distracted by the flames, Laila hurled her spear again. It jetted through the air, piercing the mounted orc right through its heart, and the monster collapsed instantly, dead. As Laila summoned back her weapon, a dagger flew by her with unnatural speed—aided by the wind spirit—and struck the other brute directly between the eyes. The hulk fell slowly sideways from its sorechon, being partially dragged by its mount before ultimately crashing to the ground.

Nikolean rode up to Laila on his beautiful charcoal steed, Midnight, with its glowing red eyes and jet black hair, and gave her a smirk. "Didn't think we'd let you have all the fun, did you, my lady?"

She smiled at him, then watched as Turathyl glided to the south ledge after slaying the four guards above the gorge. But, her attention was diverted by the sorechons that continued to charge at the group, snarling with teeth bared. Arrows flew past as Salyaman ran up beside them on foot, rapidly firing at the beasts and planting several shots into their tough hides, slowing them down. Letting out a boisterous battle cry, Hort shot past them all on Orbek, his axe held high in the air, heading straight for the two sorechons.

Glondora briskly dismounted from Helna, gripping her staff on the way down, and began circling it in the air. She then lashed the tip forward at the beasts and shouted, "*Ferétsa ageeran!*"

The beasts' movements slowed as they began to freeze from Glondora's spell while Hort hastily swung his axe, embedding it deep into the thick neck of the first sorechon, nearly severing its head, then yanked his axe back clear while it collapsed.

"Thank ye, me love!" he called out to Glondora as he rode smugly to the next beast. The freeze spell was beginning to wear off, but he swung his axe hurriedly, planting it in the sorechon's neck as he had the first beast, slaying it alike before it could pick up too much speed. The animal fell face-first into the dirt, skidding forward as it came to its final resting place.

"Any time, me husband!" she called back, smiling.

Upon discerning the group's confidence growing, Salyaman cautiously warned them, "I am afraid it is not yet time to celebrate." He motioned toward the gorge where there were at least three dozen more orcs charging at them on foot, various weapons in their grasps, and even more still in the canyon beyond.

Hort trotted Orbek up beside Glondora, hoisting her up behind him, while everyone faced the oncoming army, preparing themselves for battle.

After Turathyl slew the four orc guards masterfully on the south ridge, she saw the imminent danger the others were in and started running toward the cliff to leap off, when Laila mind-sent, *'Free the dwarves inside the gorge!'*

Hesitantly, she looked back and forth between the caged dwarves and the orcs heading for Laila and the others. It took all the dragon's willpower not to fly toward the elf, but she decided to trust her, turning reluctantly toward the gorge instead. However, she gripped the side with her claws, stopping herself from jumping over when she saw how many more orcs were still within, ready and waiting for her.

Before she could react, a type of bolas with weighted stones came shooting up over the side, wrapping thick ropes around her front leg. It seemed a feeble attempt at first, but then she realized the bolas-snare was mounted to a pulley system anchored in the gorge below. She chewed at the ropes, but the orcs started to turn the crank and reel her in like a prized catch. The evil swine were laughing below, very pleased with themselves. Bracing against the crumbling cliff ledge, forcefully opposing the pull of the ropes, the dragon fought the trap, but her leg continued to skid forward over the side, pulling her with it.

As the orcs came at Laila and the others, she knew they had to deplete the monsters' numbers quickly if they were to stand a chance. She motioned for her comrades to hold back and positioned Merimer sideways, clearing her path. The ground beneath them thundered with the trampling orcs, and the air was filled with their swine-like cries of battle. When the monsters came within range, Laila let out a mighty scream as she pulled fiercely from the fire spirit, her adrenalin pumping hard through her veins while pushing outward toward the oncoming horde. As she let loose an inferno of fiery hell before her, the orcs in the forefront were engulfed in the blast, and they screamed in horror, their skin rapidly burning away. However, the orcs behind them continued to press forward, loathsomely using the burning orcs as shields against the flames.

When Laila let go of the fire and saw the orcs continuing to charge at them in such a horrific manner, she cringed and shuddered at the sight, but there was no time for fear, no time for doubts. She had only made a slight dent in the swarm, and they were coming too fast.

With haste, Laila dismounted and pressed her hands against the ground, sending shockwaves through the earth out to the oncoming horde. The rocky surface beneath several of the orcs quickly loosened and seemed as though it were melting as they sank into the terrain, fighting the sopping soil that was pulling them downward. Although her quicksand approach had only slowed a select few of the foes, she could sense that her power was stretching further, requiring less energy, thanks to the tranquility spell Glondora had cast. It wasn't replenishing her like taking energy from the earth did, but it would allow her to utilize her powers more than anticipated.

Feeling inspired, Laila reached for the earth spirit again and pulled forth sharp spikes that protruded from the ground betwixt them and the monsters, creating a wall. Regardless, the

CHAPTER 6

orcs still didn't stop; they scaled and clobbered down the wall, barely slowing their pace at all.

Davion continued casting fire spells at them while Laila remounted. Glondora managed to freeze only a few, momentarily slowing them. Strategically waving her staff, she shouted, "*Ferosta lacarté!*" and spears of ice fired from her staff at the orcs, with each repeated "*lacarté*" cast. The spears propelled at the beasts, several of which managed to pierce their tough hides.

Salyaman mumbled an enchantment, then roared out and began shooting his arrows more rapidly than was visible to the eye. With all of the group's efforts, a few more orcs dropped off, either wounded or dead, but a sizable rage of orcs was still charging for them.

Laila converted Dragonsbane into dual daggers, and everyone held their weapons ready to engage; Salyaman with his two swords, Hort with his axe, Nikolean with his long-sword, and Davion and Glondora with their staffs.

The sky grew dark as unnatural black clouds filled the area above them, and thunder rumbled through the land. Knowing it wasn't her doing, Laila looked around to find the source of the obvious air magic, and her heart skipped a beat when she spotted Turathyl within the canyon, struggling against the orcs who had snared her.

As she stared back at the stampeding orcs, panic surged through Laila's veins. When the monsters were only twenty paces away, the tiny elf screamed an unholy bellow at them, engaging her mind-summoning ability by sending a wave of telekinetic energy. The first row, consisting of half a dozen orcs, was picked up off their feet and flung forcefully backward into the others, each knocking several down. As they scrambled to get back up, Laila borrowed Turathyl's storm, raising her hand to the sky. A bolt of lightning shot down, striking one of the orcs, and sending him scorched to the ground. She repeated the lightning strikes three more times but then remembered that she needed to pace herself, even with the tranquility spell, and released her hold on the storm.

Merimer stomped at the ground beneath Laila, preparing to charge, and Laila mentally nodded for her to "go!" while letting out a fierce battle cry. Laila rode out toward the oncoming orcs, and her comrades all joined in her bellow as they followed her lead. The sound of metal on metal clanged and echoed through the gorge as the two groups collided into a heated battle.

When Laila reached them, three orcs were thrown backward with a shock from Merimer's shield, but the impact was enough to drain it, and the protection fizzled and fell away. When another orc neared her, she hastily stood in her saddle and pounced forward at it, surprising the beast as she landed on its shoulder and thrust her dagger into the back of its skull. As the monster began to fall, Laila leapt from the corpse to the next unsuspecting orc. The orc tried grabbing at her with its graceless ungainly limbs, but she moved swiftly, stabbing at it until severing an artery, its green blood spraying out from the wound. Then she struck again and again until it finally collapsed.

Using the height of his steed as an advantage, Nikolean swung his sword at the orcs nearest him, but they were efficiently blocking his attacks. So, taking Laila's lead, he dodged the orc's bludgeonings, grabbed his daggers, and jumped from his mount to attack them more agilely. Watching him move was like watching leaves caught in the wind as he maneuvered his way around them faster than visible to the monsters—remarkably sluggish in comparison. The drow would swoop in, stabbing at them, and then leap away before they could retaliate.

Salyaman continued his assault on foot, slicing the orcs with his blades while they were being pierced repeatedly by the thorns protruding from his skin. His cat-like reflexes helped him evade most of the maulings, but more were closing in on him. As one of the orcs swung his giant sword at the elf, Salyaman was not quick enough to dodge, and the tip sliced across his upper arm. He grimaced from the pain, refusing to cry out.

Upon seeing the elf in distress, Hort came galloping over with Glondora and dismounted, grabbing his axe. "Keep safe, me love!" he hollered as he joined Salyaman. He hacked at the beasts with his weapon, carefully blocking them with his large metal-rimmed shield.

Davion and Glondora kept behind the others, casting whatever offensive spells they could to keep the orcs at bay, preventing them from ganging up on the group. Glondora froze as many as she could manage, finding that slowing them helped the others not be overcome by the masses, giving them a better chance. She also focused on her strength as a hydromancer, which was casting protective magical wards on the group, effectively reducing the injuries that befell them.

Laila was trying to get through the orc army hastily but was too focused on the dragon's screeching and became distracted from her battle, concerned for Turathyl. While looking toward the gorge, anxious about what they were doing to the dragon, an orc snuck up behind the elf with a mace held out, ready to thwart her.

"*Ominus unasceiry!*" Davion cast and a large blue ball of fire shot out from the red garnet embedded in his staff, striking the orc directly.

Laila jerked around as the monster emitted a hair-raising scream, watching as the fireball continued to incinerate the orc beyond its skin and bones until there was nothing left but burnt ash. She glanced at Davion, giving him a thankful nod before turning back to the other orcs, more focused and prepared than before.

As the group continued to hack away at the orc army, they were becoming weary. There were just too many of them to maintain their momentum much longer. Laila noticed that her friends were beginning to grow weak and slower, as each of them incurred more and more minor injuries, and she knew it was only a matter of time before one of them would receive much more than that. She had to do something now.

Upon looking out over the field, her jaw dropped when Laila saw even more orcs charging at them from the gorge, including more sorechons. They just kept coming at them endlessly, and she couldn't fathom how many there must be.

Mentally shoving the two orcs in front of her back to give her some space, the tiny elf raised her hands to the sky, and her eyes began to glow red as she invoked the fire spirit, connecting deeply with it. The storm clouds of Turathyl's calling then turned blood-red and orange, creating a daunting hue over the gorge. Everyone—friend and foe alike—gawked as fire began to rain down from the sky. The flames shot down like meteors, aimed at the orcs running from the gorge toward them. The monsters all floundered around, trying to dodge and unsuccessfully evade the incoming missiles. Rock and orc went flying as the meteors plummeted, striking them down, wiping out several enemy targets.

Her friends continued to fight the orcs before them, trying to subdue them, but they were still struggling. When Laila heard a horse squeal, she looked to find Davion flying out of his saddle after Helna was struck with a mallet, and their attacker was now approaching Davion. The hulking beast raised its mallet high above Davion's head, smiling wickedly.

"NOOO!" Laila screamed.

Fire still raining from the sky, Laila promptly grabbed hold of a meteor, redirecting it with accelerated speed toward the orc about to strike the human. The meteor exploded against the orc, sending it flying with a giant hole in its chest, and it crashed to the ground, dead. *Not this time!* she swore to herself. While Davion regained his stance, Laila continued to cover him.

With everyone distracted on the front line, no one noticed as a treacherous orc snuck past the others and headed for what it deemed an easy target. As Glondora continued casting her wards on her friends and ice shards at the orc masses, she didn't see the cunning orc coming up on her left rear but heard its swine-like, guttural snort as it advanced on her. She turned to discover a raised chained club about to strike her with a fatal blow.

As the weapon came down, the dwarf bellowed, *"Ferosta lacarté!"*

Shards of ice shot from her staff, planting directly into the orc's ugly mug, and it screeched in agony. The force of the ice piercing through its face jolted the beast, causing the club to make an indirect hit instead. Glondora cried out in pain from the impact against her right shoulder and chest as she fell to the ground on her knees.

While stumbling around, the orc squealed in pain and flailed its arms berserkly. To stop the torturous infliction from the embedded ice shards, the beast suddenly struck itself fiercely in the face once, twice, with its own club. The squeals then stopped, the orc collapsing to the ground, dead.

Upon hearing his wife's cry, Hort whirled around and ran back to her without a second thought, leaving the orc he was battling confused.

"Glondy!!!" Hort called out as he neared and bent toward her to get a better look. "Are ye alright, me love?"

Wincing in pain, she nodded with tears in her eyes.

"I wonna' leave ye," Hort declared and turned, readying himself to protect her.

Laila, having heard Glondora's cry as well, was relieved to see that she was safe for the time being and that Hort was with her. As her rain of fire subsided, she looked around at the remaining orcs. Most of the ones in the clearing had been wiped out, leaving only a few that her friends were battling.

In the distance, Turathyl let out a weak, pained howl. Laila saw that she had been pinned down by the orcs, who were stabbing at her with their weapons, while the dragon was doing her best to deflect them with what limited movement she could attain.

"Do you need me?" Laila called out to everyone. "I need to get to Tury!"

"Go! We have this!" Davion shouted back.

"Aye, lass. I be stayin' with Glondy. Ye go get yer dragon," Hort said encouragingly.

"Go! Be safe!" Salyaman added as he struck his sword upward through an orc's jaw and into its skull.

Laila then exchanged a brief glance with Nikolean. He nodded confidently to her, giving her the reassurance she needed, and she was off, running as fast as her legs could carry her. It wasn't long before Merimer was galloping up beside her, linked with her, and Laila grabbed hold of her mane, remounting. While they ran at full force for the canyon, the elf prayed to the gods, desperately seeking their aid to reach her dragon before it was too late.

CHAPTER 6

CHAPTER SEVEN

BLOOD

*A*s Laila powered forward toward the ravine atop Merimer, she saw two orcs standing before a wooden spike wall, slapping their weapons smugly in their palms with a fierce smile upon their lips, and a third one closed the heavy gate. Beyond the wall lay her dragon, bound and beaten on the ground, blue blood trickling like rain onto the rock and several more of the monsters taunting her merrily. Laila knew she had to get to Turathyl at once and didn't have time for more distractions.

When the three orcs strode out to greet her, Laila raised her hand to them without slowing down, crying out as she shoved them with her mind. They went catapulting backward toward the wall, impaling with force on the spikes. Two of them were killed instantly, while the third waved his only free arm around, completely helpless.

As they continued galloping toward the wall, Laila searched for a way to get inside and signaled for Merimer to slow down, but the hybrid kept driving forward toward the wall. The elf's heart stopped right before they were going to collide with the spikes, and she raised an arm before her and closed her eyes in a cold sweat, but then she felt Merimer jolt. Upon opening her eyes, Laila found herself in the air, high above the wall, still holding on to the beautiful unicorn-elkah beneath her. Merimer was lunging over the wall, effortlessly clearing its spikes, and landed with a graceful impact on the other side, releasing a proud victory snort.

With a mental kick, they ran for the dragon. As they approached another group of orcs, all turned to observe the newcomer—all but one. Laila watched as her dragon lay defenseless on the ground, unable to move and too weak to fight. An orc near Turathyl's head raised his long heavy sword high into the air, preparing to finish off the dragon. An evil grin was smeared on the monster's hideous face, lips curled back from his sharp tusks, and as the blade came down, Laila released a blood-curdling scream. Her hand out before her, she used the spirits to hold the orc in place; her hatred and anger for those creatures building up inside her as the orc fought with its immense strength against her hold, its sword inching closer to the dragon's head.

While Laila was holding the orc in her grasp, Nikolean managed to get through the spiked barrier with Midnight and was heading to join her. Two orcs attempted to charge at the elf atop Merimer, but they were thrown back, zapped by Merimer's replenished shield. More of the beasts were being slowed by Nikolean's daggers as he threw them from behind her, planting them into prime locations. Davion and Salyaman arrived next. But the elf didn't see any of them; she only saw the orc that was endeavoring to kill Turathyl.

Laila clenched her fists at the monster still paralyzed by her power, hatred and anger in her eyes. That orc began to shake violently. A terrified and confused look swept over its face, and then came the screams. Laila's scream and the orc's nearly matched in magnitude as the monster continued to convulse under her control. Their voices carried throughout the canyon, startling all who heard, stealing the attention of all who could see. She held the beast there, her heart pounding fiercely. Then, the orc's screaming went quiet, and it quivered so severely that it became an echoing blur of itself. The sword dropped from the beast's grasp, clanging on the stone beneath. Without further warning, the hulking mass suddenly exploded from within, its thick-green blood and flesh spewing out in all directions.

Laila stopped screaming and breathed heavily, trying to collect herself, lightheaded and dizzy. She could feel Merimer stamping at the ground under her, but couldn't hear her neighing in distress. There was a loud ringing in her ears, the only sound she could hear, and she looked dazedly around.

As the realization of what had just occurred washed over her, descrying pieces of the orc everywhere, the young elf stared in bewilderment. Despite the devastation, she took notice of her dragon lying motionless on the ground. She was running out of time.

While Laila rode Merimer towards the remaining orcs, whose attention had returned to her, she sensed their nervousness as they wavered between whether to flee or attack. The ringing in her ears stopped, and the sounds of battle flooded back into her mind; the thundering of Merimer's hooves beneath her, the screams and squeals of the orcs, the sounds of weapons clanging.

Too full of adrenaline to register how depleted she was, she raised her Dragonsbane spear as she neared them and skillfully stabbed at the hulking beasts. Nikolean joined her with haste, and Laila was relieved that her friends had defeated their earlier foes and were more or less in one piece. With them distracting the remaining few orcs, Laila darted with Merimer the rest of the way, then lunged off the hybrid and knelt down by Turathyl.

'Tury,' Laila pleaded, 'Tury, please! Can you hear me?!'

Weakly opening her eyes, the dragon used all her strength to look at the elf beside her. 'You need to go,' the dragon told her. 'Save yourself and the others. There are still more coming; I can hear them through the ground. I will not last much longer.'

'No! I won't leave you! I will save you!' Laila cried out mentally, stroking the dragon's snout with love as her friends finished off the remaining orcs behind her.

Hort and Glondora had arrived with Orbek and were making their way toward the cage holding the captive dwarves.

'It is okay, Laila. It is my time. You must save yourself and complete your mission. Everyone is counting on you.' Turathyl rested her head back in the dirt, her breathing slowing.

'Don't say that!' Laila wept. 'I won't leave you! I'll heal you!'

'There is no life in the soil here; your earth magic cannot save me. Laila, go now. I know you can do this. I am so proud of how far you've come.' Taking a deep strained breath, the dragon said, 'Goodbye, young one. Believe in yourself, for you are so much more than "just Laila."' The dragon attempted to give her a smile, but was too weak. She closed her eyes, exhaling a final breath.

"NO!" Laila shouted aloud, tears streaming down her face. "Not like this! Not now!"

Laila collapsed on the unmoving dragon's snout, embracing her muzzle as she wept hysterically. The dragon's life force was so faint now, and Laila knew that in a moment, her guardian, her friend, would be gone. Her comrades were watching forlornly, shaking and bowing their heads.

"You can't leave me," she whispered to Turathyl, unable to reach the dragon's mind any longer. As she sat there sobbing, Laila heard a hog-like squeal when Nikolean stabbed a final orc, causing it to keel over to the ground.

For the briefest of moments, all was deathly silent until a loud rumbling filled the gorge. The ground began shaking and trembling beneath them, loose pebbles dancing on the hard rock bed. Their eyes all turned, panicked, as more of the monsters came terrifyingly around the corner toward them. But Laila couldn't bring herself to leave Turathyl.

Earth... Life... Energy...

"Laila! Let's get the dwarves and get out of here!" Davion bellowed from beside her.

"Yes, get the dwarves," Laila replied, oddly calm, as she stood up, away from the dragon, but she didn't follow them. Instead, she stared with intent at the orcs in the distance that were advancing on them at an alarming rate.

Seeing a disturbing smirk appear on the elf's face, Nikolean cautiously approached her. "My lady? Are you... alright?"

All the others quickly ran to the wooden cage holding the dwarves and hacked at the gate until it came free. The dwarves rushed out, thanking their saviors whole-heartedly. Unfortunately, for the dwarf the orcs had been toying with before the battle, the one that incited the attack to begin with, it was too late. While the four imprisoned dwarves were being released, Hort respectfully—and hastily—laid a dwarven shield he found near the cage on the deceased dwarf's chest, bowing his head as he sent a brief prayer to the Goddess Mother to keep safe his soul.

"We have the dwarves; let us leave *now*, Lady Laila!" Salyaman shouted.

But Laila didn't move.

"Salyaman, Glondora, do your best to heal my friend," she commanded, continuing to stare eerily at the oncoming horde.

"M'lady, she be too far gone fer us," Glondora told her.

And then running was no longer an option; the orcs were now too near for an escape. Everyone, including the newly freed dwarves, prepared themselves for another battle.

"HEAL MY FRIEND!" Laila shouted with a voice that sounded like many as she glared back at them in fury.

They all gasped, alarmed, when they saw her. Laila's eyes had turned completely black, her hair flying wildly in the wind. She did not resemble the sweet elf they knew, but appeared now as a demonic force full of wrath. Laila had pulled forth a different spirit, one that she had only brushed upon in the past; she had tapped into the phantom realm, drawing its power into her.

Startled and fearful of what was happening to Laila, the healers tentatively made their way toward the dragon to see if there was anything they could do.

From the water spirit, Laila called upon the same blood magic that caused the orc to explode, using it to hold all the monsters in place, frozen in time. The orcs fought against her, but she was filled with all the spirits' power, and her hold would not easily be broken. Then, with its darkness embracing her, Laila felt the phantom realm's power surging through her as she directed it toward the horde, grasping on to their life forces. The surrounding sky grew dark as a thick, eerie fog swiftly filled the gorge. Sounds of spirits howled and screamed while the fog whirred and whooshed around them, haunting the onlookers to their very cores.

Without pause, the beasts' heads tilted back in unison, their bodies completely out of their control, and a dark aura began to emerge from their gaping mouths. Everyone watched, horrified, unsure of what to do. Then, in a petrifying mystical cloud, the life essences of the orcs flowed spine-chillingly across the ravine and into the dying dragon.

CHAPTER 7

No one dared approach the elf while she siphoned the life from the orcs; they simply watched in fear—and awe—as she drained the spirit energy out of each and every last orc before them. Turathyl's heart began to beat harder, and her chest rose and fell as she was able to take another breath, but she was still severely injured. With the dragon's new energy source, Salyaman and Glondora got to work tending to her injuries post haste. Salyaman had healed Glondora's shoulder, but she was still weak from the battle, and Salyaman couldn't heal the dragon's more critical wounds with his limited abilities.

"M'lady!" Glondora called to Laila. "We need ye! Tis too much fer us!"

Nearly depleted, Laila's breathing was strained as though a weight was pressing on her chest. She blinked the blackness from her eyes and dazedly looked over at the dragon with exhaustion. "I don't know how!" she cried out. "There is no life in the earth for me to heal with!"

"There isna' gunna' be much life in the earth fer most o' the journey, m'lady. The land tis nearly all dead west o' Lochlann. Come! Ye'll have ta learn ta use yer water magic ta heal!" the dwarf yelled.

It hadn't even dawned on Laila that she controlled both elements used for healing; earth *and* water. The earth healing had just come naturally to her without even realizing she was doing it initially, so she never thought even to try water magic.

Instilled with a new sense of hope, she rushed over to Glondora, who helped guide her. The way she used her magic wasn't at all like what Laila could do. However, she understood the premise thanks to the dwarf, comprehending a lot of it had to do with the water that made up most of all life forms.

As she placed her hands over Turathyl, Laila summoned the water spirit forward and, to her relief, found the process came more naturally than she had anticipated. It was as though the water spirit knew what to do before she could tell it. The spirit pulled from the elf's energy as it flowed with vigor into the dragon, weaving together her wounded flesh and organs. It healed her heart and her lungs first, and the dragon was slowly opening her eyes once again.

Laila managed to heal Turathyl's life-threatening wounds, but the dragon remained critically weak with several injuries yet to be mended. Sadly, Laila just could not do any more.

The dragon, with great effort, lifted her head and turned to gaze at the remarkable young elf. '*Thank you, Omi Méa,*' she told her faintly.

Laila started shaking, her adrenaline stabilizing, her body pushed to its limits as the spirits' powers drained her. Tears welling in her eyes trickled down her cheeks when she suddenly bent forward and vomited all over the ground, just before collapsing. Everyone began to crowd around her, panicked.

"I know what she needs!" Nikolean shouted, shoving past them and scooping her up into his arms.

"Where are you taking her?!" Davion demanded.

Ignoring him, Nikolean carried her over to the orc he had attacked earlier that lay near death, heaped against the side of the ravine. He rested her next to the orc, placing her hands on its rough, calloused skin as he began to pray. Then, just as Laila had unconsciously siphoned life from the drow on Silvers' Mountain, she began to do the same to the orc, its life force flowing freely into her, until the beast was no more.

"My lady?" Nikolean prompted, sitting her up. "Can you hear me?"

Groggily, she opened her eyes and found herself met with Nikolean's face, which instantly brought a smile to her lips, causing him to chuckle with relief.

"Tury?" she inquired weakly.

'*I'll be alright,*' the dragon reassured her, '*thanks to you.*'

CHAPTER 7

With Nikolean's assistance, Laila stood up and returned to Turathyl, nearly collapsing on her muzzle. *'I'm so sorry, Tury!'* she cried, holding her snout lovingly.

'And what are you sorry for?' the dragon asked, confused.

'I was so mad at you! But when I thought I lost you...'

The dragon purred at the young elf, clicking air at the back of her throat. She was reminded of the crying elf cub she had found in the tree hollow over sixteen years ago. And, just like then, the purring soothed the little elf, comforting her and halting her tears.

'I do not blame you, Laila. I cannot change the past, but I believe you can change the future.'

When all had settled down, the group quietly watched while Laila embraced her dragon. The other dwarves they had rescued gathered around them timidly, staying nearest Glondora and Hort.

"Pardon me..." one of the male dwarves said, calling their attention. "But does any o' ye care ta tell us WHAT THE BACCAT JUST 'APPENED?! And who be the elfie? What did the lass do ta them orcs?! And what a dragon be doin' 'ere? And a drow? And why ye be 'elpin—"

"Calm down, Okom!" the rescued female dwarf interrupted. "Methinks what 'e be tryin' ta say is, thank ye very much fer the rescue and can any o' ye tell us what in Ignisar's Lair be goin' on 'ere?!"

THE DRAGONS

Great Spirit

- 91 -

CHAPTER 7

CHAPTER EIGHT

GORTAX

Without any more attacks from the orcs, the group stayed in the gorge that night. The dwarves, including Hort, Glondora, and even Davion, honored their fallen comrade, Nelgour Frostspine, who was slain when the battle commenced. They performed the most proper burial they could muster up, given the circumstances.

While Glondora attended the make-shift funeral out of respect, Laila recommenced healing Turathyl's remaining wounds. Salyaman tended to the others, who all endured minor injuries throughout the battle. They were relieved that they could linger in the gorge and heal all the wounded in peace, giving Turathyl the time needed to recover as well. That is not to say that there were no orcs left in Gorén Gorge but is to say that those few that were left made it a point to stay well away from their invaders.

It was eerily quiet with the towering trench walls surrounding them as they gathered by the campfire that night.

Most of them broke the silence as the evening bore on with a joyous celebration from defeating the orcs.

While she lay there recovering, Turathyl was comforted to have her little elf back by her side as Laila rested against the dragon's shoulder. However, she could still sense that something was disquieting the Omi Méa.

'Is something troubling you, Laila? Why aren't you celebrating your victory with the others?' Turathyl asked her, concerned.

Quietly fiddling with her dagger in the dirt, she replied, *'I just don't think that I have it in me. I don't know that I'm up for this challenge. First, I failed against the Silvers, and now I nearly lost you to a bunch of orcs. I have nearly lost two of those I hold most dear to my heart, and both times were all my fault. I don't know if I could live with myself if I were to lose any of you for good. What if we don't all make it? Perhaps there's another way, or maybe the dragons just need more time to forgive the elves–'*

'Laila,' the dragon interrupted her. *'You're right. We may not all survive this journey, but that doesn't mean it would not have been worth it. There are so many others that have died because of the war, so many who continue to die almost every day, caught in the feuding between the races. Even with all of your magic, there is no way to just will everyone to stop fighting and love one another. I wish there were. However, I have no doubt in my mind that this is your destiny, Laila, and that only you can put a stop to the endless hate between the races. I don't know how you are to do that exactly, but I believe the gods have sent you to us, and I have faith in you.*

'If you should lose me–or anyone else along the way–do not regret anything. We all knew what we were agreeing to by joining you on your quest. We all love you and want to see this through. I have been watching your friends. Any one of them would lay down their life for you without a second thought because they believe in you, too. There has never before been so great a spirit as you. The powers you possess surpass all beings of Onis. Do not fear the gifts, Laila; embrace them. Use your

powers for the purpose they were intended, and then we can all rejoice when peace is brought to the land.

'If today proved anything, it is not that you are not up for this challenge, but that you are the only one who is. You are an unstoppable force, Great Spirit. I'm sorry... I mean "Laila."'

Laila mulled over the dragon's words, wishing she really could be just "Laila," but she knew her dragon was right; she was so much more. That didn't make her alright with the idea of losing any of her friends, but she understood it was a risk they would need to take if they were going to bring a stop to the war. She then prayed to Jayenne, wishing for her to watch over them, to keep them safe and close. Aside from her dragon, she was most fearful of losing Davion or Nikolean to the unknown, not being able to imagine the pain that losing either of them would cause her.

To her dismay, Davion had been keeping his distance from Laila since the battle, and she wasn't sure why, but she hoped he was simply giving her space to reconnect with Turathyl. Nikolean continued to be Nikolean, keeping mostly to himself and staring at her, smiling whenever their eyes would lock for even a moment, which always made her blush. She thought back on what Glondora had said about both the drow and human's feelings for her, but worried that Davion's were changing.

The four dwarves that had been held captive, Okom, Notdras, Handul, and the handsome female Haddilydd, were all excited to hear the tale of the prophecy and amused at seeing all the races together in a single group getting along so well, especially including that of a great Silver. Of course, the comrades failed to divulge that—for some of them—it was more a tolerance and less a "getting along," attributable to their lingering hostility.

Laila learned that the dwarves, along with poor Nelgour, were from Gortax and had been attempting to travel to

Lochlann when they were captured by the orcs. They had been in search of others who had departed Gortax before them, never to be heard from again. There had been rumors about increased activity of orc mobs near the gorge, but they hadn't realized how advanced of a threat they had become. With increasing dragon attacks on the other races beyond the originally targeted elves, the dwarves kept shelter in their cities. Even the mighty Gortax warriors and paladins preferred to spar with one another—whether on training grounds or in the taverns—to help fulfill their need to release pent-up aggression they would otherwise have used against the surrounding orc, drow, and other monstrous threats.

Observing the dwarves, Laila was intrigued by their playful banter and general merriment, considering everything that had just transpired. She took particular notice of Haddilydd and Handul's relationship, not quite sure what to make of it. They were continually taking playful verbal jabs at each other, like she'd seen Hort and Glondora do frequently, but they lacked the affection of her married dwarf friends. She thought that perhaps they were just courting and were not yet comfortable with that form of affection, although they seemed as though they'd been together forever.

As the group conversed, sharing stories and tales of adventure, Davion sat in the dirt with knees bent and forearms resting upon them, listening to the crackling of the fire against the cool dark night while staring into the depths of its flames. He didn't even notice Hort stroll up beside him until the dwarf clumsily sat down, kicking up dust around him.

"Me boy, why ye look lower than a basalure's belly?" Hort asked him, concerned.

Davion flashed back to the Norn River at the comparison, remembering where they had nearly lost Orbek to the black waters' slithering basalures. He could envision the slimy serpent that crawled out after them with its two stubby legs, dragging the rest of its body behind it. That day seemed like a lifetime ago now with all that has happened.

While letting out a long sigh, Davion grabbed a twig and tossed it into the fire, watching it sputter and spark as it struck against the coals. "Did you see what she did, Uncle?" he asked quietly.

"Hmmm... The orcs' spirits," Hort replied. "Aye, twas quite the sight. I didna' know she 'ad it in 'er."

"Neither did I," Davion said and continued in a whisper. "And there was something else; before you arrived. Uncle... she made an orc explode with her mind! I've never seen anything like it."

Hort grabbed his axe and started to clean and sharpen the blade. "Blood magic?" he asked, bemused. "She be a strong one, that elfie o' yers. Though, I didna' expect ta see 'er usin' the dark magics. Hmmm... She still be our Laila, ye know."

"But, her eyes... her voice..." Davion said distantly, remembering the fright he experienced from seeing her in her demonic guise, before losing the rest of his thought into the fire's dancing flames before him.

Hort sat quietly beside him, staring into the same flames, befuddled by the magic that the young elf maiden possessed, but he never really understood any of it to begin with. Just like he never understood all of the others' apparent connection with her, even Glondora's, yet he did not share a similar affinity. Sure, he found her quite fascinating and generally pleasant to be around, but the only affections he had were more because he knew Davion cared deeply for her. He was unsure how to comfort or reassure Davion of what he saw the elf do to the orcs. Plus, dealing with feelings wasn't exactly his strong suit. So, instead, he simply sat with him in silence, hoping he found some comfort in his companionship while sorting out his thoughts.

When everyone had recovered enough to resume course, it was another ten-day journey to get through the gorge and traverse along the mountain base to Onis Falls. Ever since Laila's talk with Turathyl, she had been torn. While more confident in herself—which was apparent to everyone—and feeling closer to her dragon again, she was still struggling with a heavy pain in her chest that she simply could not move past or heal.

Over the course of the next several days, she would rush out eagerly to meet any challenges head-on, fueled by her inner turmoil and newfound courage. She was disappointed when almost all foes were scared off at the sight of the great dragon stomping along with the group.

Nikolean rode alongside her on Midnight, amused by her recent fearlessness, but was sure to keep a close eye that it didn't become recklessness. After she chased off three orcs toward the mountains, she came trotting back on Merimer, dismay across her face.

Laughing, the drow smiled and said, "You'll get them next time, my lady."

With Hort and Glondora prattling on amongst the Gortaxian dwarves, who were bumpily riding in the cart behind Orbek, Davion traveled alongside Salyaman, mostly keeping his thoughts to himself, which suited both of them just fine. However, although quiet and reserved, the elf prince was doing his own observing, studying the new Laila intently, joined in Davion's concern for her.

Before Laila could even see the pristine waters and splendor of Onis Falls, she could hear it, like a cloud of static in her ears. It was early afternoon as they finally reached the falls, and it had become quite chilled over the last several days.

In the early mornings, the ground had been laced with a glistening white blanket of frost, beautifying their otherwise harsh terrain. It was still early enough in the season that the frost would vanish as the sun would rise high above them, the land warming to a comfortable degree. Nevertheless, that far north was noticeably colder than what Laila would have experienced back in her Sacred Forest at that time of year.

A peculiar calmness surrounded them as the sound from the falls drowned out everything else, even possible predators lurking in the mist. They made their way cautiously along the mountain base, passing a trench that had once been full of flowing waters in times past. Then, as they came around a corner, the landmark came into view.

Laila was in awe at the sight of the gargantuan waterfall. It was in a recessed area of the mountain range, expansed across the northern ridge. When she had first discovered Onis Falls through the earth spirit, the vision had not nearly done it justice. She was breathless standing before it, struck by the spectacular view, forgetting for just a moment all the heaviness that weighed on her heart.

The water billowed over the front of a small mountain slope, dropping over two hundred feet into a sparkling pool below, clear as glass beyond the plunging white waters. There were still signs of where the stream had once traveled south into the Du Noir Lake and farther flowed down into the dark elves' territory, but no more. It had all since dried and cracked beyond the small pool before them, forsaking the drow lands forevermore.

'I will need to wait in the mountains until you are ready for me,' Turathyl stated as they neared the falls, and Laila wordlessly sent her acknowledgment.

"I don't understand," she said to the dwarves. "Where is the entrance to Gortax?"

The dwarves continued down the path toward the falls without slowing down. "Yer lookin' at it, lass," Okom called back to her from the back of the wobbling cart.

Upon glancing over to Davion and the others, she saw that their intrigue was nearly as much as her own. She guessed that Salyaman might not have seen Onis Falls before, but assumed Davion and her dwarf companions all would have.

"Have you never been to Gortax?" Laila asked Davion curiously.

"I have not," he replied curtly.

She noticed he had still been acting peculiar since the gorge and decided not to pursue querying him if he was not interested in conversing with her. After all, she was not quite feeling like chit-chat either, still fighting the nagging in her head that left her feeling dispirited. Instead, she looked forward, intent on soaking in the experience of getting to see another new city. Unfortunately, she was also soaking in something else as they drew closer. Her neck strained as they approached the magnificent falls, looking up at its beauty and power while its mist swept over her from the plummeting downpour. She was thoroughly chilled by it, causing her to tremble. The mounts all snorted as the droplets tickled their noses, but everyone continued on, tightening their cloaks and furs around them to break the bite of the cold.

When they got nearer, Laila realized that the stone path they were on led right up to the falls, and the dwarves ahead of her disappeared behind the roaring water. Her mouth agape, she gave Merimer a mental kick and rode quickly ahead, eager to see what lay behind the falls for herself. To her dismay, beyond the initial exhilaration of being behind a waterfall, with its deafening splashing and cool waters spraying over her face, what she found was another long, dank passageway that they would need to traverse in order to reach Gortax. Except, she was told that it was even longer than the one leading to Lochlann. She did find it strange, however, that there had been no guards to stop or greet them at the tunnel entrance behind the falls, just a gloomy open tunnel with no visible end in sight.

As they made their way through the passage toward the dwarven capital, Laila pondered what "tricks" she could display for the dwarf king that would convince him that she was who they would all claim her to be; once again, putting on a show to appease her audience. She thought bitterly of it but understood her role and how important it was to gain the king's support. Even with her newly discovered abilities, she did not feel confident enough to go against Aeris again. Fighting orcs was not at all like the challenge she had faced on the Silvers' Mountain, and she shuddered at the remembrance of it.

"Nearly there," Haddilydd said excitedly, eager to show off her home to the newcomers. She was fascinated by the tales of the prophecy and the privilege of escorting the one-and-only Omi Méa to her home, which she had humbly offered to the group as refuge.

Due to the dwarves' excitement, Laila tried to act anticipatory for them out of politeness, even though she was nervous and wished it could all have been over with. She yearned for a sense of belonging somewhere, or even simply to visit a city and enjoy it without being continually pressed to throw her life on the line for others. Merimer perceived Laila's apprehension and snorted her shared displeasure, aiming to comfort her.

Noting that Davion had been keeping his distance from the elf maiden, Nikolean rode up near her to be supportive, and she welcomed his stolid presence. She was more at ease with the drow around, knowing he wouldn't press her for conversation that she wasn't in the mood for and was content simply to be in the moment with her.

During their trek through the mountain, Laila noticed that it was much quieter than the cavern that led them to Lochlann, and after some time, it dawned on her that there was no echo of dripping water from pipes leading to the city. After querying the dwarves why that was, the stout Handul explained that they had other sources for their water and gave her a wink, as though hiding some big mysterious secret. Laila thought it a rather strange secret to keep but played along with his coyness and assumed it would all be revealed to her when they reached the city. She was right.

As they approached the end of the tunnel, Laila had expected to be hit with a wave of heat from burning forges and fires to light the dark mountain core, just as she had first experienced entering Lochlann. However, it was the great city of Gortax, and she was instead greeted with a blast of snow flurries wafting in from the tunnel opening and a brisk breeze. There was fair natural lighting gleaming in from the evening sun through thick metal bars blocking the exit. Beyond that, all she could see was more rock.

"Oiy, Skorruk!" Okom hollered, clanging his sword between two of the bars like a bell that echoed down the tunnel behind them. "Geil nuhd aise!" *Let us in!*

Haddilydd giggled, which Laila found peculiar. After a brief moment, a dwarf—at least it was a safe assumption that it was a dwarf, although nothing could be seen of his face—peeked his metal-covered head out from behind the tunnel wall. He peered through the bars briefly before bringing the rest of his body around the corner, sporting even more of the same metal covering his entire body with only slits for his eyes and mouth.

"Mister Okom?" came a muffled voice from the metaled head.

"Aye, of course! Now let us in!" he repeated.

CHAPTER 8

Squinting through the bars at the others, the dwarf seemed hesitant to do so, particularly upon seeing a drow in their company. He wasn't certain of the proper procedures under such a strange visit from all the races together. "Methought ye all lef' ta Lochlann. Who these 'ere other folks be wit' ye? They look like trouble ta me." The dwarf shifted uncomfortably in his heavy armor.

Haddilydd stepped toward the bars and into the light, sneering, "What a load o' okullo dung! Ye 'bout ta see trouble if ye dunna' let us in, boy!"

The dwarf raised his visor, revealing a very young dwarf lad, and he mumbled quietly—for a dwarf—through the bars, "Auntie Haddy, I didna' see ye. I jus' be tryin' ta do me job. Please dunna' embarrass me." The boy began looking past Haddilydd and bowed his head when his eyes met with Handul.

Annoyed, Haddilydd Placed her hands on her hips and huffed at the boy on the other side. "This lot be the saviors of all Onis! Now let us in so's we can take these 'eroes ta see King Brakdrath. We 'ave some very excitin' news ta give 'im that I can assures ye will tickle 'im under 'is beard!"

Nodding and crossing his arms over his chest, Handul stepped forward beside Haddilydd and said gruffly, "Do as yer auntie tells ye, me boy, and open the blastit gate."

"Of course, Paw."

Paw? Laila then realized why Haddilydd's and Handul's relationship seemed so odd to her; they were siblings! She was unfamiliar with sibling relationships beyond that of her wolfkin, but they were obviously quite different from her own experiences. In light of that knowledge, their behavior started making more sense to her.

The metal dwarf quickly disappeared again, and Laila looked around at the others, all waiting patiently in silence. She wasn't sure why, but she suddenly felt sick to her stomach in anticipation of having to face the king. It made her feel silly and insecure that she could go up against a clan of Silvers and hordes of orcs, but feel inadequate when having to go before another leader and ask them for help.

Growing up, she rarely had the need to ask for help from anyone. Her wolfkin all worked in unison, anticipating the needs of the others and doing whatever was necessary for the betterment of the pack. They sensed when one of them was in danger or hurt and knew what to do. So, asking for help was a foreign concept to her, and thus far, it had not quite worked out in her favor, leaving her feeling very deficient.

The bars began to rise with a loud clanking noise while chains lifted the heavy metal gate, wrapping around a winch on the other side, and everyone was eager to get out of the cavern. As Laila stepped through the opening, she realized that the rock she had seen from within was actually a large stone wall encompassing the city before her. In addition to that, surrounding the city walls was a different barrier of tall mountains, reaching far into the clouds, forming perfectly around the dwarven city. Except it dawned on her that it was the city that would have been formed perfectly within the mountain barrier. It seemed rather strange to her to have the extra wall of protection that she found herself gazing upon, almost like a fortress within a fortress, but she assumed that they had their reasons for it.

Admiring Gortax, Laila was suddenly reminded of Lord Kilgar's description in all of his ramblings at the party, which now seemed like ages ago. *"Tis a grand city it tis... tis a beautiful place covered in snow and ice... ye step out ta see the great castle and city of Gortax, surrounded by mountains risin' up ta the 'eavens..."*

She shook her head at the memory, at what little that description did for the wonderment. As she looked up at the battlements, she noticed the outer wall was done in a similar style to Má Lyndor; sizable ballistae armed with long spears pointing upward to the skies instead of at the passageway entrance. There were a few guards around the base of the city wall, watching their approaching guests with intrigue and skepticism, a hand on the hilts of their weapons as they eyed the drow. Laila hoped that Nikolean wouldn't have to go through that again; the judgment, scrutiny, and distrust. Although she was going to go through it in her own way, she was unlikely to encounter the hostility and possibly severe outcome he might face.

The group approached the city gate, its portcullis and large wooden doors already open, and the Gortaxian dwarves with them dashed ahead with their short legs to tell the guards all about their welcomed guests. Inside, there were many tall pillars that Laila realized were more watchtowers, housing several dwarves, each with more weapons pointed upward. Unlike the other cities she had visited, what was most breathtaking about Gortax wasn't the meticulous architectural designs or intricacies, since most of that could not even be seen; it was the beauty added by nature, all the snow, ice, and enveloping mountains. The buildings were covered with the snow's white gloss, and icicles dripped from the roof overhangs.

Many buildings, which appeared to be primarily dwellings, lined the main road leading to a large castle in the middle of the city. Past the main road, the dwellings appeared scattered and haphazard and were at all different levels, keeping to the mountain clearing's rugged base.

The day was getting late, and although still quite bright, the stars were already shining vividly in the sky. It seemed a strange place that didn't follow the rules she knew from back home, where the stars were only visible in the complete blackness of the night. Neither of the moons, Jayenne nor

Kyrash, could be seen from where they were, blocked by the mountain peaks.

If it weren't for the cold, Laila thought it would be nice to stay there for a while before moving on, in no hurry to take on any more battles or face any more dragons or races that would likely refuse to join them. She sighed heavily at the thought while taking in the exquisite sight of another new city that defied what she had imagined anyone being capable of creating.

CHAPTER NINE

AWAKEN

*W*ith the sun setting behind the western mountains, Haddilydd led the group toward her home, explaining that they would need to send a proper request to see the king, and it would be best to do so after he's had a nice breakfast and not tired from the day. Everyone agreed that would be fine; Nikolean most of all, fearful of the rumors of King Brakdrath being a stern ruler when it came to outsiders in his city. He had received no indication as to how the king handled dark elves visiting his domain.

The dwarves accompanying them were stopped several times along the way, being asked about their early return and if they had managed to find the others that had left before them with no word since. Sadly, they had no good news to share with them, and, of course, they were all surprised and upset to learn of the mighty Nelgour Frostspine being slain by the orcs, pausing for a moment of silence each time at the mention.

Laila couldn't quite get a feel for the place as they turned around corners down oddly shaped roads, passing house after house. It was very different from Lochlann, including the general demeanor of the dwarves. There wasn't that same cheer and vibrancy she had loved about the Lochlannians, but she wasn't the same elf either and wondered if she simply perceived everyone differently now.

When they reached their host's home, Laila observed its quaintness and modest size, worried about how they would all fit comfortably, as it was even smaller than Hort's dwelling. Although used to piling in a tightly packed den with wolves all nestled against each other, she did not share that same comfort level with her two-legged companions. She was well aware of and accepted the different formalities that existed in the new world she had become a part of.

After loving farewells between Laila and Merimer, Hort and Orbek, the group unburdened the okullo of the cart and permitted Okom, Notdras, and Handul to take the mounts to the stables.

"I'll be back ta stay wit' ye tonight, Haddy," Handul told his sister.

"Tis not necessary, ye silly man. I be sure ta be in the best care wit' the savior o' Onis under me roof!" Haddilydd replied loudly, hoping to muster up some mystique and attention from her neighbors.

"Well, I be back all the same," he said gruffly before heading to the stables with the others.

"Right, now, in we go. There ye are, lass, watch yer step there—yup, and there too. Watch yer 'ead! My, ye high elves be tall!" The dwarf led them all into her home, with its uneven floors leading downward and narrow hallways that split and diverged, with several rooms along each one. Again, very strange compared to the open spaces of the Lochlann homes.

"I'll get the tea on so's we can warm up. Ye all jus' make yerselves cozy."

CHAPTER 9

As she followed Glondora into one of the rooms, Laila was left a little perplexed upon discovering it was much larger than she had anticipated, considering the home's petiteness from the outside. That single room was about the same size as Hort's main living area with the combined kitchen, yet there were several more doors leading off the hallway they had left behind, and she wondered where they all led to. It was then she realized that the part of the dwarf's home that was visible from the outside was merely the entrance. The room, among several others, had been dug into the mountain's stone, and she and her friends were now underground. She wondered how extensive her home truly was, trying to imagine the tunnels in her mind.

"Pyromancer, be a dear and light the fire, will ye?" Haddilydd addressed Davion, filling a pot of water to brew some tea.

As Davion went over to the large fireplace with an opening tall enough to house a dwarf, the others tried to make themselves comfortable, huddling near it, and he used his magic to ignite the wood already placed within.

Hort took a seat on the dusty green couch made of a wooden frame with down pillows and cushions. He removed his boots, airing out his offensive-smelling feet, wafting a hand over them.

As she shivered from the cold, Laila realized she could see her warm breath clouding out in the room's brisk air. Noticing Laila shudder, Nikolean stepped closer, wanting to put his arm around her but unsure how that action would be received. So instead, he stood there in silence, hoping that the closeness of him and his body heat would suffice.

Salyaman began unloading his burden of weapons and supplies into the far corner, and Glondora made her way to the kitchen to offer Haddilydd a hand by readying the mugs.

"Let me help with that," Salyaman said, going to assist with the tea like a gentleman.

Haddilydd giggled nervously at having a royal elf helping her with such a menial task but dared not refuse him.

It was a relatively quiet evening, everyone worn from the journey. Salyaman suggested they discuss the plan for tomorrow. He wanted to be ready to face the king early the following day. When they all looked with expectant eyes at Haddilydd, she quickly took the hint and gave an awkward bow, excusing herself to give them some privacy.

As Nikolean stood nearby against a wall, Laila and Davion sat down at the small-but-heavy wooden table. Salyaman remained hovering nearby, while Hort and Glondora stayed on the couch by the fire, warming their naked feet.

"Mister Strongarm," Salyaman addressed Hort, "is there anything you can share with us about King Brakdrath? Anything at all that may help us prepare?"

"Hmmm..." Hort thought while stroking his beard. "I was jus' a lad when me lef' 'ere, but I 'erd 'e be a no-nonsense type o' ruler. Wonna' be at all friendly like our Lord Kilgar was. Bes' we stick ta the mission and not bore 'im wit' chit-chat and whatnot."

"So, skip the pleasantries." Salyaman nodded. "Understood. Does anyone have any suggestions on how we should proceed?" he asked, looking around the room.

Laila stared off into the distance, remembering the lack of support and blackmail from the royal elves of Má Lyndor, and ground her teeth, having nothing helpful nor pleasant to contribute.

"I'm sure twill all work out fine," Glondora offered optimistically. "Jus' need ta show 'im our Lady Laila be the real deal."

Glondora wasn't at Má Lyndor, Laila reminded herself. *She doesn't know.* Laila wrapped her arms around her chest, closing herself off, and continued staring forward.

Davion stood up from the table, addressing the group with confidence. "If he's a no-nonsense king, then we should just be direct with him. Tell him about the prophecy and everything we're trying to accomplish. Show him that Laila is the Omi Méa and how powerful she is, and he will see it for himself." He raised his arms for emphasis. "Show him how powerful we *all* are!" The wall sconces flickered as he raised his voice. "We are all a part of this! We need to show him that we are united and will not stop until he and every other nation agree to help us confront the dragons once and for all!"

Hort and Glondora thumped their fists repeatedly on the couch arms, enthusiastically backing Davion. Hort was proud of the man Davion was becoming and of how strong he had grown in such a short time.

"And what if he refuses? Why should he sacrifice his men for us?" Nikolean asked in a cynical tone, still leaning against the wall.

Irritated, Davion fumbled for an answer.

"Then we burn his city to the ground," Laila said sardonically, without averting her eyes from the blankness of her stare.

Everyone glared at her, shocked and confused.

"This is serious, Lady Laila," Davion scorned. "We need to come up with a solution."

Glaring up at Davion, she stood to meet his presence in the room, unwrapping her arms from her torso. "And why not? What have kindness and polite requests got us so far? Some armor and weapons for our army of... six?!! We need troops; we are going to war, are we not? It is clear there will be challengers of the prophecy. If they won't join us, then they are against us, against our mission. Perhaps some persuasion is in order.

"I could have had Má Lyndor's support had I just agreed to marry that wretched prince, but I refused. And why? I doubt I would have ever seen him again, but we would have had our troops, and others may have followed more easily because of it. If the elves won't even back one of their own claiming to be the Omi Méa, the one to end the war that is affecting their race the most, what chance do we stand with anyone else?!"

"This is absurd!" Davion said to her, his voice cracking with either fear or disgust, she assumed.

"Davion..." Glondora said softly, standing to intervene.

But Davion continued to press, raising his voice, "What's wrong with you?! This isn't you, Laila!"

With everyone beginning to encircle her, Laila was filling with anxiety and rage.

"And who am I?!" she spat, stepping assertively toward Davion. "I was done! I wanted to go home! You wanted me to be a hero. You want me to be strong enough to face more leaders, more dragons, more battles, more hate, but only strong in the way *you* wish. I've seen the way you look at me since the battle, since I wiped out those orcs. Should I have just let Tury die?! Should I have just let the dwarves die?!"

Everyone watched her cautiously, afraid to move. Laila saw the worry and apprehension in their eyes—she wasn't blind. With all her brokenness and fear manifesting, her tears threatened to expose themselves. She felt vulnerable, and she hated it. How is she supposed to be the Omi Méa and be Laila at the same time?

While looking around at all of them, she blared, "I thought I was finally the Omi Méa that everyone has been expecting me to be, that you've all been hoping for and praying for. Someone strong enough, brave enough, and ruthless enough that can go up against anything and do what needs to be done!"

Davion ambitiously took a step toward her, the space between them closing and full of tension. "Not like this," he said with a stern demeanor. "You were kind and gentle and loving, but now you speak of threatening innocents, and you use the dark magics. I don't know who this person is before me, but it is not the Laila I love."

Like a knife to her chest, she knew she was right about his feelings changing toward her, and she was no longer the girl of his dreams. She looked him dead in the eyes as she growled, "Then, perhaps, this Laila cannot afford to love."

Fuming and shaking, Laila grabbed her coat and began to leave, but Nikolean stepped in her way, worried about where she was going or what she would do in her current state.

"My lady..." he began.

"Not now, drow!" she spat without looking at him as she stormed past. He swallowed hard. Out of all the hatred he had received from the others, she had never before referred to him as "drow" nor with such contempt in her tone.

Laila aimed to escape from the strange house, or at least she thought she had. She was lost in what seemed like endless hallways and headed in whichever direction felt coldest, hoping to find the exit. *There is just no pleasing them!* she fumed inwardly.

Upon emerging through a door that she thought was the exit, she found herself on a semi-enclosed patio with a terrible view of the backs of other dwellings—which only made her more frustrated. *I can't do anything right! What is wrong with me?!* She felt trapped, her heart pounding and chest heavy like she couldn't breathe.

'*Laila...*' she heard Turathyl penetrate her mind, but her head was too full already, so she blocked her out.

Pacing back and forth in a panic, she just wanted to run, run wildly to her forest back home, to her familiar trees and surroundings alongside her wolf brethren.

Maybe I did die on the mountain, and this is all just my nightmare playing out, punishment for leaving home where I was safe and loved, too eager to see what everyone else did; I wasn't ready—I'm still not ready. This is all just too much. I need to get out of here, out of this place.

Gasping for breath, her mind going a mile-a-minute, she began feeling dizzy as though she were going to pass out, and her body started trembling fiercely. Laila shook her arms frantically as she tried desperately to breathe. It reminded her of Aeris siphoning the air from her lungs atop the Silvers' Mountain—the setting of her recurring nightmares. As she wheezed, she shut her eyes tight, terrified that Aeris had found her there, that the monarch had come to finish her off once and for all. Laila could see the dragon in her mind, staring at her, laughing as she struggled for air. She had to escape! She had to get out! She had to run!

As she pivoted swiftly to find a way out, Laila bumped into someone, who immediately wrapped his arms tightly around her, pulling her firmly against him and holding her steady. She fought, of course, trying to push the person away, trying to strike her restrained hands against their chest. She was so hysteric that she didn't even know who she was resisting, nor care, just that she was angry and hurt and wanted to go home.

In the restraint, she slowly began to ease. Then came the tears. She cried harder than she ever had in her life, clinging to the person before her, her heart hurting with every sob, as she gasped for breath between each pained outburst. Her tears soaked her warden's chest while she blubbered over him, not caring who heard or saw. Her body may have recovered from the

CHAPTER 9

Silvers' Mountain, but her mind had been shattered, perhaps beyond repair.

After several minutes, Laila's breathing began steadying, her tears letting up, and she sniffled, trembling, trying to gain control of herself. The person holding her slightly loosened his grasp, but didn't let go.

As she started to regain some of her sanity, Laila pulled away to see who had come to her aid and was surprised to find Salyaman standing before her. Embarrassed, she stepped back away from him and started hastily wiping her tears.

"It is alright, Lady Laila," he said calmly. "You have been under a great deal of stress. None of us knows what you are going through, but we are all concerned for you."

Laila sniffled, regaining control of her body but not ready for another confrontation as she averted her eyes from the elf prince.

"It is understandable that you would be hurting after all you have endured. Unfortunately, Glondora and I can only heal your flesh."

He reached out and held her shoulders at arm's length, lowering his head to look at her compassionately, and she returned his gaze. "It is a great burden, most certainly, that has been placed upon you by the gods. You have a power unlike any before you, and I fear that this quest of ours is taking its toll on you. It is important that you are strong—like you said—but it is more important that you do not forget who you are, Lady Laila. Do not let your powers or this prophecy devour you."

She nodded at him understandingly before he continued, "Let us not forget what this mission is about; ending the hate, not creating more. Now," he sighed, releasing her shoulders, "it has been a long journey. Perhaps we should try to discuss a plan in the morning after we have all had some proper rest." He looked at her with earnest eyes, giving her a half-smile,

"However, in our mission of peace, I do think that an alternative solution to burning the city to the ground should be considered."

Laila laughed abruptly, surprising herself, and covered her mouth, embarrassed. Aside from not being used to Salyaman having a sense of humor, she realized how counterintuitive that notion sounded now. "Perhaps," she replied, attempting to return a smile.

Salyaman guided Laila down the dark hallways to the room she'd been assigned but respectfully kept a slight distance from her, his hands clasped behind his back.

"Good night, Lady Laila," he said quietly as they reached her door.

Laila gave him a pained smile, thankful for his friendship, but still feeling tormented within. "Good night, Lord Salyaman," she said softly.

The elf prince gave her a royal bow, and she headed inside her chambers.

It was a modest room with little more than the essentials and dark-stone walls. Two of them were covered in nearly a dozen poorly painted portraits of dwarves. Laila couldn't be sure if they were all male, as some appeared to be bearded females. There was a small blue-cushioned chair resting in the corner, and a strange iron contraption meant for heating the room. It had a mesh door and a pipe running up through the ceiling but housed no fire within, leaving the room frigid and harsh.

It was promising to be a cold night ahead, and Laila was reminded once again of her mother, the Wolf God Lupé Caelis, and her wolfkin, wishing she could have their warmth and refuge to comfort her. The farther she traveled from her home, the more she wished she had never left.

After she closed the door behind Salyaman, she leaned her forehead against it, trying to collect herself. She listened to

CHAPTER 9

his footsteps through the thin-wooden door, which grew quieter as he headed down the dim hallway away from her.

Devastated over the argument with Davion, she hoped all hadn't been lost between them. She took a deep breath, holding it for a moment, then let it out heavily.

'Laila,' she heard Turathyl in her mind, 'is everything alright?'

She wasn't sure how to answer her. Laila was feeling very much alone, lost, confused, and broken, but there was nothing her dragon could do for her. She wasn't sure there was anything that anyone could do for her. To answer Turathyl, she simply sent a mental nod and decided to leave it at that.

Shuddering, Laila wiped away a tear that was on the brink of rolling down her cheek again as she picked her head up away from the door. Then, she nearly jumped out of her skin when she heard a rattling knock on the other side. Swiftly composing herself, she opened the door to find the drow, who, instead of saying anything, stood there staring at her pensively.

Laila waited there for a moment, wondering why he was there, and wondering if he was waiting for her to greet him or apologize or something.

Then, Nikolean bowed his head to her and said, "My lady," holding out a thick quilt before him. "I thought you could use this. Handul returned with a few of them and... well, I just thought... if you wanted it..."

Laila looked at him quizzically. *Is he nervous?* she pondered. He was acting very out of character, and she feared she had now pushed both him and Davion away from her.

"Yes, of course," she replied, quickly taking the quilt from him. "Thank you."

As she waited for him to leave so she could close the door, Nikolean continued to stand there, staring at her. The awkward silence was making her quite tense, so she finally asked, "Was there something else, Niko?"

After clearing his throat, he gave her a gentle smile and bowed to her again, replying, "No, my lady. Sleep well." Then he swiftly turned and disappeared into the dark hallway.

That was strange, Laila thought.

'You know he loves you.' The elf maiden jumped at Turathyl's voice, her nerves still on edge.

'I wouldn't be so sure,' she snidely retorted. *'I think they are both afraid of me now.'*

She could sense her dragon sighing and blushed, embarrassed that she had lumped Davion and Nikolean together in her response. Laila really didn't know what love was in that regard, but she could see the look in their eyes, and it didn't feel like what she thought was love, not anymore. Nothing had been right with her or with anything, ever since... She closed her eyes mournfully, her failure and near-death achingly on her mind. Either way, it wasn't something she was going to be figuring out that night.

After removing her metal armor pieces, Laila was too exhausted to bother igniting the furnace. She simply wrapped the quilt from Nikolean around her, crawling into the cold hard bed, tired and alone.

As she blinked her eyes around in the darkness, Laila quickly recognized the dream and frowned disappointedly. Except, that time, instead of calling out for the dragon—which she assumed was lurking about somewhere—or waiting for the fire to ignite around her, she simply sat down in her spot, wrapping her arms around her legs. Sighing, Laila rested her head on her knees and wished only to wake up. She already

found the fire spirit and wasn't in the mood for any more riddles that didn't make any sense; she merely desired to be left alone.

After sitting in silence amidst complete blackness with nothing but the sound of her own breathing, Laila sighed again, agitated, wondering why the Red Dragon hadn't come. Perhaps he has forsaken me too, she thought miserably to herself.

"Who has forsaken you but yourself?" she heard the great voice of the dragon boom through the silence in the Ancient language.

Startled, Laila sprang up from the ground and surveyed the area for the source of the voice, sensing he was very close, but she still could see nothing. So, she called out into the abyss, "Everyone! They are all afraid of what I've become. They are afraid of me for calling upon dark magic that I used to save Tury. They expect the world of me, the great prophesied elf, but I continue to fall short in everything I do. I nearly even got Tury killed by a bunch of sniveling orcs! I don't know what I'm doing, and they all see it, and I am failing them all over again!"

She heard the dragon heave a heavy grumbling sigh that echoed through the blackness. "So, that is what is weighing on you?" the great dragon asked. "You fear you will fail them again? But why do you believe you failed them before?"

"Isn't it obvious?!" she yelled.

"No," he said bluntly. "I told you what must be, will be. Your confrontation with Aeris was always meant to transpire as it did, no matter when it happened or what you did."

Dumbfounded, Laila was frustrated with the mind games. "Then what was the point?!" she hollered. "And why can't I see you again?"

"Because you do not wish to see me," he replied. "Otherwise, you would."

More riddles... Laila shook her head in aggravation.

"You have been feeling quite sorry for yourself, Omi Méa, unnecessarily, and you are running out of time."

"Out of time for what?" Laila blurted, but there was only silence. Laila sat down stubbornly, frustrated with her dream dragon. "I'm not moving from this spot until I start getting some clear answers! The world can go to Ignisar's Lair for all I care!"

The ground beneath her quaked abruptly from laughing rumblings of the dragon. His chortling grew louder and sharper until it sounded more hauntingly evil than humored. Laila quickly grew nervous, worried he would start attacking her again like in past dreams.

"Yes, to Ignisar's Lair." He cackled again unsettlingly, but it was waning back down to an amused chuckle.

Huffing annoyedly, Laila asked, "And why is that so funny?!"

"Because I, my little Omi Méa, am Ignisar."

Laila's mouth dropped in a gasp, and she immediately took to her feet again, nervously looking around. The way the expression had been used, she believed Ignisar to be the afterlife's gatekeeper, the tormenter of those who had done wrong in their lives. So, what did that mean for her? Had she been communing with an evil entity the entire time?

She heard the dragon move, the ground cracking as Ignisar took a few steps, presumably toward her, and her heart was racing, her body panicked. She glanced around, terrified, unsure of what to do or how to wake herself up. It suddenly seemed more like a nightmare than another dream of the dragon.

Wake up, wake up, wake up! Laila willed herself, but she remained looking around in the black space of her mind. She was no longer smug and confident before the Red Dragon, but was instead shaking in her boots.

The dragon's stomping movement echoed through the emptiness, and Laila circled around, trying to pinpoint his location, but it was coming from everywhere. Scared and confused, Laila needed to see what was happening and reached her hands out around her. Fueled by her fear, she raised her arms, and walls of fire materialized around her, creating a blazing spectacle. Except, unlike before, that time it was of her doing.

"Hello, Great Spirit," the dragon said placidly when she looked upon his illuminated frame. He no longer appeared regal and magnificent to her. Now, in his monstrous form, the dragon seemed perilous and diabolical as the flames reflected against his silhouette, his eyes once again glowing bright orange, even though she knew they were the same black death as the Norn Mornder stone.

As she shielded her eyes from his glare with her forearm, she pleaded, "Please, don't hurt me!"

The dragon lowered his grand head near her, so close that she could feel his breath on the back of her arm. "And why would I hurt you?" he asked, his words rustling her hair.

"Be..because you're evil," the young elf damsel said, terror-stricken.

"Am I?" The dragon chuckled again, and the elf winced. While retracting his head back away from her, he told her, "Great Spirit, you have no reason to fear me."

Hesitantly, Laila lowered her guard, still trembling, "Then... what is it you have come to me for?"

Ignisar looked upon her majestically and replied, "The time of the rising is nigh. You have set the pendulum in motion by confronting Aeris, and now you must wake from your slumber and complete your task with haste."

Laila recalled the last dream of the Red Dragon and how he had told her to wake up. "But I did wake up, as you said before."

"That is not what I have seen," he replied. "You have been walking in a dream since I saw you last. If you are to move forward, you must stop looking back. You are on the right path, but it is time to truly open your eyes, Omi Méa. Stop dwelling in your past sufferings and start healing yourself and the land of Onis."

"But I feel so lost," the young elf said poignantly, looking down and wrapping her arms around her.

"It is time to find me," the dragon stated.

"What do you mean?" she asked.

"Aeris will soon know of your plot, and if you don't move now, it will be too late. It is time for you to come to me. Your Turathyl will know the way. But hurry, before it is not just you who is lost, but all of Onis."

When the great dragon stood before her, preparing to leave, she cried out in a panic, *"Wait! I am not ready! I don't know who I am anymore or what I'm doing! I'm trying to do my best and be what everyone else wants of me, but I don't know how! And I'm scared I'm becoming evil by using dark magic; they all look at me with fear. How can I be the Omi Méa without losing myself?"*

While looking upon her with regard, Ignisar cocked his head and replied, *"You are the Great Spirit, and the magic you use is neither dark nor light; no magic is. It is the wielder that is thus. But your magic is not like those of the two-leggeds. They cannot comprehend because you are using the spirits of our world as we Ancients do. You must find the balance in yourself the same as in the Sacred Forest when you first discovered the spirits. Now, my little Omi Méa, no more tears. If you are to defeat the hatred of this land, you must accept yourself for who you are—every part of you—and you will know what to do when the time comes."*

Elevating his head high above her, Ignisar glared down at her resolutely as he said, *"It is time to awaken."*

CHAPTER 9

CHAPTER TEN

BRAKDRATH

While securing his pouches to the belt around his waist, Davion jerked around, surprised, as the door to his humble room swung open. Hort drowsily sauntered in, scratching his haunch through the thin cloth of a grungy white nightshirt that draped to his shins.

It was early morning, the room dimly lit by two candles, and Davion assumed the sun had not yet risen. Although, being underground, he really had no way of knowing for certain. The room he had been placed in contained a single bed too short for him and a small nightstand and dresser of the same dark-stained wood. It had a rather gloomy atmosphere, but the thick handwoven rug under his feet helped. It was also better than sleeping on a cot or thin mattress on the floor, so he was thankful for the offer.

His uncle crossed the room, letting out a garish belch before taking a seat on the end of Davion's bed while the human watched on. "Good morning to you too, Uncle," he cheekily said while collecting the rest of his things.

"Hmmm... Mornin'," Hort replied grouchily, stifling a yawn.

With a smirk, Davion told him, "You know, you wouldn't be so tired if you and Glondora would have just gone to sleep last night. It really didn't help being on the other side of your wall, either."

Unabashed, he replied, "Tis not me fault that laiden be crazy fer me." Eying Davion, Hort added, "Speakin' o' laidens..."

Davion had an idea of what was coming next, and sat down on the bed and began fidgeting with a leather pouch in his lap, waiting for his uncle to continue.

"Ye were rather cold ta the lass last night. Did ye even go and apologize ta 'er after?"

Davion looked at his uncle, confused. "Apologize for what? You heard what she said, didn't you?"

"Aye," Hort said in a commiserative manner. "I was there. But, me boy, I thought ye cared fer 'er. Methinks she jus' be tryin' 'er best."

Looking back to the pouch in his hands, he heaved with agitation. "She's not the same, Uncle. I can feel it. There is something off with her. And seeing her using the dark magics to destroy those orcs... seeing her eyes, empty and black..." He paused, getting lost in the memory. "I don't know what to think anymore. I want us to succeed. I want to be part of the group that puts a stop to the war."

"And ye dunna' think she wants that too?" Leaning a little closer to Davion, Hort asked thoughtfully, "Does ye love 'er, me boy?"

After a brief hesitation, he said, "Of course I do. I just don't know who she is anymore, and I never know where I stand with her, anyway. I thought we had something, some special bond, but it just seems like her head is somewhere else."

Hort stood up from the bed, his old abused body resisting with aches and pains, as he told Davion sympathetically, "Be patient, me boy. Perhaps she jus' needs some more time. I be sure she could use yer understandin' and support in the meanwhiles."

For distraction, Davion rolled the pouch from one hand to the other and back again, listening to the hypnotic rattling of its contents while staring at a colorful strand in the rug, trying to follow it with his eyes. He didn't know what to tell his uncle. To imagine being without her made him nauseated, but he wasn't sure how to support her given her behavior. Nor did he believe he could stand behind her if she continued using dark magic.

"What ye got there?" Hort asked, interrupting his trance.

"The Dragon Stones," Davion replied. "Laila had asked that I hold on to them for her when we left Lochlann. She seems bothered by them for some reason. Or maybe she just doesn't like them. I'm not sure."

"Hmmm..." Hort grumbled, then pat his belly with both hands. "Speakin' o' Dragon Stones, methinks tis nearly time to go see King Brakdrath. Best be getting' ta the mess hall fer a bite and ta discuss the plan."

As Hort headed for the door, Davion averted his eyes, disturbed upon noticing a rather prominent hole in the backside of the dwarf's nightshirt. "Uncle, you may want to get dressed first," he remarked, chuckling.

With a glance down at his attire, the dwarf muttered a curse before making his way back out to his and Glondora's room to get ready for the day.

The comrades were overwhelmed as they were escorted into the dwarven castle and entered the throne room. It was a grandiose room with a long path to the throne at the far end. They could see the length of the room before them as they stepped forward with caution, their feet shuffling anxiously while staying close together.

Tall stone pillars encased the pathway, with what Laila hoped were only carvings of bones and skulls into their surface as they loomed over the group hauntingly. Torches burned near the bases, with guards standing at attention beneath each one. Unlike most of the city's drab, natural-gray stone, the room's walls and pillars had once been painted off-white, which had become dingy and chipped with time. The day was still young, leaving Gortax poorly lit from being in the mountains' shadows, causing the meager window slits to fail in illuminating the castle. The crisp winds howled as they breached the narrow openings, adding to the macabre atmosphere of the great room.

Overshadowed by his gargantuan throne atop a platform at the far end, they could scarcely see the king sitting within it or the attendees at his side as they made the long walk toward him. The glorious throne was forged from many metals and woven with several embellishments, the back spiking up halfway to the ceiling. However, above the throne was what really stole their breath.

The group gawked up at a preserved Silver's head mounted upon the wall, its teeth bared aggressively. As their gazes met the dragon's onyx-black eyes, a terrifying sensation overwhelmed them, as if they could almost hear the screams of the dwarves that had perished in its assault.

Davion and Nikolean both looked attentively at Laila, curious how she would react, but Laila seemed unruffled by the display. In truth, Laila was utterly disgusted and chilled by it. In spite of that, the conversation with Ignisar weighed heavy on her mind, and she understood that it was imperative she become strong—and quickly—so she remained steadfast. She was resigned to show no weakness before the dwarf king in her efforts to gain his support.

As the group reached the end of the long room, the old king sat forward in his seat, looking over the peculiar bunch closer. He studied them somberly, his steel-blue eyes above a large ruby-red nose nearly glowing from the frigid cold. There were gold bands and thick braids decorated into a long white beard that draped over his chest to his knees, swaying as he moved. The king was heavily armored in a thick silver plate with gold trim and elaborate detailing carved into the metals, sporting grand spaulders accentuating his already-broad shoulders. A cape of heavy furs was clasped to them, covering his back and cushioning his bottom. Instead of a helmet atop his head lay an exaggeratedly tall crown of gold and bronze hues that flared up into points resembling flames. He was gripping the tip of the handle from a sizable dwarven maul resting at his feet like a large boulder while peering at them studiously.

Something shuffling off to the side momentarily took Laila's attention from the king, and she glanced over to find the dwarves they had rescued, including Haddilydd. Laila couldn't help but notice the nervousness radiating from them, heightening her own unease, but she held her stance and gazed solemnly back to the king.

The group stopped before the large staircase leading up to the platform that extended the width of the room, upon which sat King Brakdrath. Laila took another step forward, exuding confidence as she addressed him, fully clad in the armor and heavy furs bestowed on her by Lochlann, "King Brakdrath Lightsword, my name is Lady Lailalanth—"

"Yes, yes. I know who ye be," the king interrupted her with an old gruff and crackly voice while waving a hand dismissively and leaning back in his chair. "Ye have created quite the stir ta me kingdom, elfie. Everyone be abuzz wit' the chatter o' ye and yer dragon; sayin' some ridiculousness 'bout ye blowin' up an orc wit' yer mind." King Brakdrath leaned forward again in his throne, squinting his eyes at her to get a better look. "The stories they tellin', be there any truth ta them?"

"Aye, me lord," Hort said proudly, stepping beside Laila. "This laiden can talk ta the Ancients and wields all the magics o' our land. There be a prophecy tellin' 'bout a Great Spirit..."

The king raised his hand, hushing the dwarf instantly. He let out a grumbling sound, his strawberry nose twitching in thought as he tugged gently at his beard, examining them. Laila startled as the king raspily cleared his throat, breaking the silence before speaking again. "I know o' the prophecy. Somethin' 'bout an Omis Miden or some such thing."

Standing from his throne, the dwarf king cricked and cracked his neck, his crown holding firm to his head as he did, and he slowly descended the steps toward the group. As with the other leaders, his interest was in that of the elf maiden alone. King Brakdrath did not care about the human, high elf, nor even the drow, but analyzed Laila with scrutiny. "So, elfie, where be this dragon o' yers now?"

Even though Laila was trepidatious about answering, glancing at the head mounted on the wall, she replied, "She is outside of your great city in the mountains awaiting word from me."

Nodding, the king said, "Tis in me mountains?"

"Her name is Turathyl," Laila responded. "She has sworn to protect me and help put a stop to the war between the races so we can unite the land."

The king let out a slight chuckle, then eyed the others, his mirth increasing. As he regarded the dwarves in the corner, he succumbed to a full, roaring belly laugh. "Tis that so?!" he crowed and hooted with laughter again. "So ye and yer dragon gunna' take on the world, are ye?"

"Yes," Laila replied firmly, looking stolidly at the king, "along with the nineteen other Silvers that have so far defected against their monarch, Aeris, and pledged themselves to Turathyl and our cause."

King Brakdrath looked at her, flabbergasted, his amusement forgotten, and astonishment washed over his face.

Laila continued, "I also possess the spirits of the earth, air, fire, water, and phantom realm, and have with me four others who each represent a nation of Onis and of its elemental magic. The human holds the power of fire, the dwarf harnesses the power of water, the dark elf has air, and the elf possesses earth. We all vowed to bring an end to the war and hate that has been reigning over this land."

King Brakdrath glared over the group. "So, then what is it ye ask o' me?" he inquired, cutting to the chase.

Salyaman replied, "We are requesting your support. We intend to confront the dragons and speak of peace between the races. However, we have seen that we will be met with much resistance. That is where we will need support from all the races in the form of men. We are building a united front to attest to the dragons that they won't stop us from uniting the land and putting a stop to their war once and for all."

Laila had half expected the king to burst out laughing again, but he remained contemplative as his eyes bore into Salyaman in silence.

Remembering the stones, Davion held them forward. "Lord Kilgar gave us his prized Dragon Stones to bring before you to show that he is willing to offer his support in any way he can."

He poured all five of the stones into his hand to show the king, and Laila instantly cringed, looking away from them. Her chest tightened and lip quivered as she recalled the cold death-chill from Norn Mornder and the pull of it at her soul, while she tried with moderate success to maintain her guise.

The king acknowledged the stones, nodded, and said, "I see."

Davion returned the stones to the pouch, and Laila could sense the moment Black Death had been tucked away within the leather. With a great sense of relief, she took a deep breath and veered her gaze back to their host.

As he looked at Laila, King Brakdrath continued, "And 'ow many other armies ye 'ave lined up then? The elves me presumes?"

Hesitating, Laila glanced uncomfortably at Salyaman for help. If she told them the elves refused to join them, how would they convince him to risk his men?

"Actually," Salyaman spoke up, getting the king's attention, "yours would be the first. We came here straight from Lochlann after we attained some dragons for our cause. The dragons are guarding Lochlann as we speak."

"Aye!" Hort said enthusiastically, "Me Lord Kilgar said we should come ta ye. That ye be a wise king twould know what a great move supportin' the Omi Méa would be fer yer kingdom!"

With a pensive eye on Hort, the king grumbled under his beard for a moment, then said to them all, "Well, I canna' decide such a thing without a pint under me belt first. I will need ta think on it some more. In the meantime, methinks I'd like ta meet this Turathyl o' yers."

He gave her a toothy smile, revealing a blackened and silver grin that made her skin crawl. She didn't know how much she trusted King Brakdrath considering the head mounted behind him, but felt confident enough that she could protect Turathyl should the need arise. That is, she prayed she could.

Escorted by several guards, the dwarf king rested his sizable hammer upward against his shoulder and sheathed a

CHAPTER 10

sword at his side as he led the group to a vast courtyard that butted up against the castle. It was covered in a thin blanket of snow, crunching under their feet as they walked. The area was enclosed with a sculpted stone fence and pillars carved like war hammers facing up toward the sky. There were sizable archways centered on each of the three outer walls. A layer of snow drizzled over the wall's ledge, and the sky above was brightening as the sun rose higher, the city in less of the mountain shadows.

Laila had been explaining to Turathyl in private what was happening along the way and requested she join them, but to be cautious since she wasn't sure what the king's intentions were.

When they had all gathered near the center of the courtyard, King Brakdrath squinted up at the sky. "So, ye need a horn or somethin'? 'Ow ye gunna' call this dragon o' yers?"

"I have already done so, King Brakdrath," Laila responded, and just as she did, the great Silver crested over the mountaintop above them, her white underbelly scales reflecting the sun's rays like tiny mirrors.

The king dropped his jaw and tightened his grip on his hammer while all the guards drew their weapons. Turathyl hesitated, hovering in the sky and glancing to the towers with the ballistae all readied. Gaining altitude again, Turathyl's instincts told her to flee.

"Your Majesty, you must have your men stand down," Salyaman stated.

"He is right," Laila added, "She will not hurt you, but you must trust us."

King Brakdrath raised an eyebrow at the elves and lowered his hammer from his shoulder to the ground, resting it in the snow, then nodded and grunted to his guards. They, too, sheathed their weapons, and then one of them let out a strange shout that sounded similar to a double caw of a raven. Others echoed the call throughout the city, and all the remaining guards and towers stood down.

'It's safe,' Laila told her dragon. 'You can come.'

Observing the dwarves closely, Turathyl slowly descended toward the courtyard near the group.

"Incredible!" King Brakdrath exclaimed as the great Silver Dragon landed gracefully before him, only lightly stirring the ground around her.

In the effort of diplomacy, Turathyl bowed her head to the king, then looked upon him, surprised to find no fear or hate in his eyes, only fascination.

"King Brakdrath," Laila said, walking up to her dragon, "this is Turathyl, the Silver who challenged her monarch, inciting a revolt so that she could join our mission. You see, it is not just the two-leggeds that are tired of the endless killing and hatred, and I am sure we can get several more dragons to join us as well."

As Laila paused, Salyaman added, "But we will need more than just the dragons. We need all of Onis to come together and show that we will not be tormented any longer."

The dwarf king stared considerately at the elf standing beside her dragon and stroked his beard in thought. He was quite perplexed at seeing the mortal enemies together, but had to admit to himself that it did give him a glimmer of hope.

"'Tis a considerable request ye've made, lass. Though I must admit, ye got me attention."

The king took a few steps toward the dragon, and Turathyl raised her head nervously as he approached, curling her lips with hostility. King Brakdrath raised his hands, yielding and stopping where he stood. "Aye, twill take some time, methinks. Yer dragon trusts us 'bout as much as we trust it." Examining the dragon, he added, "And where be the saddle? 'Ow ye ridin' it?"

Turathyl and Laila looked at each other, confused. The thought had never occurred to either of them and, admittedly, made them both feel rather uncomfortable. Turning her gaze back to the dwarf king, Laila responded, "She is my friend, not my mount. I have Merimer to ride from place to place."

"I see," he replied disappointedly. "Well, if that ever changes, be sure ta speak wit' our blacksmiths. I be sure we could work out a good deal ta be yer sole supplier o' dragon gear. Perhaps even some armor fer the beasts."

Laila actually liked the thought of the armor to help protect her friend but promptly received a vetoing response mentally from Turathyl, who snorted her disapproval to the others.

"Thank you for the offer," she responded for them, "but what of the men?"

King Brakdrath walked back over to his maul, then casually hoisted it back against his shoulder as he replied, "Ye've given me plenty ta mull over, little elfie. 'Ave yer dragon stay in Gortax fer the day, get ta know me people. Both o' ye meet me back 'ere tamorra' at this time, and I will 'ave yer answer fer ye."

The king swirled his finger in the air whilst he turned and headed back for the castle. The guards gathered in behind him, leaving the others standing alone in the courtyard.

"Well now, I think that went rather splendidly, dunna' ye?" Glondora said perkily to the group as King Brakdrath went out of sight.

No sooner than the king was gone, Davion turned and vehemently headed toward one of the archways without a word. Concerned, Hort stumbled after him, with Glondora promptly joining them.

Nikolean heaved a sigh of relief, having expected to be hauled off again in chains, and was developing a new fondness for the dwarven people.

"My lady," he said quietly, "what now?"

While Laila watched Davion leave, her heart felt heavy. She worried he was still upset with her from the prior night and would need to speak with him and apologize. Her conversation with Salyaman and her dream dragon had helped to open her eyes. It wasn't an instant fix, but she definitely was seeing more clearly now and knew she needed to get her head in the game.

Laila decidedly averted her eyes back to Nikolean and Salyaman. "Now, I suppose we do as the king suggested and get to know the city and these people."

"I agree," Salyaman said sternly. "I get the impression he wanted your dragon to stay in order to observe her behavior and determine if she can be trusted. Perhaps you spending the day here with Turathyl is what the king needs to witness to satisfy his concerns."

Turathyl lowered her head near Laila, and she gently pet her snout lovingly as the dragon told her, '*I may not trust these two-leggeds, but I think the elf is right. If they were to see how comfortable we are with each other, it just might be what the dwarf king needs to be persuaded.*'

Nodding, Laila relayed that Turathyl was on board.

"Let us go then and meet the people; show them your dragon." Salyaman bowed to Turathyl before turning to leave the same way as Davion had.

Nikolean approached the dragon and gave her a friendly stroke on her snout, which surprised Laila when Turathyl didn't flinch nor resist. The elf maiden failed to mask her confusion as she looked at them both with a skewed expression. Then the drow smirked at Laila before wordlessly following Salyaman out.

'*What is going on with you two?*' Laila asked her dragon apprehensively.

CHAPTER 10

Turathyl let out a low chortle of dragon laughter. *'Be careful, little elfie,'* the dragon said mockingly. *'You almost sound jealous.'*

"Stop that," she said aloud, ashamed and flushing.

Turathyl could sense that Laila's energy had much improved since the day before and couldn't help but enjoy the moment, praying that it would last.

'Perhaps we should have him come back and pet your nose as well. Would that help?'

"Let's go, dragon," Laila snidely said as she gave her a playful push before following the drow out. She blushed as she watched him walking away, his beautiful white hair flowing in the wind, his tight leather armor moving like a second skin. She remembered how that skin felt, how he felt—those soft, consuming lips...

'You know I am still here,' the dragon chuckled.

'Get out of my mind, Tury!' Laila mentally blared, dying of embarrassment. She looked down at the ground in front of her, hiding her bright-red cheeks amidst her golden locks.

King Brakdrath Lightsword

CHAPTER 10

CHAPTER ELEVEN

PERCEPTION

s one might imagine, Gortax was not built with the comfort and conveniences in mind to accommodate a dragon within its mighty walls, so there were limited places that Turathyl could explore. She and Laila ended up finding enough of a clearing along the main road to the castle for the dragon to rest. To their surprise, the dwarves all seemed eager to inspect the Great Dragon, and several even brought her offerings of fresh, raw meat. She couldn't help but wonder if they were meant as a sacrifice to appease her and keep her from eating them, but she wasn't about to question their hospitality while it was filling her belly.

Laila gave a polite smile to any dwarves who would approach them, all the while aware of the dark elf standing in cautious observance a fair distance away. He was concerned about how the tides could turn if the dwarves were to suddenly feel threatened or offended in any way, and he remained adamant about protecting Laila. Still, he kept removed from them, presuming that both a dragon and a drow might be a little too valorous for the dwarves to accept all at once.

Laila wasn't sure where Davion, Hort, or Glondora had wandered off to but had seen Salyaman as he purchased provisions throughout the day for their next trip. Turathyl was resting, licking her paws, and cleaning her muzzle from the last tasty sacrifice while Laila stood nearby, appearing casual as she keenly observed her surroundings.

'*You have been in much better spirits today,*' the dragon told the young elf. '*I suppose Salyaman said something that helped?*'

She gave a slight nod to the dragon, trying to be discreet, unsure how much she should indicate to their audience of their telepathic link. It was early afternoon, and she looked up at the sky, wondering why the sun had offered no warmth to that frigid place.

'*It was more than just him,*' she replied after a moment. '*I had a dream last night.*' Turathyl continued to clean her face while Laila kicked despondently at the snow around her. She crossed her arms over her chest, feeling oddly vulnerable, as she explained, '*I've been having a reoccurring dream of a Red Dragon since before I left my home in the Sacred Forest.*'

'Oh?' Discontinuing her bath, Turathyl perked her head up, peering with intrigue at the elf.

'*I hadn't said anything before because I didn't know what it meant. For the longest time, I had believed him to be the fire spirit that I was seeking. He would appear to me, usually say some crazy riddles, or even attack me sometimes, and then I would wake up confused, trying to make sense of it all.*'

'So, was *he the fire spirit you were searching for?*' The dragon crossed her paws in front of her, monumentally poised as she observed the elf.

'*Tury...*' Laila began, a little frightened to convey her discovery, as though telling someone else would suddenly make it all real, and until then, the dragon would remain simply a dream.

'What is it?' Turathyl pressed, becoming anxious from the pained aura she discerned emanating from the young elf.

'The dragon... It was Ignisar.'

Turathyl's eyes grew wide, trying to understand as she stared at Laila, speechless. While the maiden held her breath, she sent a mental image of the dragon from her dreams.

Laila heaved out, releasing her breath as she blurted, *'It was the gatekeeper to the afterlife.'* Then, she gathered herself together and continued with despondent eyes, *'I'm scared, Tury, but he came to me saying that I was to come find him, that I'm running out of time.'*

When Laila looked at Turathyl, she was insulted to see her reaction. The dragon, although concerned, seemed to be holding back a laugh.

'What is so funny?! This is serious! I don't think it's just a dream, Tury! I believe it really was Ignisar!'

As she shook her head, trying to compose herself, Turathyl replied, *'No, of course. It's just... Laila, Ignisar is not the gatekeeper to the afterlife; he is the monarch of the Red Dragon clan in the Syraho Desert.'*

Gawking confoundedly at the dragon, Laila's mouth dropped, not knowing what to say. She felt completely foolish and wondered why the others would refer to "Ignisar's Lair" the way they did.

Perceiving her thoughts, Turathyl added, *'Ignisar is the most feared of the dragons, the oldest remaining, and the wisest of us all. As far as I am aware, no two-legged has ever seen Ignisar, nor his clan, and lived to tell the tale.'* Pausing for a moment in thought, the dragon continued, *'I don't understand how it's possible that he has been appearing to you in your dreams. What has he told you?'*

Mulling over her memories of him, she replied, '*He said what happened with Aeris on the mountaintop is what was always meant to happen; that it set a pendulum in motion, and now we must hurry and come find him before it's too late and all of Onis is lost. He didn't tell me how much time we had or what would happen, just that I needed to hurry.*'

Laila went and sat against the dragon, forcing a smile at the dwarves who were watching their every movement, while Turathyl thought about what she had just been told.

With a rumbling dragon sigh, she lowered her head near the elf while keeping her gaze on the surrounding crowd. '*I don't think going to the Reds is a very wise idea right now. Perhaps we should wait until we have all the two-legged armies at our backs to go before him. We somehow managed to come out of our battle with Aeris alive, but, Laila, if Ignisar is luring you to him so that he can kill you as Aeris wanted to, I fear there would be no saving you then.*'

Laila understood Turathyl's concern while she absentmindedly fiddled with her dagger, creating swirls in the snow. She certainly did not feel ready for another battle against a horde of dragons. However, she felt in the pit of her stomach that Ignisar's intentions were not to destroy her but to help her, just as he had been doing from the beginning. She believed him to be more of a guide on her journey than a challenger. Yet, how much could she really trust a dream versus Turathyl, who had known him much longer than she could comprehend?

While contemplating her dream dragon's motivations, she noticed a very young dwarf girl tottering joyfully toward them. Upon glancing around, she did not see the girl's parents, and held her breath as the child threw a snowball at Turathyl, hitting her in the wing.

"NO! MERLA!" a female dwarf screamed, terrified, as she ran toward them and grabbed the child by the arm, jerking her back. Her eyes fixated on the dragon in horror.

Turathyl lowered her head, inhaled, then wafted out a strong breeze at the ground toward the girl, stirring up all the snow. Merla giggled with glee as her mother let go of her arm, and she twirled in the snow flurries falling all around her. The great dragon smiled as she watched the child's merriment, and the mother even let out an uncomfortable smile in return.

Sharing in the moment, Laila summoned even more snow to whirl up around the child, then theatrically fanned it out in an icy explosion. The snowflakes danced back to the ground while two other children ran to join in on the fun.

When the flurries had all settled back on the ground, Merla ran toward the dragon, and Turathyl remained calm and poised while the girl hugged her foreleg. Then she waved at Turathyl and said with her sweet innocent voice, "Ghyn, ghyn, draiky." *Bye, bye, draggy*, before skipping back to her waiting mother, who had frozen stiff, unsure of what to do.

While bowing her head, giving a slight nod of respect to the girl's mother, Turathyl caught in her glimpse King Brakdrath watching them from a castle balcony in the distance.

'We have a royal audience,' she indicated to Laila.

The king observed them without a hint of amusement a moment longer, then gave a nod of acknowledgement before disappearing into his castle.

"Are ye gunna' tell me why ye got dragon's fire in yer britches?" Hort demanded of Davion. "Why'd ye jus' take off like that after seein' the king? We should all be tagether comin' up wit' a plan ta convince him ta join us!"

Davion paced back and forth in a large room of Haddilydd's home. He passed before an empty firepit, only half the sconces lit, as they cast shadowy flickers against the walls and floor. Hands balled into fists, Davion only saw red while he steamed back and forth across the floor. Glondora waited quietly in the corner, out of the way, worried about the boy.

"Why does she hate me so much?" he fumed. "I know we got into an argument, but she couldn't even look at me when I was talking to the king. Do I repel her that much?!"

"What in Ignisar's Lair ye be talkin' 'bout?" Hort belted out.

Davion stopped pacing for a moment and looked at Hort, seething in his response. "When I was showing King Brakdrath the stones, she looked away like she was embarrassed of me speaking or something. Maybe she doesn't want me here anymore. If she doesn't want to be with me, that's her loss, but I deserve better, and I deserve to be here!" The bare sconces in the room flared, igniting without command, and a spark flashed in the fire before dying out again.

Hort looked with worry at the flames and back to the human. "Davion, me boy," he said in a calm tone, his hands held slightly out as though approaching a wild animal he hoped to befriend, attempting not to antagonize him further. "I dunna' know what be goin' on wit' ye, but methinks ye may be readin' too much inta things. Maybe ye need ta have a chat wit' the lass; find out what really be goin' on."

Huffing, Davion tried to hear Hort's words but was having trouble letting him in. He hated how much the elf maiden affected him; how with a smile she could make the sun rise; with a touch, she could make him want to move mountains. But, when she pulled away from him, it was like ripping his heart out of his chest, and then would come the burning.

Davion took a deep breath, releasing it slowly, trying to calm himself. "I don't even know what I'd say to her, Uncle," he said, slightly more collected. "I just wish she would open her eyes and realize that I'm the best thing for her. That we could do anything if we were together. She doesn't need dark magic or that blastit drow! I could help her stop this war if she'd just stop pushing me away!"

Puzzled, Hort was disturbed by what was happening to Davion; this wasn't like the boy he raised. He didn't approve of how he was acting or thinking. He also didn't understand how he was creating fire without casting a spell, and it troubled him greatly.

"What's wrong with her?!" Davion cried out, looking to his uncle for answers, who stood there with eyebrows furrowed, unsure how to respond. "I don't know how to fix her."

With a cautious step out of the corner shadows, Glondora said, "Lad, I know the lass been strugglin' since the Silvers. I dunna' know how ta 'elp her either, but methinks yer uncle be right, and ye need ta have a nice chat wit' 'er. If she loves ye, and ye love 'er, then me 'opes ye can sort it out, but ye need ta be willin' ta listen too. Either way, I know she been put upon a great deal wit' this prophecy, and it canna' be easy on 'er. Jus' 'ear 'er out. What does ye say?"

While taking another deep breath, Davion focused on easing the fire he could discern boiling up within him. He didn't want to admit it, but he found himself feeling rather heated more and more, both physically and emotionally, as though the darkness that Firemaster Thornton had warned him about was somehow trying to escape. It was subtle at first and easily ignored, but as time passed and as his beautiful elven angel continued to grow more distant from him, he could perceive it burning hotter within him.

Davion hadn't told Hort or anyone about what was happening to him, but he saw how they were watching him and knew they noticed the fires ignite in the sconces without an incantation. It was getting worse, and he knew it, worried he would soon have to tell someone.

Not knowing what anyone could do to help him, Davion didn't want to burden them with his struggle, but seeing fear and concern in their eyes made him realize that he may be losing control. He didn't know why the fires would burn hotter or brighter when he was angry. To his knowledge, he had never started fires prior to that instance without the use of a spell at the very least, and he was taken aback. Was it possible he was just becoming more powerful? But why? He wondered if it had to do with his connection to the prophecy or what pulled him to Laila. But what worried him more was that he had only noticed it for the first time after the orcs had nearly killed him, and Laila had brought him back from the brink of death. What else had she brought back with him?

When he managed to quell the burning inside of him, he looked upon Glondora earnestly and replied, "You are right. You both are. Perhaps I overreacted and saw something that wasn't there." He attempted to give them a smile, which came out half-hearted. "I will speak with her when I get a chance."

Davion continued pondering what it all meant while Glondora smiled at him and insisted that they all have some tea and cake before they find the others. Was the rising power within him something he should fear or something to be embraced? It clearly seemed like it would have its benefits if he could learn to control fire without the need for spells and incantations. Maybe he would become the most powerful pyromancer Onis had ever seen! His lips curled up in a sinister grin at the thought while he mused to himself.

As the evening pressed on, Turathyl and Laila were bombarded by more and more dwarves wanting to approach the dragon after seeing her friendly demeanor toward the child.

Rarely, some would even brave that pivotal moment of reaching out just far enough to let their fingers graze against the cool hard scales of the beast, where they would then giggle childishly and back away swiftly.

Had Laila known what a circus was or how they showcased the strange and unusual, she would have very much felt like one of those on display before all the curious dwarves. But, since it was a new experience for her, and she didn't see any harm in it—so long as Turathyl continued to tolerate them—she decided to indulge their wonderment, making quite the spectacle of themselves.

At first, it was primarily the women and children who wanted to gather around and greet the dragon, while the men typically stayed farther back, eying Laila and Turathyl with distrust and apprehension. Laila didn't mind. By seeing how much fun the others were having, she hoped that they would soften their hatred for the dragon and give the two of them a chance.

After some time, she even found herself enjoying casting little spells from the various spirits for their amusement. While the men seemed intrigued mostly by her display with the fire, the women would line up for a chance to give her various fruit seeds. Laila would rapidly grow them into young budding trees and vines, creating a following of very grateful dwarves. The children mostly loved her display with the snow and ice as she continued to play with them happily.

At one point, Glondora and Hort joined them as well, encouraging the Gortaxians to approach while raving about the magnificent Turathyl. They stayed for a while, excitedly telling tales of their journey and how they were going to bring peace to the land.

Laila was disappointed and a little sullen that Davion never came by to spend time with them, worried about how he was faring after the way he had stormed off. In an attempt to stay optimistic, she forced a smile and prayed he was just too busy off somewhere celebrating what they believed to be a successful first meeting with the king, likely in one of the many taverns. The human was indeed off enjoying some Gortaxian dwarven mead. However, it was not in celebration.

In all the attention from the dwarven people, Laila hadn't realized how much time had passed until the crowd gradually dispersed, returning home for the night to dream of friendly "Masters of the Sky." It was much later than Laila had believed, but the city of Gortax would not grow dark for several more hours, long after the rest of Onis. As snow fell from the sky to the mountains below, the reflection of light on the tiny flakes kept the sky unusually bright well into the middle of the night, causing Laila to be out much later than she had intended. Now, she was completely exhausted, and morning would come much too soon for her liking.

Turathyl sent Laila a loving farewell as she spread her wings, then headed back into the mountains for the remainder of the night, where she would feel more secure. The moment the dragon was gone, Nikolean approached Laila from where he had been watching over her all day, greeting each other with a smile and a nod.

Familiar with Nikolean's nature, Laila wasn't surprised by the silence as they strolled tiredly back to Haddilydd's, but there was a strange discomfort walking with him through the empty streets. Without the noise or distractions of the others—and possibly in part due to her exhaustion—she couldn't help but wonder what was going through his mind, curious if she truly had pushed him away along with Davion. Regardless, she was most grateful to have him there, particularly since she found herself quite turned around in the strange maze of a city, walking rather aimlessly.

CHAPTER 11

"This way, my lady," Nikolean said, veering down a street that led to their host's dwelling.

With a sheepish smile, Laila nodded and turned to follow. When she stepped toward him, her foot unexpectedly slipped on a patch of ice, and Laila felt herself falling backward with the ground flying out from under her. The next thing she knew, she was looking up into Nikolean's eyes, his face only inches from hers, while grasping his arm tightly. He had swooped over and caught her, holding her hovering barely half her height away from the hard ground. It always amazed her how swiftly he could move, and she was thankful for the assist.

To be so near him, feeling the warmth of his breath and his strong arms around her, caused her to gulp as her heart raced, both from the fall and the anticipation of what might happen next. But her imagination had got the better of her, and Nikolean instead gently aided her back to her feet while she continued clinging to his arm.

"Thank you, Niko," she told him, embarrassed, looking deeply into his red eyes.

He stared back at her intently, unmoving. Her heart began to beat harder in her chest as she gazed at him, her breathing heavier, and she wondered if he'd dare to pull her against him as he had done once before. She wondered even more whether or not she'd stop him. Despite everything else, she couldn't deny the spark that she felt every time he was near. But then Laila realized she had yet to release his arm, and that was likely the reason he still lingered so close.

Chuckling nervously, she released him and retrieved her hands before looking to the ground as though searching for more slippery patches of ice.

They resumed their stroll in silence, and he kept a respectable distance from her the rest of their course, noticeably averting his gaze whenever she would glance his way. It occurred to Laila that perhaps he had remained watching over her merely to honor his life debt and that the passion they had once shared was now just a distant memory for him, or even a mistake. She considered touching on his mind, but decided it wouldn't be right. That, and that she might not like what she found.

When they returned, the rest of the party had already been slumbering for some time. Upon reaching Laila's room, she turned back to face him and smiled warmly as she said, "Goodnight, Niko."

Without expression, the dark elf bowed to the Omi Méa and replied, "Goodnight, my lady."

He then turned and began heading back down the hallway. Flustered by his seemingly cold demeanor, Laila quickly made her way into the bedchamber. She wasn't sure what she had expected, but realized he might have been too fatigued for chit-chat or pleasantries beyond a simple "goodnight." Even still, she couldn't help but be disappointed, though not understanding why.

Too tired and confused to dwell on the mysterious dark elf's perplexing mannerisms, she took a deep breath and headed over to her bed. Their meeting with the king would come all too quickly, and that needed to be her primary concern.

The morning following their little display for the dwarves, everyone prepared themselves suitably to go back before the king and enjoyed a quick breakfast courtesy of Haddilydd and Handul. Laila sensed that Davion had been trying to speak with her all morning. Even so, she had been too groggy from the late night and too caught up in the chaos of the morning preparations to give him the attention he sought. She found

CHAPTER II

herself avoiding his attempts, hoping for a chance to converse after their meeting—and that he wouldn't run off again.

When they reached the courtyard, they were guided to the center of the clearing where they had been the day prior, and Turathyl joined them soon after. Laila greeted her warmly, touching her face to her muzzle. It wasn't much later that King Brakdrath came out to greet the comrades, clasping Laila's forearm in a warrior's greeting as he reached them.

"Lady Laila," King Brakdrath said respectfully. "If ye dunna' mind, I'd like ta take a stroll wit' ye." The king held out his arm chivalrously for Laila to grasp, and she did so modestly, looking at the others who all nodded in encouragement. They didn't go far; they simply strolled around the courtyard, leisurely following a pathway framed with rock edging.

Unlike the last visit, when she had been too nervous in front of the king, Laila regarded the courtyard amiably for the first time as they walked. With nothing able to grow there, the space had been landscaped with carved stone archways exhibiting delicate flowers and vines chiseled into their surface. A gazebo-style platform stood off to one side, holding stone benches within. It was covered in snow, like everything else in the city, with extraordinarily large icicles dripping from the overhang. Various sculptures of dwarves were strategically placed along the path, each in a different pose, facing inward. The old king cleared his throat a few times as they wandered, presumably to say something, but words would never come.

To break the ice, Laila said, "Thank you for allowing us to stay in your great city, King Brakdrath. Turathyl and I enjoyed meeting with your people very much."

"Yes, of course," the king replied.

As they reached the end of the courtyard, Laila admired a sculpture of a dwarf paladin made of white stone holding a sword erect above its head. The dwarf was depicted in a way that seemed humbled, as though praying to a god or goddess for a blessing on the sword. The king casually guided her along the path as it curved around the statue until they were heading back the way they came. After a few more anticipatory moments, he finally said, "Lass, ye and that dragon o' yers..." the king shook his head, and Laila's nerves pitted in her stomach as she anxiously waited for him to continue. "I never woulda' believed it ta be possible 'ad me not seen it wit' me own eyes."

Worrying the king was struggling with his lingering doubts, she volunteered, "You have not asked to see my powers, Your Majesty. Perhaps you would like a demonstration to show you they are real?"

Raising his hand at her, the king shook his head and clenched his eyes, rejecting the offer. "That not be necessary, lass. Me 'erd all 'bout them powers o' yers. Me people seen ye take out the orcs that 'ad taken control o' Gorén Gorge. I didna' realize it 'ad got so bad. I woulda' lost many a man tryin' ta take back that gorge and clear the roads back ta Lochlann. Ye did me a considerable favor and saved many o' me men in doin' so. Ye've already made 'istory in me books, and I've no doubt yer 'bout ta make more."

Laila told him honestly, "I saw them about to eat your people, and I couldn't let that happen."

King Brakdrath stopped and turned, smiling graciously at her as he said, "Aye, so I 'erd. Me people been speakin' mighty high o' ye. It doesna' take a wizard ta see ye 'ave a kind 'eart and a powerful soul. I dunna' know if that and yer powers be enough ta put a stop ta this war, but me seen and 'erd enough ta convince me ta be a part o' this rise against the Ancients."

Smiling widely at the king, Laila tried to contain herself. "What are you saying, Your Majesty?" she asked, wanting him to clarify before she became overly excited.

CHAPTER 11

"I be sayin' ye 'ave the support o' Gortax—and Lochlann—behind ye. I will start preparin' an army fer battle ta be ready fer ye when the time comes. Ye will 'ave all the soldiers me can spare fer yer quest ta stop the dragon war once and fer all."

Unable to resist, Laila flung her arms around the king, and he patted her back uncomfortably.

"Thank you, King Brakdrath!" she exclaimed, releasing the king shamefully.

The others, having seen Laila's excitement, realized they had the answer they had been praying for and gave each other celebratory handshakes and hugs—where agreeable. Smiling at the group's relief and delight, King Brakdrath invited them all to join him for a feast that night where they could discuss the plan for his army's involvement.

CHAPTER TWELVE

STRATEGY

The evening feast went splendidly, hosted by the king in a large banquet hall within the castle. In the spirit of the evening, Laila even decided to wear one of the exquisite elven gowns and jewelry she had brought along, including the necklace with Turathyl's silver scale that she had tucked away until then. The elf maiden sparkled radiantly in her attire, feeling once again like a real princess dining with the king in his castle. It was a nice change of pace from how she had been feeling for quite some time.

Glondora had enthusiastically helped her prepare for the evening. She curled large ringlets into Laila's hair, adorning it with gems and jewels that complimented her bronzed face. The dwarf even painted her eyelids, cheeks, and lips with refined pigments befitting the royal elven lady that she was.

The companions all sat with King Brakdrath near one end of an extravagant heavy wooden table with clawed feet and geometric patterns carved along the edges, its thick glossy finish reflecting the flickering light of the sconces and candles. Laila was entranced by the luxurious room and relieved that it was just her comrades and herself dining with the king that evening instead of a large crowd.

Tapestries draped over three walls, displaying the Gortax coat of arms of a snow-covered mountain and plate helmet. Lochlann's emblem hung on the fourth wall with its two crossed swords over a fire. Regal paintings of dwarven kings, past and present, also adorned one of the walls encased within fancy gold-painted frames.

King Brakdrath showed a more welcoming side of himself while partaking in the mead and meal before them. "Please enjoy!" the king insisted. "Twill be some time before we can obtain more provisions from Lochlann, but thanks ta ye lot, twill be possible once again! We shall all eat like kings tanight!"

He had insisted they not discuss business until the conclusion of the feast and, instead, the king shared stories of his home while they indulged in a wide assortment of meat and scrumptious sides. There were even ample vegetarian options offered considerately to Salyaman. The aromas of the spread from the cooked meat and spices were intoxicating, and it was the best meal any of them had enjoyed for some time.

Laila and the others took pleasure in hearing about Gortax and its history. They learned how the warriors and more adventurous of the dwarves had long ago sought something more thrilling than the endless mining of minerals for trade and fortifications. Longing for adventure and challenge, they traveled Onis, but still had the pull of the mountains calling them home. However, Lochlann no longer felt like home to them. It had become too crowded and cramped for their liking, having become used to the expanse and freedom the open land had granted them. So, they settled in the beautiful clearing within the western mountains and relocated the capital city to Gortax.

Prior to the wars and the drought, Gortax wasn't always covered in snow, and used to be quite beautiful and lush in the summer, with everything changing following the slaughter of the mother dragon, Onis Caelis. However, they refused to leave and return east, where there was still some vegetation remaining, praying every day for the land to heal and bring back the beauty it held once upon a time. The city's hydromancers did what they could to grow crops within greenhouses, but the bulk of their food supplies had been coming from Lochlann. Distressingly, the orcs and dragons had made it impossible to transport, causing their people to use what little they had sparingly.

Laila understood the king's insistence on the great feast to celebrate her group. To the dwarves, they weren't just "going to be" heroes; they already *were* heroes. With a score of renegade dragons watching over the dwarves and taking out orcs that had been causing their supplies to dwindle, they had freed up the trade route once again.

When the meal concluded, several dwarven kitchen staff brought in a wide spread of sweets and placed them on a table along one of the walls, creating a dessert bar for them to admire and indulge in. There were pastries filled with various fruits and creams, sprinkled with sweet sugars and honeys, and cakes of many shapes and sizes. Upon the king's insistence, Laila made her way over to the spread and eyed some other treats she didn't recognize, including types of puddings, custards, and tarts. They were all so beautifully decorated that she was afraid to take any of them and ruin the display. It wasn't all sickly sweet things, though; there was also a tower of assorted fruits that had all been carved to resemble flowers like a bouquet. It seemed like something more from a dream to be admired rather than anything created to actually be eaten.

Sensing Nikolean approaching her, she looked at him nervously, unsure of which she should try. He smiled at her, amused by her struggle.

"The great prophesied elf meant to save us all can't decide between a cake or a pie?" He smirked playfully at her.

Blushing with embarrassment, Laila reached out and grabbed one of the fruits from the tower and held it up triumphantly to the dark elf, returning his smirk.

Nikolean nodded to her approvingly before grabbing one for himself. He took a large bite while grinning at her; the juice dribbling down his chin.

With a soft chuckle, Laila shook her head at him and looked away as her cheeks became flush again, but it was not out of embarrassment that time, as her heart was also pattering within. It pleased her to see his humor had improved since the previous night.

After swallowing the piece of fruit, Nikolean wiped his face with the back of his hand, a silly grin upon his lips. He then bowed regally to her and said, "My lady," before heading back to the table with the remainder of the fruit in hand.

With the feast at its end, King Brakdrath's demeanor changed in an instant, becoming serious again as he brought up the plan for his army. The group explained to him that they intended to go to each of the nations and request their aid, then have all the armies assemble at the Trader's Post by Miran Lake—being a central location—before confronting Aeris again.

The king agreed with their plan. He knew it would take time to meet with all the races, but reassured them he would be ready.

Laila, still tormented by the warnings of her dream, let the king know that it was her intention to leave first thing in the morning for the dark elf capital to request their support. He couldn't endorse her decision to do so but was intrigued as

Nikolean told him about the Drakka while advertently leaving out the part of the drow being the cause of the war.

The king realized that "all the nations" would need to include the drow as well and wished them luck in their efforts, proclaiming, "May Jayenne and Kyrash be ferever on yer side."

Satisfied with the plan, King Brakdrath excused himself to attend to other matters. However, he bade that they stay and enjoy the dessert bar.

After the king had left, Salyaman told the group that they still needed to discuss their plans for acquiring support from the other races. "Are we certain going to the dark elves first is the right decision? Perhaps we should try the elves again, but go to our capital, Thas Duar Moran. Much has changed since we last spoke with my people, and I believe they would be more willing to listen now that we have the advantage of the dwarves and a score of Silvers. Then we could travel south to the human capital, Roco, and meet with King Lyson."

"There isn't time," Laila said firmly. She wasn't sure how much to reveal about her dream, but she knew that time was of the essence, and the drow were the nearest nation to them. "I believe that once Aeris knows of our plan, she will come for us. We need to be ready before that time comes." As she stood dauntless before them, she declared with confidence, "We will depart in the morning for the dark elf territory. Nikolean, you will need to be our guide once we arrive."

Nikolean nodded in compliance. The others seemed less than eager to accept her decision, but did not challenge her further on the matter.

"So be it," Salyaman stated. "I will start preparing for our departure." He bowed respectfully to Laila and then excused himself.

Hort was mumbling something incoherent to all except Glondora, not pleased with the plan. His wife smiled lovingly at him, assuring him that it would be fine, then left to get him some sweet cake and more mead to pacify his grumblings.

With everyone distracted, Davion hesitantly approached Laila, who had returned to the dessert spread for another treat. He smiled awkwardly, catching her attention, and rested his hand on the table as he leaned against it, trying to appear casual.

"Lady Laila, I've been meaning to have a word with you."

Laila was actually relieved that they would finally get to speak. It had been bothering her that he had been keeping his distance from her and that they hadn't really said a word to each other since their argument. She looked at him expectantly to continue.

Davion said nervously, "When we first spoke with King Brakdrath, and I had presented the stones to him..."

"Oh, yes!" Laila exclaimed, interrupting him, and placed her hand on his. "I am so grateful that you did! You are the only one I feel like I can trust with them."

Dumbfounded, Davion gaped at Laila, not knowing what to say, then eyed her hand on his, registering its warmth. That wasn't at all what he was expecting. "But, why did you look away?" he queried.

Upon seeing what she perceived as concern in his eyes, Laila decided to open up to him about the stones. "The black rock—Norn Mornder—it affected me strangely when we first received it from Lord Kilgar. Neither Tury nor I know what it means, and we thought it best I not handle the stones again until we could figure it out."

"Oh." Davion looked down, back at her hand still on his, and felt foolish for a moment. "I thought... Nevermind. Although, I am still worried about you using dark magic, Laila." He, like everyone, could see that she was not as withdrawn as she had been and was acting more herself, but he still wasn't sure what to think of the changes in her.

Laila gave him a warm smile and told him reassuringly, "Davion, it is sweet of you to worry, but I am not worried. I would never use any magic for evil. Therefore, I believe it is not evil. Everything I do, I do to protect you and the others and to fulfill this prophecy."

Her explanation only slightly settled Davion as he pondered on her words, still worried that she could lose herself to the magic without even realizing it, just as he was slowly losing himself.

"I still don't like it," he told her honestly. "Just promise me that you'll be careful and not let it destroy who you are. I couldn't bear to lose you to it."

Touched, Laila readily reached out, and Davion met her halfway, comfortingly holding each other in a friendly embrace. He lingered a little more than was warranted, missing the closeness, but was more at ease knowing that he had misunderstood what was going on. Briefly, he considered telling her about the changes that had been happening to him as well, but he struggled to put the words together and decided he wasn't ready.

"I will continue to guard the stones for you as long as you like," Davion told her while they partially separated from one another. He held her there for a moment, grasping her elbows with his hands, her arms resting gently on his. Wondering where her heart stood with him, he wished they were alone, not wanting to let go.

"Thank you, Davion," she replied, pulling back farther for him to release her. "It gives me peace to know that they are in your hands."

CHAPTER THIRTEEN

REACTIONS

*T*heir departure from Gortax was much more amicable than when they had arrived, having made many new friends during the performance that Laila and the great Silver put on for the dwarves. However, they were almost all eager to resume their journey.

Hort still wasn't thrilled about their next destination and didn't trust the drow at all. He wished he and Glondora could wait for them in Gortax, but, with the hurry that Laila seemed to be in, acknowledged it wouldn't be possible. He did have to admit, however, that Laila had made a remarkable recovery from whatever had been ailing her since the Silvers' Mountain. They were all relieved that she appeared better, although they recognized that it wasn't the same Laila they had got back. The new Laila seemed much more sure of herself and of her purpose, and it was reassuring and encouraging for all except Davion. He was less than thrilled with her transformation and contemplated what it would mean for the two of them going forward.

Turathyl joined them again after leaving the city and walked alongside Laila while she rode Merimer. The dragon found it slow and daunting, considering they were technically in a hurry, but plowed through the monotony as patiently as she was able.

As they headed south past Onis Falls, following along the dried-up river that was no more, Laila was feeling exposed with no trees, mountains, and scarcely any hills. There was nothing but more of the same rock and dirt. She was also a little nervous about meeting the dark elves and wondered how much truth there was to the stories of their wretchedness. Only being familiar with Nikolean, she was having difficulty imagining how horrible they could possibly be.

While pondering on the matter, she inadvertently glanced at Nikolean and blushed again as they locked eyes. She wasn't surprised to catch him looking at her; it had become expected. But it was making her more nervous than it had in the past, more self-conscious. She tucked a renegade lock of golden hair behind her ear and sheepishly looked his way again, disappointed that he was now looking forward, away from her. Feeling silly, she returned her attention to the invisible road that followed the dried-up riverbed and shivered as a cool wind crossed their paths. Still being winter, the air was bitter cold, but not nearly to the extent it had been in Gortax.

On their second day of traveling, they came to the end of the dry river, where it expanded into a large crater that was once the northern end of Du Noir Lake. All in agreement, they decided to rest there for the night and dismounted.

As she looked out over the barren lake and land surrounding it, Laila's heart ached not just at the sight of it, but at the pain of it. She knelt down, placing her hands against the hard rock surface, and could feel the death within. It was similar to when she would withdraw life from the vegetation around her to restore her health, killing the surrounding plants, except it was on a much, MUCH greater scale.

"I sense it also," Salyaman told her, seeing her pain. "But perhaps to a lesser degree than an Omi Méa would."

"I don't understand how this could happen," she said, wrapping her arms around herself protectively, still connected with the pain of the land.

"It's because of the drow using dark magic and feeding off of the land," Davion said bitterly.

Scoffing at Davion, Nikolean responded, "This was not from the dark elves' magic. It all happened after the mother dragon was killed. Our magic may have made the land dark, but it did not kill it."

'The drow is right,' Turathyl contributed. 'This land, this death, is part of what is believed you will heal from the prophecy. I am not clear on how that is, but I now believe this land has perished as penance for the drow killing Onis Caelis. It is worse in their territory than in any other part of Onis.'

While Laila relayed to them what Turathyl had said, Davion huffed and began creating a pit for a fire.

Salyaman took a deep breath, considering the dragon's words, then added, "It is increasing over all of Onis, not just here anymore. Even the elven territory has become harder to keep thriving. It is a great concern of mine for the future of my unborn child. That, and of course, the ruthless dragons."

"Speaking of dragons..." Davion began. "Laila, you said to King Brakdrath that you believed we could get several more to join us. How do you propose we do this? Are we to confront another dragon clan after we have gathered all the armies? The Golds, perhaps?"

Davion's question had piqued all of their interests, and they gathered around her, curious about her plans.

As she looked out over them, all eyes watching her intently, she said while feigning confidence, "We cannot wait that long. There is no time to waste."

Even though aware she was doing better, they were all worried about what another confrontation would do to her so soon. They also dreaded the idea of going it alone again, without the backing of the armies.

Laila had still not explained to them about her dreams of Ignisar, nervous about how they would react. Her body inexplicably began trembling as she tried preparing herself to tell them of her plan to visit the Red Dragons, not realizing how scared she, herself, was to go.

"There is one particular clan we must face first before I will know what to do next." After taking a deep breath, she continued, "I intend to see the Red Dragon monarch, Ignisar, after we speak with the dark elves."

She kept a close eye on her audience's reaction, witnessing as everyone gawked at her as though she had just said the stupidest thing they had ever heard. Resting nearby, Turathyl watched on keenly without intervening.

In confirmation of her assumptions, Hort exclaimed, "Okullo dung! That be the dumbest thing I 'ad tickle me ears! Lass, ye done and said a lot o' things that made me think ye might be crazy, but now I KNOWS ye be crazy!"

"Husband," Glondora said gently, putting her hand on his arm, but he pulled away abruptly, raising his arms in the air.

"No, Glondy! There be no way in Ignisar's Lair that any o' ye are ever gunna' be convincin' me ta go ta, well... IGNISAR'S LAIR! Tis bad enough ye wanna' go see the blastit drow, but no way! Me and Glondy will not be goin' 'fore any Reds!"

Nearly everyone started speaking at once, agreeing with Hort, insisting that they leave the Reds out of it. Nikolean stood watching Laila intently, trying to see past her maniacal words and understand.

"This be complete madness! Lass must be determined ta get us all killed!"

"Me Hort be right, m'lady. No one 'as even seen a Red and lived."

"I can see no benefit in involving the Reds at this time."

"I still think we should go to see the humans first. I may have some sway, having gone to the Magi Academy."

"MADNESS!" Hort raved.

As the group began a near-riot, Laila grew more nervous. She knew they wouldn't be happy about the idea, just as Turathyl wasn't, but she feared that if they did not go soon, then all would be lost as the Red Dragon had predicted.

"I'm with my uncle," Davion stated. "Going to the Reds is suicide. I know you're powerful, but the rest of us wouldn't last ten minutes."

Laila was disheartened, looking around at their faces. She didn't know if there was a way to make them more amenable to the idea. Even telling Turathyl of the dreams didn't help convince her, and she's actually met Ignisar. What chance did she have of convincing the others? Yet, she had to try.

Cautiously, Laila divulged, "I have seen the Mighty Red Monarch Ignisar in my dreams." They all stared at her, concerned and aghast. "He has been guiding me on our journey and told me that I must come find him."

Fuming, Hort shouted, "So we gunna' risk our lives fer a dream?! Me 'ad plenty o' dreams, but I not be trustin' a talkin' okullo that be compairin' me ta parfaits—whatever the baccat that be—ta decide me fate!"

"Let her speak," Nikolean said firmly.

"Go on, Lady Laila," Salyaman added, and Hort backed off, grumbling.

Inhaling deeply, Laila tried to calm her nerves as they all looked at her like she'd completely lost her mind. She couldn't be certain that they were wrong; all she knew was what her gut was telling her.

"Ignisar was the one that helped me discover the fire spirit. He has been pushing me forward even when I didn't want to go on. I can't explain why he appears to me, but I believe he will help us. He foresaw all of what has happened and forewarned that Aeris will learn of our plan and come for us. The Red Dragon told me we are running out of time and must hurry, or everything we have been working for will be lost."

While taking a deep breath, she tried to gauge their reactions. They were all just staring at her, some with concern, but she wasn't sure if it was for her sanity or for their situation.

"That explains your urgency to get to the dark elves," Salyaman said thoughtfully. "If this is true," he added, staring intently at her, trying hard to give her the benefit of the doubt, "and it, in fact, was Ignisar that appeared to you with knowledge of the future, why would he not have warned you about what would happen with going to Aeris when we did?"

Laila wasn't surprised by his question since she had wondered the very same thing. "The Red Dragon told me that it was meant to happen the way it did, that it was meant to set things in motion, but that we are on the correct path for the prophecy."

The group seemed unsettled and dissatisfied by her answer. She feared that she had just convinced them all that she had gone mad instead of what her true intention was; they needed to go see Ignisar.

"And if it's a trap?" Davion asked.

Nervous, Laila wasn't sure how to answer him. She had no way of knowing for sure other than her gut feeling.

CHAPTER 13

Sensing her distress, Nikolean interrupted, getting everyone's focus off of Laila, "We still have to meet with the dark elves. Let us start there, and then we can decide what is next. It does not need to be decided tonight."

Annoyed, Davion stepped toward Nikolean and hollered, "Don't pretend that you aren't in the least bit terrified to go before the Reds as well! You may have her fooled, drow, but the rest of us know your true nature, even if we don't know your true intentions—yet."

"I am in agreement with the drow," Salyaman proclaimed, looking Davion sternly in the eye. "Let us prepare to see the dark elves, and then we can discuss the plan for the dragons further. It indeed does not need to be determined tonight."

Grateful for the redirect, Laila locked eyes with Nikolean, a timid "thank you" in her expression, and he nodded understandingly in response. At the same time, Davion backed off, tending to the fire bitterly.

As they settled for the night, Hort continued mumbling about the absurdity of even mentioning going to see the Reds. He grumbled about how he didn't care how long they spent with the dark elves; there was no way anyone was going to convince him to go before the Red Dragons, and especially not their monarch, Ignisar.

CHAPTER FOURTEEN

PYNAR

*T*he brisk morning winds struck them awake as the crack of dawn gleamed over their faces, the sleeping piles covered in warm furs stirring groggily. Laila had been up for nearly an hour, watching the sun break over the horizon while sitting against her sleeping dragon. Her breathing slow and tranquil, she relished the beauty of the painted clouds of pinks, reds, and orange as the day woke around them.

Laila's thoughts were of back home, of her family, and of all the joy she had with them growing up. The war she was destined to stop was not her own, yet she knew that the people of Onis had never experienced the peace that she had enjoyed with the Wolf God and her pack. It almost instilled a sense of guilt, having had enjoyed that simple yet tranquil time all to herself while the world around her was unknowingly suffering.

"Laila?" Davion said, approaching from beside her.

She closed her eyes, inhaling the cool morning air, and let it out slowly through her lips. The human came closer; she could sense him even through the earth. The spirits were all with her now, all the time, and she had been focusing on finding that balance within herself, as the mighty Red Dragon had suggested. It was helping. There was a calmness sweeping through her as she embraced them as a part of her instead of just tiny lights that she grasped hold of.

"Davion," she said, opening her eyes again and turning her head to look up at him.

Stammering, he said, "I... I..." He cleared his throat and changed his tone as he remarked, "We should get going soon."

Troubled once again about their relationship and what that word even meant for them after another night of disagreements, she replied plainly, "Yes, we should." Then she jumped to her feet and gave Turathyl a gentle pat, the dragon beginning to stir as well.

Merimer trotted up to the elf, neighing, and Laila kissed her snout, ready to be on their way. The surrounding death where the gods had forsaken Onis was painful to her, but she was determined to find a way to heal the broken land again someday, just as she had been putting her own brokenness back together.

As they continued heading south toward the Du Noir Forest, Laila took the lead, the others following solemnly, still mulling over the conversation of the past night. The dragon took the tail, keeping watch for anything out of sorts.

Sometime after they had stopped for lunch, Laila spotted a strange formation in the distance but couldn't make out what it was. As they drew closer, it appeared to be a city on the horizon, but something didn't seem right. Merimer stopped while the elf inspected it and called for Nikolean to come join her.

"There," she pointed toward it. "What is that? A dark elf city?"

Squinting, Nikolean realized where they were. "No, my lady. It is a city of no one. We are coming upon the Ruins of Pynar. It is believed to have collapsed shortly after the fall of the mother dragon, though I am not sure why."

Pynar. Laila thought it an interesting name for a city but was more curious why two-leggeds would be using a word from the Ancient tongue to name it.

"Was it dark elf?" she asked.

"No, my lady. But I must insist we go around. My people believe it to be cursed, and even the spirit classes will not go near. The elders forbade my people from entering long ago."

Salyaman rode up beside Nikolean and narrowed his eyes while surveying the ruins. "I am familiar with the name. However, I do not recall what nationality it was. The elves had heard rumor of it being haunted by angry spirits from the drow releasing their dark magics within."

"So, it has been left alone all this time?" Laila inquired.

"I do not know any more beyond that," Salyaman replied. "But I agree that we should go around the ruins. There is no telling what may lurk within its walls."

Laila heard their words, but her heart was in disagreement. Something was once again calling to her. She hadn't felt a pull like it since she was called to find Davion back in the Sacred Forest. Her heart rate increased, elated, as she wondered what it could be. *Perhaps another two-legged meant to be with us is hiding within,* she speculated excitedly.

"We will go inside," she told the group absolutely.

Nikolean opened his mouth to object, but Laila immediately gave Merimer a mental command, darting forward at a fast trot. She knew there could be dangers within, but curse or no curse, she had to discover what lay beyond its walls. Although eager to find out the source of the pulling, she wasn't going to dash in recklessly—not again.

'*I will scout,*' Turathyl sent her, lifting off into the sky and stirring up the dust around them as she headed swiftly to the ruins.

While moaning and grumbling their displeasures, the rest of the group hesitantly slashed their reins, picking up the pace to follow the elf maiden.

Mental images of the long-abandoned ruins were sent to Laila from Turathyl while she flew overtop, and Laila was both captivated and disappointed all at the same time. She had often wondered what the world would look like from a dragon's point of view. The city was quite large, and seeing how the shapes changed from above fascinated her. The lines that were its streets spread out like a spiderweb from a central structure. She noted there was no castle or building that appeared more significant than the others to indicate precedence, like in the prior cities she had visited. Only the lone structure in the middle seemed to hold any more interest merely due to its location. The various surrounding buildings—that now mostly lay in shambles—seemed to be equally placed. There were, however, substantial rock platforms encompassing the outskirts of Pynar that caught her attention. Even with all its intrigue, her disappointment came from seeing no living thing within the city walls.

'*They could be hiding,*' Turathyl pointed out, sensing her letdown.

As they approached the dilapidated entrance, they brought their steeds to a slow walk. The mounts flicked their tails nervously and tucked their ears back on their heads, anxious about the energy of the ruins.

Apart from Laila, the rest of the group held their reservations about their presence there, eyeing for signs of anything that appeared amiss, which was difficult since the entire place felt amiss. However, upon entering, they were instantly in awe as they regarded the marvel before them and dismounted to get a better look at their surroundings. They could not deny their curiosity as the mysterious city unveiled before them. Its architecture was unlike any that they had seen, yet similar to that of all.

Even near the entrance, Hort and Glondora spotted the workmanship of the dwarves with etched stone and construction not unlike Lochlann, although chipped, broken, or crumbled. Salyaman studied a dwelling of marble with its roof caved in that reminded him of his home, Má Lyndor, in its design and appeal. Davion even noticed influences of his own people, things comparable mostly to Roco, the human capital. A remaining parapet, half its walls crumbled on the ground, sported an orange-shingled roof in a similar style to the small village, Amillia, where he had once lived with his mother, father, and brother.

"This is incredible," Salyaman said, looking around at how all the different pieces seemed like they had somehow managed to be cohesive in their day.

Laila spotted Nikolean analyzing some carvings on a stone. It was lying before a peculiar dried marble pond full of boulders and debris that was once a large fountain. A carved draconic wing was all that remained distinguishable from what would have been the center statue. The drow had a peculiar look on his face as he ran his gloved fingers over a tablet.

"What is it?" Laila asked curiously while approaching him.

"This writing is Drow," he replied. Though worn and cracked with time, it was still legible with some effort. He began reading the inscription. Laila reached to his thoughts, hearing the meaning behind them, and translated for the others who were gathering around.

"Moén att waras kon chürra."

"Like the water that flows within."

"Ir nid ëlla liet den Onis."

"We are all a part of Onis."

"Ir nid ëlla liet den jernam."

"We are all a part of each other."

"Ir nid att Ginairev."

"We are the United."

"Ir nid Pynar."

"We are Pynar. Pynar also means 'united' in the Ancient tongue," Laila explained to the group.

Everyone stood in wonderment, silently fascinated by the ruins as they looked around. The only other town where several of the races could be found together was the Trader's Post, but that was merely in tolerance for the purpose of exchange. Even there, the drow were not a welcomed crowd. It was hard to imagine all the races living together peacefully within those walls all those years ago, yet there they stood, seeing the evidence for themselves. At some point, it had been more than merely a possibility. Then everyone's mind fell to the same question: What happened?

"Well, if ye ask me, they prolly destroyed themselves," Hort declared, breaking the silence. "Me bet ye any coin that be what 'appened 'ere. Dunna' get me wrong; I be all fer endin' the war, but blastit if ye'll catch me livin' next ta a drow!"

"Husband," Glondora nudged him, "ye've been livin' wit' a drow fer nigh two seasons now, ye silly oaf! And a blastit fine drow 'e be! A drow who saved yer 'ide on more than one occasion need me remind ye." Glondora gave Nikolean a friendly wink, and he smiled at her, nodding appreciatively.

"Okay, Okay. Well, me still thinks that's what 'appened 'ere," Hort grumbled then tottered off toward some rubble.

Laila shielded her eyes with her arm as she looked up at Turathyl attempting to land near them while everyone made room for the dragon.

'I could see nothing living within. I believe we are safe for now, but you should still be careful.'

With a nod to her Silver, Laila touched the hilt of Dragonsbane at her side reassuringly. Still feeling the strange pulling at her heart, urging her on, she started to make her way farther into the ruins. The others followed in behind, guiding their mounts through the rubble while gawking at the surroundings that made no logical sense being all in a single place, yet somehow gave the impression of being perfectly integrated.

As they stepped through a large pile of debris, Laila discovered the enthralling building she had seen through Turathyl's gaze at the center of the extraordinary city. She immediately recognized it as the source of the spiritual pulling.

Mesmerized by the building with its white stone exterior and tall curved archways surrounding it, she moved steadily over the rubble toward the entrance. Compared to the rest of the city, the building was in the most preserved state.

Strange whispers began to tickle in her ears, getting louder the closer she became. Even though she felt an other-worldly aura emanating from the unusual stone building, she couldn't help but keep walking forward, unable to ignore the strong magnetism drawing her towards it. She needed to find out what dwelled within.

"What do you think it was?" she asked aimlessly as she continued to head for the structure.

While walking alongside her, Salyaman replied, "It appears to be a type of temple. However, I am not sure to what deity. It is unlike any I have seen before."

They paused at the entrance, gathering around, as they tried to peer inside. It was relatively dark, but cracks in the structure and ceiling allowed light beams to shine through, spotlighting areas of no significance but offering just enough light to keep their footing as they stepped inside. Laila entered first, wondering what was so important about that place that it would pull her there. The others, except for the dragon, followed her in.

Once her eyes had had a moment to adjust, her heart skipped a beat as she looked around, finding an unusually familiar room. At first glance, its shape and the ambiance of the debris and gloom reminded her of a cave. Then, the sunlight shifted, piercing through and illuminating the room further. Highlighted in the center of the room was a large stone table shaped like a cross. It was unscathed and only slightly weathered with time, with a thick layer of dust over its surface. Elaborate and peculiar markings were engraved around its perimeter.

"I know this place," Laila said enchantedly.

Laila's attention was then brought to the walls as she tried to recall where she had seen that place before. She was unsurprised by what she found, but still captivated by it. Illustrations of dragons adorned every wall surrounding them, barely visible from the light streaming through the cracks, but she recognized them in an instant.

There were depictions of dragons fighting man as well as fighting other dragons, dragons flying high in the skies, and dragons posed beside two-leggeds. One image was causing her to squint for closer analysis as she peered at an odd figure painted onto the back of a dragon, trying to discern what it was.

Whilst Hort stayed near the door, uneasy of the temple, Glondora touched the art on the walls, admiring its vivacity and longevity, wondering what they had used that would have lasted all that time.

Nikolean walked around the edge of the room, not touching anything as he searched for more traces of his people.

As he stepped toward the table, Salyaman noted, "This writing around the table, it is in the Ancient tongue."

"What does it say?" Davion asked him, nearing to get a better look.

After staring at the writing for several moments, the elf prince shook his head. "It appears to be some sort of verse—perhaps a spell—and mentions the four elements. Water..." he touched the edge of the table point where he was closest, then walked briskly to another point. "This one says fire. I suspect the other two would be air and earth. However, I am not sure I should read the verse aloud. There is something very peculiar about this temple. I believe they may have been worshiping dragons."

'Do you know anything about this?' Laila asked Turathyl, sending her mental images of the room.

'I do not,' she replied. *'Please, be careful. I sense magic here that I am not familiar with.'*

Laila drew near to the table, the whispered buzzing in her ears increasing, and she placed her hand upon the dusty stone surface. The moment she did, a strong breeze blew through the building, stirring up all the dust from the tabletop and floor.

As everyone coughed and sneezed from the disturbance, Laila stood frozen, bombarded with flashes of moments, of memories that weren't hers, but they came so quickly she had trouble making sense of them. There were dragons of the four element classes flashing through her mind, and two-leggeds from each race gathered around. She saw a dragon flying with an elf upon its back. She saw the destruction of cities and of men, but then her thoughts jumped back to the temple, except it wasn't in ruins, and it wasn't dark. The temple was brightly lit with sconces burning, the mural freshly painted, and the table smooth and clean. There were four ghostly figures, all in black robes, standing one at each point of the cross, and it sounded as though they were humming. Listening carefully, she realized they weren't humming at all; they were chanting something. The figures raised their hands, stretching them outward toward one another, and something on the table began to glow in front of them. Then the images vanished as quickly as they had appeared, and Laila was standing again in the dark, dusty room; the whispering, gone.

Blinking, she looked around at the others, who were recovering from the dust storm, oblivious to what she had just experienced. As she shifted her focus back to the table, she recoiled in surprise, jerking her hand away from it.

Revealed beneath the dust was a small circle carved into the stone at each point. Wrapping around each circle were five lines, which then extended towards the middle of the cross, swirling around a fifth carved circle at its center. Each of the circles was only the size of a grape, but the encompassing lines made them prominent.

With the image flashes fresh in her mind, she studied the circular dips in its stone surface; their shape, their size, the connection between them, and then it hit her.

"The stones," Laila murmured. Raising her eyes, she gaped at the others. "The stones!" she repeated fervently. "Davion, hand me the Dragon Stones!"

Swiftly, Davion released the leather pouch from his belt and poured the four Dragon Stones into his palm. As he held them out for Laila, she grabbed them eagerly. After pawing through them, she handed him back the red one with orange flames; the Fire Stone.

'Laila, I don't like this,' Turathyl said, alarmed, having been watching through her mind.

Ignoring the dragon, she hurriedly went to Salyaman and handed him the gold stone with the burnt-orange cracks; the Earth Stone. Glondora excitedly dashed toward Laila, realizing what she was intending, and held out her hand expectantly.

With a smile at her enthusiasm, Laila placed the rippled stone with blue and green waves into her palm; the Water Stone.

"What ye be doin', lass?" Hort shouted from his spot by the entrance, afraid to go any farther in, an uneasy feeling holding him back. "Glondy, give 'er the stone back! Ye and me can wait out 'ere!"

"Sorry, husband, but I canna' do that," Glondora replied firmly. "Now, where be the water again?"

Circling the table, Salyaman indicated where each of the elements was etched into the stone cross. In clockwise order, they read "Earth, Air, Fire," and "Water."

While the others stood at their respected ends of the cross, Laila approached Nikolean with the final stone.

"Are you sure we should be doing this?" Nikolean asked her quietly, drawing intimately near her.

When she looked up into his enchanting red eyes, the blood rushed to her cheeks, and she smiled coyly as she replied, "Completely." Then she took his hand with hers, her fingers tingling against his warm skin as she pressed the white stone with silver swirls into his palm; the Air Stone.

"Laila, I'm not sure this is a good idea," Davion said nervously, standing before his spot at the table. "We have no idea what will happen."

"Me boy's right!" Hort declared. "Ye all 'ave lost yer 'eads! Let us leave now 'fore ye do somethin' ye'll regret! Please, Glondy. Ye dunna' know what yer doin'!"

"Maybe so," Glondora replied, "But methinks there be only one way ta find out then." She held up her stone toward the table, preparing to place it in the circle.

"Not yet, Glondora," Salyaman said, stopping her. "Lady Laila, are you certain about this?"

Acknowledging the fear in the eyes of the others, she gave them a reassuring smile. "Ever since before I left my home, something has been pulling at me. It is what brought me to Davion and to all of you. I can't explain what the reason is behind any of it, but I know we are supposed to be here, that everything has been leading us to this point."

"That is enough reason for me," Nikolean said.

"But do you know what will happen to us?" Davion asked, concerned.

Laila shook her head, causing Davion to let out an exaggerated sigh. "Well, if we're going to do this," he said, "then I suggest we all place them at the same time."

"I as well," Salyaman stated, and the others nodded their agreement.

'Please be careful,' Laila heard Turathyl say, dismayed.

There was a nervous excitement filling the room, but they all seemed intrigued enough that they wanted to go through with it, although hesitant. Hort held his place, trying his best not to interfere, even though he was extremely concerned for Glondora and Davion.

Laila stood back, observing them all, and rubbed her hands together enthusiastically as she asked, "Is everyone ready?"

They all nodded in response, afraid to speak.

"GO!" she hollered, and the four of them each laid their stones carefully in the circles before them, and then...

Nothing.

Nothing happened.

They looked at each other confused, Laila most of all. Glondora adjusted her stone, thinking that perhaps it wasn't in there just right.

"I don't understand," Laila said disappointedly, dropping her hands to her sides. "They should be glowing or something."

Pressing the heel of her hand against her temple, her fingers clawed in her hair, she tried to remember the vision, realizing they must have missed something.

"Laila, there is a fifth circle," Salyaman pointed out, looking at the center of the cross.

"Of course!" she exclaimed, overly eager, startling the others. "You don't suppose...?" Looking back to Davion, she motioned to the pouch with the fifth stone they were given from Lord Kilgar.

"Norn Mornder?" Davion asked rhetorically. "We can try it. I will place it there for you." He smiled at her, the shifty type of smile between two friends sharing a secret. After removing the perfect black stone from the pouch, he took it to the middle of the table. Laila averted her eyes from it, trying to get the chill of its touch out of her mind.

When Davion placed Norn Mornder in the center, again, nothing happened, and he retook his place at the fire end of the table.

"Well, that be a relief!" Hort sighed, contented.

Frustrated, Laila looked at the center of the table to Norn Mornder, and her eyes instantly locked on to it. She felt it jolt her entire body as it wrapped around her mind, the same as when she had been entranced by looking into Aeris's eyes, and she shivered at the likeness. Her heart palpitated, her breathing stopped, and she felt frozen in place and time.

Everyone watching, none realized at first what was happening, thinking Laila was just staring upon the stone. However, in the next moment, they knew something was amiss. Laila's eyes became clouded over until they went completely dark and hazed, appearing like two black gaping holes.

"Ma Kyrash!" Davion said in alarm. "Laila?! Laila, what's happening?!"

The others tried calling her name as well, but she could not hear them. She only heard the whispers, loud in her ears now, as her body moved of its own accord toward Norn Mornder. No one knew what to do. Nikolean was about to leave his spot to try to break her trance, but before he could move, Laila began to speak.

The language of the Ancients spilled out of the Omi Méa's mouth, but in a voice that was not her own. Before anyone could react, they too began to speak the same words, words unknown to most of them, in voices that were not theirs. Their feet were plastered to the floor where they stood, and their arms unwillingly stretched out toward one another, forming a circle around the Omi Méa as they chanted the strange words. Salyaman knew they were speaking the verse he saw engraved around the table, but he no longer had control. He and the others were onlookers to their own bodies and actions, unable to do anything to stop it.

Hort hollered and yelled, panicking about what was going on. He forced himself to enter the temple and tried to pull Glondora away, to wake her up, but he could not budge her. The dragon roared frantically, shaking the rubble of the city, afraid of what was happening, yet unsure if she should stop it.

The Dragon Stones began to glow brilliantly in front of each group member, except for Norn Mornder. From the Black Death stone came forth a dark and sinister fog of the phantom realm. Then, the table's engraved lines also glowed a bright blue, connecting the stones to one another as they continued their chant. Laila, standing next to the center, raised her hands above her head, her chanting intensifying, and the others did the same, irresistibly following her command. Along with each of the stones, the elf maiden slowly began to levitate, the spirits holding them, wrapping around them.

Hobbling back to the entrance, Hort grabbed hold of the doorway when a great gale began to blow wildly through the city of rubble and into the temple. He cried out for them, begging them to stop, but no one would hear. The earth shook as

Turathyl stamped wildly at the ground outside, feeling helpless as the Dragon's Eye took over the Omi Méa.

Their chanting grew boisterously loud over the whirring and moaning that was coming from the black smoke as it slowly filled the room. Then, Laila winced her eyes, shaking as she unexpectedly screamed. A brilliant flash of light shot out from her chest like lightning through Norn Mornder and out to each of the four Dragon Stones. It then continued out, beaming into her four surrounding comrades. They shook at the intensity of the energy pouring into their souls. Suddenly, a resounding BOOM echoed and quaked the temple like an explosion. Laila dropped and collapsed to the floor. All four of her friends at the table went catapulting backward away from it and slammed into the temple walls, falling unconscious to the ground.

CHAPTER 14

CHAPTER FIFTEEN

VOICES

"Baccat! DAVION!" Hort screamed, panicking as he ran to him. "Me boy! Wake up!"

Shaking Davion, who was unresponsive, Hort glanced over to Glondora.

"Me love!" he called, running over to her next and doing the same. No one was moving, and he was terrified that they were all dead, too overwhelmed, and too scared to check. The dragon, roaring wildly and shaking the earth with her stomping, wasn't helping him focus. Rocks were breaking free from the temple and clacking to the ground around him.

"DRAGON! YE CUT THAT OUT OR YER GUNNA' MAKE THE WHOLE PLACE COLLAPSE!!!" he yelled as loud as he could to penetrate the racket she was causing.

Turathyl whined a throaty moan as she stopped quaking the ground and lowered her mighty head, trying to peek through the small entryway, pressing an eye up against the opening.

"Yer blockin' the light, beast!" Hort hollered at her as he examined Glondora, and the dragon moaned again, pulling away.

To Hort's relief, he discovered that his wife was still breathing. "Oh, praise Jayenne!" he exclaimed, throwing his hands up to the heavens, relieved. He kissed her forehead and whispered how much he loved her and needed her to wake up.

Without leaving her side, he called back out for Davion several more times, hoping to wake him as well.

"Uncle," Davion managed to mutter after several minutes while he tried to prop himself up on his elbows. "I'm alright."

Soon after, Salyaman and Glondora began to stir, disoriented and hurting from the impact against the temple walls. Even Laila began to wake, rubbing her eyes with her fists, her head filled with a loud ringing from the explosion she deemed had come from within her.

Before she could collect herself, the temple creaked and cracked loudly, then let out a rumbling roar. Laila could sense the ground trembling just before she was being whisked up by someone and carried out with haste. The others scrambled to escape as well. Still trying to focus, the image of the room a blur, she clenched her eyes at the brightness when they neared the exit. Immediately following the cracking came a loud BANG as they breached through the doorway, followed by a clangorous CRASH while the roof split and crumbled. They jumped clear, diving away while the temple collapsed thunderously behind them, along with most of its walls.

After being thrown to the ground outside the temple, Laila blinked her eyes open, and her gaze was drawn to the scene of utter destruction. Her friends were covered in dust while they attempted to get back to their feet, and she felt a warm touch on her arm, the ringing in her ears subsiding.

"Laila, are you injured?" Davion asked her, his voice still a little muffled in her ears.

She looked up into his eyes, bewildered as to what had just happened, and smiled, relieved to see him. "I don't think so," she told him. "Thank you."

"Ye know this be all yer fault, dragon!" Hort huffed. "If ye hadna' been stompin' 'round like that, twoulda' been fine. Ye nearly got us all killed!"

'Laila, I am sorry, I was so worried,' Turathyl told her sincerely. 'Are you certain you are unharmed?'

As she took a moment to assess herself, Laila descried some minor scratches but seemed to be intact overall. 'Yes, it appears so,' she mind-sent.

"Glondy, ye 'ad me so scared! What the baccat 'appened back there?! Does ye feel any different?"

Patting her hands over her body from her shoulders to her thighs, then back up to ensure her bosoms hadn't been blown off, she smiled at her husband. "Jus' a little sore tis all."

Davion held out his hand, and Laila took it appreciatively, allowing him to help her to her feet while she scanned the area. She caught a glimpse of Nikolean's legs stretched out by Salyaman, who was sitting upright on the ground, blocking the rest of the drow from her view. When she noticed his legs weren't moving, her heart jumped up into her throat.

"Does anyone feel any different?" Davion asked.

They all looked at each other in disappointment, shaking their heads.

While staring at Nikolean's legs, Laila observed them starting to move. Relief for the drow hit her, but she could not hide her chagrin about the ritual. "So... it was all for nothing," she said, disheartened.

Salyaman began to stand, clearing Laila's view to Nikolean, and stated, "It is possible something went wrong during the ritual."

Nikolean was conscious, *praise Jayenne*, and rubbing his hand against his head, wincing his eyes in pain.

"Niko," Laila said, stepping toward him, "are you hurt?"

'He likely hit his head in the temple,' Turathyl told her.

Still rubbing his head, the drow muttered, "Yes, probably."

"Probably?" Glondora asked. "Are ye hurt or ain't ye?"

Disoriented, he didn't reply.

Laila went to his side and knelt down. "Here, let me take a look."

Nikolean raised a hand to stop her from fussing over him. "Don't waste your strength, my lady. I'm sure it's just a headache and will pass."

The drow tried to stand but immediately stumbled and fell back down, his head spinning and throbbing with intensity.

'Stubborn man,' Turathyl snorted. *'He's just trying to act tough to impress you, you know.'*

While clasping his hands to his head, Nikolean abruptly shouted, "I am not!"

"What in Ignisar's Lair ye goin' on 'bout, drow?" Hort asked.

"Ye must've hit yer 'ead 'ard," Glondora said, approaching him. "If ye wonna' be lettin' m'lady 'ave a look, then at least let me."

'That was strange,' Laila said to Turathyl. *'I hope he's alright.'*

Turathyl cocked her head at Laila, concerned about the drow's outburst as well. The dragon then nodded to her, agreeing as she watched Glondora cast her healing over Nikolean's head.

CHAPTER 15

After she had completed her spell, Nikolean said, more stable, "Thank you, Glondy." Then he tried to stand again, with success that time.

"Well, at least we all be whole and well now," Glondora said with relief.

"Yes," Salyaman said, brushing himself off. "We seem to be otherwise unharmed, which is more than can be said for the temple."

Everyone looked at the pile of rubble that remained, sighing.

Davion approached Laila and took her hand. "Are you sure you're alright? That was pretty intense back there."

She nodded and smiled at him reassuringly. "Just disappointed," she admitted, then gasped, "The stones! They're still in the temple!"

Nodding to her, Davion said, "I will go find them for you. Don't worry."

Laila thanked him as she politely retrieved her hand, and he headed toward the pile of debris that was the temple.

'I was sure I was being led to this place for a reason,' she told Turathyl in private. 'But I guess we'll never know why now.' While idly kicking at the rubble, she strolled over to her dragon and nuzzled into her snout. 'We'll start heading to the other side. You should meet us there so you don't demolish the rest of the buildings by walking with us.' Laila gave Turathyl a loving pat and stepped back, allowing her space.

As the dragon spread her grand silver and white wings, she assured the elf maiden, 'I will be watching you.'

Nikolean startled everyone as he grabbed his daggers and held them outward aggressively while shouting, "Who said that?! Who's there?!" He spun frantically around, searching for an assailant.

"Whoa there, lad!" Glondora yelled, raising her hands, trying to calm him. "Sorry, methought I got it all. Put the knives down, and lemme 'ave another look at yer 'ead."

"Wait!" Laila hollered at them both, a theory manifesting in her mind. *'Niko, can you hear me?'* she mind-sent inquisitively to him, but he did not respond and continued holding his aggressive stance.

'I don't understand,' she told Turathyl.

'Perhaps he's just gone mad,' the dragon replied, tucking her wings back against her sides.

While shaking his head back and forth with clenched eyes, the drow cried out, "No... no... no..." He pressed his fists against his temples, still clasping the hilts of his daggers, as he loudly declared, "I am not mad!"

"No one said ye are, lad. Tis alright. Jus' be calm." Glondora told him with a tranquil tone.

"Niko, you heard that?" Laila asked, hurrying toward him.

"Laila, stay back!" Davion called, rushing out of the temple toward her. "He'll hurt you!"

"No, he won't," Laila told him with confidence. As she approached the drow, Laila said in a calm and soothing manner, "Niko, drop the daggers. You are not going mad. You were hearing Turathyl."

Everyone's eyes gaped open, Nikolean's most of all as he dropped the daggers to the ground, and they clattered against the rocky surface. The drow looked back and forth between the Omi Méa and her dragon incredulously.

"How is that even possible?" Davion blared. "Are you sure?"

"Perhaps that is what the ritual was for," Salyaman pondered.

Laila's lips stretched into a wide smile, overly excited at the possibility. "Tury," she called to her dragon, "say something else!"

As she lowered her head, Turathyl stared with intensity at the dark elf, then mind-sent with a pronounced enunciation, as though talking to someone who spoke another language, *'Can you hear me?'*

Nikolean jumped, startled by the words in his mind, "Yes! Yes, I heard you!"

"But how do you understand her?" Laila questioned. "She was speaking the language of the Ancients."

Nikolean looked at Laila strangely and replied, "That is not how I heard it. She was speaking Drow. I presumed at first that there were dark elves nearby I was hearing."

Salyaman circled Nikolean, his thumb and finger gripping his chin as he analyzed the dark elf before him. "Very peculiar."

Huffing, Davion asked, "Why is he the only one who hears her, then? We were all there; we all got shot with those beams."

'Perhaps because Niko and I already shared a connection before your ceremony,' Turathyl contemplated. *'I wonder... Niko, can you mind-touch me? Think something while directing it toward me.'*

Laila and her dragon stood there, staring at Nikolean in silence. Meanwhile, everyone else was glancing confoundedly back and forth between them without a word.

Until... "What be goin' on? Ye all talkin' ta each other right now? Oh, Kyrash, give me strength!" Hort, exasperated, throwing his hands in the air and stomping off toward Orbek.

But Turathyl never heard anything that Nikolean had tried to tell her. *'Interesting,'* she said at long last.

"She can't hear me?" Nikolean asked.

"No," Laila replied. "Maybe you just need practice," she offered with an encouraging smile.

Nodding, he said, "Maybe."

"I still don't understand why only he can hear her," Davion said, getting annoyed.

Laila explained Turathyl's theory to the others. Davion was not at all thrilled about it, anxious about how it would bring Laila and Nikolean closer and jealous of what it also meant for him to be the only one able to hear the dragon's mind-speech. It was clearly something that they were going to have to investigate further. It did seem a rather odd outcome to whatever it was they had performed in the temple.

After deliberating over what may be going on with no conclusions, Salyaman stated, "We should keep moving."

"Aye," Hort agreed. "This place be givin' me the ruckus-bruckus. I'd like ta not be 'ere when the sun goes down."

"Wait," Davion said, recalling what he was doing when Nikolean started his ranting. "Laila, I never found the stones."

Everyone headed for the temple remnants, Laila avidly in the lead, and they searched for the stones, but not a trace of them remained.

Laila sighed heavily as she threw a rock into the debris, the sound of it clattering against the scattered objects. "I guess that's it," she said, disheartened. Then announced with a hardened tone, "Let's go." But she did not want their loss to dampen the excitement over their discovery from the ritual. So, in an attempt to be optimistic, she forced a smile and added, "Niko, I'll see if I can teach you to mind-speak on the way."

He gave her a nod of acceptance, and everyone began collecting their things in quiet contemplation of the day's events.

While the group continued to head southwest toward the Du Noir Forest, Davion glared with scorn as Nikolean and Laila rode on ahead alongside the great Turathyl, laughing and talking about the drow's new Onis-defying connection with the dragon. He sneered at them, following behind on Helna, but no one noticed.

Hort was simply relieved they had all survived and was actually enjoying his wife's endless prattle as she told the story again from her own perspective and how being blasted by the light shook her undergarments. They didn't seem to mind that only Nikolean came out of it with a new "special gift" and were just ecstatic that it hadn't been a total waste.

Salyaman kept his eye on their surroundings with apprehension as they approached the dark elf territory. He knew how dark elves were received on the east side of Onis and dreaded discovering how high elves or the others would be received on the west. It wasn't long before they spotted the forest in the distance, and he emitted a loud whistle for the others to stop.

"It is getting too late to enter Du Noir Forest safely. I suggest we camp here for the night," Salyaman announced to the others.

Laila had been too distracted by Nikolean to even realize where they were. Merimer stopped beneath her as she viewed the forest. The beauty she had discovered on her journey north to the mountains after leaving her home in the Sacred Forest made looking upon the Du Noir Forest that much more painful. Not one leaf adorned its black withered trees that were gnarled and twisted up from the base, full of death. Even the roots were shriveled and breaking through the dried and cracked surface. An eerie fog blurred the forest floor to the unkeen eye, creating a haunting veil over whatever lurked within.

"It's winter now, so at least the lava is at rest," Nikolean murmured to her, attempting to be encouraging when seeing her consternation of the forest. "In the heat of summer, lava courses through our land like blood through our veins."

"Why have you stayed here?" she asked, bewildered.

"We are not welcome anywhere else, and it is our home."

As she stared into the dark forest from afar, she saw something moving through the trees like a shadow. It reminded her of her wolfkin back home, but its front was massive and hideously shaped, with a hunched back. The figure turned its head, sensing her there, and locked its sight with hers, its red eyes glowing through the mist. A shiver rushed up Laila's spine as she averted her glare for a moment, and when she looked back, the figure was gone.

"Yes," Laila said timidly. "We shall camp out here tonight."

Nikolean dismounted from his steed in a swift, fluid leap, and held out his hand for Laila to assist her off of Merimer.

Awkwardly smiling down at him, she took his hand while swinging her leg over. With a smooth and gentle motion, he lifted her off and down until her feet touched the ground, staying near while gazing hypnotically into her eyes. As she looked up into his gaze, her arms trembled with nervousness, and a warm flush spread across her cheeks.

With a slight bow of her head, she softly uttered, "Thank you, Niko."

"My lady." He smirked coyly at her before breaking their connection and stepping back to give her space.

Davion looked on, remembering when he first lifted her down from Helna after she had regained consciousness back near the Sacred Forest. Was it really so long ago that things could change so much? He ground his teeth while tending to his horse to prepare for the night, trying with all his might not to lose control of himself or the fire he sensed burning inside.

In his typical authoritative mien, Salyaman stated to the group, "We will need to rotate watch; have two lookouts at all times. It is imperative we stay on high alert this near the dark elf territory, even with the dragon."

As she took ease by the group, Turathyl said, *'I will not slumber tonight.'*

Nikolean smiled, patting the dragon's neck. "Tury and I shall take first watch," he called to the others boastingly.

"Not on me life," Hort spat.

"I will keep watch with them as well," Laila said enthusiastically. "We can work on your mind-speech to Tury some more."

After a moment of hesitation, the others nodded in agreement. Davion knew he wouldn't get any rest that night since there was no way he'd be falling asleep with them keeping each other company during the first watch.

Once everyone had settled in for the night and the fire lit, Laila and Nikolean sat on the hard ground near the pit, keeping warm, while the others huddled nearby under their furs, ready for the night's cold winds. Turathyl stayed to the side where she could easily watch over all of them, particularly her favorite two-leggeds sitting by the flames. She observed them contentedly, perceiving them growing closer.

A few hours in, with a steady snoring coming from the dwarves, Laila and Nikolean were beginning to think that it was unlikely he would ever be able to mind-speak to the dragon.

Poking at the fire with a stick, Laila tried explaining again how she thought he could attempt to communicate back to Turathyl. It was hard for her to conceptualize since it had always come naturally to her, but she would not give up hope that it could be done.

The dark elf stared intently at Laila as she talked, trying hard to absorb her words, but he kept finding himself distracted by the glow of the fire against her perfect, tanned face, and painting warm hues in her golden tresses. Attentive of her supple lips and the way they moved fluidly while she spoke, he couldn't help but stare, enamored.

"So, try that and see if it works," Laila said, turning her gaze to Nikolean.

Perking his head up, he tried to recall all that she had just said. "I'll give it a go." He smiled.

'You weren't even listening,' Turathyl sent solely to Nikolean, crossing her paws before her and looking down at him candidly. The dragon had discovered she could easily distinguish between their minds while they had been traveling.

The dark elf glared at the dragon, an intense guise on his face, as though trying to see right through her.

As she opened her mind broadly for him, Turathyl detected a very faint, 'whaaaass toooo.'

While stifling her dragon laughter so as not to rouse the others, Turathyl exclaimed to both of them, 'He did it! You did it!' And she continued to laugh joyfully.

Laila's eyes grew bright, a smile wide across her face, and she leapt over to him, wrapping her arms around him. "Yes! I knew you could do it!" she declared enthusiastically, yet as quietly as she was able.

He reciprocated her embrace, his arms encircling her with a firm grip, as he pressed his face into her hair, inhaling her intoxicating scent.

Without letting him go, Laila wishfully tried mind-sending him again, 'Can you hear me?'

The drow did not respond.

'She's asking if you can hear her,' Turathyl relayed.

Nikolean pulled back just enough to gaze upon her face and stared deeply into her eyes as he shook his head "no."

Disappointed, she frowned at him, averting her sight to the ground.

With his index finger, he delicately lifted her chin, compelling her to look back into his enchanting red eyes, and they stared at one another with a deep, unwavering intensity.

She wondered if he was trying to use telepathy to communicate with her, but, before she could ask, Nikolean leaned in toward her and softly pressing his lips to hers.

Turathyl looked away with a grin, closing off her mind to give them privacy.

Laila's eyes fell shut, and she felt as he placed his hand delicately against the side of her face. He moved his lips, parting them as she did the same, his tongue sweetly brushing against hers. As she enjoyed the intimacy of his kiss, she remembered from before the feel of his lips, of his mouth, the rapture of them, but it was different. He continued to kiss her, and she leaned farther into him, holding him affectionately, her heart thumping with vigor against her chest.

She didn't want him to stop even though it wasn't the same fiery passion she had experienced with him before; it was tender and alluring. It was reminiscent of indulging in the blissfulness of her sweetberries back home. The warmth of his embrace reminded her of being among her kin, wrapped up cozy and safe within their den. Upon recognizing the similarities, she became rather doleful.

Being reminded of her home, which she missed dearly, she withdrew gently from him, looking away. But it was more than just that.

"My lady," he whispered softly. "Are you alright? Should I not have?"

As she gazed back into those red piercing eyes, she became a little frightened. She wanted nothing more than to kiss him again, to feel his embrace, to give herself over to him, and it scared her.

Feeling vulnerable, Laila attempted a smile and shook her head. "It's fine," she told him before standing up to walk back to her spot by the fire, trembling. "But we are getting distracted from our duties," she added, smiling easier now that there was some distance between them. "You should practice more with Tury before we have to wake the next watch."

Nodding, Nikolean looked over at the dragon that was still pretending to mind her own business and began attempting to commune with her again. He wondered if Turathyl held any insight to the Omi Méa's seat of affections.

While the two of them resumed their guard assignment, Laila tried torturously not to look the drow's way for the rest of their watch. Neither of them noticed the tear trickling down the human's face onto the satchel beneath his head; his eyes fixed agonizingly on the elf maiden.

CHAPTER 15

Turathyl & Nikolean

CHAPTER SIXTEEN

DU NOIR

*I*t was a long night for Laila, tossing and turning as her thoughts kept her awake. When she wasn't mulling over the implication of every intimate moment she had ever shared with Nikolean—particularly their kiss from the prior night—she was agonizing over what they would face in the coming days as they enter Du Noir Forest. The stories she had heard of the dark elves so far were not pleasant nor reassuring at all, and she prayed to the gods that they had been an exaggeration.

Arm tucked under her head and a fur cloak pulled up over her, Laila stared blankly at the glowing coals of the dying fire. She contemplated whether it was worth trying to sleep anymore when the sun would rise in less than an hour's time. After a while longer of mental unrest, she sighed and propped herself up, looking around at the others. Salyaman and Davion were walking the perimeter, keeping watch and trying to stay warm by moving. The other three seemed to be snoozing contentedly nearby.

'*Did you get any sleep?*' Turathyl asked, concerned as Laila stood up. While she tried not to overstep, she could sense all the turmoil spinning in the young elf's mind all night.

Laila strolled over to her dragon and embraced her snout lovingly. '*No. But, I will be fine. You know I dread going before the two-legged leaders and their critical eyes. I think I'd rather be facing Ignisar today than the dark elves from what I've heard of them.*'

Sending compassionate feelings of understanding, Turathyl told her, '*And yet, you seem quite comfortable with one particular dark elf.*'

Laila blushed, smiling into the dragon's muzzle, still holding her close.

'*The sun will be rising soon,*' Turathyl continued. '*I need to go hunt, but I should be back before you reach the forest.*'

Acknowledging, Laila nodded and released her grasp while stepping back. '*Alright, but please don't be too long.*'

The dragon could sense the elf's nervousness and replied, '*I will do my best. But you must understand, even when I return, I will not be able to walk with you through the thick forest.*" Upon descrying the look of disappointment on the young elf's face as she looked away toward the ground, Turathyl added, "*Do not be discouraged. I will stay as close as I can and come if you need me.*'

As Turathyl lifted her colossal form, Laila took several steps back, giving her space. The dragon beat her massive wings to the ground, creating a strong breeze that whipped around the camp as she lunged skyward. The others began to stir from the disturbance while the land slowly came into view, with the first light of day gleaming over the horizon.

"Where's your dragon off to?" Davion asked, approaching Laila quietly, his staff resting cavalierly against his shoulder.

Turning away from the disappearing dragon silhouette, Laila looked at Davion, finding an icy expression on his face.

"To hunt," she replied. "She will meet us at the forest."

Laila observed as he gave her a slight nod, then turned and continued back to his belongings to start packing up. It felt so cold as she watched him walk away. The elf maiden missed when he would greet her with warm smiles and a friendly embrace, and it broke her heart to see him so withdrawn and distant from her now. She knew she was the cause of it and wished that she wasn't, but with the way her feelings had been developing, she decided it may be for the best. With Davion pulling away, she would no longer need to be remorseful over who she suspected her heart was leading her to; Nikolean. At least, that was the theory. In reality, she still felt tormented by the guilt, having had such a strong bond with Davion since the beginning.

The group had a quick breakfast, chatting briefly about how they should approach the dark elves when they encounter them. Nikolean sat beside Laila while they ate, instructing them to let him do the talking, saying they would need to trust him. Hort, of course, scoffed at the idea that he could ever trust a dark elf, but no one else rebutted the request, so they let it be.

As they approached the border of Du Noir Forest, everyone halted their steeds, surveying what they could see through the trees. Laila searched the skies for Turathyl but couldn't see her anywhere. After a moment, Nikolean began to lead Midnight forward. However, the group hesitated to follow until Salyaman gave Friet a gentle kick, heading into the murky forest as well.

With no living vegetation, they were able to ride their mounts efficiently between the dead trees, the wagon bumpily wobbling along at a steady pace over the broken ground and unearthed roots. The surrounding death made Laila both uneasy and sick to her stomach.

It wasn't long before they were completely enveloped in the dark fog and surrounded by the dead and gnarled trees. Out of the haze, a creature went bolting by in a flash, crossing over the path before them, and all the mounts faltered except for Merimer and Midnight. It was about half the size of Orbek, with matted fur and pointed ears, but it had gone so quickly that all Laila saw was a dark-blue blur.

"What was that?" Laila asked, peering into the trees uneasily but unable to spot it again.

Nikolean smirked, amused by her reaction. "A wurryn. Do not worry, my lady. They are not aggressive and mostly hunted for food."

Relieved, yet still on edge, Laila kept her eyes peeled for anything else that might surprise them.

Aside from the gloom of the forest, they all noticed there was a pungent smell similar to burnt hair that seemed to be everywhere. It was a lingering acrid smell like that from the burning of sulfur atoms—a very displeasing odor. Most of them tried to ignore it, but the look on Hort's scrunched-up face, his nose twitching as though it were trying to escape, made it undeniable.

"What the baccat is that stink?!" Hort finally blurted, unable to withhold any longer.

"It's in the soil here," Nikolean stated. "You'll get used to it."

Wafting his hand in front of his face, Hort cursed, "I bloody well hope not!"

"Tis no worse than yer feet every time ye take them boots off!" Glondora jabbed at him playfully. "But does ye 'ear me complainin'? Now hush up and keep yer eyes open."

With a grumble under his breath and his chin tucked, Hort glared up grouchily as he gave a gentle flick of Orbek's reins, keeping the pace, while the wagon tottered noisily behind them.

Hours slowly passed by as they nervously followed the dark elf through the bodeful forest in silence. There were much of the same dark and withered trees with the occasional malformed critter scurrying about and disappearing into burrows. It was beginning to all look the same, as though they were going in circles.

Davion was about to ask if the drow had any idea where they were going, but the high elf beat him to it.

"Are we nearly to your people?" Salyaman asked Nikolean.

The dark elf simply nodded.

"Cuz, ye know," Hort called at them, "if tis gunna' be a whiles, can we at least stop ta eat first?" He patted his grumbling belly.

Laila looked up to the sky to determine how much time had passed and realized for the first time that she couldn't see any sun, or sky, or clouds. The whole forest canopy was covered in the same thick blanket of fog as the surface.

'Tury?' she sent out past the forest, praying to find her.

To her delight, the dragon responded to her and Nikolean, 'I am on my way. I had to go much farther than I planned.'

Relieved, Laila let out a sigh, a little more at ease.

The group agreed to break for a brief lunch. With their trek into the dark woods being relatively quiet thus far, they confidently dismounted and stretched their legs.

As they settled and ate their rations, Laila stayed near the back, seated upon a stump next to Merimer, feeling the need for some space. The others didn't think much of it. Davion was happy to keep his distance from her, not knowing how to act around her anymore, his heart breaking and anger pooling. Although Nikolean wished to be near her, he wasn't clear on where her feelings lay and respected her apparent desire to be alone.

CHAPTER 16

As she swallowed her honeyed bread, Laila thought she detected a strange whirring noise coming from behind them. Upon glancing at the others, she discovered they were all engrossed in their meals and looking to the path and trees ahead for any signs of danger.

Laila was convinced she recognized the strange sound from somewhere but didn't want to disturb the group, assuming she could handle whatever it was. And so, she snuck away toward the sound. While she peered through the trees and the dead, tangled brush, the whirring became louder. It was a peculiar high-pitched mystical hum that sounded almost ghostly, while a faint light flickered in the distance.

As she chased after the light, the humming engrossed and enchanted her, blocking out everything else. Laila didn't even hear her friends at the camp yelling for her or anything after. All of her senses were focused on the entrancing light while she fluttered through the trees as though lost in a dream.

Climbing over a fallen log, she saw the mystical light hovering in the middle of a small clearing. It looked like a glowing red orb that jeered and danced around, singing with its ghostly voice as it moved.

While she stared intently into the light, it suddenly flew right up near her face and hovered before her. She swore she could see someone within it. The miniature person appeared spiritual in nature, glowing even brighter than the surrounding orb. The figure raised a teeny-tiny finger before its lips as if to say "shhh" to her.

Fascinated by the tiny light-person, Laila raised her hand, pointing to the glowing red sphere. She was just about to touch it when Turathyl's voice rang loud in her mind.

'Laila! Get down at once and stay where you are!'

Panicked and confused, Laila did as the dragon instructed, with her sight locked on the will-o'-the-wisp as it vanished before her eyes.

While everyone was finishing their lunch, Nikolean's heart skipped a beat when he realized that Laila wasn't there anymore, and he jumped up, scanning the surrounding trees. Upon spotting the elf maiden prancing off farther into the dismal forest behind them, he shook his head and let out a sigh, then began heading after her. As he traversed deeper into the forest, the camp fading from his sight, Nikolean remained inconspicuous, keeping his distance from the elf, curious where she was off to. Before he had a chance to discover what had caught her interest, there was a desperate holler from someone in the camp.

Dithering, he watched Laila disappearing into the brush beyond, looking back and forth between her and the camp, agitated and torn. Nevertheless, when someone from the group screamed, he bolted back toward the others without another thought.

Worried about what he would find, he quickly told Turathyl to have Laila stay hidden, '*Keep her safe, Tury, until I send further word!*'

As he breached through the trees, back to their resting spot, Nikolean came out to nearly a dozen hooded dark elves amongst the group. Davion was lying in the dirt with a welt on his forehead, and several dark elves were encircling Salyaman, his swords drawn and thorns spiked from his skin. Glondora was on the ground with a slash across her arm while two drow restrained Hort from behind. Another dark elf soldier was approaching Hort heatedly with its sword readied, aiming at his chest, while the dwarf struggled and shouted profanities at their assailants.

CHAPTER 16

"TÖS!" Nikolean yelled urgently in Drow for them to *STOP!* He held his open hands up to them, making his face clear. "Eis nid ra hiym!" *They are with me!* "Nikolean Den Faolin!" Upon seeing Nikolean, all the dark elves swiftly disengaged their weapons from the group and released the dwarf, shoving him to the ground. Davion began sitting upright, and the companions raised their hands in surrender. The drow soldiers held their daggers and swords downward before them with the opposite fist pressed against the hilts and elbows bowed outward in salute.

"Taggürrah! Ir gaht ise myvern!" *Commander! We thought you dead!* one of them declared, appearing almost fearful seeing Nikolean standing there.

The comrades looked nervously back and forth between Nikolean and the other dark elves, unsure of what was going on.

Continuing in Drow, Nikolean replied, "Clearly, I live. I have been on a secret assignment and am delivering these vermin to Nordor Hellia to speak with our leader, Kull Merzumar Den Fraül. They lay claim to be able to restore our land." Nikolean drew his sword, and pointed it at Glondora, glaring threateningly at the drow who had spoken. "And why is the mountain mouse bleeding?"

"It was preparing to cast on us," another one of them replied in a female voice familiar to Nikolean.

The shrouded figure pulled back her hood, letting it fall to reveal her face. The female was strong yet slim and had the same snow-white hair as Nikolean, but her ashen skin had a slight purple hue to it. Her face was young in appearance, but there were strategically placed scars, one horizontally across each cheek, from someone trying to teach her a lesson.

"Akayra, it is good to see you," Nikolean said, nodding firmly to her.

"You have been gone a long time, cousin," she told him in a bitter tone. "Even still, none of this should surprise you; it is not as though the other races have ever come here with good intent, most certainly never to heal our land." Cocking an eyebrow at her cousin, she sneered, "I am actually surprised to see you stopping us. They are all very fortunate you arrived when you did. Regardless, you must come with us to Duep Norder first."

"We are in a bit of a hurry," Nikolean stated.

"I am afraid we have to insist," the first dark elf proclaimed, stepping forward and pulling back his own hood. Nikolean did not recognize him. The man was much older than he, his skin already turning white, and Nikolean sensed he wasn't going to be able to talk himself out of it. "No one sees Kull Merzumar anymore without being cleared first by one of the outlying lords, not since the Drakka's attempt to overthrow him—not even commanders that no one has seen in years." With a distrusting glower at Nikolean, he gestured to the path beyond them. "We shall accompany you to Duep Nordor and assist with taking the outsiders to one of the dungeons."

Nikolean gave him a nod of compliance, then gestured to the others. "Let's go, wretches," he said harshly to them in Onish. "Time to see how the drow judge *you*."

Hesitantly, they lowered their hands, and Nikolean spat at their feet while dark elves grabbed the reins of the mounts—except for Merimer. The mystical creature reared as one approached, kicking at the shrouded figure to get back. The dark elf swiftly drew its sword, ready to slay the beast, but Nikolean shouted for them to stand down. Merimer neighed and snorted with hostility before bolting off into the trees away from them.

"Just let it go," he said in Drow. "Stupid beast is more trouble than it's worth."

The comrades were having a hard time not speaking up or asking Nikolean what was happening. Davion was convinced that he had set them up and that they shouldn't have surrendered to the drow, but Glondora insisted he keep his head down and "trust Niko," as if it were possible.

Salyaman wasn't sure what to think yet, biding his time, waiting for a moment to speak with Nikolean. He had also considered the possibility that the dark elf had turned on them, but couldn't fathom why he would do such a thing.

Watching from a distance, Laila stayed low to the ground, covered over with her enchanted elven cloak, camouflaging the elf maiden to her surroundings. Its enchantments would work in whatever surroundings she should find herself in, and she was grateful that the dark elves did not seem to notice her there.

Laila resisted every urge in her body telling her to rescue her friends, to run in and show the drow who they were dealing with. Intertwined with her mind, Turathyl implored the Omi Méa to stay put, insisting that Nikolean had a plan, in large part of which was to keep her and the others safe. Laila wanted to believe she could trust him, but the others had been warning her about doing so since they first shot him with an arrow in the Ashwood Forest. Furthermore, she had been eavesdropping into the minds of the dark elves, catching enough of their conversation to know that Nikolean had not been very forthcoming about his role with them. *A commander?* It seemed like something he should have mentioned. If the dark elf soldiers were as ruthless as she'd heard, what did that mean for him?

Feeling backed into a corner, Laila recognized that Nikolean had entrusted his life to her throughout their entire journey, and she hoped and prayed that she could trust him now with theirs.

CHAPTER SEVENTEEN

TRUST

*N*earing Duep Nordor, the group grew nervous as they approached the outskirts of the city, terrified of the fate that awaited them should Nikolean fall through or betray them. The dark elf city did not appear to be large nor prominent, but that did not dampen its effect on the drows' prisoners. It was surrounded by a wall slightly taller than Salyaman, created from dark, unearthed stone, jutting up into sharp points. As they passed through the entryway, they found it peculiar that there was no one standing guard, as in all the other cities. But, seeing the dark elves within, they got the impression they could all handle themselves just fine should anyone uninvited dare enter.

Near the entrance hung two large iron cages. One cage contained a corpse that had most of the flesh picked clean by the wildlife. Its smell still lingered in the air, not yet overtaken by the burnt hair smell of the soil. The other had a drow female inside, sitting at the bottom with her face pressed against the bars. Unfamiliar with how the drow aged, the newcomers weren't yet sure if she was young or old, but she was clearly too weak to move or react as children struck her and the cage with rocks from slingshots. The cage with the female drow creaked hauntingly as it faintly swayed back and forth.

While being escorted down the main road, every dark elf the group passed stopped and stared at them with hatred in their eyes and a sneer upon their lips. The homes within the city walls appeared nearly as dead and gnarled as the surrounding forest's wood—which was used in their construction. Their shale roofs, made from the volcanic ash of the summer seasons, matched their dreary appearance in darkness, and there appeared to be a general theme of death throughout the town. Beside the doors of several houses hung what appeared to be trophied ulna bones from victims' arms displayed horizontally. One home had a string of eighteen bones that looked like a nightmarish ladder next to their door.

Davion was contemplating which fire spell he should use when the drow would inevitably attack them. As he looked around with apprehension, he was actually quite surprised to learn that they didn't all look like Nikolean. He had been taken aback to descry the older drow with the whitening skin and Akayra with her purple hue. While he studied the diverse pigments, from a cobalt blue to black as the midnight sky, he realized that the lighter their skin was, the older the drow appeared to be. From what he witnessed as they followed their captors, they didn't all have pure white hair, either. There were dark elves with hair of black, white, and various shades of gray, as well as those with pigmented tresses of vibrant purple, blue, or red; shades he had never before witnessed among the other races.

Hort—for a change—kept his mouth shut and his head down, trembling as he stayed near Glondora. He felt as though he were walking into a rock fiend's den. Even though he knew the drow to be loathsome creatures, he was shocked at how minacious they made their own homes appear.

Glondora tucked her arms close around her, staring horrified at the blatant display of the dark elves' hatred, even against their own kind. In an attempt to ignore the pain in her arm, she clenched her jaw and unconvincingly tried to show no fear.

As for the high elf, he strode stoically through the drow streets, his head held high and stony-eyed. If he were experiencing any fear—which he was—he would not give the dark elves the satisfaction of seeing it.

Their dark elf "friend" walked assertively with the captors, leading them all toward a daunting-looking building. It had stone-chiseled beasts guarding the base at the front entry and humanoid skulls cascading along the edge of the stairway. A dark-wood and iron-rimmed door began opening as they approached, and a drow stepped out, heavily adorned in black-metal armor, his face hidden by a sizable helmet. Appearing much larger than a typical drow, it was a malevolent figure draped in a dark flowing cape, its grim ebony plate clanking as it strode out to meet them before stopping at the top of the steps.

Nodding firmly to the death knight before him, Nikolean began to ascend the stairs, but the armored figure held up his hand for him to stop.

"I am Commander Nikolean Den Faolin," he said in Drow, reminding the dark figure before him. "Let me pass."

A very deep voice replied through the metal, "You *were* commander. You have been gone for quite some time, Nikolean Den Faolin."

The older drow that had discovered them in the forest told Nikolean, "Your audience with Lord Brilldessah will require a formal request."

Although a "lord," Brilldessah was a female dark elf. The drow did not alter their titles dependent on whether those that rose to power were male or female; they were equally respected for their feats. Even though Kull Merzumar was a male, their prior Kull had been female as well.

With a nod of understanding, Nikolean declared, "Then I request an audience with Lord Brilldessah. I have important matters to discuss regarding the prisoners and the healing of our land."

"The lord will review your request upon her return tomorrow. You will be notified at such time of her approval," stated the armored drow. "Take the prisoners to Despair Dungeon."

Before the group was hauled off, Nikolean grabbed Salyaman's arm gruffly, covertly whispering to him in Onish, "Trust me." Then they were separated as the dark elves eagerly prodded for the comrades to keep walking, leading them to a postern entrance that would take them underground to the dungeons.

As he stood there devising a plan, Nikolean watched as the group disappeared. Then Akayra strode up beside him, catching his attention.

"Where have you been?" she whispered, distressingly.

Observing her, he spotted a tear glistening in the corner of her eye, and was confused by her concern. "I told you; I was on a mission," he replied firmly.

"You should have been here. You should never have left."

"Has something happened?" he asked.

Nodding sullenly, she replied, "Go see your father. He needs you."

"What's going on?" he asked, becoming tense.

Akayra took Nikolean's arm, wrapping it with hers, and led him away from prying eyes, pretending they were merely going for a stroll. "He's become much worse since you left. Your mother... she couldn't take it."

"She never could," Nikolean said bitterly.

"Well," Akayra sighed, "be that as it may, she finally left, and it nearly destroyed him. He's worse than ever."

His cousin veered down a side alleyway, hiding him in the shadows, then turned to face him once they were out of sight. "There were rumors you had joined the Drakka, Niko." Before he managed a response, she continued, "I know you would never go against our elders, but you need to watch your back." She gave him a quick embrace before raising her hood back over her face while she headed out of the alley, leaving Nikolean to stew in his thoughts.

'Tury,' he sent out, searching for the dragon.

Turathyl had been waiting eagerly to hear from him, and responded without delay, 'I am here.'

'Have Laila meet me outside my family home.' He sent her mental images of how to get to the dwelling where he used to live. It lay outside the Duep Norder walls by roughly a twenty-minute walk. 'I will meet her there and let her know what is going on.'

The dragon sent him mental confirmation and was then silent.

Laila clung to Merimer, gripping her reins tightly as they bolted through the woods toward the dark elf dwelling from Turathyl's mind. The trees whipped by her like a shadowy blur. The exquisite all-white elkan horns bobbed rhythmically, paralleling her own fluid motions as they flew through the forest as one. Terrified about what was happening to her friends, the elf maiden was imagining all sorts of horrors befalling them, and her heart raced along with the pounding of the unicorn hybrid's hooves over the hard ground.

CHAPTER 17

With her friend's uncanny speed, it was only moments before she spotted Nikolean's family home, quickly halting before they broke through the trees into the clearing of the outlying city dwellings. There were three other visible structures, all amply spaced from one another as much as the sizable clearing would allow.

Laila jumped down from Merimer and kissed her snout. After giving her a gentle pat on her strong neck, she sent a mental command to head to Turathyl as fast as she was able, lest she be caught by the drow as well. The beautiful creature bolted off in the direction of her dragon, and she watched as its brilliant white coat disappeared into the thick gray fog.

Not a dark elf in sight, she stealthily crept along the forest floor to get nearer to the dwelling that matched the picture in her mind. She held her breath in nervous anticipation while drawing closer.

The building was a wattle and daub house with a thatched roof. In contrast to the rest of Onis, it was a symbol of wealth to the drow in their barren land. It had been neglected of maintenance but was much larger than she expected based on the mental image she had received. Extending lengthwise, she assumed three or four of the modest Lochlann dwarven homes could have fit within. It was just a shame to see it in such condition, as though forgotten amongst the trees. Laila imagined had there been any life left within the forest, the house likely would have been swallowed by it.

After a few minutes, she saw Nikolean galloping into the clearing atop Midnight, kicking up dust as he came to a stop in front of his old home. He flew like the wind off his steed's back.

'Laila, it is safe,' Turathyl relayed on behalf of Nikolean.

Relieved, she jumped up out of hiding and ran toward him, her feet pitter-pattering across the grainy surface. She was so thankful to see him that she wanted nothing more than to jump into his arms. However, as she drew near, it hit her that she still had no idea what had happened to her friends. *Where are they? Why aren't they with him??* She suddenly felt quite disconcerted and stopped just before him.

Without a moment's pause, Nikolean grabbed her hand and led her into the house before she managed to say a word. As soon as they were inside, he quietly closed the door behind them and proceeded to fasten wooden shutters, blocking all light and view to the outside.

"Niko..." she said, troubled.

He placed his finger over his lips for her to keep quiet, staring very intently into her eyes while she stood there, confused. Then he was gone.

Fleeting agilely with implausible speed, Nikolean searched each of the rooms within the lightless house. Laila wondered if he could see in the darkness better than she, considering she was unable to see anything besides his shadowed outline as he darted through the main room with each pass.

Seconds later, an unlit candle was held directly before her face, startling her.

"Here," he said.

Laila took the candle and waved her hand over the wick, igniting it with her mind, allowing for a meager illumination of the room.

"My father isn't here," he stated. "We should be safe for now."

"Safe from who? What's going on, Niko? Where are the others?" Laila questioned, agitated.

"Come, sit. I will explain."

He motioned his hand toward a couch in the living area. It appeared dusty and worn, its cushions dark auburn with spots worn through to the padding. There was a matching chair against the far wall and a spooky fireplace in the corner, which held no wood, only cobwebs and ash. Laila spotted nothing decorative like in the dwarven or elven homes, and it felt rather desolate.

As she took a seat uncomfortably near the edge of the couch cushion, Laila found herself feeling uneasy in his home, although she wasn't sure why. Nikolean then came swooping into the room and sat beside her. He turned to her, taking her hands, discerning them trembling in his own.

"I have a plan," he declared, cupping her hands with his, hoping to calm her. "I will need to go before Lord Brilldessah and explain what I was doing with the others. She may or may not listen to what I have to say about the prophecy, but I think hearing of a chance for our lands to be restored will help us gain approval. Then, we can go before the Kull in Nordor Hellia."

"Do you think she will listen to you because you are a commander?" Laila asked, pointing out brazenly that she knew.

Nikolean was thrown off guard, gaping at her for a moment, while it hit him that she had heard and understood everything he said to the dark elves earlier. "I am not a commander anymore, it seems," he told her. "I knew they would recognize me, and I had to think fast in the forest to buy us some time. I'm sorry for anything you heard."

"You still haven't told me; where are the others? What's going to happen to them?" she pressed.

After hesitating for a moment, Nikolean looked grimly at her as he explained, "They have to stay in the dungeons for now. Tomorrow I will go before Lord Brilldessah and convince her to release them."

"And if she doesn't? What will they do with them?"

Glancing down at his hands cupping hers, he forced himself to look back into her eyes while he divulged, "Most likely, she will order them to be executed. But I won't let that happen. My lady, I need you to trust me."

She looked into his desperate eyes, not comprehending how he could overthrow the lord's decision. "I want to," she said with restraint. Ever since they had crossed paths, she had been warned not to trust Nikolean, and the recent events weren't instilling much confidence either.

"My lady..." He paused, moving closer to her, looking at her earnestly. "I think you already know that I would do anything for you. This quest that you're on—that we're *all* on—I believe to be the only hope of redemption and healing that my people's land has, and I know you think that the others all serve some purpose towards your goal. So, if it is my purpose to sacrifice my life so that they may rejoin you and fulfill the prophecy, then I shall die knowing that I did my part; for you and for my people."

She stared at him, rattled, trying to grasp what he was implying. "Why would you need to give up your life? I'm sorry, Niko, but I don't understand what your plan is."

"I'm hoping it will not come to that, but I just need you to trust me." He gave her a half-hearted smile, hating to see her brow furrowed so perplexingly.

"So, what can I do to help?" she asked, trying hard to have faith in his plan, but still terrified of losing her friends.

"You can stay here, where you will be safe," he replied.

"But I can help. I—"

"No, my lady," Nikolean interrupted squarely. "If you go in there, powers flaring, then we may never have a chance of gaining their support; the elders nor the Drakka. They cannot see you as a threat. You are a powerful force to be feared, but that is not our goal here."

While looking down at her hands again, he massaged them affectionately. His half-smile faded as he said without taking his gaze from her delicate fingers, "I don't know for certain how my meeting will go, and I can't be worried about what will happen to you if I am to concentrate on getting the others out of the dungeons. You may not like what I have to do, and if you are there, I may not be able to."

"What are you saying?" Laila asked.

Nikolean gazed up at her, the same pained eyes as when she saw him for the very first time, about to die. He was terrified of what she would think of him if she knew the truth.

"I am drow," he stated bluntly. Then he took a deep breath before continuing, "I will do what needs to be done, but my life is expendable; yours is not. I must protect you so that you may fulfill your destiny. But... if I don't make it back to you..." he choked up as he tried to say the words.

"Don't say that," she whispered, her own eyes tearing as she considered the possibility. "Niko, you *have* to come back to me."

"My lady, if it were up to me, I would never leave your side for a moment." He squeezed her hand tightly, entwining his fingers with hers, fusing them together. "Can you trust me?"

Like Lupé Caelis had told her, even if she pried into his mind, she could only know what lay on the surface and could never know for certain someone's true self. How can you ever really know someone's deepest intentions and desires beyond what their words tell you? Only by trust. Could she trust him not to betray them in order to save himself? Could she trust that it was not all part of some other ploy? Could she put her faith in him, her heart on the line, trusting that he would not break it? There he was, asking her to do the most basic thing, yet the most difficult. Can you ever truly trust someone without any doubts?

"You must know how I feel for you," he said intently, interrupting her thoughts when she failed to respond.

There was a lump in her throat. She couldn't speak and shook her head slowly. Of course, she had her suspicions. She knew that he was attracted to her and wanted his land replenished, but lacked confidence in anything beyond that.

As he leaned in closer to her, he touched the side of her neck tenderly with his hand, holding her gaze with his own. The intensity of his stare sent chills through her body as she was bewitched by his eyes once again. "My lady, you have captivated and intrigued me from the very first moment I saw you. There was something pulling me to you, something I could not ignore, but what I had found was beyond what I could have ever dreamed for.

"When you left the bread in the forest, knowing I was there, but not even knowing who I was or if I was good, you showed me what a kind heart you have. I was less than deserving of that kindness, and I could never claim to be worthy of such a heart."

Nikolean looked away for a moment. His hands trembled slightly against her skin as he gazed back into her eyes and continued, "Then you saved my life, something no elf would ever have even considered, and I feel like you have been saving my life ever since. There are things in my past that I am less than proud of, but you saw a good in me that I had not even seen in myself. You made me want to be the man that you saw; no longer what I once was. You are the most pure and beautiful creature I have ever seen. Every time I look upon your face, I see hope, I see strength, I see..." His eyes twinkled in the dim candlelight with his pause. "...love. I pledged my life to you before the others to honor a life debt, but I never needed a life debt to know that I would risk everything for you. Laila..."

Her heart fluttered as he said her name, and her breathing became erratic while trying to absorb the moment.

"Laila... I am in love with you. I have *been* in love with you. You can't possibly imagine how hard it has been to be around you without being able to do anything about it. That night in Gortax when we were alone, when I walked you back to Haddilydd's and caught you from falling..." Laila grimaced with embarrassment at the remembrance. "It took everything in my power not to kiss you, not to tell you then and there what you mean to me."

As she recalled how he had seemed cold and aloof toward her that night, she stared at him, confused, and asked, "So why didn't you?"

He gazed back at her intensely, and replied, "Because of who I am—*what* I am. I am a dark elf, after all, and you are... Well... *You*; the prophesied elf meant to save us all. I did not believe it would be received well by you—nor anyone else." Looking at her hands, he took in a deep breath, then sighed heavily. "That night after the party in Lochlann when I first kissed you, it seemed clear to me that you believed it to have been a mistake. Then, when I kissed you again last night, you pulled away. I can only assume that you decided you did not want me to. It didn't surprise me, given all that I am. I supposed I had misread the situation in hopes that you could possibly feel anything for me as well."

Having not been raised around all the hatred between the races nor comprehending who he was before they met, she really had no idea the depth of where his concerns lay. She looked down at his hands holding hers, confounded, as she attempted to decipher her own feelings and the real reason she had pulled away from him. At the same time, she was trying to grasp everything that he was saying.

"I don't know what will happen before Lord Brilldessah," Nikolean continued, "but I need you to trust that I will let no harm come to you or your friends, no matter the cost."

The thought of losing him scared her greatly, but it was more than just that. As she looked back upon him with tear-swollen eyes, she was finally starting to see what had been in front of her face the entire time.

Not wanting to resist anymore, Laila seized the moment and drifted toward him, pressing her lips against his. Her heart raced in anticipation for him to grab her in another passionate embrace. Even so, he did not return her gesture and pulled delicately away. Swiftly sitting upright, she stared blankly at him, hurt and confused.

"My lady," he said, his voice soft and gentle as he looked on her with serious eyes. "I do not wish you to kiss me out of affliction for my willingness to die for you or for my confessions." Pausing for a moment while studying her expression, Nikolean continued tentatively, "Everything that I have told you is the truth, but if you do not care for me in that way, I will accept your decision, and you should feel no obligation to me further for my affections. However..." he looked longingly into her eyes with his piercing-red stare, "...if— by some chance—you have decided that we could be as one, then give me your lips again, and I shall show you the extent of my love for you... forever, even if my forever lasts only one more night."

Laila stared at him intently, her heart aching in her chest. She had avoided confronting her feelings for him out of fear of being distracted from her mission and fear of hurting Davion. Now, he was forcing her to stop suppressing any feelings that might be there and make a decision. She realized it wasn't about sharing another fleeting moment nor an amorous embrace. As she swallowed the hard lump in her throat, her hands trembled nervously in his while she contemplated his proposal. Everything in her body told her to throw herself into his arms and kiss him again. But was that enough?

While gazing into his eyes, she could perceive the heat that was between them, the longing for him to embrace her whenever he was near. She thought of how her skin would tingle every time he would touch her hand, even if seemingly by mistake. But did that mean she loves him as he claims to love her?

And what of the alternative? The possibility of never seeing him again after that night, or being apart from him for any reason, unexpectedly overwhelmed her. She realized he could very well be killed in the morrow while she sits helplessly in his home. Tears broke free from her eyes as she shakily gasped for breath, not realizing she had been holding it in while considering his words on the edge of her seat.

Nikolean had been growing concerned from her silence and was startled by her gasp. Wondering if he had just made himself a fool, he let go of her hands while smiling awkwardly and asked, "Are you alright, my lady?"

Nodding her head zealously, she accepted that she had known what her answer would be for some time now. Quickly tilting forward again before he could pull away any farther, she took the risk and once more pressed her lips firmly against his. Except, that time, he returned her kiss. His lips tightened against hers as he smiled, then he wrapped his arms around her, pulling her to him, kissing her sensually in their embrace. Her body filled with excitement from his kiss, and she felt as though a weight had lifted from her chest by letting go of her restraints against her feelings for him.

As Nikolean hoisted her up against him, Laila wrapped her legs around his waist, arms over his shoulders, and he continued to kiss her—her hungry mouth, her soft neck, her sensitive petite elven ears—whilst carrying her down the dark hallway toward one of the back rooms. She didn't notice where he was taking her. So long as he was kissing her and holding her amorously, she didn't care. Her heart pounded like it wanted to erupt through her chest, and there was nowhere in the world that she would rather be.

When they reached his old bedroom, she lit a candle on the night table, using the fire burning inside her without opening her eyes. She continued to brush her lips lustfully against his, gripping him tightly.

His room was still the same as when he'd left it, not a thing out of place, nor had it been cleaned for some time. After standing Laila near the bed, Nikolean slid off the dusty top sheet, tossing it aside, and then immediately proceeded to remove all his clothing from the waist up. Her heart raced as he revealed his ashen chest, several large scars decorating it, and she reached out to run her fingers softly over them, her hand tingling as she touched his skin. She was nervous and shaking, but he grabbed her hands and pressed them lovingly against his steely chest, helping to ease her. He then continued to kiss and caress her where they stood as he slowly removed her armor, one piece at a time.

With her body and soul bared to him, she stood there shivering until he swiftly scooped her up into his arms, and the warmth of his skin against hers exhilarated her while he laid her gently on the bed. He explored her skin soothingly with his hands, tasting her lips down to her neck, and her body ached with a yearning for him to consume her.

Although her heart was racing in anticipation, she no longer doubted that was what she wanted, that he was *who* she wanted. There was no way of knowing what would happen in the morrow, but she knew that whatever was to come... she trusted him.

CHAPTER EIGHTEEN

FAOLIN

*T*iredly opening her eyes after finally managing to get some rest, Laila smiled with ecstasy as she looked upon Nikolean's sleeping face right before hers. His naked frame was interlaced pleasingly with her own as she laid in his arms. As she looked upon the drow in a whole new light, her heart was finally becoming clear to her. Yet, it was such a conflicting feeling to be lying there in total bliss, all the while knowing that he was about to go risk his life for her and her friends.

My friends...

The smile faded from her face as she worried whether they were unharmed, wondering what was happening to them, causing her affliction over her moment of happiness with Nikolean.

As she rolled to her other side away from the drow, Laila almost screamed when her gaze fell upon a strange man sitting in a shadowed corner staring at them in silence. In her newfound modesty since meeting her companions, she quickly yanked the loose sheet over her nakedness all the way up to her throat as she stared back at him, shaking.

In fear, Laila used the fire spirit to light the sconces in the room, illuminating the corner, and the man remained still, not reacting to the sudden flames at all.

The man's skin was pale white and rippled with wrinkles. He had thin, tangled silver hair and wore a shabby-black robe, gray with grime, embellished with a once-prominent gold-embroidered trim. Propped next to him against the wall rested a rickety staff. A black gem containing dark-red swirls was encapsulated into its twisted tip.

Laila's eyes widened at the old dark elf as he continued to sit there, his elbows resting on the chair's arms and hands clasped upward before him while he glowered at her.

"Niko," she whispered, nudging the young drow. Nikolean snorted, then rolled to his side away from her. "NIKO!" she yelled, panicking.

Darting upward in the bed, Nikolean drew a dagger from no-one-knows-where and held it outward, looking for the cause of the commotion, not yet fully awake nor cognizant of where he was.

The alarming figure in the corner spoke in a low mature voice, "Nikolean."

Upon jerking his head toward the sound of the old drow's voice, Nikolean let his hand with the dagger fall back to the bed. "Hunna, Ëita," he said, and Laila bore into his mind to follow the conversation; *Hello, Father.*

Her nerves on edge, Laila continued to gape at the man.

The old drow stood up slowly, the creaking of his bones echoing in the silence. He grabbed his staff tightly and took a frail step forward, never once taking his eyes off of Laila. She was on pins and needles about what he planned to do to her as she prepared to defend herself.

To her surprise, he turned his back to them dispassionately and started heading for the door, saying, "I shall put the tea on."

After he left, Nikolean scooted off the bed and began grabbing his clothes. Laila let out the breath she had been holding, still clutching the sheet up against her neck while staring down the gloomy hallway past the open door.

Nikolean held her garments before her, blocking her view and getting her attention. She readily took them and began to dress with haste, her heart pounding in her chest from the fright.

When they were both decent, clad in their armor, Nikolean sheathed a dagger at his side, then took her hand with a firm grip and led her out of the room toward the kitchen. Laila noticed that the windows were still fastened shut from the night before, but sconces and candles had been lit enough to see reasonably.

As they neared the kitchen, Laila overheard Nikolean's father talking with someone and grew even more distressed, worried about what all the drow were going to think of finding an elf in the Faolin home. However, when they reached him, he was alone and pouring tea into small chipped cups. She positioned herself slightly behind Nikolean and anxiously scanned the room, trying to ascertain if the person he'd been talking to was in the shadows, but there was no one to be seen.

"Father," Nikolean said in Drow while Laila followed along through his mind. "I need to talk to you about where I've been."

The old man raised a shaky hand to him while he took a sip of the warm tea with the other. "Who is your friend?" he then asked. "She looks different from your usual guests."

Abashed, Nikolean glanced at Laila, who had not reacted to his suggestive comment, too fretful of what was happening. He was about to answer when his father suddenly hissed to the side, then startled them by blurting out with anger, "I know she's an elf! I have eyes! Let the boy talk!" Then he looked back to his son, attempting a smile, which came out crooked and disturbing. He nodded and gestured to Nikolean, saying forcedly calm, "Go ahead, Son."

Not unfamiliar with his father's eccentricities, Nikolean cleared his throat, and addressed the man with respect. "Father, this is Lady Lailalanthelus Dula'Quoy. Laila, this is my father, Nikososo Den Faolin."

Laila clung to Nikolean's arm, unsure of the proper etiquette, especially considering the unusual outburst.

"No, she's not!" Nikososo shouted, startling her.

"Father?"

"Lies! They tell you lies!" he yelled nonsensically, then glowered at the air around him. "Yes, well, it's an elf, isn't it? An Elf! Anyone can see that!"

Embarrassed, Nikolean turned to Laila and took her hand while his father continued to ramble to himself, "I'm sorry," he whispered. "My father isn't well. I didn't realize how bad it had become."

Not daring to take her eyes off the raving drow, she asked quietly in Onish, "What's wrong with him?"

"Wrong?!" his father exclaimed, still in Drow, returning his focus to them. "Nothing's wrong with me! It's them! All of them! That's who's wrong, not me!" Then he turned away, ranting more about things that continued to evade them.

With a heavy sigh, Nikolean led Laila back out of the kitchen to the living area with the old dingy couch, where they could speak freely, and Laila took a seat.

"I'm sorry. I should have warned you about my father. In his prime, he was one of the most powerful necromancers of our time. Everyone feared and revered him. But, as he got older, he began losing his grip on reality. In time, it became so bad that they had to release him from the guard, and I think that it ultimately destroyed him.

"I shouldn't have left. I knew it was too much for my mother to handle alone, but I had to do my part to help the Drakka find a solution to our dying land." Nikolean clasped his hands around the back of his neck, pacing the floor, flustered and full of guilt. "It's much worse than I imagined. I fear he's gone completely mad."

Just then, the old drow came hobbling in, bracing himself with his staff in one hand and a tray in the other, supporting three teas that were spilling over in a mess with each struggled step. He smiled at them as though nothing had occurred while he handed his son the tray. While Nikolean took it and placed it on a side table, his father walked by Laila to take a seat in the chair on the other side of the room. As he passed her, Laila encountered a surge of cold energy waft over her, flowing behind him like an icy breeze, sending shivers up her spine.

"Yes, yes, I know," the drow said to no one, waving his hand around as he took his seat. With a stern look at Nikolean, he said, "They say you are Drakka."

The young drow remembered Akayra warning him about the dark elves' suspicions and was ashamed his father knew of the rumors. It also made him nervous about how much others might believe those rumors when he was to go before the lord soon. Such treasonous accusations would most definitely end poorly for him. He wasn't quite sure how to respond to his father in a way that wouldn't make him angry or disown him.

While he took a seat on the couch next to Laila, he looked at Nikososo with sincerity, and began, "Father, I'm sorry if I have brought shame to our name, but I—"

"She's here," his father interrupted him before he could continue.

As Nikolean cocked an eyebrow at him, a soft rattling sound at the front entrance startled both Nikolean and Laila, drawing their eyes to the door in time to see it opening. They both sprung to their feet, and Nikolean stepped in front of Laila protectively as they glared at the door while he drew his dagger.

After entering the house without a word, the shrouded figure pulled back its hood and looked around. Nikolean was moderately relieved to see it was Akayra but remained poised with his dagger while maneuvering Laila farther behind him out of her view, unsure of how she would react.

"Akayra," he said, calling her attention.

"Ah, there you are," she replied, walking at a brisk pace toward them. "Lord Brilldessah has reviewed your request. You meet with her at noon at the... Rashukk!" she cursed, noticing the strange being Nikolean was hiding behind his frame. She drew her sword rapidly and aimed it toward them, hissing aggressively at Laila.

"Put the sword down," Nikolean insisted, raising his free hand to her, palm forward, while keeping his dagger ready in the other. "Let me explain."

"What are you thinking?!" she said heatedly in a hushed tone. "Why isn't she in the dungeon with the others? Are you trying to get yourself killed??"

"Put your weapon down, and I will tell you."

Laila was peeking out timidly from behind Nikolean's shoulder, prepared to retaliate if needed. However, Laila had no desire to attack the drow people and hoped for her to calm down. The female dark elf glanced back and forth between the two of them with consternation. With hesitation, Akayra withdrew her sword waveringly, doubting her decision to stand down as she sheathed it.

"This had better be good," she snarled at her cousin and crossed her arms over her chest.

"She's an elf!" Nikososo remarked and began laughing unsettlingly. "Can you believe it?! An ELF!" He continued laughing, like that of an old crone cackling, as though at some private joke between him and the voices in his head.

"No, Uncle," Akayra said. "I most certainly do *not* believe it. Go ahead, Nikolean. Explain why there's an elf in your home."

With a deep breath, Nikolean relaxed his stance and put away his dagger. "After the Drakka uncovered the truth about what the elders had done to Onis Caelis, I left Du Noir. I was searching for any hope of stopping the resulting plague, which has been killing our lands over all this time. In my searching, I did manage to find that hope, but I also found so much more..."

To their surprise, his father quieted his laughing to listen, and Akayra continued to stare at him apprehensively while he went on to explain. He relayed everything he learned about how killing the mother dragon had caused the spirits of the land to forsake the dark elf territory more severely than the rest of Onis. He had sought to discover if there was any way for the drow people to redeem themselves and restore their lands, and what he came upon was Laila.

Motioning for Laila to step forward, he told them all about the prophecy of the elf destined to end the war, the elf that would go before all the dragons and races to unite and restore the land once again.

"Lady Laila *is* that prophesied elf, and I have pledged my life to help her fulfill her quest so that our lands may thrive once again," he concluded.

She ground her teeth, thinking about his fantastical tale, then asked him outright, "So, does that mean you have joined with the Drakka?"

"Akayra," Nikolean said, flustered that that is what she took from everything. "I don't think you realize the gravity of what is happening here. I need you to hear what I am telling you. We have a chance to restore our land. Shouldn't that come above the elders and their customs?"

Nikolean protectively grasped Laila's hand, and Akayra stared at the two of them, realizing that there was quite a bit more to the story than her cousin's treasonous ways.

Waiting for them to respond, Nikolean half expected his father to laugh again at the notion or to yell and scream at him for joining the Drakka, but he did neither. He simply sat there, staring at them for a long moment. Nikolean wondered if his old man had heard anything he had said or if he was too lost within the boundaries of his mind.

Breaking the silence, Nikolean asked, "Father? Did you hear me?"

But Nikososo just continued to glare at them, remaining silent.

"How long has he been like this?" he asked Akayra, forlorn.

"Your mother left soon after you did," she replied grudgingly. "That's when it started to get really bad. The healers don't seem to know how to help him. They say he's gone mad, and they can't find any physical reason for it."

"The dragons are coming," his father suddenly said in a grave tone and demeanor, commanding their attention. "Better hurry. The dragons... Hurry."

Akayra went to the old drow in quick, long strides and knelt beside him with compassion. "Uncle, the dragons have not bothered us for a long time. You're safe."

He shook his head and started to rock back and forth in his chair, appearing frightened.

"See?" Akayra stood up and faced the others, gesturing to Nikososo. "Mad."

But there was something unnatural about the old drow that was bothering Laila. She could still feel the chill in the room, an almost familiar cold emanating off of him. As she listened to him ramble, it hit her that it was a similar message Ignisar had warned her of in her dream. Was the mighty dragon trying to communicate with her through Nikolean's father now?

As she stared at him in her observance, Laila said in Drow, "Hiym ket gah ëitni revvük," *I not believe he's mad*, surprising Akayra, who hadn't known she had been following their conversation. Nikolean donned an inappropriate grin at hearing Drow coming from her lips, momentarily forgetting the seriousness of the situation.

After releasing Nikolean's hand, Laila walked with caution toward Nikososo.

"Get back from him!" Akayra warned, threateningly gripping the hilt of her weapon.

"She won't hurt him," Nikolean declared. "Let her see him."

Reluctantly, the drow stepped aside and watched the elf with trepidation as she knelt down before the old man.

Locking eyes with Laila, Nikososo gave her a wide smile as he said, "Hello." Then he lifted his shaky hand and touched the side of her face with an unexpected gentleness. "I see you." He pulled it away again, leaning back in his chair, and appeared more at peace.

By being that close to him, she strongly felt the biting chill surrounding him and believed it to be coming from the phantom realm. She concentrated on the strange aura, trying to determine why it was there.

"Niko, you said he was a powerful necromancer. What is that exactly?" she asked in Onish without taking her eyes away from his father.

"They are casters that use dark magic to raise and commune with the dead. Great necromancers, like my father, can create powerful armies from the bones of the deceased that cannot be easily destroyed," he told her with pride. "Why do you ask?"

As Laila studied Nikolean's father, the whites in her eyes began to haze over like a darkening cloud until they had gone completely black as before. That's when she saw it. Hovering near the old man was what appeared to be a tear in the fabric of space. It looked like a black lightning bolt with an ominous haze wavering around it, looming over Nikososo. Laila could hear whispering all around him like the whispers she had experienced in the past when connecting to the phantom realm. However, there was something different—more menacing—about the forces there. She slowly stood up, gazing into the dark, sinister crack, and her heart jumped into her throat, seeing it begin to expand.

Gasping, Laila watched as a shadowy wraith with glowing red eyes came seeping through its haze. It then soared around the old man's head, wailing a harrowing sound. She immediately stepped back, keeping her sight on it, her hands poised, ready to defend herself.

"My lady? What is it? What do you see?" Nikolean asked, frightened by her reaction.

Noticing her blackened eyes, Akayra jumped back away from the elf. "What's going on?!" she hollered.

The phantom emitted a horrifying howl as it whirred around the old drow, and Laila tried to understand what it was doing. Nikososo began ranting nonsensically again, and when it shrieked at him as though in response, she realized that he was communicating with it.

With her most soothing and placid voice, Laila said in Onish, "Your father..." She paused with caution, not wanting to cause any alarm to the ghost. "...he's not crazy. The veil to the

CHAPTER 18

phantom realm has been torn around him, most likely from so many years of communing with the dead. It seems he never stopped."

Nikolean, taken aback, wasn't sure whether to be relieved or even more concerned. "So, what can we do?" he asked pensively.

"No! No!" his father cried out. "Get away! They won't let you! You get away!"

Ignoring the old drow, Laila raised her hands to the spirit, but it quickly vanished back to the other side before she could try anything. Within the blink of an eye, four more wraiths shot out from the veil, moaning frighteningly.

"I told you!" Nikososo declared. "You're not welcome here!"

"Father!" Nikolean yelled. "She's trying to help you!"

As she stepped farther away from the elf, Akayra asked with clear doubt, "You think she can?"

Nikolean remained silent, deciding it best for his cousin to witness for herself what the Omi Méa was capable of while he watched her continuing to study his father.

With her hands raised, Laila attempted to expand her consciousness and establish a link with the ethereal beings. In all honesty, she had no idea what she was doing, but in sending out her thoughts, she could feel the torment and the pain seeping off their ghostly figures. They screeched at her direly, then, without hesitation, dove toward her in an attack, one after the other. Laila dropped to the floor, out of the way, and the spirits flew past her, brushing across the elf maiden's back with their chilling touch. Then they soared back over to the old man.

"Laila!" Nikolean yelled, panicked and frustrated that he couldn't see what was happening for himself in order to help her.

After jumping back to her feet, Laila took a deep breath, angered by their assault, and thrust both her hands forward at them, her fingers clawed. She pulled from the phantom spirit within her and wrapped her mind around the specters' essences, holding them there in place. They screamed and wailed with intensity, while the old man rocked back and forth fiercely in his chair.

The old drow, Nikososo, unexpectedly jumped up, surprising them all. He grabbed his staff, his red eyes glaring at her as he shouted, "*Myvern akahn!*"

A mystical hand with long skeletal fingers of black smoke came forth from the tip of Nikososo's staff. It reached out rapidly toward Laila's neck, a trail remaining behind it like an arm attached to the staff's stone.

"Father! NO!" Nikolean pushed Laila aside, jumping in front of the hand, and it grasped on to his neck instead as Laila fell out of the way.

"NIKO!" Akayra screamed, unsure of what to do.

As she beheld the ghostly hand with its long, pointed fingers strangling Nikolean, Laila was shocked to find his father not stopping the spell. Upon turning her focus back to the old man, she saw a grim haze near his eyes, and she wasn't convinced it was just his father in that old, frail body anymore.

Laila stood back up without delay, and used her mind to shove the old drow backward with force, sending his staff flying out of his hand, breaking the spell. He cried out in pain as he slammed back into the chair.

Akayra ran over to Nikolean to make sure he was alright and was comforted to find him still breathing.

Meanwhile, Laila watched as a shadowed mist left the old drow's body, floating back up above him. She immediately used the phantom spirit to grab on to all the shades, but they fought and resisted her. Unable to hold on to them, the spirits soared around the room wildly as they shrieked. But, to her astonishment, they always returned near the portal. She realized they must be linked to it and was grateful that they hadn't been escaping the entire time.

While summoning a greater power from the phantom spirit, she instead directed it towards the tear in the veil, concentrating on its energy. The specters grew furious with her and prepared for another strike, but Laila directed a continuous spiritual surge at the veil, a mist shooting forth from her hands like black fire.

As her black mist struck the veil, everything came into view for Nikolean and Akayra, and they gasped while they watched in amazement. The spirits were forcibly drawn back through the crack, screaming their pain and displeasure as Laila continued the stream.

With the wraiths gone, Laila focused all her strength on pulling at the edges of the veil, hoping to tether it closed with her powers. There was great resistance as she pulled on it. She could even feel the spirits knocking against its narrowing gateway, like a jolt against her heart every time they attempted to break through. As she released a wail of her own, she could sense the fibers of the veil coming back together at last, her arms shaking rapidly as she heaved the edges closer, weaving the tear shut.

A final hair-raising scream pierced through the veil as the last of the crack was sealed and mended. Laila dropped her arms to her sides, wavering, her eyes returning to normal, but then they immediately started rolling into the back of her head.

As the elf maiden's body gave way to gravity, Nikolean darted over to her, grabbing her before she could reach the ground. He recognized that she was losing consciousness, and did the quickest thing that came to his mind by pressing his lips solidly against hers, his hand cradling her face. Almost instantly, he felt an intense tingling sensation through his lips and the hand resting on her cheek as his energy began flowing out of him and into the elf, restoring her.

Her eyes began to flutter open, and she smiled to find him there, right before her. To let him know she was better, she gave him a light tap on his arm.

Relieved, Nikolean kissed a soft peck on her lips, then gazed upon her as he helped her to stand upright. Afterwards, he returned his focus to his father, observing him sitting quietly in the chair, still watching them.

"Well??" Akayra said impatiently, trying to comprehend what had just transpired.

"Is it finished, my love?" Nikolean asked once she had regained her bearings.

With a much-needed deep breath, Laila smiled and nodded. "It's finished."

"Father?" Nikolean went back to Nikososo, kneeling as he took his hand and looked observingly into his eyes. "Are you alright?"

He stared down at his son, a tear in the corner of his eye, as he nodded. "It's quiet now." With the aid of Nikolean, he stood and said, "I think I'd like to go lay down for a while."

"Of course, Father."

Nikolean couldn't help but wonder when the last time his father had really slept was as he helped Nikososo walk down the hall to his room.

While they were gone, Akayra circled around Laila, looking her over and making her uncomfortable.

"My... love..." she said sardonically. Halting back in front of Laila, she crossed her arms over her chest and asked, "How were you able to close the veil? And what spell have you cast on my cousin?"

"Leave her be, Akayra," Nikolean said, returning. "We owe her a huge debt."

Akayra grunted, knowing he was right but not wanting to accept being indebted to an elf.

"Cousin, you realize it is nearly time to go before Lord Brilldessah?" she said snootily, still unsure of how she felt about all of it. "What are you going to do with the elf?"

"Actually..." he said, looking at her keenly. "I was hoping you could stay with her; keep her safe while I'm gone. If things don't go well, I may need you to help her escape."

"What?!" she blared. "You want me to babysit your pet elf AND commit a felony?! Besides, I was planning to be at the meeting. I'm probably the only friend you have left here."

"Please, Akayra. I need you." He smiled at her hopefully.

With a sneer at Laila, she sighed exaggeratedly. "Fine! But you better get back here. Whatever you do, don't implicate yourself in being Drakka. Just tell them whatever they need to hear and get out of there."

Nikolean pressed his hands together and bowed thankfully to her. Then he took Laila's hand, walking with her slowly back to the entryway.

"My love," he said, taking both her hands as he faced her. "I don't know how I can ever repay you for what you've done for my father today. I had feared there was no hope for him."

Laila smiled earnestly at him and nodded as he continued, "When I first heard Tury, I honestly thought that I was going mad, just as my father had, and it terrified me. Even after I found out that I had been given a gift instead of a curse, it has always been in the back of my mind that I, too, might someday have to face the voices in my head. You have no idea how much what you have done for my father means to me. Now I know that he was never crazy at all, just broken. And just like everything else, you healed him."

Nikolean wrapped his arms around Laila, pulling her tightly against him as he buried his face into her hair, praying that it would not be the last time that he would know her scent. As she returned his embrace, Laila suddenly felt her heart aching in her chest, realizing he was about to leave her and that it could very well be the last time she'd ever see him.

With tenderness, Nikolean pulled slightly away and looked deeply into her eyes. She was captivated by the intensity of his blood-red gaze before he leaned in and kissed her long and passionately, the world fading away as they desperately clung to that moment for as long as possible.

Nikososo Den Faolin

CHAPTER NINETEEN

BELLS

*P*ositioned near the far end of the chamber, Nikolean stood facing the dais along the back wall, holding a military stance while waiting for Lord Brilldessah to arrive. Like nearly every building or dwelling of the dark elves, the room was dimly lit, emitting the same somber effect which they tended to prefer. There were posh seating arrangements covered in furs against gray lava-rock walls on either side. A large chandelier with black diamonds and rib bones from two-leggeds hung morbidly between himself and the lord's decorated chair with its rich purple fabrics. He noticed that the whole room had been decorated in an elaborate manner, much more so than by the lord he had served before departing, flaunting a general guise of opulence.

When he heard the heavy chamber door jolt open, he maintained his statuesque stance, staring forward, as was customary. He listened with intensity to the many footsteps entering the room behind him, counting ten soldiers and a female with boots that clicked and clacked from spurs with every step, assuming that to be Lord Brilldessah. As the soldiers passed by and took their places on either side of the hall facing him, he was disheartened that he did not recognize any of them. He could only assume that it was deliberately done.

So as not to appear discouraged, Nikolean kept a straight face while he drew his weapon upon discerning the lord approaching his flank. He held it at chest level, facing downward with his opposite fist pressing against the hilt in salute.

"Lord Brilldessah," he said with confidence as she passed him, heading to the chair.

From the back, Nikolean could see that she was rather tall for a female dark elf, with silky jet-black hair down to her waist and an extravagant charcoal-gray fur cloak that trailed a few feet behind her. Spaulders jutted up like claws from her shoulders toward the ceiling, and she walked with a strong warrior stride. When she reached the slightly inclined dais, she stopped in front of her chair and whipped her cloak around to face Nikolean. He was surprised to see such a dark-blue tone to her skin, assuming she'd be much older, but she didn't look a day over one hundred—unprecedented for a dark elf lord. However, no one of Nikolean's tender age had ever risen to commander status before him either. He was never certain if it was due to his father's prestige or due to his ruthlessness.

Lord Brilldessah stared at him with her bright-violet eyes for a long while before snapping her fingers angrily in the air. A young boy then hurried before her and unbuckled three finger-bone clasps on her cloak, removing it with care. As he folded the cloak delicately over his arm, he backed away timidly from her in a subservient position, returning to his spot in a back corner. She rolled her eyes in annoyance at the boy while taking her place upon the vibrant chair.

"Nikolean Den Faolin," she said with a smirk. "Former Commander of the Duep Nordor Troops."

"Yes, my lord," he said with a humble bow.

The dark elf lord relaxed sideways in her chair, crossing her ankles and resting her feet on its arm, her tight leather armor croaking with her movement. "You've been away for... three years?"

"That is correct, my lord."

"So, tell me. Why has the great Commander Den Faolin returned and with quite the intriguing entourage?"

"Lord Brilldessah, I have returned to ask for help." He paused, studying his audience.

"Go on," she said impatiently.

"I have been searching for a cure to our land," he resumed. "Despite all the magic we pour into it, I have watched as our people continue to suffer, and it has only been getting worse. My exploration led me into the Ashwood Forest, where I encountered the group currently in your dungeons. They are on a quest—I am on a quest—to go before the dragons and demand them to stop the feuding. We believe it will also restore our lands."

Unsure of how much he should reveal about Laila and her involvement before he could go speak with Kull Merzumar, he waited strategically to observe her reaction.

As she drummed her long-spiked nails across the armrest in a steady rolling motion, the lord stared at him, unamused, and Nikolean couldn't tell if she was annoyed or bored.

"Look, Nikolean," she said frankly, "I realize I am young for my position, but I am not naïve, and you should not assume so. I'm not sure why you brought your pets into our land, but there is no way that sordid lot is going before any dragons and living. They couldn't even take out my soldiers to stay out of our dungeons."

"That is because we came here to speak of peace, not to incite a war," he replied intently.

Sighing at him—definitely annoyed—she continued, "You came here to discuss peace between the drow and the other races? And why would we do that? I suppose you believe we need to be redeemed for the bold act of our elders who sought to turn the tides in our favor?"

"With all due respect, my lord, does it look like it has been working in our favor? Our land is diseased and nearly uninhabitable."

Lord Brilldessah swiftly sat upright in her chair, taking on a much more prominent stance. She gripped her fingers over the edge of the armrests and glowered at Nikolean. "You will not disrespect our elders! There were rumors that you had betrayed us, that you had joined league with the Drakka. I had hoped to give you the benefit of the doubt for the sake of your family's honor, but everything you are speaking of is based in the lies of those treacherous scum!"

Desperate for her to listen, to gain her favor so that they could seek aid from Kull Merzumar against the dragons, Nikolean blurted, "There is a prophecy! It speaks of what I was telling you. A prophecy as old as the war, that is now coming to fruition!"

Lord Brilldessah stared at him with slightly more interest, as she asked, "What prophecy?"

Nikolean, seeing his opportunity, spilled some details of the prophecy to the lord. He told her of meeting the Omi Méa and all the wonders she can perform, insisting that she would put a stop to the dragons' massacres. He explained their plan of gaining support from all the races and his journey to the dark elves to ask for their help, while the lord listened studiously to the tale.

Once Nikolean finished, she leered at him and asked, "Why would we want the dragons to stop killing our enemies?"

Nikolean replied, "The dragons have not been discriminating solely against the elves anymore. They have been increasingly striking down the humans and dwarves in their assaults. It is only a matter of time before they seek out the drow as well."

A look of vexation across her face, the lord mused, "Perhaps because the other races have been sticking their noses where they don't belong through their trading and alliances with the elves." Then, staring at him sternly, she continued, "You still haven't explained how those wretches in my dungeon will heal our land."

After a deep breath, Nikolean explained, "The prophecy states that the Omi Méa will bring replenishment of life over the land. Those wretches in your dungeon are all a part of it. If uniting the races is what is needed to heal Du Noir, then the drow should be the first in line to do so; since our land is suffering the most."

Lord Brilldessah glared at Nikolean for a long moment, then stood imperially from her chair and asked, "And where is this Omi Méa now?"

Her soldiers standing to either side took a step forward toward Nikolean, their hands on the hilts of their weapons, and Nikolean realized he had just made a grave mistake. Those drow were as stubborn in their hatred as the Great Aeris.

"She's... gone on ahead of us with her dragon to find other supporters," he lied. "I told her I would speak to the drow on her behalf."

While peering at Nikolean, Lord Brilldessah humphed, then waved her finger at the guards. Two of them quickly stepped forward, taking Nikolean's weapon, and grabbed his arms, holding him facing the lord. His heart sinking, Nikolean knew better than to resist.

"Nikolean Den Faolin," Lord Brilldessah spoke firmly, "it has been made clear to me that you have joined with the Drakka by your actions and your intent. That, or that you have gone as mad as your father." She sneered at him.

Since he now knew his father to be quite well, Nikolean did not react to her comment with insult, as she had hoped.

Disappointed, she continued even more agitated, "From this day forth, your family will be stripped of its name and will furthermore be known as 'Süd' Faolin! Your lineage will bear your name upon introduction as their disgracer; a great dishonor upon your house! As for you, Nikolean *Süd* Faolin..."

The lord took long dramatic strides from her dais toward him, glaring at him fiercely. When she reached him, she clutched his face in her hand, and her sharp nails dug into the sides of his cheeks. Only inches away, she addressed him with scorn. "Such a shame. You held such promise, young drow." While leering at him, she added through pursed lips, "And such a pretty face, too."

Without averting her eyes from Nikolean, she pushed his face to the side, releasing it. Then she stepped away, her hands clasped behind her back as she roamed the floor, speaking loud for everyone to hear. "By law, the Drakka have been declared enemies of the Dark Elf Empire, and any member is guilty of treason."

Returning before him once again, she raised her hands high to all her soldiers and pivoted to face Nikolean. "Can anyone here remind our Ex-Commander Nikolean Süd Faolin what the penalty for treason is?"

They all shouted in unison, "DEATH!"

Giving him one last sinister smile, she spat at his feet, disdain for him seeping off her like a poisonous cloud. Then, turning her back to him, Lord Brilldessah commanded with a cavalier wave of her hand, "Take him away. He shall be executed at dusk with the others."

Filled with anxiety, Laila sat atop a wobbly wooden stool in the kitchen next to the counter. Despite her nerves, she was trying her best to listen to Akayra yammering on in Drow about her people, insisting they weren't all monsters; they just weren't afraid of anyone or anything, including death. She attested that since the other races don't understand that type of mentality, drow are therefore viewed as demons in the night. She then referenced several horrific-sounding acts and tried to justify them to Laila, but Laila could not see any justification in cruelty or torture.

As she looked at the elf, Akayra realized she had been rambling out of nervousness and worried that her tales of the drow were doing more harm than good.

In an attempt to change the subject, she said, "About my uncle..." Pausing, she poured some tea for Laila, then continued, "...that was pretty amazing what you did," and she gave her a sincere smile. But then her face quickly scrunched up in an appalled guise as she exclaimed, "That doesn't make us friends or anything! I just mean... thank you."

Uncomfortable with Laila's silence, Akayra wondered if the elf could actually speak drow, contemplating that perhaps she hadn't understood a thing she'd said. She didn't think about the fact that Laila would be agonizing about what was happening to Nikolean and her friends at that moment.

Niko... Laila sighed woefully. She could not put him from her mind. Any task she performed since he left, any step she took, no matter what was happening around her, she continued to dwell on thoughts of him. She repeated everything he had ever said in her mind, particularly his confessions, every "my lady," and lastly, "my love." She pictured his face, remembering how it felt to kiss him, to hold him, what he sounded like, smelled like, his smile, his eyes, his gentle touch. Unable to deny it to herself or anyone else anymore, she knew that she loved him. With every fiber, with every breath, with every heartbeat and every thought, she loved him. She never wanted to imagine being without him, aching at the thought of possibly never seeing him again.

As the minutes had become hours without any word, any optimism Laila held had vanished. All that remained was her being wrought with worry. *What if he failed? What if he can't save them? What if he can't save... himself? This can't be it, can't be the end.* Laila's eyes glazed over while staring into nothingness, brooding in Nikolean's absence, oblivious to her surroundings and... that Akayra had still been speaking to her.

"Laila? Laila, are you listening?" Akayra said to her, annoyed, waving her hand before her face.

"Sorry," she replied in Drow, fighting to hold back the tears glistening in her eyes. "I worried about Niko."

Akayra nodded, feeling foolish. "Of course you are. Drink the tea; it'll be good for your nerves."

While attempting a smile, Laila thanked her for the tea and took a long sip while covertly reaching out to Turathyl. *'Have you heard anything yet?'* she pleaded anxiously.

The dragon sighed into her mind as she replied, *'Not since you asked me a moment ago, no. You know I will tell you as soon as I do.'*

'Sorry,' Laila sent back.

'You have no reason to be. I don't mean to be harsh; I'm just trying hard to keep my mind open for the drow. He cannot communicate as easily as you and I, and I'm worried I won't hear him.' Sensing feelings of affection and comfort from her dragon, Laila felt a little more at peace. Then, Turathyl added, *'For the record, Omi Méa, I knew that you were in love with the drow long before you did.'*

Laila could tell her dragon was smiling. It would typically have made her smile as well were it not for the horrible feeling of doom lingering over her head as she awaited word of his—and her friends'—judgment.

Clad in heavy chains, hands tied tightly behind his back with feet bound, Nikolean was dragged forebodingly down the dark underground cavern that led to the dungeons of Duep Nordor. They had taken extra measures to ensure he was secured, knowing his reputation and not willing to risk seeing his feats for themselves.

Since his sentencing, Nikolean had been trying to reach Turathyl to get Laila out of the house, afraid that Lord Brilldessah hadn't believed his story of her going on without them. Alas, he was still new to mind-speaking with a dragon, and the distance between them, combined with the stone walls, seemed to be making it more difficult than he anticipated.

Four guards from the hall where his judgment had been passed were guiding him down the steep, bodeful stairway, its musty and bodily waste smell much more potent than he remembered.

Nikolean had been studying the guards, how they moved, the way they walked, trying to determine what magic—if any—they might possess. He was quite familiar with that particular dungeon, just never as a prisoner before, and hoped that they hadn't changed it while he'd been gone.

After they reached the bottom of the stairwell, they proceeded down a long corridor toward a gate that would lead them to the cells. Nikolean could sense one of the guards was beginning to lag back, his footsteps growing quieter, and the prisoner tested the looseness of his bindings, pretending to have an itch. Although his hands were tied behind his back, he smirked mischievously, anticipating that escape would be difficult, but certainly not impossible.

As they neared the gate and the guards slowed their pace, Nikolean prepared to make his move. But instead, he was distracted when he heard behind him the distinct and familiar sound of a neck being broken and a body falling to the floor.

The guard holding his right arm let go, and the other man grabbed hold of it, detaining him from behind while they all turned to investigate the disturbance. To their surprise, they discovered that the fourth guard who had been holding back had killed his companion. He stood there, smiling tauntingly at them, sword drawn steadily before him with both hands, preparing for their attack.

Before they could react, Nikolean thrust his head back into his custodian's nose, breaking it. The guard yelped, impulsively releasing his prisoner to grab his bloodied nose, while Nikolean instantly turned and kneed him fiercely in the groin. As the guard yowled and keeled over, Nikolean swiveled, using his chained hands still behind his back to grasp the man's head and snap his neck. He let go, and the limp body tumbled to the floor, dead. In awe of Nikolean, the drow guard that was aiding him was disappointed in himself for blinking and missing the entire spectacle.

Surging with both adrenaline and power, Nikolean darted in a blur toward the other gasping guard, slamming his shoulder into the man, while he rammed him with force into the stone wall. The moment Nikolean stepped away, the defecting guard thrust his sword into the remaining opponent's chest. It pierced straight through until he hit the stone behind, and he twisted the blade as he pulled it back out. Blood sputtered from the guard's mouth, eyes wide with shock while he gradually skidded down to the floor, leaving a red smear on the wall behind.

Without wasting a moment, his aide speedily grabbed a set of keys from the wounded drow and began unbinding Nikolean's chains from his hands and feet.

"We must hurry," the unfamiliar man said. "There will be others coming soon."

"Are you Drakka?" Nikolean queried as he massaged his wrist from where the chains had been chafing him.

After grabbing the gatekeeper's keys from the second dead guard with the broken nose, the man looked up at Nikolean, a jovial grin across his face. "For Du Noir," he said proudly. "I'm Rogg." Then he went hurriedly to unlock the gate. Rogg was a little older than Nikolean, with dark gray hair and blueish skin. His smile seemed eerily friendly for a drow.

"For Du Noir," Nikolean repeated. He then grabbed his dagger from the first guard who had met his fate.

Without a second thought, Nikolean went to the guard propped against the wall holding his chest wound and mercilessly slit his throat, finishing him.

Before they broke through the gate, he was startled to hear, *'Niko...'*

'TURY!' he sent back with excitement. *'Tell Laila to get out now! I will come for her as soon as I can! She is not safe there!'*

He listened for her intently, terrified he hadn't reached her when she didn't respond. But he couldn't wait; he had to hope and pray that he had.

Nikolean and Rogg advanced with stealth down the seedy corridor toward the dungeon cells, a tortured scream from a prisoner ricocheting off the walls. He hoped it wasn't one of his comrades. They slowed as they neared the doorway entrance to where the cells were, knowing there would be more opposition.

As he peeked around the corner of the doorway, Nikolean spotted three more guards: two guarding either side of the entrance and a third dragging his sword tormentingly across

CHAPTER 19

the dungeon's cell bars as he walked back and forth, the clanging echoing throughout the room.

From what he could discern, the screaming was coming from an oubliette-type cell in the floor where a prisoner had been thrown and likely tortured. His comrades were within a single cell, fettered to the walls with anti-magic shackles—standard for caster prisoners—that would prevent them from being able to use any magic. Overall, they appeared to be alive and well, having only bruising and minor lacerations. He was honestly surprised that their condition was not much worse, but assumed the torture would come prior to their execution at dusk. No good drow execution wouldn't include some type of torture before the final event.

Nikolean suddenly realized that Davion was not with the others. While glancing discreetly in his limited field of vision, he failed to locate the human. All he could see was a male drow prisoner in the cell beside them, stripped to his undergarment. He was severely malnourished, with his bones outlined through his ghostly skin. The withering old drow was staring in Nikolean's direction, but the pupils in his eyes had gone white, reflecting the glare from the room's sconces. If it weren't for the filth on his body, the prisoner would've passed for an apparition.

None of the others had seemed to notice Nikolean there, and he withdrew, pressing his back against the corridor wall. He took a deep breath in preparation while he signaled the guards' positions to his cohort. Rogg nodded, tightening his hands on his weapon.

Moving like the wind, Nikolean swept into the room with Rogg trailing behind him. Before the guards knew what was going on, Nikolean approached the one on the right from behind and covered his mouth, stifling a scream while expertly stabbing him through his temple, killing him instantly. Nikolean withdrew his dagger and released the dead guard, letting his corpse heavily collapse face down on the stone floor.

Meanwhile, Rogg had engaged in sword-to-sword combat with the other guard, clanking their weapons loudly.

Glondora called out, "Niko!" excited to see him, and the jailer turned heatedly toward him.

Nikolean took his dagger and threw it at the jailer. The dagger soared through the air, planting itself squarely between the jailer's eyes before he even knew it was coming.

"Get your friends!" Rogg called out as he parried the guard's attack. "I have this one!"

Nikolean hadn't taken two steps toward the cells when he heard the foreboding sound of a deep, focused voice from behind him.

"Watch out!" Glondora yelled, and he jerked around to look.

"*Niyalum vintay!*" a dark arcanist cast from the other side of the room.

A bolt of energy came shooting out from the man's hands, darting towards Nikolean, who evaded at the last second. As the pulse hit against the cell doors, it sent an electric shock of blue lightning waves dancing over all the bars. Hort and Salyaman pulled aggressively at their bindings, their shackles digging into their wrists, enraged that they couldn't do anything. The person in the oubliette began cackling hysterically at the commotion above.

Nikolean hadn't been able to see the dark arcanist from the doorway, but now that he was faced with him, he espied what had happened to Davion. Strapped and stretched out on a wooden table, the human lay motionless. His robes were opened, revealing his chest, and there were burn marks over his skin from being tortured by the wizard. Nikolean was nearly hit with a second bolt while distracted by the sight.

Upon hearing a blood-curdling scream from the guard that Rogg had been battling—and had now defeated—Nikolean knew it was only a matter of time before others would be coming to investigate. Grabbing for his dagger, Nikolean cursed when he realized it wasn't there. The only one he had with him was still lodged in the jailer's skull.

Like an arrow from a bow, Nikolean darted across the room, evading another attack as it shot past his leg, fizzing out when striking only rock. The wizard's eyes grew wide in alarm from Nikolean's speed, but he cast again and managed to land a bolt right before he reached him.

Stunned by the blast, Nikolean dropped to the floor, reverberating from the energy surging within his body. Rather pleased with himself, the arcanist smirked at the fallen rogue and began casting another—more fatal—spell.

Nikolean strenuously recovered himself and darted at the caster again, evading his electrifying attack. Thrusting both fists forward, he slammed against his assailant's chest as he reached him with incredible speed, sending him flying backward. The wizard hit his back against the edge of the table where Davion lay, trying to brace himself against it. Nikolean then swiped his leg with haste, out and under the caster, forcing him to crash to the ground. Without a moment's pause, he grabbed a nearby renegade spike off the floor and stabbed it down into the arcanist's heart, once, twice, thrice, ensuring he would not be getting back up.

Before they had a moment to rejoice, the echoing chime of the city alarm bells began to toll ominously throughout Duep Nordor.

"That's our cue," Rogg said with urgency.

Panicking, Nikolean told Rogg to grab the human while he dashed back to the cell, grabbing his dagger callously out of the guard's skull on the way, then began setting the others free from their shackles. Once released, Glondora started to check on Davion, but Nikolean insisted that there wasn't time; they would have to address his wounds later.

With the human flung over his shoulder, Rogg began heading to the exit, but Nikolean shouted, "This way!" directing them all to a tall torture device, with hanging straps and long nails, that was anchored to the far wall. He pressed in on a loose brick beside it, and the device quaked and began to turn, revealing a narrow passage to a dark hallway beyond.

"Quickly!" he insisted, and they all squeezed through. Nikolean closed the passage door behind them, and they made their way down the secret tunnel. "This will take us to the edge of the city walls. I need to get to Laila before they find her."

As they neared the tunnel's exit, the alarm bells rung clearly in their ears, reverberating down through the sewer grate above their heads, promptly followed by the sound of soldiers stampeding through the city streets.

"I will take them to the Safehouse until we can move them out of the city." Rogg then instructed Nikolean where to meet up with them once he had the Omi Méa.

'Tury...' Nikolean tried desperately one more time. *'If you can hear me, get Laila out of the house! I'm on my way!'*

CHAPTER TWENTY

DRAKKA

*P*acing the floor trepidatiously, Laila shook her hands in nervous anticipation, feeling helpless, not knowing what to do. Even though Turathyl still hadn't been able to reach Nikolean, she knew in her gut something had gone wrong, could feel it within the depths of her heart.

"You need to calm down," Akayra told her nonchalantly while leaning against the wall, arms crossed. "It's Niko. I'm sure he's fine."

Just then, the city's grim bells tolled, and they both jerked their heads in the direction of Duep Nordor, gasping.

"Time to go!" Akayra said with more zeal, drawing her sword and walking toward the exit.

"No!" Laila blared in Drow. "I no leave them!" She stared at the drow firmly and stood her ground.

With a glare of disbelief at the elf, Akayra groaned angrily and stomped back over to her. "This is not up for debate! I was told to get you out if things went wrong. You hear that?" The drow pointed towards the bells tolling from the city. "That means something has gone very wrong!"

'*Tury!*' Laila called out in desperation. '*Have you heard anything? What's going on?! I don't know what to do!*'

'*I've heard nothing,*' her dragon sent back.

"Please!" she begged of the dark elf. "Just give little time!"

While she fidgeted with her sword, spinning the hilt in her hand repeatedly as she thought, Akayra stared at the crazy elf before her and gave a heavy sigh. "Fine. A few more minutes, and then we are out of here. And if you get killed in the meantime, that's not on me!"

With a frustrated growl, Akayra took over pacing the floor, mumbling curses under her breath.

Meanwhile, Laila awaited word from the dragon, her angst eating her inside out. It seemed like an eternity had passed, and the elf maiden practically jumped from her skin when Turathyl suddenly sent loud and clear, '*Laila! Get out now!*'

Laila opened her mouth to tell Akayra they needed to leave when a loud bang thundered through the house as someone knocked forcefully against the door. They gawked at the entry only a few paces from them, the only way in or out, afraid of what was on the other side. Another loud bang crashed against it as someone abruptly kicked in the door, sending it flying off its hinges. A man in all black metal armor clunked inside, glaring around through the slits in his helmet.

Akayra hollered as she charged at the death knight, her sword erect, but the knight blocked her attack with his shield and dexterously grabbed her by the neck within the grip of his gauntlet. With great strength, the mysterious figure then began squeezing, and her sword clattered against the floor as she gripped at the knight's hand on her neck.

"Akayra!" Laila screamed, afraid to jolt the knight with her powers in fear of causing him to snap her neck in the process.

Following a throaty incantation, a dark aura seeped eerily out of the cracks in his plate, swarming toward his fist on the drow dame's collar. A voice then came from the bedroom hallway, and Laila quickly looked to find Nikososo chanting something as he walked toward them. He was maneuvering his staff in a rhythmic motion and thrust the tip toward the death knight. A red streak shot out from the staff's gem, entwined with a black fog from the phantom realm. It struck the knight, and the fog wafted over him like smoke as spirits attacked and burned his skin.

The knight released Akayra, and she fell to the floor, gasping while grabbing her sword again. The death knight staggered and waved his hands around, screaming from his searing skin as he tried to stop the attacks from the shades.

Seeing her opening, Akayra promptly thrust the sword upward through the parting under his helmet, killing the death knight instantly as she struck him straight through to the skull. When she pulled back to withdraw her blade, she found it to be stuck, and the knight's head jarred with each tug. As the body began to fall, Akayra put a firm grip on her sword, veering the corpse sideways away from her while it came crashing to the floor.

"He won't be alone," Nikososo warned them. "You must go."

While Laila turned to the old drow and thanked him, Akayra stepped on the dead knight's head, bracing him as she vigorously yanked her blade free. Laila wished she didn't have to leave Nikolean's father so soon and wondered if they would ever meet again.

"When the time comes..." he said to her with a warm smile, "do not forget about us. The drow land could use your mercy and forgiveness." He gave her a humbled bow of his head.

Before Laila could reciprocate the gesture, Akayra was grabbing her hand and dragging her out the front door.

"Head for the woods," she told the elf once they were outside. "Just run. I will try to throw anyone off your trail."

Laila hugged Akayra gratefully, blindsiding the dark elf.

Instead of shoving her off, as was the drow's instinct to do so, she first gave the strange little elf a gentle pat on the back while rolling her eyes. Then, Akayra firmly pushed Laila away, and commanded her, "Get going!" before she turned and headed post-haste toward the city.

As Laila sprinted for the forest, she was overwhelmed with fear and confusion about the drow people. She honestly hadn't known what to expect. It was hard for her to believe that any beings could be so cruel to one another, yet all stories of dark elves indicated they were vile demons that held no empathy nor love. Although that wasn't quite her own experience, she did recognize that they were not at all welcoming, like the elves or dwarves had been. Amongst her confusion and doubts, she was also frantic at the possibility that she might not ever see Nikolean or the others again.

Upon running into the entangled dead brush, Laila tripped and fell to the ground, her foot caught in vines. As she tugged at her leg, she quickly discovered the vines had long thorns, feeling them slash at her leg and ankle between the gaps in her armor. While trying to untangle herself, her emotions began taking over, terrified that Nikolean and her friends were all dead, and she was finding it harder to focus and hold back her tears. Then, from behind her, came a menacing laugh.

Laila looked up to find a dark elf soldier heading toward her, a grin upon his face as he imagined how much fun he was going to have with the elf damsel. Within the blink of an eye, a spray of crimson blood splattered out from the dark elf's neck as a dagger's sharp blade slid across it. The man cupped his hands

- 255 - CHAPTER 20

over his throat, gurgling while he was shoved forward to the ground from behind. Standing in the maniacal drow's place stood the most miraculous sight Laila could have hoped for... Nikolean.

Aghast from how readily Nikolean, like Akayra, killed his own kind to protect her, she found herself even more conflicted about the dark elves. While she was aware of Nikolean's skill with a blade at killing orcs, it stunned her to see him take another drow's life so effortlessly and without remorse in his eyes. Despite that, it didn't change how relieved she was to see him there, nor how her heart raced as he untangled the vines from her leg, his hands gentle and kind on her skin.

As Nikolean stood and reached out to Laila, she smiled lovingly at him while taking his hand and letting him pull her to her feet. When he pressed his lips to hers, she did not resist. She could not understand how someone so gentle and so loving could kill so easily. She assumed that the soldier was not the only dead drow by his hand on his way to her. It seemed to be their way of life there, and she could only hope that in completing her quest, they might find more peace.

Prior to Nikolean and Laila's arrival, Rogg had been relaying to the Drakka all about the prophecy nearly verbatim from Nikolean's telling of it to Lord Brilldessah. Except that when Nikolean spoke the words, they sounded desperate and implausible. In contrast, Rogg's rendition came off as much more optimistic and even exciting, a clear storyteller, with the Drakka on the edge of their seats as they listened.

Rogg paused as they entered, greeting Nikolean and grinning, star-struck at the famous prophesied elf. "Welcome, Omi Méa, to our humble Safehouse!"

With an awkward smile at his exuberance, Laila uncomfortably allowed him to take her hand and kiss the back of it. She was quite surprised to receive such a warm welcome from any of the dark elves.

After stepping aside to usher Laila past him into the dwelling, Rogg turned back to Nikolean and said, "I am so sorry about Lord Brilldessah. I couldn't believe she would strip your father's honor from your family and further insult you by tarnishing your name with 'Süd.'"

Nikolean looked around at the eyes watching them, embarrassed, and replied loud enough for them all to hear, "Lord Brilldessah knows not of what she speaks. She may have the authority to declare such a command, but what she says will never change my father's honor. No one can take from him what he has done for the dark elf people. And her ignorance to what the Drakka stand for will never tarnish my family name."

All the drow in the room either nodded or raised their drink to him in agreement. With that made clear, Nikolean stepped past Rogg and settled at a tall side table while Laila walked past the others.

The Omi Méa espied what appeared to be a kitchen at the back of the dwelling containing a table where Davion had been lain. Upon descrying Glondora casting healing spells over him, Laila's heart stopped for a moment.

"What happened to him?" she asked, quickly making her way to his side, hoping to be of use.

With a frown portraying her grief, Glondora replied, "The lad didna' take it too well when they tried to put his shackles on. Thought he could 'andle them all by 'imself. If me own 'ands weren't shackled already, I woulda' 'elped." Sighing, she shook her head sadly.

"Me boy tryin' ta be a hero," Hort huffed, standing nearby to keep an eye on him.

When Laila placed her hands on Davion's arm, she sensed there wasn't anything more to be done. Glondora had already healed the wounds inflicted on his flesh, and he only needed to wake up. She felt beyond terrible that it had happened to him, worried about what unimaginable pain he must have endured. Even though his wounds were healed, the smell of burnt flesh lingered on his skin.

After a few more minutes, Davion managed to open his eyes, trying to gather his bearings. He was relieved to see Laila there and almost smiled back at her when she gleamed upon finding him awake, but his heart was still torn over seeing her and Nikolean kiss. That was something Glondora would not be able to heal.

The human sat upright, and Hort assisted him to the main room, where everyone was gathered, explaining to him what was going on. He was still a little physically sore, but nothing he couldn't manage. Nevertheless, looking upon their current company, he wondered if they hadn't just jumped out of the dragon's claws and into its jaws.

Laila joined them in the main room, and three Drakka departed a wooden bench for her to take a seat. With a polite smile at them, she obliged.

"Nikolean," Salyaman said, trying not to appear intimidated while surrounded by all the dark elves. "What is the plan now?"

While jabbing the tip of his dagger and twirling it in a wooden slat on the table where he stood, Nikolean sighed, feeling defeated. "I had planned on going to Nordor Hellia to speak with Kull Merzumar, but now I'm not sure."

Rogg, speaking in Onish, confirmed his doubts. "It would be a poor decision and one we might not pull you out of. Kull Merzumar is even more loyal to the elders and fears any challenge to their ways."

"That's what I was afraid of," Nikolean said heavily. Then he sheathed his dagger and strode over to sit beside Laila.

"But if it's an army you're looking for, all is not lost," Rogg grinned assuredly. "The Drakka's numbers have grown plenty since your time, my friend. We have been preparing to take down the empire so that we can rebuild. However, if this prophecy is what is meant to restore our lands, then I see no better purpose for our mission."

With an inkling of hope, Nikolean asked, "Who must I speak with now to gain the Drakka's support?"

"Don't worry about that," Rogg declared. "I would be honored to take care of it for you. I just need the details on what you require from us, and I will make sure it happens. From what I understand, you have quite the journey ahead of you still."

Davion didn't trust their eagerness to assist, and he wasn't the only one. Regardless, being quite outnumbered with heavily armed dark elves in such close quarters, none of them were willing to speak up, except for one.

Standing before them, Salyaman asked warily, "Why would you offer your full support to us so willingly?"

Rogg laughed, amused. "As I'm sure Nikolean is aware, we have been watching him for some time through our scryers."

As he turned his gaze to address Nikolean, Rogg continued, "We keep eyes on all Drakka who left with your same intent. I must say, though, that you have been the most entertaining to keep tabs on." He and several others laughed in merriment.

"Of course," Nikolean said, remembering.

"Since spotting you coming this way, we have been eagerly anticipating your arrival. We just didn't know what it was you would need. Unfortunately, we can only see through the scryer's pond and cannot hear. We did not know the prophecy's words of what was driving you until today."

CHAPTER 20

Nikolean, with a great sense of relief, thanked Rogg and rested his hand on Laila's armored thigh. He began telling the Drakka enthusiastically of their plan to meet at the Trader's Post. From there, they intend to confront the Ancients who refuse to allow peace in Onis.

While the dark elves discussed the plans, Davion heard nothing but a humming noise buzzing in his ears as his eyes fixated on the dark-ashen hand gripping Laila's thigh. He realized there had clearly been a development in their relationship while he had been off getting tortured by the drow. The words of his companions echoed tormentingly in his mind, "*trust Niko.*"

As the heat boiled up within him, unable even to blink away from the sight, Davion stood abruptly and excused himself from the others.

Laila watched after him, concerned, but knew she'd probably just make things worse if she went after him with the way things had been between them. She didn't know how he would react to her relationship with Nikolean, but was certain he wouldn't be happy for them.

When he discovered a darkened room, Davion briskly closed the door and raised his hands before him, wordlessly igniting every sconce and candle with a flaring intensity.

"Stupid, stupid, STUPID!" He clenched his fists, pacing back and forth, cursing himself angrily under his breath, not wanting anyone to overhear. "How could I have been so stupid?!" His eyes glistened as tears welled, threatening to release. "I'm such an idiot!" he fumed, thinking back on everything since he had first seen Laila appear to him in a dream. Memories of every look, of every moment they had ever shared together since, mulled over in his mind as he picked them apart, trying to make sense of it all. *Where did I go wrong? How could I have been so mistaken about her? I thought we had something incredible. I thought we shared an unbreakable bond. I don't know how I could have been so stupid!*

His tears broke free, creeping down his face, which only made him angrier—to be so upset over someone who obviously didn't care for him at all the way he cared for her. How dare she invoke his tears! How dare she ever let him believe that he stood a chance! *She knew how I felt about her! I never hid that. She should have had the decency to tell me she didn't feel the same! I'm such a fool! And a dark elf?! WHY??* He feared it was because of Nikolean's bond to Turathyl; that if it were he that had made the connection, then it would be him holding her in his arms, him kissing her soft lips; him wrapped up in her at night, smelling her, feeling her... *Blastit! Get out of my head!* He hated being constantly encumbered with thoughts of her.

Just then, the door creaked slowly open, and Hort's head peeked through the crack. Davion stopped pacing upon seeing him and wiped his face indignantly with the back of his sleeve.

"Are ye alright, me boy?" he queried, stepping cautiously inside.

Feeling foolish, he nodded unconvincingly.

"I'm sorry I couldna' 'elp ye in the dungeon, me boy. Twas killin' me ta see ye like that. I was terrified ta me bones ye wasna' gunna' make it, and I dunna know what I'd o' done then." Hort stepped closer to him, angry at himself for being so helpless.

Davion shook his head. "I know, Uncle. It's not that. It doesn't matter. I'm fine. Everything's fine." With a painted smile on his face, Davion placed a reassuring hand on his uncle's shoulder. "I just needed a moment to breathe," he said. "I will be out shortly."

Hort paused, trying to determine if the boy was truly alright enough for him to leave, and Davion gave him his most persuasive smile. Reluctantly, Hort decided to let him have his moment to "breathe" and left to rejoin the others.

A little calmer, Davion looked around the room at all the flames burning in their wicks and then stared curiously at his hands, turning them this way and that. It was strange to him, the new skill he was developing, and as he rolled his hands over, a small flame spontaneously formed, hovering in his palm. Davion smiled fanatically as he manipulated the flame over in his hands, feeling the power surging throughout his entire body.

CHAPTER TWENTY-ONE

RUN

*I*t was nearing dusk, the group well aware that it was approaching their scheduled execution time as they followed the Drakka stealthily beyond the city walls. With Rogg in the lead, they guided the companions through Duep Nordor's outskirts until they had managed to evade all the soldiers and reached the edge of the woods.

"I have to part with you here," Rogg told them. "Keep heading east, and I will see what we can do about getting your mounts to you. At least we were able to recover all your weapons and purses."

Nikolean clasped forearms with Rogg and bowed his head. "Thank you, my friend. For Du Noir."

"For Du Noir," he repeated. "Now, go! Run before they find you!"

None of them had to be told twice, and they took off into the dreary forest as fast as their feet could carry them. For the elves and drow, that was not an issue. However, the human and dwarves were having a much tougher time putting any distance between them and the merciless drow city they were happy to be leaving behind.

"Tis these boots!" Hort grumbled as he stumbled along.

Unable to descry anyone following them, the elves forced themselves to accommodate the much slower pace of the others. Regardless, it wasn't very long before Hort was keeled over after breaching into a small clearing, his loose helm falling and rolling around on its brim as he gasped for breath. Everyone halted, peering at the dwarf.

"We can't stop here!" Nikolean snapped. "We need to keep going!"

Before anyone could argue, the ground began to rumble beneath them, and a thundering sound echoed through the trees, the branches trembling.

"What be that?" Glondora asked nervously while offering Hort a water flask.

"They are coming for us," Salyaman answered. "We will have to fight."

With a heavy sigh, Laila wrapped her arms around her torso, dreading what those words meant. It was one thing to her to have to kill savage monsters like the orcs or trolls, but she had no desire to kill the drow. She may not agree with their ways, nor understand how they could be so cruel to one another, but she had also seen how kind they could be... and loving. Nikolean had been right before; starting a war with them would not be the way toward peace.

Listening to the foreboding drumming of the hooves against the hard soil, Laila reached out with her mind, looking for Turathyl, wondering if she could help. However, she sensed that there were already others nearby that they weren't aware of. Closing her eyes, she concentrated harder, trying to detect the source of the life forces. They seemed very peculiar to her.

"Prepare yourselves!" Nikolean shouted to the others as he armed himself, readying for battle.

The rest of the group followed suit, except for Laila, who was frustratingly trying to discover who was watching them from nearby. Then, she discerned a strange force telling her to run. It was similar to that of Merimer, yet quite different at the same time.

"No," Laila said, opening her eyes to the others. "We must run."

"Laila, we won't make it," Davion said with despair in his tone.

"My lady?" Nikolean inquired, wondering what she knew that they didn't.

"RUN!" she yelled, echoing the presence in her mind, and headed deeper into the forest.

They all joined her, even Hort, reclaiming his helmet and pushing through the pain and exhaustion, hobbling after the elf maiden.

Seconds later, a swarm of dark elves atop strapping charcoal-gray steeds came stampeding toward them, bellowing out a terrifying war cry that flooded the encompassing woods. As the horses hurtled towards them, the others stopped running and turned, preparing themselves for combat.

Before the dark elves reached them, a giant tree branch came unexpectedly barreling down across the field where they had just been standing, knocking five soldiers from their horses in one fell swoop. More branches came forward, swatting at the horses and their riders, sending them flying through the air with mighty blows. Everyone gaped in shock as the tree trunks separated into perceived legs, and they stomped thunderously toward the oncoming force, bashing and tossing them all about.

On the outside, the trees did not look much different from any of the gnarled and dying trees surrounding them except for the fact that they were moving and using their branches like mighty arms. Their roots would come entirely out of the soil as they took a step, slithering over the ground like tentacles, then would bury themselves again whenever they would stop for a moment. The great trees plodded heavily from place to place, but their "arms" were swift and fierce, creaking spookily with every swing.

"Lass!" Hort called out, "Yer doin' it! Keep it up!"

As she stared out over the field, Laila was confused and in shock. "I'm not doing anything!" she shouted.

Everyone searched for who was helping them but saw no one.

The dark elves charged at the trees, swinging their swords at them, barely making a dent in their thick bark. As they swatted the tiny creatures away like gnats, the trees were proving to be formidable opponents. But before they could claim victory, a female drow pyromancer started chanting and conjuring flames. When her flame bolt hit one of the trunks, burning and sizzling its bark, the tree let out a shrill screech of pain, and they all realized that it was the trees themselves that were helping them, not another caster.

From camouflaged faces hidden within their bark, the other animated trees let out a nightmarish wail that carried on the wind like ghostly wolves howling in the night.

"They're treants!" Nikolean hollered to the group.

With their new knowledge, the group expeditiously joined in the fight against the dark elves. Laila forcefully flung the fire mage back with her mind, disrupting another cast. Then, Glondora stepped forward and shouted, "*Ferétsa ageeran!*" in combination with her staff, casting her freezing spell on the drow pyromancer. While the heat from the drow's fire element within prevented her from freezing like the sorechons or orcs, it did temporarily freeze her ability to send any more scorching casts against the trees, despite her repeated attempts.

Davion promptly began casting fireballs at the enemy, testing his new abilities with zeal. Nevertheless, everyone was too engrossed with their own perils to realize that not all of his attacks were being verbalized.

Salyaman grabbed his bow and started shooting arrows rapidly toward the targets, helping to keep them at bay.

Meanwhile, Hort ran into battle with his axe held high, charging at the closest drow—a dark cleric, a dark phantom magic class of the drow. As he swung his weapon toward the drow concealed in gray and maroon plate, it blocked his attack with a metal shield and then plunged its mace with great power down upon the dwarf. Hort was quick to block the attack, but stumbled backward, allowing the cleric to utter a quick incantation in a bodeful and sinister voice. The plated drow raised its mace to the sky, and a surge of unholy black and red lightning shot down to smite the dwarf. Without a moment's pause, Hort raised his shield above his head and blocked the lightning strike with success, but the jolt of it split off a third of the wooden shield and knocked the dwarf to the ground.

With the dark cleric standing over him, Hort hastily scrambled back to his feet, then thrust his broken shield upward into its chin. As he swung his axe again, he managed to strike the drow, denting its chest plate. But the cleric didn't seem phased. Instead, it swung back at him, thunking its mace down against his broken shield.

"*Ferosta lacarté!*" Glondora cast from behind her husband, sending bolts of ice at the cleric. Unfortunately, they were no match for its armor, and shattered on impact.

While the dark cleric mumbled another enchantment of its own, its weapon began emitting a shadowy stream that spiraled through the air toward the dwarf. Glondora screamed for her husband to run, but he refused to retreat, wafting ineffectually with his axe and broken shield at the stream encompassing him like a black cloud. The hydromancer then cast her freeze spell at the cleric to halt its assaults, but it fizzled against an anti-magic ward that was protecting it, and she cursed in frustration.

Alarming the entire battlefield, one of the treants suddenly stomped, stretching out its branches as it loomed forward and roared a ferocious sound at the cloud attacking Hort. The treant's deep spine-chilling voice resonated through the forest as everyone froze in place and stared with dread. The mist attacking Hort dissipated with the treant's scream, then the dwarf startled as roots abruptly sprung out of the ground before him. They looked like snakes coming out of the soil as they wrapped themselves swiftly around the dark cleric, clutching it tighter and tighter in its coils, strangling the drow while crushing in its plate. In seconds, the cleric went limp, and the roots flung the metaled corpse at the other dark elves, knocking several to the ground. The brutal roots then withdrew back into the dirt. Hort watched the cracking of the ground as they recessed under the soil, discovering they had extended from the base of the treant that had roared at the dark cloud.

Upon seeing their fellow soldiers being tossed and defeated facilely by the treants and escapees, the dark elves realized they were losing. The drow simply did not know how to defeat such a foe as the mystical treants, and a horn blared, calling their retreat.

As their attackers bolted off after their horses, the comrades cheered and shouted after them victoriously. Laila observed while they gathered back together, ecstatic that none of her friends had been hurt. She was also pleased that there really hadn't been any casualties aside from the dark cleric. Her heart ached to see the civilizations at war with one another, especially amongst their own kind, as witnessed of the dark elves.

When all was safe, the assailing drow out of sight, the treants slowly stomped over to the group, halting and lingering before Laila. No longer roaming across the ground, their trunks were once again undivided, their roots returned deep into the soil, and they stood there serenely, as though they had never moved at all.

Salyaman studied them cautiously and told his companions, "We have treants in the Emerald Forest as well, but it was my understanding that they are aggressive to everyone and only show themselves when the forest is threatened."

"It is usually the same in Du Noir," Nikolean pointed out. "But I had thought them all dead with the forest."

Laila stepped forward toward the closest one and placed her hand on its bark with a gentle touch. "They very nearly are," she said, forlorn, feeling its pain.

Just then, they heard more horses approaching and turned quickly to find Rogg and another drow from the Safehouse leading Orbek, Helna, Midnight, and Friet. Everyone was relieved and excited to see they had survived and welcomed their mounts. Unfortunately, Glondora's old cart was nowhere in sight, along with most of their supplies and victuals.

Rogg leapt down off Midnight, handing him over to Nikolean, and clasped his forearm. "Isn't it incredible?" he said, gesturing to the treants. "They have helped the Drakka in the past, but no one knows why."

"We should get going," Nikolean announced, mounting up.

"I can't," Laila said.

"You can ride with me," he told her.

"No..." she looked mournfully back at the treants. "Why did you help us?"

"Um... Lady Laila..." Rogg said, eying her. "They can't talk."

The tree before her creaked and swayed a little, and she saw what appeared to be eyes come into focus within the bark. There was a piece of knotted wood resembling a nose and a parting in the surface that grew wider as it opened its mouth. The forest rumbled around them with the intensity of its voice as it spoke in the language of the Ancients. "Omi Méa mow nied Onis."

"Whoa!" Rogg exclaimed. "I had no idea! Does anyone know what it said?"

Laila nodded, and Salyaman translated, "Great Spirit must heal Onis."

"What about the Drakka? Why have you helped us?" Rogg asked.

While letting out a haunting moan, the tree twisted to look upon Rogg as it replied while Salyaman continued to translate, "It they turn to help Great Spirit. Must heal Onis before too late. We die more every day."

"So, they know the Drakka are trying to find a way to heal the land," Rogg said in speculation. "I just hope we can do it before they're all gone. There aren't many of them left that I'm aware of. I must admit that it has been nice to count them as allies of the Drakka during our plight."

"I can't leave them like this," Laila said agonizingly, sensing that the deathly plague from the land had been slowly infecting the treants over time.

Knowing Laila as they did, none of them were surprised, nor when she placed both her hands on the treant and began to send her thoughts into its bark, wrapping her mind around its spiritual essence. While she connected with it, the ground trembled beneath their feet, and the others watched as it spread its roots out towards the treants on either side, intertwining with them, who in turn did the same until they were all connected.

"There's too many of them for her to heal," Davion said. "It'll drain her."

"You're right," Nikolean agreed, alighting quickly from Midnight and heading toward Laila.

As the elf connected with the treant, she sent her energy forth, and it flowed through the mystical being's branches, out into each of the treants in the union. She could feel them gradually growing stronger, their life source ever-so-slightly more vibrant. However, Davion was right, and it was draining her much too fast with them all together.

She was startled when she felt a warm hand grab hold of her shoulder. Bracing herself to resist whoever-it-was trying to stop her, she was bemused when they remained still. As an unexpected surge of energy poured into her from the touch, she understood what they were doing.

Worrying about who was sacrificing themself to help her, Laila was surprised when a second hand was then placed on her opposite shoulder by another. With new life energy coursing through her, she continued healing the treants. Then she felt a third hand, and a fourth, and a fifth, and even a sixth and seventh as the two Drakka joined her as well. Her hands glowed brightly with the spirit energy as she continued to press forward.

As she felt her comrades' hands begin to shake, Laila broke the connection to the treant. She immediately shoved at the others with her mind just enough to break their link to her so she would not continue to drain them for herself.

When Laila looked up at the massive tree, she smiled contentedly at the sight. The gnarled black treants were no more, but instead, their bark appeared a healthy deep gray. Even though no leaves adorned their branches, Laila spotted several silver buds starting to form. She wondered what those enchanting trees must have looked like in their prime, assuming the rest of the forest would have appeared the same. She could sense the warmth and gratitude emanating from the treants, and the one before her leaned forward, looking fondly on the tiny elf with its magical visage.

"We thank the Great Spirit," the treant boomed. "Hurry now, or all will be lost."

Then, without another word, the treants turned creakily and began trodding away. Nikolean placed his arm over Laila's shoulder and rested his head against the top of hers, joining her weakly as they watched the monstrous trees disperse back into the mysterious woods.

"Thank you," she said to the others while she watched the treants leave. "I couldn't have done that without you." Sighing, Laila added, "It isn't much, but it will hopefully give them a chance of survival until I can heal this land by completing the prophecy."

Inwardly, she was unnerved and shaken from the treant's warning. She knew what it meant and what they needed to do next. It was time to see the Red Dragons.

CHAPTER TWENTY-TWO

HEAT

*J*oined by Merimer and Turathyl on the outskirts of the Du Noir Forest, the group decided to make camp for the night. They rightly believed it rather unlikely that the dark elves would attack them with a dragon at their sides.

When everyone was settled, Laila mentally prepared herself for another confrontation with her friends, formulating in her mind a compelling argument to tell them it was time to go see Ignisar. It couldn't have been a coincidence that both Nikolean's father and the treants were sending her warnings of the same nature as the mighty Red Dragon.

With everyone gathered at or near the fire, Laila took in a deep breath, letting it out slowly, then said in a loud and clear voice, "I realize you're not going to want to hear this..." She paused, making sure she had all of their attention. "...but I need to go before the Reds now. I understand your reluctance to come with me, but I *need* to do this."

Without hesitation, Salyaman said, "We will go."

"Aye, m'lady," Glondora chimed in. "Ye can count on us."

Dumbstruck, Laila couldn't believe her ears and was skeptical that it was going much too easily. She was even more shocked when Hort halted his repair work on his shield and added gruffly, "Aye, lass. Ye can count on me as well."

Nikolean simply smiled at her, giving her a slight nod, as if there was any doubt about what he would do. Meanwhile, Davion poked at the fire with a stick in silence, not taking his eyes away from the flames.

"I don't understand," Laila said. "What has changed?"

With a smirk, Salyaman said wryly, "I suppose you could say that we had some time to discuss it while we were... hanging around."

Laila smiled, trying not to laugh at his ill-humored comment, surprised by him again.

"Yeah, well..." Davion said, throwing his stick into the flames, watching it crackle and sputter. "I apparently missed that conversation."

Laila frowned at Davion, her heart aching for what he must have endured at the hands of the dark arcanist. "I'm so sorry, Davion," she told him sincerely.

Glaring up at Laila, Davion clenched his teeth as he tried to ignore the dark elf hovering over her shoulder. He pushed himself up to his feet, then looked at Hort. "I thought you believed it to be madness, Uncle. What do we really hope to accomplish from going before a dragon clan that we know will kill us on sight even more readily than the Silvers? I understand wanting the dragons' support behind us in addition to the two-legged nations, but why not start with the Golds or even the Blues? They have not been as vengeful over the last few centuries. Did we learn nothing from the Silvers' Mountain?!"

Nikolean retorted, "We need to stand united if we are to succeed."

The drow's words only served to anger Davion further. They reminded him of Pynar, the "united" city, and Nikolean's connection with Turathyl, convinced that was how the scum had won Laila over. The fire in the pit flared higher and hotter for a moment, causing Laila to step back, alarmed from the heat. The pyromancer took a deep breath, trying to calm himself before he lost control of it, and the pit's fire settled.

"Me boy," Hort said, calling his attention, afraid for him. "I dunna' want this either, but we vowed ta put our faith in the elfie and see this through. By some miracle o' Kyrash, we've yet ta die, and if the laiden tis tellin' us the Syraho tis where she must be, then tis our duty ta protect 'er the best we can."

"Hort is right," Salyaman added. "We must trust in her and pray to the gods that they will be in our favor."

"Are we at least taking the Silvers we already have with us?" Davion asked.

'Aeris's attacks have increased against Lochlann since we departed,' Turathyl told them while Nikolean relayed to the group. 'It is your decision, Omi Méa. I can have them start heading to meet us there if that is what you desire.'

"No, Tury," Laila replied for them all to hear. "I will not leave Lochlann defenseless, being so close to Aeris. Ignisar has given me no reason to suspect he will harm us, and we have Tury to help with any of his scouts. We will confront the Reds ourselves."

Davion stormed off toward Helna, pretending to need something from her pack, and Hort started to go after him.

"Let 'im be, husband," Glondora said, touching his arm.

However, Laila couldn't let him be. She saw the pain he was in and the hatred in his eyes when he looked upon her now. Despite what was going on with her and Nikolean, she accepted

CHAPTER 22

that she and Davion were bonded somehow, and she knew she could not leave him behind.

Approaching Davion cautiously, Laila's body tensed while she cleared her throat to speak, getting his attention, and he turned to face her.

"Are you alright?" she asked timidly.

He chuckled at the absurdity of her question and replied sarcastically, "Sure. Never better."

"I'm sorry for what the dark elves did to you. I wish I had been there to stop them," Laila said, longing to know how to comfort him.

Davion fiddled with Helna's straps, trying to stay calm. "Yeah, well, you weren't." Stopping to look at her, he added coldly, "Instead, you were with *him*..."

He glowered over her shoulder at Nikolean, animosity bleeding from his eyes, and he tried hard to push back the burning that was boiling up inside him. Then he looked back at her, surprised to find a tear in her eye. *What the baccat does she care?* he wondered.

"Davion..." she whispered, nearly inaudible.

Laila looked down at her hands deplorably, wrenching them together. She was aware that there were no words that would change how hurt he was feeling. A large part of her wished to just hold him comfortingly, but feared that would only give the wrong impression or cause him further pain.

As he stood there, waiting for her to continue her thought, Davion felt the fire easing within upon witnessing the tear trickle down, glistening against her smooth, tawny cheek. With a heavy sigh, he gave Helna a gentle pat, then stepped toward the elf maiden.

"I will go," he declared sternly, and she looked up into his eyes, appeased. "I told you before that I would be there for you, no matter what. My promise to protect you and be with you through this remains unchanged."

"Thank you, Davion," Laila told him solemnly.

In an attempt to alter the mood, Davion added, "But if your little plan gets me killed, just know that I'm going to come back and haunt you for eternity over it."

Laila smirked at his jest and asked, "Promise?"

Painfully smiling back at her, swallowing his fire, he replied, "Promise."

There was no breeze to cool your skin, and the heatwaves in the desert blurred the vision as the group trekked southeast through the scorching Syraho Desert. Three days in, and all that was visible was an endless vastness of flat dried and cracked ground, light tan in color. Glondora was becoming weaker and having difficulty keeping up with her water summoning to quench their thirsts.

It was beyond comprehension how that stretch of land remained so hot even in the midst of an Onis winter. The general theory was that it remained hot simply because of the Reds and their fire spirit. Many of the group took turns hiding in the shade of Turathyl's wings while the others remained on high alert, keeping watch to the skies for any sign of the Reds. The torridity was even too much for Turathyl to bear at times, and she would frequently leave to fly into the cooler winds up above them to "scout."

It would be correct to assume that, at some point, every one of them doubted their decision to follow Laila into what seemed like a torturous walk towards their impending deaths. On the other hand, it also surprised them that they weren't snatched up by a Red the moment their feet had touched into the mighty dragons' territory—as all the stories had suggested. Turathyl had warned Laila that it would be best to wait until they were closer to the lair before she reaches out to the Fire Dragons. In truth, they would not be overly thrilled with her being there either, as the Reds were quite territorial even with the other dragon clans. Knowing that Ignisar had appeared as a vision to Laila, she hoped that if they were closer when discovered, they might have more of a chance convincing any scouts to let them speak with the mighty monarch.

While they all led their mounts at a steady walk, Davion worried that Helna would not survive much longer in the heat. Orbek didn't seem to be managing very well either under the two dwarves. Sadly, it was Midnight, with his dark coat soaking up the heat of the sun, who was the first to squeal as he reared, tucking his head to his chest, before falling to the ground. Nikolean rolled out of the way, then strolled back to look upon his horse while dusting himself off.

Glondora jumped down off Orbek and hurried to Midnight's aid, trying her best to cool him off, but she was having trouble in such dry, harsh conditions.

"We need to rest," Salyaman declared, dismounting as well. "I fear if we do not find the Reds soon, we will not make it much farther before we all perish."

While Glondora tended to the horse, everyone dismounted and huddled in the shade of the dragon, attempting their best to cool off as well during their break. Rogg had sent them off with some provisions, but they had nearly exhausted them already.

Observing her friends, Laila saw how despondent they seemed; tired, hot, and burnt from the sun. She sighed, wishing she had answers for them or even an idea of how to give them some hope, but she wasn't sure she had any for herself.

'Do not lose faith, Laila,' Turathyl told her, sensing her doubts. Then, speaking to Nikolean as well, she added encouragingly, 'We are getting close and should see them soon. They know we are here. I have been hearing them for some time already, but I do not know why they have yet to approach.'

Laila nodded at Turathyl, while Nikolean patted the dragon's neck.

'You know, dragon,' the drow said to her, 'if you had just flown us there, we would have been at the Reds ages ago.'

The great dragon cocked her head sideways, staring at Nikolean unamused. 'Never going to happen, drow,' she sneered.

Nikolean shrugged at her and chuckled before heading back over to Laila.

Now that Nikolean and Turathyl were in proximity again, they were able to mind-speak with ease. Unfortunately, even though the dragon always sensed him during her flights, they would encounter great difficulty hearing one another, their ability to communicate diminishing as the distance between them increased. He had been disheartened to discover that they would need to keep close for it to work, unlike Turathyl and Laila, who were able to communicate over greater distances, as dragons could.

"Well, my lady, it seems we will be facing another dragon clan soon," he said, concerned about how she was faring.

Laila nodded without a word.

"Are you prepared?" he asked.

She nodded again, simply to satisfy his query. Even so, she remembered the last time he had asked her that just before they reached the Silvers' Mountain, a foreboding feeling sweeping over her. She could still picture the mighty Red Dragon asking her those exact words in her dream. Even after all that she had been through, she still wasn't sure what that meant.

CHAPTER 22

While crossing her arms in front of her, she looked out sullenly over the group while they went about their business, trying to keep cool. Nikolean wrapped his arm around her comfortingly.

"Midnight seems to be faring better already, thanks to Glondora," he mentioned.

Although grateful that Midnight was improving, Laila was growing more frustrated with the dying land and how it was limiting her powers. Even though she could use the water spirit now to help mend bones and flesh, she couldn't seem to replenish with it, like Glondora, without having to steal energy from herself or others. It had been nagging at her, wondering how she was supposed to heal all the death and disease over the land when it took so much out of her—and her friends—just to heal a handful of treants. She had even tried calling upon a storm to wet their lips, but in the intense heat, it evaporated before reaching the ground. She was feeling powerless as their alleged "savior."

Davion had been the most unphased by the desert heat. He hadn't gloated about it, though, hadn't even indicated to the others that he was doing quite fine. Mostly, he just kept quietly to himself, trying desperately to keep his eyes on the skies instead of on the elf maiden and the dark elf, who were not always discreet about their affections with one another now. His feelings hadn't changed for her, and he doubted they ever would. He still could not bring himself to hate or even dislike her a little, which would have at least made it slightly more bearable. It was apparent to all that she had made her choice, and he feared there was nothing more to be done about it. After all, how could he possibly compete with someone who could also commune with her dragon?

Exhausted from the sweltering atmosphere over the last three days, it wasn't long before Laila dozed off, curled up on the ground near Merimer under Turathyl's shade. Knowing how much she would need her strength, the rest of the party did their best not to disturb her as they ate their rations. Davion sat watching over her while he consumed the last of his dried meat and water. The drow was keeping guard, watching the skies with Turathyl.

Gazing dolefully at Laila while she napped in the late morning heat, Davion was pondering if she was really lost to him forever when an annoying buzzing noise started tickling in his ear, causing him to swat at it. Quiet again for a moment, he started to relax, but then it returned. Except now, it was more like a scratching sound. He wiggled his finger frustratedly in his ear, trying to make it stop. Regrettably, that seemed to have the opposite effect, and instead, he was now hearing what sounded more like whispers all around him, although completely incoherent.

In a panic, Davion jerked his head all around, terrified that the drow had found them, recalling their dark magic classes and the spirits they could summon. Unable to see anything, Davion jumped to his feet, swatting around at the whispering voices.

"What be the problem, me boy?" Hort asked, concernedly watching him battling the air.

But Davion didn't know what was wrong, and that *was* the problem. When his efforts failed, he couldn't take it anymore and was getting angry. As he waved his hands around aggressively, as though under attack from a cluster of bees, flames unanticipatedly ignited in his palms. Startled, he instantly closed his fists, and the fires vanished as quickly as they had appeared.

"What is going on?" Salyaman demanded, approaching.

Before he could respond, Nikolean asked suspiciously, "Where did that fire come from? I didn't see you cast a spell."

While feeling a little like he had been losing his mind, Davion peered around at the others. "I... I thought I heard something," he replied, embarrassed.

"What did ye 'ear?" Glondora asked curiously while also trying to deflect from Nikolean's question. Knowing he could create fire without incantations now, she and Hort still weren't sure themselves what to make of it but had been keeping his secret without a word of discussion.

"I... I'm not sure," Davion stuttered honestly. "It's probably just the heat getting to me," he lied, knowing full well that the heat wasn't affecting him like the others.

"Hmmm..." Hort muttered. "Tis getting' ta us all, me boy."

Glondora brought him some more water, which he drank, pretending to be parched.

Not being naïve, Nikolean knew he was avoiding answering his question about the flames, but decided it may not be the right time or place for an inquisition.

"Tis alright, lad," Glondora said, sitting down with Davion, maternally resting her hand on his arm. "I'll sit wit' ye fer a bit."

With closed eyes, Davion rubbed his temples, attempting to put everything from his mind. He was grateful for Glondora and Hort's deflection from Nikolean's comment. Nevertheless, he knew that wouldn't be the last he would be hearing of it and would need to explain himself soon. As he sat there quietly, trying not to draw any more attention, the whispers returned again, getting louder within his mind.

"We appear to have company," Salyaman said, unalarmed, distracting Davion from his turmoil.

Everyone followed the high elf's gaze and saw a reptilian creature, roughly the size of a small dog, standing on two hind legs about fifty paces from them. It had a lengthy tail for its size that waved back and forth as it swayed, staring with its head tilting jerkily while it examined them. Its body was striped with gray and the same tan as the desert rock and had two short arms held before it with little claws curling over. Beady eyes blinked rapidly at the base of a long, pointed snout.

"Aww. Tis kinda cute," Glondora said, taking a step toward it.

"Looks like dinner ta me," Hort said, grabbing his axe.

The creature took a few steps toward them, seemingly curious, and Turathyl turned to see what was going on.

'Wake Laila,' she told Nikolean, getting to her feet. 'This is not a friend.'

Obliging, Nikolean went to wake the young elf maiden but thought it amusing that the dragon seemed worried about the little tike.

"Sal, maybe ye can reach it wit' yer arrow from 'ere." Hort proposed, picturing it over a spit.

Laila joined the others, still groggy, and looked out at the creature. Reluctantly, Salyaman slowly drew his bow and arrow, not making any sudden movements as it watched them. Then it made a cute high-pitched rolling noise in the back of its throat as though it were trying to say "hello."

In another instant, they saw the head of a second one peek out of the ground near the creature, which then jumped out of an unseen hole. The first critter took another step toward them, then another jumped out of the hole, and those two joined it. Within a matter of seconds, there were now five, no nine, no... fifteen... of the creatures, and even more continuing to jump out from multiple holes nearby. Blinking their beady eyes, they slowly advanced toward the group.

"Hmmm... Tis not lookin' so cute now," Hort said mockingly to Glondora.

"Ma Kyrash!" Davion cursed, grabbing his staff.

R.E. DAVIES

'*They are terrocs,*' Turathyl told them, alarmed. '*Meaner than they look.*'

"Prepare yourselves!" Nikolean warned, grabbing his sword from his back. "They're terrocs! Not friends!"

As soon as Nikolean called out their name, the little creatures bared their razor-sharp teeth at them, hissing viciously, while nearly fifty terrocs darted towards the group. Salyaman started shooting arrows at the charging critters while Davion began casting fire spells, and Glondora cast her protections.

Turathyl let out a threatening roar, but the little vermin didn't stop. Instead, they leapt from the ground and attacked the dragon, latching themselves on to her hide. The great dragon yowled as they dug their claws and teeth through her scales, piercing the flesh beneath while more of the varmints headed for the group.

Laila gaped in shock at how quickly they reached them and grabbed for her Dragonsbane spear, stabbing one and whipping the terroc at another as it leapt for her head. Hort swung his axe repeatedly at them, but they were too agile, gnashing their tiny teeth at him before he could get them off. As Nikolean moved with haste and vigor, he felt his power surging through him as never before, reaching a new momentum he didn't know he possessed. Even still, he found the creatures to be too fast to evade so many at once, slashing and hacking at them frantically.

Meanwhile, there were still more hopping out of camouflaged holes in the terrain. The dragon stomped at them and caught a few of the pests in her jaws, but they were darting around too rapidly for her to be effective, continuing their attacks on the ancient being.

To Laila's dismay, she saw several heading for the mounts but was too caught up fighting off the ones encircling her. She didn't know what to do or how to attack so many of them without hurting her friends in the process. They had swarmed the group like a plague of locusts.

When she heard Merimer squeal, Laila looked to find her unicorn hybrid protecting the other mounts, using her forcefield to knock the beasts back and gallant white horns to toss away those that broke through.

'I don't know what to do!' Laila cried to Turathyl, feeling helpless as she slashed and stabbed at the attackers that kept grazing her with their claws and snapping at her.

Then, as though a horde of terrocs weren't enough, loud dragon roars pierced the sky, shaking the ground beneath. In horror, the group looked up to discover five monstrous dragon silhouettes heading straight for them, the sun at their backs. Trembling and overwhelmed, they were all terrified, convinced it was to be their end; the Reds had just been waiting for the opportunity to attack them when they were vulnerable and wouldn't stand a chance.

CHAPTER 22

CHAPTER

TWENTY-THREE

FIRE

*W*ith their shrieking war cries, the dragons dove toward the companions as they struggled against the fiendish terrocs, and Laila caught sight of the fire in their mighty jaws, ready to unleash their attack. Encumbered with vicious pests, she tried to reach out and tell the dragons to stop, tell them they were there in peace, but she wasn't able to reach them. All she managed was, *'Tury! Help!'*

Turathyl beat her wings, trying to shake off the terrocs to no avail, and roared aggressively at the incoming dragon quintet. Not threatened by the Silver, fire came blaring out of their mouths towards them. The cacophony from the noise of screams, hollers, and shrieking terrocs was deafening as they braced for the burn, and the fire struck down over the crowd.

Her heart in her throat, Laila gasped as she surveyed the group, stunned to descry that her friends remained unharmed from the flames. None of the attacks had struck them, and she heaved a sigh of relief. Only the terrocs had been scorched and set ablaze.

To give herself some space, Laila sent out a telekinetic blast around her, casting four terrocs off of her and propelling them away. In following the dragons' lead, she emitted a wave of fire, engulfing over a dozen terrocs in a sea of flames.

More fire came blazing down from the sky, and more of the terrocs were engulfed in flames, screeching as their flesh burned away to a black crisp. Davion had been using a combination of casting and his new abilities to defend himself, also finding that fire was the best offense against the critters.

As the Reds swooped back around and sent more streams of fire at the ground, the surviving terrocs fleeted skittishly away, disappearing back into their little holes. Everyone finished slaying the ones nearest them by any means possible before they could escape.

Freed from the terrocs, Laila ran protectively before her group to face the Reds whilst they descended. The monumental Fire Dragons landed heavily before them, quaking the ground as their masses touched down.

Praying to Jayenne to make a better first impression than with the Silvers, she mind-sent to them as they eased against the firm terrain, 'Thank you, mighty Red Dragons!'

Seeing a Red for the first time in the sunlight was awe-inspiring. The rays gleamed over their ruby-red scales, causing them to sparkle brilliantly, like glistening gems. The dragons were poised regally in their colossal forms, displaying dark-maroon underbellies. Their muscles rippled with each movement, and the rise and fall of their chests calmed as the fires quelled in their monstrous jaws. They had similar quills as the Silvers from the tops of their scalps, down along their backs to their tails, which were spiked with a mass of the sharp quills.

CHAPTER 23

However, only one of the five possessed nearly as many quills as Turathyl, creating the assumption that he was almost as ancient as she. To Laila's surprise, the Reds were even larger than Turathyl, with only one fairly young Red slightly smaller than her.

The rest of the group kept their weapons ready, unsure of what was happening, and prepared to fight. With steps like thunder, the Reds tramped across the desert rock to stand close before them, unwavering. The lead dragon then lowered his head near Laila while the other four started gobbling up several of the cooked terrocs surrounding them, swallowing them whole. The comrades were encouraged to see them indulging in the terrocs instead of them; although Hort was also fretting that they wouldn't leave any for him as he eyed the *greedy dragons*.

Laila held her ground, standing firm, as she stared back at the dragon looming over her. She could feel his judging eyes, and her heart raced as her mind flashed back to her last confrontation with unfamiliar dragons. The eldest Red sniffed at her with curiosity while she stood utterly still. Its foul breath wafted briefly over her face before it gallantly raised its head back high. Glancing over the rest of the group, it then stared back upon the little elf.

Laila said both mentally and aloud in the Ancient tongue, "I am Lady Lailalanthelus Dula'Quoy, the Great Spirit of prophecy! We are here to speak with the Mighty Ignisar!"

With a majestic nod to her, the Red boomed in a deep, resonant mind-voice, *'We are aware.'*

Davion fell to his knees, screaming in agony as he grasped his head in pain, and everyone turned to look.

"Davion!" Glondora yelled in panic and ran to him, worried the terrocs had done serious damage.

Unphased by the distraction, the Red turned his attention back to the elf before him and tucked in his wings, displaying a non-threatening stance.

'*My apologies,*' the Red said in a softer tone. '*We shall use our hatchling mind-touch. I was not aware the frail human could hear us as well.*'

Gasping, Laila turned her head to Davion, who was staring with eyes wide and mouth agape at the Reds. "He... can't.... Davion??"

As he staggered to his feet with Glondora's assistance, a drop of blood seeping from his ear, Davion told her, "It's alright. I'm alright." Then he walked humbly toward the dragons, shaken to his core, rattled and bewildered.

While everyone watched on perplexed, they tried to discern what was happening but were too leery of speaking in the presence of the new dragons, still not convinced they weren't all about to die.

"This is incredible!" Laila elatedly exclaimed as Davion reached them. "You can hear them?!"

Davion gave a slow nod, still in shock, trying to understand what it meant.

"He can hear them!" Laila shouted ecstatically to the others.

'*I am Gothäzer of the Reds, son of Ignisar,*' he told Davion and Laila.

Laila bowed her head before the dragon, honored to have one of Ignisar's descendants come to meet with them.

"I am Davion Collins," he said aloud, quivering, having no idea how to mind-speak, "Pyromancer of Lochlann."

'*Yes, of course,*' Gothäzer replied. '*Although, you appear tall for a dwarf.*'

The dragon grinned at Davion, and it suddenly dawned on Laila—on all of them—why only Nikolean could hear Turathyl

CHAPTER 23

since the Ruins of Pynar and why, now, only Davion could hear Gothäzer; it was determined based on their elemental power. As she realized the implication for Salyaman and Glondora as well, Laila tried hard not to jump up and down with excitement and composed herself before the dragons.

'We must take you to see Ignisar without delay.'

The Red Dragons immediately advanced towards them, causing alarm to spread among the group.

"Laila!" Glondora called out, frightened.

"It's alright, they're taking us to Ignisar!" she called back, praying that it truly *was* going to be alright.

Although surprised it was going so well, Turathyl remained skeptical about their intentions, believing Ignisar of wanting the pleasure of killing Laila for himself.

Gothäzer quickly grabbed Davion and Laila in his clutches. At the same time, the other four dragon companions snatched up their friends, including the mounts. Turathyl protectively grabbed hold of Nikolean, but when she reached to grab hold of Merimer, the hybrid darted away and would not be captured. The Silver plunged into the air with the drow away from the other dragons, leaving Merimer behind.

"No!" Laila screamed as the mighty Red took her up into the sky, stretching out her hand toward her beautiful Merimer below. The hybrid watched with intent as her elf maiden was lifted away from her. While the dragons beat their gigantic wings, lifting off into the air, Merimer reared, neighing loudly as they soared out of sight. Laila's heart sank, watching as her precious companion disappeared.

Despite her dismay and concern for Merimer, Laila couldn't help but be enthralled as she gazed out over the terrain, ascending higher and higher into the sky. She was overwhelmed with emotion, getting to witness first-hand what it was like to see from a dragon's perspective. Even still, she wished they had gone farther and seen more than the expansive desert.

The others were not as thrilled as Laila. Although it was not their first time flying through the sky encaged within dragon talons, it was even more nerve-racking that time on the basis of their destination. Hort kept his eyes closed for the entire trip, muttering every curse in his vocabulary while Glondora screamed most of the way. Nikolean was the only one who felt truly safe in the clutches of Turathyl, united and reassured by her that she would not let the Reds harm him.

Davion was still in shock over what was going on. While hearing the whispers in his mind, he looked at them in a whole new light, trying to concentrate on seeing if he could decipher what they were saying. Alas, they were still just whispers to him, unlike when Gothäzer addressed them directly.

Salyaman used his acute ranger sight to take advantage of surveying the land, but he was still unnerved by the thought of what might befall them once they reached the Reds' lair.

What would have taken them another day of traveling was over in just a few short—albeit terrifying—minutes. They all gaped as the dragons' lair came into view, smoke rising in steady billows throughout. It was much more expansive than any of them had imagined, with mounds of hard molten rock, and lava coursing through the cracks in the soil.

Off to the side loomed the entrance of an ominous cave with an open mouth not unlike that of a giant dragon's, stalactites hanging like sharp teeth past the lip. Its opening was massive enough to allow the mighty dragons passage into its depths, with smoke wafting out from the shadows. Fire randomly spurted from geysers nearby the cave, mimicking the Fire Dragons' spine-chilling attacks.

As eerie as the den was, what brought most of the terror to the companions was seeing the dozens of dragons watching them, their heads all raised in observance, as they descended right into the middle of the cluster.

Laila was immediately overcome with panic as she tried to process all the dragons' voices buzzing about her head, remembering the last time she had been in such a position. The dragons surrounded them, instilled with curiosity, and their wings were assertively spread as they loomed over the group. Even Turathyl was feeling intimidated by the beasts as the dragons released all their captives from their grasps.

Laila searched the masses of dragons, trying to spot the Mighty Ignisar, but was unable to. However, she suddenly discerned a familiar sound that had her heart stop with elation, and she whipped around to look. Her exquisite mystical unicorn-elkah was on the outskirts of the den, standing proudly on her back legs, kicking her forefeet in the air toward her as she neighed proudly.

'I can't believe it,' Turathyl gaped.

Laila had no words; she simply grinned from ear to ear in amazement.

'Heal your wounded,' Gothäzer instructed.

Caught up in the moments since the Reds first greeted them, Laila had forgotten all about the wounds she'd endured from the terrocs, which had gratefully been lessened by the dwarf's wards, and went with haste to inspect her friends. Noticing the blood dripping from their exposed flesh, she sighed upon seeing the damage but was relieved it was at least damage she had the ability to assist with. Glondora and Salyaman joined her while they mended everyone, nervous beyond measure of their audience. There was a lot of pressure trying to concentrate on healing, with so many fierce onyx eyes studiously watching their every move.

When her comrades had been healed, Laila and Glondora started tending to the mounts, which they were having trouble keeping steady as several of the Reds licked their chops, trying hard to resist the temptation of some nice fresh meat.

A loud cawing radiated from above, and everyone looked to see more dragons approaching, raining several small objects from the sky. While the dragons below eagerly snapped at the charred objects before they reached the ground, the group realized it was more of the terrocs from earlier.

To Hort's pleasure, one of the young dragons approached them passively, dropping a crispy terroc at Laila's feet. She gave a grateful bow to the dragon, sending her thanks, and Hort went without hesitation to grab the terroc carcass. After hacking it apart to split between the group, the dwarf was the only one who was able to stomach partaking in the cooked meat while in the presence of such terrifying hosts.

"Lady Laila," Salyaman said, approaching her, "I do not understand why they have not tried to attack us. Are you sure we are safe?"

As she scanned the surrounding dragons, which were all staring intently at them, she couldn't say for sure and replied, "I hope so."

Not all the beasts were pleased with them being there, harboring hostility of their presence. There was only one thing that kept them from slaughtering the two-leggeds on sight and taking pleasure in the crunching of their bones between their teeth; the fear of Ignisar's wrath. Laila shuddered at the thoughts and desires emitted by the aggrieved Reds. Contrarily, several others seemed to be curious or even excited about their arrival. It was hard to know for sure which direction their visit was going to go. She could only hope and pray that speaking with Ignisar would go in their favor. Her heart pounded nervously, aware that there would be little chance of escape that time, with no mountains to fall off and no safe space between her friends and the potential enemy dragons.

Nikolean walked warily to Laila, unsure how to act surrounded by so many of the ancient beasts. He hoped to offer her any comfort possible, given their situation. Gothäzer approached the group with a firm stride and loomed over them intimidatingly. As he glared down upon the tiny beings, he stood poised, supremely holding his head high, and addressed Laila and Davion.

'It is time,' the mighty Red declared and looked toward the cave entrance. 'He awaits you within.'

CHAPTER TWENTY-FOUR

IGNISAR'S LAIR

*S*omehow, Gothäzer's announcement that Ignisar was ready to see her suddenly made Laila's chest and legs seem very heavy. Her body felt closer to the ground as she was filled with terror at the realization that she was about to face another monarch dragon. She wanted so much to believe that he was going to be the same dragon from her dreams, the one that has guided her throughout her journey. That being said, her dream dragon also had attacked her on multiple occasions...

As she shook her head with trepidation, Laila looked desperately over at Nikolean. "He wants Davion and I to go inside."

"I am coming with you, my lady," Nikolean said matter-of-factly.

"We all are," Salyaman added.

Tearing off a piece of meat from the terroc leg with his teeth, Hort gaped at them, unsure of which would be safer for him and Glondora, but ultimately didn't want Davion to go without him.

"Aye," Hort muttered with a mouthful of meat, and Glondora gave a nervous grin in agreement. Grateful for their support, Laila looked up at Gothäzer pleadingly. He glowered over the group for a brief moment, then closed his eyes and nodded his acceptance.

Huddled close together, the group timidly approached the cave entrance, while Nikolean's fingers entwined with Laila's, offering reassurance and support. As they were about to enter, one of the geysers sputtered, causing them to jump out of their skins, their nerves on edge. When Turathyl drew in behind them, Gothäzer stepped before her, blocking the entrance. *'He will only allow the two-leggeds.'*

The Silver looked on after Laila and Nikolean, panicking that she would not be able to protect them if Ignisar decided to attack. Nikolean tried to assure her that they would be alright, and Laila gave her a forced smile and nod to confirm—even though she wasn't convinced herself.

With great pain and reluctance, Turathyl headed back over to the mounts to ensure they would not be eaten in the two-leggeds' absence. Gothäzer was joined by his elder brother Kainüs as they followed after their tiny guests into the cavern, making Turathyl even more leery of the plan.

A heatwave fiercer than the blazing desert swept through the cavern, and sweat poured off of the group. It felt as though they were walking into a giant oven. With the dragons close behind them, they were painfully aware that they were trapped. Laila did her best to maintain her composure, appearing confident and strong, but she was just as frantic as the others, possibly more so.

In a quiet chant, Glondora attempted to create an icy mist over the group, but only managed to invoke a slightly cool breeze instead. Nevertheless, it was still much better than cooking to death within the cave.

Once they had surpassed the light supplied by the entryway, they were unable to distinguish much past the outline of their hands in front of their faces, and they stumbled over loose rocks and debris. The cavern echoed with their steps and the thunderous stomps of the two dragons. Then the dark passage rumbled forebodingly from vibrations as the unseen monarch dragon let out a heavy breath. Everyone froze in place until the vibrations ceased, contemplating going back were it not for their nightmarish escorts. Despite the fear of impending doom, they cautiously trekked deeper inside.

When Hort abruptly stubbed his foot on a protruding rock and stumbled forward, Davion instinctively cast, "*Luminas,*" and the tip of his staff lit up just enough to catch their footing.

Laila glanced back at the two Reds, but they didn't react to the spell. Gothäzer and Kainüs continued stomping along behind them as the group timidly continued at a snail's pace. Laila could sense the accompanying Reds had purposely blocked their thoughts from her, making her even more afraid of what they were walking into.

As they reached deeper into the cave, the monarch dragon's breathing became louder and more ominous, and the group drew closer together, silently praying for the gods to be in their favor. They could tell they were nearing the end when the walls began to widen, opening up into a substantial underground chamber.

Davion's meager light orb was not enough to illuminate beyond a few feet from them, but they could see several softly glowing red stones along the surface of the walls and ceiling. Hort admired the stones, recognizing them as firestones; very rare and valuable. The ones mined in Lochlann are traded with wealthy Gortaxians to serve as a never-ending heat supply for their cold nights. Unfortunately—although enchanting—their soft glow wasn't enough to brighten the cave either and was only making it even hotter.

The mighty dragon within the blackness rumbled in the back of his throat, and it sounded as though it was coming from all around them while it ricocheted off the walls. They peered across the chamber, attempting to get a glimpse of what was lurking in the dark. Meanwhile, the accompanying dragons came into the hollow behind them, obstructing the exit.

Laila felt Nikolean squeeze her hand tighter in either comfort or terror—she wasn't sure which. Regardless of his intent, it gave her strength.

"Hello?!" she called into the darkness.

The mighty dragon in the shadows began to take in another deep, rumbling breath. A second later, a fiery glow appeared within a muzzle full of razor-sharp teeth before them. The group's instinct was to run, but they stood frozen in place, readying themselves. They knew with certainty that the dragon in the dark was preparing to breathe fire, and there was nowhere to go.

Without taking her eyes off the dragon's incandescent jaws, Laila shouted in the Ancient tongue. "Mighty Ignisar! You have called for me, and I am here!"

To their horror, the dragon released his fire anyway, flaming out around them, and they braced themselves, shaking with dread. Laila trembled in fear that Turathyl's suspicions had been correct, and she had just led them to their deaths. Angry for the dragon's trickery, Laila raised her hands promptly and prepared to retaliate against the monster's assault.

The room was horrifically illuminated from the inferno spewing forth from the dragon and flames alit all around them, dancing on the encompassing stone—like fiery walls. Laila recognized it instantly; it was just as she had dreamt so many times. And, just as before, the colossal dragon came into view, flames gleaming reflectively across his ruby-scale armor.

The Mighty Red Monarch was gargantuan in size, well over twice as large as Turathyl, and even more prominent than Aeris. He was everything that Laila remembered from her dreams, yet so much more. To be in his true presence for the first time, gaping up at his monstrous form in the unbearable heat, the smells of ash and death, thousands of bones stacked in corners from two-legged desert wanderers, the echoing sounds of every breath and growl, everything that she had not experienced before in her dreams, she was both awe-struck and petrified. Alas, she realized that she would not be able to wake from that dream should her confrontation not go well.

When the Red monarch made no other movements, remaining statuesque as the flames died out from his lips, Laila realized she might have been too hasty to think the worst.

Kneeling reverently before him, Laila was careful to avoid looking into his entrancing onyx eyes, determined not to make that mistake again. She announced her comrades, each taking a knee upon introduction, bowing humbly before the dragon in his grandeur.

"...and Davion Collins, Human Pyromancer of Lochlann," Laila concluded, saving Davion for last in hopes of impressing the monarch. "He can commune with the Reds, as Nikolean can with the Silvers."

The ground creaked and quaked as the dragon leaned forward, bringing his grand head closer to Davion to inspect him. The human trembled as he stared at the mighty dragon snout inches from his face, holding his breath. Never before had he been so close to a dragon's jaws, and to know they belonged to the most terrifying and feared Dragon in all of Onis, he found himself paralyzed before the Red monarch. Closing his eyes, he clenched his teeth and fists while the dragon sniffed over his face, fearing he might just lose control of his bladder. Ignisar snorted, startling him, and droplets of mucus splashed onto the pyromancer's cheek before the monarch raised his head back away without expression.

With the dragon's muzzle retreated, Davion could breathe once again.

'You have kept me waiting, Omi Méa,' he said heatedly, huffing out a smokey breath, and Laila lowered her head in shame.

"I am sorry to have kept you waiting."

'Great Spirit, it will not be me to whom you will need to be sorry. I have told you before; you have set everything in motion by going before Aeris.'

"What must I do now?" she asked.

'The Omi Méa will confront the Ancients of the land and ask forgiveness for the two-leggeds' past actions,' Ignisar responded, quoting the prophecy.

"Of course," she said meekly, then stood up and proudly declared, "Mighty Ignisar! I come before you to seek your forgiveness for the past wrongs of the two-leggeds in their murder of..."

Ignisar roared violently, blaring flames angrily across the hollow, and demanded of her to 'STOP!'

Dropping as low as they could to the ground, Laila and the others cringed before him, quivering in fear as the cave filled with streaming fire.

The Red monarch took a deep breath, trying to quell the fire in his chest as he settled back down. After a moment, he peered back upon the shaking little elf. 'I did not mean me. The two-leggeds have already served their punishment in accordance with the prophecy. They do not need my forgiveness. It is the others that will need more convincing.'

As Laila recalled Turathyl's warning of him, she couldn't help but wonder, "Why is the Mighty Ignisar willing to help us stop the war? Do you not hate the elves or other two-legged races as Aeris does for killing Onis Caelis?"

The cave boomed eerily as Ignisar let out a rumble of dragon laughter. He looked down at her with amusement and responded, 'One would first have to presume that Onis Caelis is truly dead.'

Not surprised by his convoluted answer, she mind-sent, 'I don't understand.'

As he heaved a sigh that reverberated throughout the hollow, the dragon relaxed his haunches, the ground cracking beneath him as he did. 'It is of no importance what this old dragon believes. What matters now is that Aeris has become aware of your plan and has already begun her preparations.'

Laila's heart sank at the news of Aeris, panic-stricken at what that would mean for them going forward.

Ignisar continued, 'Now you must hurry and seek out the Golds and the Blues.'

'What about the humans and elves?' Laila asked. 'Should I not seek them out first and approach the Golds and Blues with their support?'

'There isn't time,' Ignisar boomed sternly. 'You must reach the other clans before Aeris does. I will send with you my strongest on your journey, my son Gothäzer, and the clans shall witness that you have my support.'

'Father,' interceded the eldest son, Kainüs, appalled. 'Why would we help the elves and turn on our own kind?! And you would send your prized son up against the great Aeris to protect the same creatures who travel into our domain for no other reason than a chance to mount our heads as trophies on their walls?!'

'None have ever succeeded,' Gothäzer hissed at his brother.

CHAPTER 24

'*That is not the point!*' Kainüs retorted. '*They are not worthy of our allegiance!*'

Ignisar roared threateningly at his children, the cave walls trembling in response to his magnificence, and the comrades cowered on their knees before him. The brothers bowed their heads submissively to Ignisar as the mighty dragon partially spread his wings, spanning the width of the cavern, and scowled threateningly at them, amber flames burning hot in his nostrils.

'*It is not for you nor I to question the will of the gods!*' Ignisar growled at Kainüs. '*I have grown tired of a war that serves no purpose, and our clan has suffered greatly from the dying lands. The plague over Onis has continued to expand and is now even spilling over into the surrounding oceans. It has gone on long enough.*'

Gothäzer took a half step toward Ignisar, head still bowed, and declared, '*I will go with the two-leggeds as you command, Father.*'

Kainüs glowered at his father and brother but remained silent in fear of getting his head bit off.

'*Omi Méa,*' Ignisar said, relaxing his stance slightly while tucking his wings back against him, and Laila stood before him in response. '*Our species is a proud one, and many will not bend easily. In each of the Ancient clans, you will find followers, and you will find aggressors. Do not be discouraged, for all is meant to pass as it shall. Sacrifices will be made by all. However, in the darkness, you shall find the light.*'

"How can I ever thank you for all that you have done for me?" Laila asked, humbled.

'*By fulfilling the prophecy, you will have your answer,*' Ignisar replied, then bowed his head respectfully to her. '*Be ready. The Great Silver Monarch will not be dormant much longer. Go now, little Omi Méa. Until we meet again.*'

CHAPTER TWENTY-FIVE

BURNING

*E*veryone was more than eager to be leaving the Red Dragons' lair far behind them, just not in the manner in which they left. In the spirit of time and avoiding their deaths in the desert heat, Ignisar had insisted they allow his most trusted to carry them to the outskirts of their territory. There was slightly less cursing and screaming from the dragons' passengers than before, which waned out after the first hour of flight.

Turathyl carried Laila and Nikolean in her claws, flying low enough to keep Merimer in their view as the magnificent creature bolted across the desert, keeping up with them. The Reds required noticeably more effort to lift themselves into the sky than Turathyl. Even once elevated, they were significantly slower than she, bolstering the Silvers' claim of being "Masters of the Sky."

The dragons headed west, the most direct route to escape the scorching heat of the desert, reaching the border after only a few hours. Once they were beyond its borders, they noticed that winter was indeed still happening in the rest of Onis, but after the temperatures they had just endured, it was a welcomed blessing. As they resumed course back atop their mounts, the two-leggeds were still in shock that they were now the first in Jayenne-knows-how-long to have not only seen a Red up close and survive, but the Mighty Monarch Ignisar himself! To have now been carried in the clutches of dragons three times was a most surreal experience for all of them. Glondora was enthusiastically listing all her friends and friendly rivals back home who simply "would not believe it!" as well as detailing all the moments that comprised the last few days, committing them to memory for all the stories she would tell.

Although Salyaman maintained his serious guise, Laila knew he was excited deep down about what possibilities awaited him when they would finally face the Gold Earth Dragons. Glondora, on the other hand, was not nearly as reserved. She was driving Nikolean and Davion crazy with unending questions about their connections to the dragons. She also enjoyed telling them repeatedly, in a variety of tales, how much she was looking forward to reaching the Blues, eager for her chance to experience the union.

Turathyl, while reluctant, even confessed to Laila that she had been wrong about Ignisar's intent and was pleasantly surprised by him. Overall, it gave her hope. She only wished that Aeris had been so gracious, ashamed of her old monarch. And while Silvers and Reds didn't typically fly in the same circles, she had to admit—albeit only to herself—that it was nice to have another dragon companion after all her time being alone with the two-leggeds.

The most elated of them all was Davion. With his newfound dragon gift, he and Laila were working closely together to teach him how to mind-speak with Gothäzer. Aside from how completely amazing it was to be able to hear a dragon, he couldn't help but enjoy those moments with the elf maiden. It wasn't like before, but he felt that the inexplicable bond was still there.

When they reached the edge of Du Noir Forest, they veered southbound toward the Blue Sea, where they would find the Blue Water Dragon clan. They dreaded the journey, disheartened that it would likely take a couple of weeks to reach their destination.

Gothäzer was astounded as to why the two-leggeds would bother to travel anywhere when it was so incredibly daunting for them.

'How have you managed to survive walking alongside these laggard two-leggeds and their mounts for so long?' the Red asked Turathyl. *'We could be there in a few hours if we didn't have them holding us back and just flew.'*

Turathyl smiled at him, commiserating with his pain as she'd been feeling it for quite some time now. *'It is a trial from our mother goddess for sure in the pursuit of patience.'*

'What is?' Nikolean asked, only picking up Turathyl's side of the conversation.

'How tedious it is to walk so slowly alongside you all,' she replied.

Chuckling, Nikolean told her, *'As I said before, if you would just carry us on your back and fly...'* He smirked at the Silver, knowing he didn't need to finish his comment to make his point.

Turathyl growled softly in reply.

After only a day of traveling and near-constant training and practice, Davion finally managed to break through to Gothäzer and mind-speak back to him for the very first time. Laila was excited about his accomplishment, but he was a little disappointed when she didn't leap into his arms over it as she had with the drow. Davion didn't know what to expect from the union since they had only just met the Red Dragon. Still, he hoped that they would someday share a bond at least as strong as Nikolean and Turathyl's, even though he knew Laila would likely always favor her Silver over any other dragon.

While Davion and Gothäzer walked at the back, practicing and strengthening their mind-speak, Davion noticed that his dragon was looking hungrily at Laila and licking his chops. Rather alarmed, he asked him why he was staring at her like that.

The Red chuckled in amusement. *'I am not looking at your Omi Méa, human. I was looking at her mount. I could have sworn I ate the last of the unicorns a hundred years ago. Yet, there one is.'*

'You very may well have,' Turathyl intruded. *'But if you plan to honor your father's wishes, you may want to leave the unicorn's offspring alone and put the hybrid from your thoughts.'*

With a low growl, Gothäzer replied, *'Very well.'*

As they stopped for the night, Davion prepared a firepit, wondering if he was ready to share with Laila his developing ability to create fire without incantations. Perhaps he could indicate it was somehow due to his link with the dragon. That way, it wouldn't appear as though he'd been hiding it from her as long as he had. He leered at her, contemplating what he should do.

While peering at Davion, Gothäzer said, *'You accused me of staring at your Omi Méa hungrily, yet you seem to be the one that does.'*

'I do not,' Davion said, blushing. *'I was just thinking.'*

Gothäzer turned his sight to Laila in the distance as he emitted a snort, disheveling the boy's wavy brown locks, which were growing shaggy from their excursion. The maiden was gathering some of the dead wood from the Du Noir Forest perimeter they had been skirting.

'*I see you stare at the girl hungrily at every opportunity. I can sense your burning inside for her, yet she seems to be with that dark elf. Why does he still live? Are you afraid you are not powerful enough to challenge him? If it were me, he would have been dead long ago.*'

With a huff at the dragon, Davion turned his attention back to his pit and replied, '*I am not like you. She has made her choice.*'

'*Then unmake it,*' Gothäzer said, cocking his head at the human. '*The drow has left with the elf to hunt. Now is your chance.*'

While looking leerily back at the Red, Davion asked, '*And what would a great ancient dragon care about my feelings for the Omi Méa?*'

The dragon rumbled with laughter, shaking his head. '*I don't. But what else have I to do other than amuse myself with your afflictions?*' Emitting a soft growl in the back of his throat, he added, '*Besides, if I'm to be stuck talking with a human, it would be nice if he weren't a coward.*'

'*I am not a coward!*' Davion snapped back, throwing a final stone at the pit. Grunting in annoyance, the human turned from the Red and walked toward Laila, who was struggling to carry a large bundle of kindling and wood his way. The dragon smirked mischievously at him as he stormed off.

When he reached Laila, Davion forced a friendly smile and kindly offered to help her carry the heavy wood. She smiled back at him warmly, thankful for the assistance, and handed him some of the branches. They walked in silence together back to the pit; Davion not knowing what to say, and Laila being content with the company.

As they began stacking the branches in preparation, Davion asked Laila, "Do you think they'll find anything worth cooking?"

"I believe they will," she replied. "I sensed several creatures nearby in the woods, but Niko knows better what is good for food here."

"Yes," he said quietly. "I'm sure he does." After throwing a final stick on top of the stack in the pit, he dusted his hands off on his robe and stood back up, adding, "Well, that should do it. Now, to light it up." He smiled at her, working up his nerve.

When nothing happened, Laila began to wonder if he was waiting for her to start it.

"Shall I?" she asked, confused.

Flustered, he gave a nervous chuckle as he shook his head. "I actually wanted to show you something. I'm still practicing and not very good yet, but I wanted you to see it."

Her interest piqued, and she stared at him expectantly. Davion took in a deep breath, held it for a moment, and then let it out slowly while rubbing his hands together. Then he pressed his palms toward the pit and concentrated. And concentrated. But nothing was happening.

Laila said quietly, "I'm sorry, I don't understand."

Aggravated, Davion began rubbing his hands together as before. As he stretched out his palms toward the pit again, Gothäzer told him, *'I hear the drow returning.'* Then the dragon added goadingly, *'You may want to hurry it up, human.'*

At the thought of the drow coming to whisk her away before he could have his moment, he sensed the fire burning within him again, and the pile of wood before them combusted brilliantly, flaring up past their heads and outward toward them intensely. Both of them jumped back in alarm, but the fire was quicker than them, and it grazed across Davion's skin, yet it was cool to his touch. Laila screamed, startled, but was lucky to have not been caught in the blaze before it died back down.

"Laila, I'm so sorry! It's never done that before! Are you hurt?"

Davion reached out for her, full of shame, embarrassment, and concern, but she pulled away.

"It's alright," she told him. "It just surprised me."

She smiled timidly at him, then turned to leave, and Davion apologized again, "I just wanted to show you that I can cast like you now without the need for spells." He dropped his arms at his sides, feeling defeated, while Laila continued to scurry away.

'Interesting...' Gothäzer mused, annoying Davion.

'What is?' the human snapped, sitting down by the fire.

'I detected my heartfire flare when you did that. Perhaps that is why your attempt was a little... overcooked.' The dragon chuckled to himself.

Somewhat more intrigued, Davion looked at him and asked what he was implying.

'Whatever has happened to you two-leggeds to allow you to commune with us seems to have bonded you in other ways as well. If you are pulling from my fire spirit, then you will undoubtedly be stronger so long as we are near one another.'

Fascinated with his theory, Davion pondered for a moment, then asked, 'If that is true, then why didn't it work the first time I was trying to cast it? How do I get better control of the fire?'

'I think you are focusing on the wrong problem. You can't gain control of the fire until you have gained control of yourself.' Gothäzer raised his head regally, eyeing the human to make sure he was paying attention.

The human was very much like a dragon hatchling to him, young and naïve in his gifts. Gothäzer wasn't typically the paternal type, but he was curious about his strange new bond with the two-legged and what it all meant. 'Your gift is still stemming from your anger. When you first attempted, you were excited to show the girl, happy almost. However, when I mentioned the drow, you nearly exploded.' The dragon smirked at him. 'Perhaps you are more like me than you think.'

Overwhelmed, Davion sat by the fire, immersed in thought, as he peered at Laila. Meanwhile, Nikolean and Salyaman returned to the camp with two small creatures dangling by long ears in the drow's grip. Although the elf maiden greeted Nikolean warmly, Davion noticed that she continually glanced his way while the two of them conversed.

Davion wasn't sure how he would learn to control the fire spirit if it only seemed to surface for him out of anger. However, if he could find a way, and with a fierce Red Dragon at his side—the most feared and formidable of all the dragons—there was no doubt in his mind that he would become the most powerful pyromancer that Onis has ever seen. He wondered if there had ever before been one able of calling upon the fire spirit as a dragon did—as he did. He had thought Laila lost to him forever to the drow because of his bond with Turathyl, but suddenly things didn't look so grim to him anymore.

Grinning at the thought of how superior he was becoming with his powers, combined with his own dragon bond now with Gothäzer, Davion speculated, This changes everything.

As the unusual collection of beings made their way south, Laila was having more confidence in their mission. She couldn't help but watch the dragons and her friends admiringly as their comfort grew with one another and how they all seemed to be getting stronger.

Although startled by Davion's fire the night prior, she did realize later, after her nerves had settled, what it was he was trying to show her and was excited for him. Since Nikolean's magic has always been passive—happening naturally as he moved with the air spirit instead of with spells—she couldn't be sure if it was something the others would also experience when they encountered the Blues and Golds, or if there was something else going on with the human. Either way, she was happy for him, and he seemed to be very proud of his new gift. No longer seeing a need to keep it secret, he had been practicing whenever they had need of a fire, and Laila was relieved to see that it wouldn't always result in an explosion.

After another day of traveling passed, and the sun began to set to their right behind the trees of Du Noir Forest, the group decided it was time to stop for another night. Laila was honestly getting concerned with how long it was taking them to travel, feeling discouraged, wishing there was a faster way. Mainly, she was dreading that they wouldn't accomplish their goal in time before Aeris decided to attack.

As they came to a halt, Laila saw a rather peculiar cave just inside the forest that had her intrigued. Although unable to sense any beings living within, she couldn't help but wonder if there was anything else worth discovering inside.

Once the camp had been set up and everyone was starting to get settled, Nikolean and Salyaman headed in search of any edible vegetation and more of the tasty creatures from the night before, which Laila had instructed were nearby. While extremely scarce, the ranger prince managed to locate an occasional patch of plant life that he could make last until they could reach somewhere more bountiful where they could replenish their meager supplies.

Hort and Glondora snuggled together by the fire, waiting for the hunters to return as the night began to chill with a cool breeze blowing over the land. Davion sat near the fire as well, taking long swigs from his flask of Glondora's summoned water, wishing he had something a little stronger.

Knowing there were no life essences within the cave, Laila decided to go explore but didn't wish to disturb anyone. Instead, she let Turathyl know that she was going to take a peek inside while they waited for the others to return.

'Be careful,' her dragon warned.

With a mental nod to her, Laila made her way into the forest, just past the boundary to the darkening cave; the sun not quite set. It did not appear to be anything magical or mystical in any way, which left her a little disappointed, but she went inside all the same. It was larger than she expected as she stepped through the entrance into a relatively spacious den where it appeared nothing had lived for some time. She saw that there was something etched on the walls, but it had become too dark for her to discern what it was.

Just then, the cave illuminated, revealing the etchings on the wall, and Laila turned in a startle toward the source of the light. Her heart pounding, she was relieved to see it was Davion there, holding a stick he had set aflame as a torch.

"It's no Muk Narda Cabi, is it?" Davion jested, looking around at the dingy cave.

Laila smiled at him warmly, recalling the beautiful cave of gems in Lochlann where they had shared a kiss, then turned her attention back to the wall. There were paintings over the cave of what appeared to be drow children. On the far left, the children were playing happily in a not-dead forest. Then, as her eyes scanned to the right, the children were scared and screaming as a dark mist with red eyes was sweeping over the forest and a field of dead crops. While shuddering as she looked upon the diabolical mist depiction, Laila felt Davion come closer and place his hand on her shoulder.

"Isn't this part of what we are trying to fix?" he pointed out.

Laila nodded sullenly. "I only hope that I can."

"Laila," Davion said, pulling her attention from the wall toward him, "you are not alone in this. I am here for you, and I have been growing stronger as well. Now I have Gothäzer with me, and I feel like you and I could accomplish anything together."

She gave him a half-smile as she replied, "Yes, the group has been getting better at working together as well."

"They have..." Davion agreed. "But I was not talking about them. Laila, you have to admit there is still a bond between us, something that keeps pulling us together."

While staring up into the human's eyes, Laila was becoming nervous about where he was going with the conversation.

"Don't you see, Lady Laila? It's the will of the gods for us to be together. You knew it from the first time we met. You and I could be an unstoppable force. Maybe that is what the gods have been trying to tell us; that to fulfill the prophecy, you and I are to be one."

Laila shook her head uneasily. "I am with Niko," she muttered softly, not wanting to hurt him but not knowing what else to say.

With an exasperated sigh, Davion tossed his torch to the ground and grasped her upper arms, telling her, "Not in this moment, you aren't. In this moment, it is just you and I, alone here in this cave. You can be honest with me. You can admit to me that you see it too, that you see we should be together, that you *want* to be together."

Before she could speak, he added, "I know he bonded with your dragon, but I have a dragon now too, a fierce and powerful Red, and we can protect you even better than your Silver can." Smiling at her, he continued, "I love you, Laila. I always have, and I always will, and I think you love me too. I *know* you do."

Then he pulled her to him and pressed his lips against hers. She tried to pull her face away, but he pursued her. Not acknowledging her resistance, he vehemently began to wrap his arms around her.

Wishing not to hurt him any more than she already was, Laila asked him delicately to stop, to let her go, but he wasn't listening. Instead, her resistance was making him angry and more aggressive, grabbing her arms forcefully, and she was starting to panic. He didn't understand why she wouldn't accept the truth—that they were meant to be together.

"Laila, stop fighting me! You know this is what we both want!" he told her, trying to get her to stop ignoring her feelings for him.

But it was not what she wanted, not at all. As she tried to pull her arms free from his grasp, Davion gripped her more fiercely, and his hands suddenly became aflame, scorching her skin.

Screaming, she thrust the human back with her mind, forcing him to release his grip on her and go flying across the cave. He crashed to the ground near the opening, and the fire in his hands extinguished. Her heart racing in her chest, Laila grabbed at her burning arms, crying, staring in shock and fear at the human on the ground.

Upon discerning for the first time how scared she was and her reddening skin of where he hurt her, Davion stuttered, "La... Laila... I... I'm so sorry. It was an accident! I... I never meant to hurt you!"

Trembling, Laila wanted to run out of the cave, but Davion was too close to the exit. So, she stood frozen, waiting to see what he would do.

A second later, Nikolean came storming into the cave, a look of consternation on his face. When he saw the burns on her arms, he blared, "My lady! What happened?! Did *he* do this to you?!"

Davion stumbled to his feet, and Nikolean grabbed him by his collar, irately shoving him back against the wall. Davion raised his hands, yielding, full of contrition.

Laila shouted at the drow to "STOP!" before he took it any further.

Quivering and still crying from the burns, Laila professed, "It was an accident! He was just showing me the paintings on the wall. I was startled and overreacted."

Laila stared at Davion scornfully, knowing that if she had told Nikolean the truth, then she would have to fight the drow as well in order to keep him from harming Davion.

"I will be fine," she added, wrapping her wounded arms around her torso, trying to block out the pain. "Nothing Sal or Glondy can't fix."

Davion stood there, watching stupefied over what was happening, while Nikolean released him. After darting to her side, the drow wrapped his arm around Laila and led her out of the cave to get her burns tended to, scowling at the human while he passed.

After they had gone, Davion trudged over to his torch on the ground and picked it up bitterly. The heat seared within him from seeing them leave together; the drow holding her closely. *How could I have been so blind? Even with the fire spirit and a mighty dragon at my side, it still isn't enough for her!* He realized he had just made a complete fool of himself... again. Determined it was the last time he would ever be made a fool, he sensed his wrath boiling up inside him.

Humiliated and infuriated, Davion closed his eyes and let the fire boil over, escaping from his body. The cave ignited in a fiery inferno around him. In the back of his mind, he could hear Gothäzer cackling maniacally. He felt no heat from the blaze as he opened his eyes again, peering through the flames at the pictures melting off of the wall while the fire continued to rage throughout the cave.

Davion Collins

CHAPTER 25

CHAPTER TWENTY-SIX

ENCOURAGEMENT

*A*s he headed back to the camp, Davion was filled with shame, hanging his head low and walking quietly, hoping not to attract any attention. He hated what he had done to Laila and was furious with himself for letting her affect him so severely. With a brief glance around, he saw everyone grouped near Turathyl, tending to Laila's wounded arms.

Glondora was casting her healing magic over the elf maiden while Salyaman made a salve to help with any pain from the burns that might remain. He looked away again and tended to the fire, preparing it for cooking the blue rabbit-like creature that the others brought back, as he tried desperately to stop internally berating himself for his actions. He didn't know what else to do, but was sure Laila wouldn't want his company nor comfort given the circumstances.

Gothäzer sat in silence, observing the human with a keen eye, and Davion appreciated him not saying anything about it. He felt horrible enough.

While Salyaman finished preparing the salve, Glondora broke away from the group and headed over to Davion, looking rather flustered.

"Care ta tell me what really 'appened in that cave?" Glondora asked, her hands on her hips.

Glimpsing briskly at Laila and then back to the dwarf, he replied, "It was an accident."

Davion turned his attention back to the fire, adjusting the logs with a stick, solaced by its crackling and the beauty of the flames. He could sense her eyes on him for a long while, and his heart was pounding, hoping she wouldn't pry any further, fearing the judgment and disappointment he'd most definitely receive.

"Humph." Glondora removed her hands from her hips and strode up to him. "Alright then, but I still need ta check ye out. Dunna' think I didna' notice the light o' fire from that there cave after m'lady left."

Flushing with guilt, Davion stood to face her. "I'm fine, Glondora." He lifted his sleeves, exposing his bare arms. "See? Not a mark."

The dwarf stepped toward him, looking him over, then placed her hand on his chest and closed her eyes. "Breathe in," she ordered.

He gave a roll of his eyes, knowing better than to argue with her while he did as she said.

"Okay," Glondora muttered after a moment, still looking at him with scrutiny, and removed her hand. "Yer lungs seem fine somehows, but ye reek o' smoke, lad. Go change inta somethin' else so's I can give the robe a right wash."

Davion turned his head, sniffing his shoulder, and realized what she meant. He also noticed that many of the robe's fibers had been singed in the blaze, despite its enchantments to withstand fire. Chagrined, he gave an obliging nod to Glondora, then grabbed a nightshirt from Helna's pack. It had become dark, but he took the clothing over to the forest to change behind a tree, taking his staff with him.

"*Luminas*," he cast on his way to the forest, and the tip of his staff began to glow.

Once he reached his destination, he thrust the bottom of the staff into the ground and stepped behind a sizable, withered trunk. As he was about to disrobe, he sensed someone behind him and turned around, surprised to find Nikolean staring at him from several paces away.

"I know you are still in love with her," the drow said. "And by some inexplicable rationale beyond my control, she cares for you deeply as well. It's the only reason you still live."

Davion was really not in the mood to deal with the drow, and was insulted at the audacity of his implication that he even stood a chance against him. On instinct, Davion reached behind his back for his staff, ready to teach the drow some manners, but cursed inwardly upon discovering it wasn't there. It was being used as a torch in the ground.

Before he could react, Nikolean swept over to him in less than a blink of an eye, and Davion perceived the tip of the drow's dagger, pressed against his side through the robe. The point was poking sharply against a rib, and he winced to pull away. Nikolean grabbed his far shoulder, squeezing it firmly with his other hand, impeding him from moving.

While holding him there captively, the drow continued, "There is almost nothing I wouldn't do for her. But make no mistake, human..." The drow snarled and brought his face closer, speaking with disdain, "...if you ever hurt her again, you will not live to see another day, and even an Omi Méa won't be able to prevent it."

As the drow leaned in closer to him, he felt the scum's breath on his cheek. Davion's heart was pounding in his chest, his body tingling with pins and needles as his face went pale and panic surged through his veins. He wanted so much to get rid of the drow, to take him out of the picture permanently, but he couldn't move as Nikolean pressed the blade's point increasingly against him. He even tried to set his hands aflame, but was unable even to create a spark without a spell. Davion feared his rage in the cave had drained him temporarily of the fire spirit.

With a hard squeeze on his shoulder, his steel grip disabling him, the drow murmured into Davion's ear, "I encourage you to keep your distance until you learn to control yourself. I will not always be so understanding."

Davion gulped, the hairs rising on the back of his neck, shivering like a feather had been grazed across it. Then he blinked, and the drow was gone. With a tense unease, he panned the vicinity, but he saw no sign of the vile demon anywhere.

While he took a deep, calming breath, his nerves completely on edge, Davion was startled when Gothäzer abruptly mind-sent, *'I think I like that drow.'* And he sensed him chuckling in his thoughts.

'Of course you do,' Davion sent back, grinding his teeth. *'What's not to like?'*

As the following days drudged on, there was an uncomfortable silence hovering over the group. Everyone mostly stayed amongst themselves, discerning the tension between Laila and Davion. And, despite her depiction of the event, Nikolean knew there was more to the story than Laila would admit, so he maintained a close eye on the human, staying near Laila at all times.

The repetition of the scenery was becoming tiresome. There was nothing but withering, dead trees to the right and dry, cracked land to the left while they trotted along. Laila and Nikolean took the lead alongside Turathyl, while Davion took the rear with Gothäzer. It was definitely a group that no random foe would dare face alone.

Laila hadn't spoken directly to Davion and had appreciated Nikolean staying close to her ever since the night in the cave, having no idea what to say to the human. She knew that he harbored feelings for her, but had not expected them to come out in that form and was very confused how to feel about him now. Had it been anyone else, she would probably hate them for it and thought she should probably hate him for it, too. However, she didn't. Part of her worried that it was somehow her fault, that she had given him the wrong impression of her feelings for him.

Of course Laila cared for Davion deeply, but she was never certain in what way those feelings were developing, not like she had been about Nikolean. She knew she had loved Davion, but it was different than the kind she felt for the drow. In some ways, it almost seemed deeper. But she never understood any of it. All the different connections were still relatively new to her. Things were much simpler with her wolf pack before all the new emotions and attractions. Regardless, now her feelings for Davion were more out of concern for what was happening to him to have changed him so much from the sweet, caring boy she thought she knew.

As the group came around a corner of the misty trees, they suddenly heard children screaming in Drow, "Roarcas! Roarcas!" *Dragons! Dragons!*

Laila and Nikolean galloped forward with haste, seeing three children running frantically away, back toward the forest where a caster stood, holding its staff readily.

"Naëm ketta lafett!" *Do not fear!* Nikolean shouted out, a hand raised out nonthreateningly. "Ir nid edünerz!" *We are friends!*

The children hid behind the caster, clinging to its navy robes, its hood concealing its face. With a firm grip, the caster continued to hold the staff in a defensive posture as they shouted back in Drow in a female voice, "Then why are you with dragons and elves?!"

Laila halted Merimer, both hands raised, and addressed the caster in Drow as well. "Please, no be afraid. We on mission of peace."

Confused by the spectacle before her, the drow hesitantly lowered her staff and pulled back her hood. She was quite young, with dark-ashen skin, the same as Nikolean's, and silver-white hair braided back into a loose knot.

The rest of the group stopped where they were, and Laila and Nikolean dismounted to appear less intimidating while the dragons stayed far back.

Upon observing where the children had been, Laila descried that they had dropped several small blackened berries in their fear. She picked up one of the berries and held it up, showing the dark elves. "You gather food?"

The drow caster nodded, shaking.

"I Laila," she told her.

The drow replied, "I am Sirka, hydromancer. These are my brothers and sister. We tend to the vines, but there are not many left."

Laila could tell the young mage was terrified in their presence. She appeared about the same age as her, but, understandably, seemed very unsure of herself.

"May I?" Laila asked, taking a step toward where she spotted some of the berry vines.

CHAPTER 26

The young drow nodded nervously while the children continued to cower behind her.

Laila approached the wilting vines and knelt before them, their faint scent of decay noticeable in the air. She could sense that there was fresh rot within the roots, and they would not survive the season. Then she held the berry up and inspected it, searching and sensing the seeds within. As she did, she also sensed that she had company, and glanced to find the children slowly gathering around her with curiosity. After giving them a welcoming smile, she made sure all the children had a view while she dug a small hole with her fingers. She placed the berry inside, then covered it with the dirt.

"It won't work," Sirka told her, cautiously approaching. "I have been unable to get any more to grow."

But Laila placed her palm over the soil anyway and closed her eyes, sending her thoughts down into the seeds. Within seconds, a healthy sprout came shooting up out of the ground, growing and expanding rapidly.

Sirka gaped at the miracle. The sprout's stem thickened and hardened as it continued to grow and span out over the area, diving its green fingers back into the soil and shooting out more sprouts that in turn branched out and grew more shoots. As the vines continued to grow, tiny buds formed over them and immediately started to bloom. Laila kept pouring her energy into the soil until the expanse of vines was covered in the little black berries.

The drow children jumped and danced around the growing vines gleefully, while Sirka gaped in awe. Laila's vines took over the surrounding area, and the children grabbed handfuls of the perfectly ripe berries, placing them into baskets. Even her comrades were fascinated by the display of her powers and what she was able to do with a single berry.

Nikolean came nearer, worried about her, but she looked up at him and beamed a reassuring smile. That had become child's play to her, not at all like trying to heal several ancient treants at once. Also, the treants had been dying, whereas the single berry had been full of life. As he regarded the happiness on Laila's face, Nikolean grinned widely, relieved, and enjoyed the moment of watching his people frolic in pure joy amongst what he prayed his lands would become like once again.

While they watched the children, they noticed several more drow emerging warily from the forest, stopping just as they came out into the sun. Nikolean greeted them warmly and motioned for them to come forward.

Laila enjoyed watching Nikolean as he conversed with the dark elves. They were all so excited to learn about the great Omi Méa and all that she had done so far and all that she had yet to do. She honestly couldn't think of a time that he had seemed so engaged with others and... happy. There were even several instances when he laughed gleefully as the children tugged at him to hear more, or to show him something. It warmed her heart to witness how things could be with the dark elves, as opposed to all the hatred and killing they had beheld during their last encounter. It gave her hope.

With the aid of Nikolean and Laila translating for them, the group learned that the dark elves were from a small village called Syraho Fangas, where the Drakka also had gained much influence. After hearing the prophecy and stories of their journey, Sirka timidly asked for permission to touch the dragon. Turathyl, while remaining cautious, agreed that it was acceptable and stepped forward toward the dark elves. Sirka, along with one of her brothers and another drow who had joined, all braved the rare opportunity of reaching out and touching a real-live dragon. They were scared, but that was part of what made it that much more exhilarating.

Glondora convinced Hort to join in on the fun and meet with the dark elves that wanted to learn more about them and what Lochlann was like. He pretended with his wife that it was paining him to do so, but even he was encouraged by how friendly and accepting the dark elves were being with them. He surprisingly gave way to an inadvertent smile in a few instances, unable to resist the good cheer of the moment.

Sirka and Glondora were immediately the best of friends. They delighted in sharing stories involving their gifts and comparing spells. She was relieved that Sirka had not been trained in the way of blood magic yet, as she had assumed all drow hydromancers were. All of Sirka's training had focused on maintaining the crops and what few surviving plants Du Noir Forest still had left. Luckily for the drow mage, Glondora had plenty of experience in that area and shared some of her knowledge with the young hydromancer. Unfortunately, the drow magics did not include any gifted with earth magic, which was what had helped the elves preserve life in their forests. Of course, having a god sharing that part of Onis with them hadn't hurt either, unbeknownst to the Elven Kingdoms.

Even Salyaman had difficulty maintaining his solemn guise as he came over to meet them. An expectant father, he found himself drawn to the children, despite being mortal enemies, and entertained them with some simple tricks. He also showed them his thorn spell, making six-inch thorns sprout out over his body, then dawdled around on all fours, pretending to be a pinecrest—a creature from the Emerald Forest similar to a wolverine in form but spiked like a porcupine. The children all laughed at his impersonation, and Laila knew she had never seen that side of the high elf before. She prayed she would get to see it again when he would have the chance of playing with his own child.

The only ones that hadn't joined in on the fun were Davion and the Red. Laila peered their way for a moment, the smile fading from her face as she looked upon the human. He was leaning against Gothäzer, his arms crossed over his chest and a scowl upon his face as he watched the others. She was so lost when it came to him now and wondered if they would ever get back to a place where he didn't look at her with contempt. It angered her. If anyone should feel hatred, it should be her. She had blindly put her trust in him since the moment she had first seen his face at the Trader's Post and hadn't believed him capable of ever hurting her. Nonetheless, she sensed there was something off with him beyond what had occurred between them. She knew that he was not the same Davion and wished she could figure out what was happening to change him.

In an attempt to shake it off, she looked back upon everyone having fun and smiled again, although a little bit less. She had really needed that moment with them, to give her hope, to give her encouragement, that everything they were doing was worth it. By completing the prophecy, it was presumed that life would be brought back to Onis, bolstering the lives of all those people who needed it so very much.

The dark elves appreciated Laila's generous gift of the berry vines and were moved by seeing all the races working together to help save them.

'Is it always like this?' Gothäzer asked Davion, unamused. 'Performing tricks for two-legged audiences wherever you go?'

With a heavy sigh, Davion replied, 'More or less. Although, usually, it is for some purpose, like to gain their support. I don't see the purpose of this.'

'Perhaps you should ask, then. Your Omi Méa is coming this way,' Gothäzer announced.

Davion stood up straight as Laila approached them, an awkward look across her face as she attempted a smile, but changed her mind just before reaching them.

"Won't you join us?" she asked them, trying to be civil.

"I'd rather not, Lady Laila," Davion replied bluntly. "We really should get going. We are wasting time here."

Frowning at him, she looked back and forth between him and the Red. "Don't you find it encouraging to be reminded of what we are doing all this for? To see the hope it brings to the people?"

"I am not doing this for the drow people," Davion told her bitterly.

She looked at him, stunned, curious how she had never realized how much hatred lived within him. It had never been a secret that he felt hostile to the dark elves and detested Nikolean, but so had all the others. She assumed his egregious hatred for their companion was just because of the way he had always stared at her. Now, after Davion's torture in their dungeons, she feared there could be no redemption in his mind for the dark elf people, even for the innocent children.

"I'm sorry to hear that, Davion," she told him disappointedly. "But I am doing this for all of Onis, and that includes dark elves, humans, elves, dwarves, and even dragons. And bringing hope to others is a part of our quest."

As she stared at him, she realized that he still had no intention of going over and playing with the drow children.

While taking a step toward him, she looked deep into his eyes and did something she typically refrained from with her friends, out of respect for their privacy. Brushing through the surface of his mind with her own, she sought out his intentions and desires. The Red could sense what she was doing but was too amused and curious to warn him.

At first glimpse, all she could see was loathing, but she could sense that there was much more than just that.

"Do you hate me, Davion?" she asked him frankly, while staying within his mind.

Caught off guard, he gaped at her, unsure of what to say. However, she didn't need him to say anything; she could hear him much better without his words getting in the way. Suddenly, in response to her question, there was something that surpassed the hatred he held for the drow people. Although she could sense that there was still much love for her in his heart, he felt devastated, betrayed, and full of overwhelming pain. Davion felt abandoned by Laila, just as he had felt abandoned by his family when he lost them to the orcs at only six years old. Laila could even see the image of his mother lying on the floor, her beautiful copper hair and olive-green dress, covered in blood...

'Leave his mind!' she heard Gothäzer blare threateningly to her. 'Have you not done enough damage?'

Withdrawing swiftly, startled by the dragon, Laila sensed Davion had not caught any of the exchange.

"Of course I don't hate you," he said to her. "I just need some time."

Davion knew he needed to let go of her, yet he couldn't just leave and didn't know how to handle that. He wanted to ask her if she'd ever loved him at all, but he was too afraid of what the answer might be and was done being humiliated.

Laila didn't know what to say and stared sullenly at the ground.

"Do not worry about me, Lady Laila," he said, then added lamentably, "I am sorry that I hurt you before. That was never my intent, and it won't ever happen again. You have my word."

With her heart tightening in her chest, she simply nodded her head, accepting his apology.

CHAPTER 26

Even though he knew his actions in the cave were inexcusable, his words had been the truth. Davion had always loved her and always would. He didn't believe there was anything that would ever change that fact. That being said, he knew for his own sanity he had to let her go.

As she looked into his eyes, seeing the pain behind them, she couldn't help but feel it, too.

"Go back to your new friends, Lady Laila. I will stay here until we are ready to depart."

Knowing she wasn't going to change his mind, she gave him an understanding nod, then turned and headed back to the others, her hand placed achingly over her heart as she withheld her tears.

CHAPTER TWENTY-SEVEN

SHORELINE

*W*ith the dark elf children and new friends in her rearview, Laila's heart swelled with anticipation, feeling as though all the pieces of the prophecy puzzle were falling into place. Her hope had been restored in the dark elf people, and they were managing to gain even more support for their quest. The drow had assured them that they would be spreading the word to all, so that anyone able would join them in their cause.

Laila was convinced even the elves would join them now that they were acquiring such a prestigious following of man and dragons alike. And, although she and Davion were still out of sorts with one another, she had noticed that he seemed to be experiencing less turmoil and agitation as they traveled.

Davion realized that he likely ruined any chance he might have had at winning Laila back anytime soon when he hurt her in the cave. He wasn't proud of that moment and prayed that they might find a way to move past it. Additionally, knowing the war that they were preparing for and the two dragon clans still yet to be faced, he anticipated that the outcome for Nikolean and Laila's connection was not quite set in stone. He maintained hope in the back of his mind that if he bided his time, perhaps he would have another chance. Until then, he decided that it was time to focus on himself, on strengthening his new powers and union with Gothäzer. Davion was still determined to become the greatest pyromancer that Onis would ever see—with or without the Omi Méa by his side.

As they headed for the Blue Sea shoreline, they were compelled to travel through the southern part of the Du Noir Forest to save time, forcing Turathyl and Gothäzer to fly overhead, keeping watch. The dragons were much too large—Gothäzer in particular—to pass easily through the woods without creating havoc.

It was quite a long journey of another eight days through the misty forest to reach their destination. Luckily for them, they did not encounter anything that couldn't be handled with little effort. The group had reached a point where—short of an orc base or a horde of dragons—there weren't many foes that would stand a chance against them or their skills. Unfortunately for them, a horde of dragons is precisely what they were preparing to face once again.

During their last day, while they progressed through the forest, they all noticed that the trees there actually seemed healthier than the rest of the blackened, gnarled foliage they'd been staring at for the last couple of weeks, indicating their departure from the drow territory. Even the mist was lighter there, and Laila could almost glimpse the sun above.

Yet, despite the optimism that their surroundings brought, there was a lingering suspicion in the back of Laila's mind that something was terribly wrong. She was praying to Jayenne and Kyrash that it was not an omen about her upcoming confrontation with the Blues. Without knowing what it was, she hadn't bothered to share her concerns with anyone but remained on edge, jumping at every little thing that skittered about or seemed out of place. Nikolean had noticed her jitteriness but had assumed she was simply nervous—as they all were—about facing the next dragon clan.

Nearing midday, Laila momentarily forgot her uneasy feeling when she heard a familiar sound that brightened her spirits as the melodic chirping of birds surrounded her with glee. She smiled and closed her eyes, listening to their songs, lost in a world of her own. Nikolean couldn't help but grin at her euphoria.

"I have never been this far south," the drow pointed out. "I had no idea there was still life down here."

While taking a deep breath as a cool breeze blew through the forest, Laila noticed that there was an unfamiliar scent. She recognized a fish smell similar to her river back home, but many other aromas were being carried on the wind, which were unusual yet intoxicatingly wonderful. They all knew they were getting close to the water's edge.

It was still early in the day when they reached the southern perimeter of the forest. As they broke through the trees, the last of the woods' murky fog dissipated, revealing a horizon as blue as the sky, with white ridges of waves curling up to the shore, sparkling and gleaming in the sun. They found themselves in awe as they brought their steeds to a halt, admiring the picturesque view. Laila couldn't believe the magnitude of the ocean before her. There was nothing but water as far as the eye could see.

CHAPTER 27

With grace, Turathyl and Gothäzer landed near the shore, keenly watching the glistening-blue waters on high alert. The dragons seemed rather unsettled by whatever they were espying. Laila and the others weren't sure what they were seeing or sensing with their dragon eyes, unable to see anything beneath the surface for themselves. They could only perceive the beauty of it all and the sounds of the waves crashing hypnotically against the shore.

"So, what now?" Davion asked, dismounting from Helna to stretch his legs. "Do we just call out to them or something?"

Huffing, Gothäzer let him know it wouldn't be that easy.

'Laila,' Turathyl said morosely, 'You will need to face the monarch, the Fearsome Fonzar, on Syrpa Island.'

Although following the dragon's gaze out over the ocean, Laila saw nothing but an endless expanse of water before her.

'What island? I see nothing,' she told her dragon, disconcerted.

'It's out there,' the dragon replied, then she connected with Laila's mind, showing her what she saw through her dragon eyes. Laila gasped as her vision suddenly raced out across the water while Turathyl engaged her remarkable dragon vision, zooming in as much as she was able until a very slight smudge appeared on the horizon. Turathyl declared that the smudge was their destined Syrpa Island.

Taken aback, she couldn't fathom how far it must be and announced to the group, "We will need to go to Syrpa Island." Laila pointed in the direction the speck had been on the water. The others all squinted their eyes to see, but no one would be able to. "Any suggestions?" she added, looking around at them with hope.

"Yeah, fly." Nikolean smirked.

Turathyl directed a soft growl at the drow. 'Even if we carried you in our talons, there are too many of you, and I assume you would not wish to leave the mounts defenseless against the wildlife here for too long.'

After dismounting from Merimer, Laila stroked the hybrid's soft white coat with love, while sending her mental agreement to Turathyl.

"And why canna' they jus' be comin' 'ere ta talk? Nobody said nothin' 'bout crossin' any water!" Hort exclaimed uneasily.

"We will need a raft," Salyaman suggested, dismounting and offering Friet some grains from his satchel. "We have plenty of materials," he added, staring at the forest behind them.

Upon discovering from his mind what he was referring to, Laila let out a grievous sigh, knowing Salyaman was right. If they couldn't fly across, that was probably going to be their best alternative. Her experience in the water was only of her river, which she knew thoroughly and held no surprises. The sea before them was foreign territory for all of them.

"Well," she said, staring at the forest behind them, "then I guess we better get started. Salyaman, how do we make a raft?"

The group got to work collecting what they would need to build a raft, employing any already downed trees first in order to spare as much of the forest as they were able. Life there was already scarce, and they had no desire to make it worse. To make a watercraft that would accommodate the six of them, they measured out the required logs to create a vessel that would be roughly two of Salyaman's height long by two of Davion's height wide. They prayed it would be durable enough to hold up over the long stretch of rough waters. Even the dragons assisted with knocking down necessary trees and lugging them over to the group. Meanwhile, Laila grew vines long and robust to use as rope for tying the logs together.

By utilizing the brute strength of the dragons and Laila's earth spirit, they were able to supply the needed materials swiftly. The rest of the group prepared and strapped the logs together, working the vines in criss-cross knots with three perpendicular logs to stabilize the platform.

With everyone participating, it wasn't nearly as daunting a task as Laila had predicted, and she actually found herself rather enjoying it. Unfortunately, most of the sunlight had been used up for the day by the time they had completed a decent-sized sturdy raft with crude paddles and a simple mast and sail made from their night sheets. Having had only ever crafted a dagger and spear out of stones and branches, Laila looked over their work with admiration, arms crossed and a smile on her face. It was an odd sense of accomplishment, that silly task, but it was a nice feeling, nonetheless.

"What are you smiling about, my lady?" Nikolean said, approaching her.

Laila chuckled, embarrassed, and pointed at the raft. "We did this."

Laughing, he shook his head at her. "Yes, it is rather terrible, isn't it? I don't think any of us should make plans to become shipwrights once this is all over with."

As she looked back at their handiwork, Laila frowned disappointedly. She had nothing to compare it against, but still thought they had done rather well. Although, recalling the great cities she had seen and all the beautiful things that man had created, she supposed that Nikolean was probably right.

Upon recognizing the disappointment in her eyes, Nikolean wrapped his arm around Laila and gave her a soft kiss on the cheek. "It should hold up, my love. That is the most important thing."

"We will need to cast off first thing in the morning," Salyaman stated to the group. "Davion, let us prepare a fire."

Once everyone had settled and their bellies contented, the sun began its slow descent toward the horizon, lighting up the waters captivatingly as the orange and red hues of its rays reflected on the sea.

Laila trekked down to the narrow beach beyond a low-set rock ledge while the others conversed around the fire and readied their mounts and packs for the night ahead. After taking off her boots and some of her armor, she went and stood at the water's edge, its cool crisp surf kissing her feet each time it brushed against the shore. While standing there in reverence of it all, she couldn't help but feel at ease. She wrapped her cloak around her, with a dreamy look in her eyes, as she took several steps farther into the water until it had reached her bare shins.

"Breathtaking." She heard Nikolean say as he approached behind her, admiring the way the sunset was painting her face and hair.

"It is," she replied, gazing out at the water while he continued to smile at her.

"Have you never seen the ocean before?" he asked.

Laila shook her head slowly. She couldn't help but wonder what lay beyond its expanse or if it just went on forever.

"And you're not worried of what lies under the surface?" he queried.

As Laila gaped down at her feet in the water, her eyes grew a bit wider whilst she turned her attention back to the darkening sea. "What lies under the surface?" she asked warily.

Nikolean chuckled at her and shook his head. "You mean, aside from the Water Dragons?" He laughed again as if that weren't enough to be afraid of and then added, "Oh, I'm sure there are plenty of things to fear under those beautiful waves."

"Well, NOW I'm worried!" she said, backing up hurriedly out of the lapping water.

Nikolean joined Laila farther up the shore and lovingly put his arm around her. He kissed the side of her head comfortingly with a big grin while she wrapped her arms around him. In the midst of savoring the moment together, with their eyes fixed upon the captivating ocean that held an air of mystery, he couldn't help but long for an opportunity to be alone with her. He had noticed that she would still irritatingly refrain from being overly affectionate with him whenever others were around, particularly Davion. Even though he understood her restraint, it didn't make it any easier to be with her when others were *always* around.

While they stood there watching the sun slowly set beyond the horizon, everyone was startled when large blue fireflies darted out of the darkening forest and shot out over the water, blinking and sparkling brilliantly. None of them had ever seen such sizable fireflies before and thought them beautiful as at least a couple dozen of them twinkled over the ocean waters, the sea shimmering reflectively in their light.

"So," Nikolean said, breaking the silence, "when we were preparing to face Ignisar, you seemed confident that the Red monarch was not going to stay true to the legends by killing us the moment we arrived. I don't suppose you have any foresight about the Blue monarch now?"

Sighing softly, Laila truly wished she did. It was unnerving to think that it really could go either way when she was to come face-to-face with Fonzar. Laila had known in her heart that Ignisar was not the enemy but had no idea what to expect of the Blues or the Golds. She only hoped that they were as wise as the Mighty Ignisar and not hell-bent on hatred and destruction like Aeris. Turathyl couldn't offer her much guidance in the way of the Blues. The Silver explained that they primarily stayed amongst themselves within their waters. When it came to the war, the Blues approach was more territorial in that so long as the two-leggeds stayed out of the waters, they would stay away from their land. Yet, there they all were, preparing to invade their waters. It didn't instill a lot of confidence in Laila and her cohorts for their impending negotiations.

"I wish I were going alone," Laila said, turning to him. She still couldn't shake the notion inside her that something was terribly wrong. "I hate the thought of putting you all in danger again."

Upon discerning the sadness in her crystal-blue eyes, he gave her a gentle smile, saying earnestly, "I understand. Though, I like to think we're not completely helpless."

"That's not what I meant," Laila said, flustered.

"I know," Nikolean said as he pulled her closer. As he held her tightly, with his chin hovering just over her head, he stared out at the sea and its dancing fireflies. "Regardless, we need to show a united front before the dragons, remember?"

Laila nodded, following his gaze, and replied, "Yes, I know."

When the ocean breeze swept a renegade lock of hair across her face, Nikolean brushed it away and grinned as she turned back to look at him before he tenderly kissed her lips. After their kiss, Laila smiled blissfully and took a deep breath before opening her eyes again, gazing at him for a moment. She leaned farther into Nikolean's embrace while turning her head back toward the ocean, captivated by the romance of the mesmerizing lights shining on the dazzling sea. She believed it couldn't be a more perfect moment to be sharing with him.

They were both startled in the next instant when a large silver fish the size of Laila's arm and thrice as thick suddenly jumped out of the water at one of the fireflies. Just before it ate up the large bug, they watched in astonishment as all the fireflies darted towards the fish in a frenzy. The romance gone, Laila covered her mouth, shocked while the fish was then torn viciously apart into several pieces in mid-air by the blue bugs within a matter of seconds. Shreds of its flesh dangled from

CHAPTER 27

several of the little glowing lights, not a piece of it wasted back to the water.

Nikolean hissed and swiftly let go of Laila, grabbing his dagger. Then he placed himself between her and the fiendish bugs.

"What just happened?!" she asked him, aghast.

"What be goin' on?" Hort called to them, alarmed by Nikolean and the blue firefly frenzy.

Before he could answer, the little lights came swooping back toward the shore, right at the group. Most of the ones with fish portions darted back into the forest, but several of the others buzzed around the two-leggeds and even harassed the dragons. They zipped around them rapidly, emitting a soft, high-pitched humming noise as they did, and the group tried swatting them away.

Guarding Laila, Nikolean kept several at bay with a stick in one hand, ready with his dagger in the other. The dragons snapped at the air, annoyed, but were too slow. Gothäzer then spewed a long flame into the air around himself, back and forth, to catch some of the nasty bugs in his wake—unsuccessfully.

Sensing they were not as they appeared, Laila concentrated on one buzzing around near her, determined to find out what they were.

"Ow!" Hort yelled. "The blastit thing bit me!"

The dwarf continued swatting at the pests before they would have a chance to nip at him again. Glondora was casting her freeze spell at them but was also unsuccessful due to their agility.

While swinging his staff around, Davion swatted at the fireflies and grinned when he knocked one. Unfortunately, it recovered before hitting the ground and charged at him. Nikolean had also managed to thwack one of the bugs with his stick, matching their speed with his own.

"STOP!" Laila shouted abruptly, and everyone froze, looking at her, alarmed. Even the fireflies stopped assaulting the group and hovered calmly out of their reach. The one Laila had been studying was still near her, and she carefully held out her hand to the dancing light, sending out non-threatening thoughts toward it, while the others observed her mindfully.

"Be careful, my lady," Nikolean warned.

The bug slowly descended toward Laila and neared her hand. Only about as tall as one of her fingers, it landed in her palm gracefully. She observed as its wings began to slow and its light began to flicker, extinguishing while the being came to a rest. To her delight, it wasn't a bug at all.

Within her hand stood what appeared to be a tiny person with two legs and arms, tiny feet and hands, each with five digits, but it had a long tail and aqua-blue skin with decorative pink lines over its body. It didn't wear any clothes but was concealed modestly with white, pink-streaked fur. Atop both its head and at the tip of its tail were more white and pink tufts of fur shaped like raindrops. Beautiful translucent blue and gold wings fluttered upon its back. With its head cocked to the side, the tiny person's large and solid cobalt-blue eyes fixated on her as they examined each other, and Laila thought the creature to be quite exquisite.

'They're called pex,' Turathyl told her two-leggeds. *'Troublesome little miscreants.'*

Upon closer inspection, Laila was surprised to see an itty-bitty dagger within the pex's grasp. Then it smiled at her, parting its deep-blue lips, and revealed a mouthful of sharp-fanged teeth.

As she smiled back warily at the enchanting tricksy creature in her palm, Laila said in the Ancient tongue, "Halvah." *Hello.*

The little creature put its hand over its mouth as though to hide a giggle, and it made a twinkling sound as it did. Then, it bowed its miniature body to her humbly and made more of the high-pitched twinkling noises. Believing it to be communicating with her, Laila ever-so-gently touched on its thoughts to see if it was. She was enthused at how receptive the tiny creature's mind was and heard the pex speak to her in the Ancient tongue with a delicate, child-like voice.

"Halvah, Omi Méa," the pex said, giggling again.

"How do you know me?" Laila inquired, continuing in the Ancient tongue.

"We know all that Onis knows."

'They are tied to the earth spirit,' Turathyl clarified, able to hear it as well.

Laila asked, "Why were you attacking my friends?"

The other pex darted around in the sky again, whirring wildly.

"No attack. We play."

"My friends thought you were attacking them," Laila said. "I'm sorry if they hurt you."

The pex's smile faded as it shook its head and said with sad eyes, "We not hurt. Onis hurt."

Suddenly, Laila was hearing from all the surrounding pex conjointly. They spoke in their sweet voices in near whispers as they repeated whimsically with varying pitches, "*Onis... Onis... Hurt... Hurt...*"

The little pex continued, "Great Spirit running out of time."

"Time... Out of time..."

"Balance must be restored."

"Balance... Balance... Restored... Restored..."

"Firstborn fire gone to air. The dragons..."

"The dragons... The dragons..."

"Hurry."

"Hurry... Hurry..."

Before Laila could respond, the pex leaped out of her hand and flew back into the forest, whirring enchantingly. All the others zipped away behind it until every one of the little lights had disappeared into the mist beyond.

"What in Ignisar's lair was all that 'bout?" Hort huffed, checking on his tiny prick of a wound from where he believed the pex had bitten him.

As he eyed Hort, Gothäzer let out a low growl in the back of his throat, telling Laila and Davion, *'I'm pretty certain my father had nothing to do with any of that.'*

Davion chuckled at his dragon. *'It's just an expression.'*

With a glare down at the human, the dragon scoffed, *'Well, your expression makes no sense to me.'*

Laila was feeling queasy and panicked as she pondered the words of the tiny creatures. The overall warning about running out of time did not surprise her, as it was not news to her, but she wasn't clear on the part about fire and air. She wondered if it was related to the sinking feeling she'd been having all day.

Since only the dragons had followed the pex's dialog, she told the rest of the group what had transpired between her and the tiny creatures.

"What do you think it means?" Salyaman asked. "Should we still be heading to the Blues?"

"Aye, we might wanna' be figurin' that out 'fore we 'ead ta the middle o' the ocean," Hort added, troubled.

Speaking aloud on behalf of the Red, Davion relayed, "Gothäzer believes the pex may have been speaking of his brother, Kainüs. 'Firstborn fire gone to air.' Kainüs is the eldest son of Ignisar and was not happy about their father's decision to aid us."

"You think Kainüs went to Aeris?" Laila asked Gothäzer, and he nodded solemnly. Laila felt her stomach twisting into knots with anxiety. "Are you able to communicate with Ignisar or others to see if they know anything about it?"

'I will need to gain some altitude, but I should be able to reach my clan from nearby,' Gothäzer responded while spreading his wings, preparing his mighty mass to leap into the air.

"Thank you," she told him.

Gothäzer plunged his wings forcefully down several times, slowly ascending, as he stirred up the debris surrounding him.

Hastily striding over to her dragon, Laila asked, "Tury? What about you? Does your clan at Lochlann know anything?"

Turathyl shook her head drearily as she replied, *'We have been much too far for me to reach them for some time.'*

On edge about the repeated warnings, Laila felt herself becoming panicked. She embraced Turathyl's muzzle and mind-sent, *'Then we will need to hope that Gothäzer can find out what's happened before sunrise when we leave for Syrpa Island.'*

Nikolean joined them, stroking the Silver's neck, and Laila said quietly to the two of them, "What if it's already too late?"

Closing her eyes, the great dragon sent back her warm affections, replying to both of them, *'We are already here. We should at least try to get the Blues and Golds on our side if we are to go against Aeris again.'*

"Lady Laila," Salyaman interrupted, approaching. "What do you think is happening?"

Shaking her head with uncertainty, Laila looked at him and then around at the others while they gathered near, anxious from her sudden increased concern. Laila's heart was racing from the pex's warning. She had sensed all day in the pit of her stomach that something was awry.

"I'm not sure," she replied. "But if Kainüs has gone to Aeris, as Gothäzer believes, then I fear we truly are running out of time."

CHAPTER TWENTY-EIGHT

BLUE SEA

*N*uzzling Merimer as she stroked her neck lovingly, Laila took deep breaths, preparing herself for what was to come while the others readied the raft for their embarkment. Gothäzer had returned late the prior night with the news they had been dreading; Kainüs has joined with Aeris, taking several other Reds with him in his rebellion against his father's wishes. Like Aeris and her followers, Kainüs had no desire to relinquish the Reign of the Ancients. They viewed two-leggeds as feeble insignificant pests that should be purged from Onis.

While she couldn't be sure about what Aeris planned to do next, Laila was confident that it wasn't going to be good. The Great Aeris and her Silvers had already posed enough of a threat, and she dreaded how much more powerful she would become with the aid of multiple Reds. She had received enough warnings from Ignisar and other spirits to know that everything had just been propelled into fast forward. They must move with great haste if they are to achieve their objective.

'We will meet you at Syrpa Island,' Turathyl told them. 'I will stay here with your mounts until you are near.'

Sighing, Laila nodded her understanding. She didn't like the idea of leaving the mounts behind, but hoped that Merimer could keep them safe from predators whenever Turathyl would have to join them.

To relay her hopes, Laila sent the unicorn hybrid mental visualizations and emotions to convey the message, fairly confident that she understood as Merimer nickered and nodded to her.

Laila considered having the Red stay, but it had been brought to her attention that if they wanted all of the mounts to survive, it would not be a good idea to leave Gothäzer in charge of their keep. She still wasn't quite sure what to think of the Red Dragon. He didn't speak much to her unless she spoke directly to him, but she observed the bond between the Red and Davion growing and was grateful for that.

"Are you ready to depart, my lady?" Nikolean asked, approaching her.

Laila was relieved he hadn't asked if she was prepared again. Her head was too full of anxiety over what must be happening on Silvers' Mountain, and she was having trouble focusing on much else. But, yes, she would manage to sit on a raft. How hard could that be?

In an attempt to appear optimistic, she smiled at Nikolean and took his hand while he led her down to the water's edge, where everyone else was already waiting.

"Go ahead, my lady," Nikolean said, holding the raft steady for her while she stepped aboard.

Hort and Glondora made their way on as well; Hort sitting himself down right in the center of the raft, holding tightly to the mast while Glondora stayed near the edge, the water calling to her intriguingly. Davion sat near Hort, quietly taking his place.

Salyaman and Nikolean stayed in the water and began to ease the raft out into the expansive ocean while everyone got settled. Once they had cleared the banks, the high elf and dark elf cooperatively assisted one another onto the raft, causing Laila to smile warmly at the sight. It amazed her how much they had all changed since they first met—how much she'd changed.

With everyone aboard, Laila waved "goodbye" to Turathyl as the great dragon stood grandly, adjacent to the sea. The dragon bowed her head sovereignly to the Omi Méa, sending her warm affections, and told her, *'I will be watching over you if you need me. May Jayenne and Kyrash be on your side, Great Spirit.'*

The dragon opened its mouth and blew forth a strong, focused gale to the sail, launching the group out into the sparkling waters.

'Thank you, Tury,' Laila replied, watching after the dragon, her features becoming blurred and slight as they darted out across the Blue Sea.

Upon sensing the raft slowing, Laila advised her friends to hold on while she closed her eyes, calling forth the air spirit from within. If they were going to reach the dragons in time, they certainly couldn't rely on paddling themselves there. While Laila glared forward as though in a trance, everyone stared at her glowing white eyes. She raised her hands to the clear blue skies, and the sail filled with forceful wind.

As they sped rapidly across the waters, aided by the wind spirit and guided with the paddles, the land slowly faded from sight, becoming a diminishing streak on the horizon. The group

CHAPTER 28

held on to the best of their ability as their handiwork with the raft was put to the test, bumpily skidding over the surface of the sea. At the same time, the group warily kept their eyes peeled to the sky for dragons.

Even though it was a simple enough magic to perform, Laila started to tremble from the exertion after a couple of hours and realized she wouldn't be able to maintain the momentum for the entire trip. As she dropped her hands to her sides, she blinked the white from her eyes and glanced around at the others.

"I'm sorry, but I need to rest."

"Of course you do," Nikolean responded.

She took his hand and sat with him, leaning against the dark elf, appreciative of his love and support, while she closed her eyes and tried to steady herself. Not wishing to hurt him, she made sure not to let the spirits pull from his energy as before. She thought perhaps some good old-fashioned rest might be a more appropriate solution.

"It is nearly midday," Salyaman stated. "This is as good a time as any to stop and take a break. We need to make sure we are strong and prepared before we reach the Blues."

Using the mast for support, Hort managed to get to his feet in order to stretch out his stiff legs, cracking and creaking as he did.

"Oiy, how much farther ye think we 'ave?" he asked, staring out around them, squinting to find anything on the horizon.

"I'm not sure," Laila said honestly, but she knew she was still going in the right direction because Turathyl had continued guiding her from afar, keeping connected with her.

After everyone had finished with their rations, Salyaman and Davion tightened the vine bindings that had loosened from the fast-bumping pace they were going while Glondora tinkered with her spells and the surrounding water. The dwarf was having fun doing silly tricks, such as making the water spurt like a fountain, comforted to be doing something enjoyable with her spells for a change. It reminded her of her early lessons with water magic before everything became about tending farms and battles.

Watching the dwarf toy with the water, Laila continued to relax against Nikolean, still rather drained. She snuggled under his arm while the slight waves rocked the raft gently, soothed by the sound of water slopping against the gaps between the logs. She wasn't looking forward to the next few hours of having the air spirit draining her and was worried that she would be far too weak by the time they reached the Blues. As she brushed her fingers lovingly over Nikolean's, she contemplated what to do.

"Husband! Come see this!" Glondora giggled, arching water back and forth between her palms.

"I can see it jus' fine from right 'ere, Glondy," the dwarf huffed, not leaving his pole.

"I sense me power surgin' like never before!" she gasped, grabbing more water to play with. "The energy 'ere be incredible!"

Energy! It suddenly dawned on Laila that the water, like the earth, was full of energy.

"That's it!" Laila exclaimed, shooting up to her feet and startling everyone.

"What is?" Nikolean asked, standing next to her.

"Energy! I can pull energy from the ocean to get us there!"

"'Ave ye ever pulled from water before?" Glondora asked, dropping her water bubbles back into the sea.

"No," she replied. "But I'm sure it's pretty much the same thing."

CHAPTER 28

Leery, Glondora cocked an eyebrow at the young elf. The dwarf had no experience pulling energy from water for herself nor accessing the spirits as Laila did, so she honestly had no sound advice. However, she was fairly confident that working with earth versus water probably wasn't "pretty much the same thing."

"Jus' be careful, m'lady," Glondora told her skeptically.

"It's worth a try," Davion said.

"Aye," Hort added, "The sooner we get off this blastit raft, the better."

"In a hurry to see more dragons, Uncle?" Davion snidely remarked.

"Hmmm..." Hort grumbled. "On second thought, this raft 'ere isna' so bad."

Laila scooted up to the edge of the raft, then dipped her fingers into the cool water and closed her eyes, concentrating. It did have a very different energy from connecting with the earth, and she wasn't quite sure from what to pull. She could sense several sources of energy and life, some minuscule and some massive, but was having trouble discerning what each of them was, hoping just to pull from the energy of the water itself.

While taking a deep breath and holding it, she slowly began to pull with her mind at the water surrounding her fingers. At first, she didn't detect any energy flowing into her, and it seemed just to be making the water stir. So, she reached deeper under the surface with her mind and pulled again. To her relief, she felt a tingling sensation as a force commenced fueling up into her fingers, hands, and arms.

After a few minutes of pulling the energy into her, she was beginning to feel rejuvenated when a sizable wave suddenly rocked their raft forcefully. She jerked her hands out of the water to hold on to the raft's edge while everyone else braced themselves as well, waiting for the waves to die back down.

Laila stood up and looked around at the endless water surrounding them. A dark blur of something massive was moving beneath the surface right below them, the raft rocking in the wake it was causing on the surface. The others took note of her eyes wide in alarm and began squinting nervously, trying hard to see beneath the waves.

"We have company!" Davion declared, gripping his staff readily.

'Laila!' Turathyl called faintly to her. 'Laila, I'm coming!'

Panicked about what Turathyl had sensed, Laila sent her thoughts out to whatever creature was beneath them, but it wasn't being receptive to her. Instead, it sent a shrill screech in response that stabbed through her mind while she grabbed at the sides of her head and screamed from the piercing pain. Glondora joined in her screams, also grabbing the sides of her head as she fell to her knees, while Hort rushed to her side, forgetting his fear.

When the noise stopped, Glondora's hands were painted with blood from her ears, and she cried from the pain that remained. Laila, not wholly unfamiliar with mental anguish from too forceful a voice, had dampened the degree of it. Even still, her head was throbbing painfully. Salyaman immediately went to aid Glondora and began healing her.

"What is it?" Nikolean asked, coming to Laila's side.

The group was distracted as the water moved around them. Then, they saw several tandem fins emerge, parting the water and leaving a wake behind them before disappearing back beneath the surface.

In the next moment, something nudged the raft from underneath, startling and jostling them as they wobbled and tried to keep their footing.

Everyone promptly grabbed their weapons, and Nikolean shouted as he clutched his daggers, "It's toying with us!"

"M'lady, what be out there?" Glondora asked, frightened.

Laila looked around, dismayed, afraid to reach out again. "Glondora, if you heard the screeching as well, it must be a dragon. I think there is just one of them, but it's not friendly."

They could vaguely see the dark mass progressing back toward them through the water, advancing fast. Bracing for another impact, they all screamed as the raft lifted a few feet in the air and was tossed callously. Luckily, it remained upright and intact, but while they were all fumbling over each other, Hort lost his footing. The dwarf cursed as he fell backward off the raft and splashed heavily into the water.

"He canna' swim!" Glondora shouted and hurriedly grabbed her staff.

Whether he could swim or not, Laila was more terrified about what the creature would do with him and peered through the water's surface, seeking where the dragon had gone. Meanwhile, Hort splashed and plodded at the waves, screaming and gurgling for help.

Glondora swung her staff hastily and shouted, "*Énaht ageeran!*" and a strong force of water scooped the dwarf up within a powerful wave, casting him back onto the raft. Hort gripped hold of the wood platform, kneeling while Glondora ran to him, throwing her arms around him as he coughed and sputtered water from his lungs. He was beyond grateful to be back on something solid as he embraced his wife lovingly.

While everyone prepared for another encounter, Laila called out to the creature with her mind, refraining from the open connection of a direct link in fear of a second mental attack. She pleaded with it to stop, insisting that they were friends there to see the Blue monarch, the Fearsome Fonzar. Despite all her attempts, they saw the mass coming back their way, its fins protruding out of the water as it sped toward them.

"Hold on!" Nikolean yelled.

The creature slammed into the raft, tossing it spiraling into the air, and Laila and her friends went catapulting from it, flailing about as they flew apart from one another high into the sky. After reaching their peaks, they were scared witless of what awaited them below as each of them began their descent, quickly falling and splashing down into the sea. The raft smacked against the surface upside down, gratefully missing the companions.

As Laila plunged into the water, the briskness of it striking through her body, she opened her eyes and searched around for the dragon. Her heart stopped in distress when she spotted the beast heading straight for Salyaman, its mouth agape.

From what she could glimpse through the blurriness of the water, the dragon was notably smaller than Turathyl and was using its entire body, including petite wings, down to the tip of its finned tail, to slither through the sea rapidly.

Aided by the water spirit, Laila forced a powerful current against the beast, careful not to catch Salyaman in its wake, while also grabbing hold of it using telekinesis. She tugged against the force of the serpentine foe, slowing it down and bringing it to a halt just before it could reach the elf's foot. Salyaman swam back toward the raft as fast as he was able, oblivious of how close he had come to being snatched by the sea creature. Laila continued to draw the dragon farther back as it snapped its jaws angrily.

'STOP! *We are friends!*' Laila tried again, but she still could not penetrate its mind.

The Omi Méa needed air, and she was losing her hold on the dragon. Be that as it may, she continued pressing herself to hold on, terrified that it would kill them all if she were to let go. To her horror, she perceived the water's current shifting, and herself being pulled by its force, as it began to swirl around the dragon, circling her sideways. The water currents continued increasing, and her friends screamed while they clutched helplessly to the unstable capsized raft. As a whirlpool developed, the group was captured in its waves, being pulled towards the vortex.

With the last of her breath bubbling up to the surface, her body began to shake from her strain against the dragon and strengthening whirlpool. Like a flash, Laila then saw through the distorted waters a massive splash as something plummeted in front of her unanticipatedly. She felt the dragon ripped from her grip, watching as it ascended in an obscured haze out of the water.

Desperate for air, Laila floundered to get back to the surface, gasping for breath the moment she emerged. Immediately, she panned the area, terrified of what she might find.

While the rest of the group swam or clung to the edge of the raft as it bobbed capsized in the waves, Laila's heart skipped a beat at her discovery. She was reinvigorated to descry Turathyl above them with the Blue Dragon in her clutches, snapping at the comrades' aggressor, the skies filled with their fierce roars.

Using the water spirit, Laila briskly jetted back over to the raft while the dragons battled overhead. "Get back!" she yelled to those around the raft and flipped it with her mind so they could get on board. Nikolean grabbed her hand and pulled her out of the water when she reached them, the raging dragons screeching all the while.

A thundering sound filled the air as a third set of much more prominent beating wings approached, and everyone turned to see Gothäzer advancing toward them. The Blue managed to break Turathyl's hold on it and flapped its delicate wings rapidly to get away.

Even though the Blue resembled the Silvers and Reds in many regards, such as their onyx-black eyes, instead of quills cascading down the beast's back, it displayed a double band of dorsal fins leading to an extensive tail, finned and flared out like a fish at the tip. Its body appeared long and slender, and its wings were proportionally smaller than the other dragons, beating twice as fast to maintain the altitude.

Gothäzer let out a mighty stream of fire toward the Blue, and a giant wall of water instantly flew up in front of it, blocking the flame. The Red's attack hissed as it extinguished against the wall.

"STOP THIS!" Laila yelled and mind-sent in the Ancient tongue, her hands raised to the feuding dragons. "We are here to make peace! Not this!"

The three dragons held their place in the sky, pausing their attacks, and the Blue turned its head to the little elf.

'Two-leggeds should not be in our waters! Especially those who come solely to attack us!' it growled.

"We are not here to attack you! We are on our way to speak with Fonzar!" she replied.

'You attacked me in the water! I could feel you stealing my life from me!' it retorted, roaring at her.

Laila winced with shame, realizing that she must have been pulling energy from the dragon instead of the water, as she had presumed.

"That was not my intention! Please forgive me; I only meant to heal myself!" Laila pleaded.

The Blue studied her for a moment, then gracefully descended back into the water, barely creating a stir. With its long neck held erect, the fearsome dragon drifted closer to the raft, its back fins piercing through and parting the water, while the rest of its body remained hidden beneath the surface. It then brought its snout uncomfortably close to Laila's face and sniffed at her.

'How do you speak to me? I sensed you in the water as well,' the dragon queried, retracting its head.

With a timid smile, Laila introduced herself and told the Blue of her destiny and purpose there. The dragon seemed curious by her and her story and glanced around at the others in the group.

"Please," Laila said, "could you take us to Fonzar? I wish to speak with him about ending the war and uniting the races."

The Blue wasn't sure what to think of them, dithering over her request. Fonzar didn't like to be disturbed, especially by two-leggeds, but it was a rather unusual circumstance.

Turathyl roared softly in the back of her throat to the Blue, reinforcing Laila's request.

After a moment of contemplation, the Blue released a rumbling sigh.

'I will take you to Fonzer, but I can't promise he won't kill you on sight,' the Blue finally responded. *'I am called Drorzyn.'*

"Thank you, Drorzyn," Laila told him, pressing together her hands before her and bowing to the Blue Dragon.

Before they could say anything else, Drorzyn snatched the brim of the raft in his teeth and began swimming toward their destination, Syrpa Island. Everyone braced themselves as the raft jolted into motion, Hort cursing as his helmet fell over his eyes, while they kept their distance from the Blue as much as the modest raft would allow.

At first, they were moving at a gentle glide across the water. From Laila's limited vision that extended to just beneath the surface, she marveled at how the dragon was maneuvering its wings and tail in the water as they began to pick up speed. Shortly after, they were traveling at twice the speed Laila had been sailing them, and were continuing to accelerate. The poor raft was jostling violently, the vines threatening to snap. The group held tight and tried their best to hold the raft together.

Laila looked up, comforted to see Turathyl and Gothäzer above staying close to them. She was feeling hopeful now that

Drorzyn was no longer trying to kill them and prayed that Fonzar would not be as hasty to attack them as the Blue implied.

At the speed the Water Dragon was pushing them across the sea, it was less than an hour before they saw the island coming into view on the horizon. They could have been there sooner, but Laila had to ask the Blue to slow down on more than one occasion due to the instability of the raft.

The moment they spotted Syrpa Island, Laila noticed that Drorzyn was no longer the only Blue with them. While she couldn't see them very well, she could sense that there were now three other dragons swimming alongside them, hidden beneath the waves. Their whispered thoughts occupied her mind while she concentrated, assessing their demeanor as Drorzyn explained why he was escorting the two-leggeds to their den. Laila was unable to tell for certain if they were hostile, causing her to feel flustered.

As they neared Syrpa Island, the group gaped in shock upon witnessing dozens of Blues sunbathing on the island rocks. The creatures perked up their interest as they approached, their sapphire scales shimmering as they moved. The island was much grander than they had expected. They could only see a small portion of it as they reached the shore, but the rocky hills before them were completely covered in dragons.

After pushing the raft up onto the graveled beach, Drorzyn hobbled, sopping wet out of the water, snapping his jaws warningly at the curiously approaching Blues. Several of them hissed at him assertively.

Upon seeing the much-larger Red descending toward the island along with Turathyl, the Blues leaped out of the way to make room for their landing, and the great and mighty dragons shook the ground as they touched down heavily.

'My monarch slumbers,' Drorzyn told them. 'I will go speak with him, and he shall decide what to do with you. You must wait here.'

CHAPTER 28

'*Fonzar dwells in a cave on the other side,*' Turathyl explained.

They watched as Drorzyn hopped bizarrely away, back toward the water, and Laila noticed that he—and the surrounding Blues—did not have the same feet and claws as Turathyl and Gothäzer. Instead, they had thick webbing between their lengthy talons, making them more ungainly on dry land.

While everyone unconsciously found themselves huddled close to Laila, terrified out of their wits as all the dragons leered at them with an eerie quiet, the elf maiden stood firm. With her mind, she reached out and sent soothing thoughts of goodwill and exaltation. Laila was hoping to keep them calm while they waited for Fonzar. It seemed to be doing the trick, but—unbeknownst to her—their hesitancy was all attributable to the Red and Silver hovering protectively over the comrades. Even though there were more than enough of the Blues to take on two such dragons, their substantial threatening size and presence compared to the Water Dragons were intimidating. They also had no desire to initiate a feud with either of their clans.

After only a few short minutes, which felt like hours to the companions, Drorzyn returned to the shore. As he hopped back over the pebbled surface, he warned Laila gravely with a light growl in the back of his throat, '*Prepare yourselves. The Fearsome Fonzar approaches.*'

CHAPTER TWENTY-NINE

FONZAR

veryone's sight—two-leggeds and dragons alike— focused on the sea as they saw two long white horns followed by a substantial sapphire-blue cranium, faded with age, break through the water's surface. They all stared in anticipation as the dragon slowly emerged, its nostrils blowing out a spray of droplets, a beard of spines dangling beneath its chin. The Ancient's dark onyx eyes focused on the two-leggeds on the shore—*his* shore.

As the dragon rose from the water, multiple rows of dorsal fins were revealed along his neck and back. The fins resembled the same pattern as the other dragon clans they had seen so far; the Silvers and Reds with their quills, which accumulated in mass with age.

Water streamed down off the Blue monarch, dripping back to the sea, and he stomped heavily onto the rocky shore while the other Blues all cawed and roared out in exuberance. His long muscular tail swayed back and forth, the spiked fins at its tip spread wide. He was not as massive as Ignisar nor Aeris, but was nearly the size of Gothäzer, which was still quite intimidating. More so than his size, his general demeanor and guise as he glared at Laila and her friends were what had them truly concerned. Laila did not get the impression he was at all pleased to see them.

Raising her hands slowly to the Blue monarch, Laila spoke aloud in the Ancient tongue, not wanting to startle the dragon with mind-speech just yet, "Fearsome Fonzar! We have asked to see you to discuss a future of peace between the races of Onis!"

The other Blues lacing the rocky hills like spectators in a stadium were wriggling restlessly, resembling waves over the island, each trying to get a good viewpoint as they prepared for the main event. They were eager to see what their monarch would do with the disrespectful pests that invaded their waters.

While he continued to thunder his way up the shore, the loose pebbles spreading beneath his steps, Fonzar did not seem very interested in what she had to say. He barely acknowledged she had spoken at all while shaking the water from his ears.

Laila continued anyway, "My name is Lady Lailalanthelus Dula'Quoy, daughter of Lady Leonallan Dula'Quoy, and the gods have bestowed on me all the spirits of Onis and the ability to commune with the Ancients of this land. I have come to ask for your forgiveness for the wrongs of the two-leggeds' past actions. We wish for your mercy and to establish peace between all the races so we can restore the land to its former prosperity."

Moving leisurely over the island surface, Fonzar finally reached the spot he was aiming for on the shore, all the Blues hobbling out of his way as he approached. Then he rested his tired, heavy body down on the pebbled beach and glared again at the intruders. Despite Laila's introduction, Fonzar was more interested in the Silver and Red that had accompanied them.

THE DRAGONS

'Why have you brought these two-leggeds into my waters?'
Fonzar asked Turathyl and Gothäzer, annoyed, seemingly not
having paid any attention to the elf maiden.

Laila, naturally, heard Fonzar and took a step confidently
toward him. While avoiding looking him directly in the eyes, she
bowed her head to him, her heart racing, and replied in mind-
speech, *Fearsome Monarch, they have vowed to aid me, the Omi Méa
of prophecy, on my quest to bring an end to the war.*

Her dragons solemnly nodded their heads, confirming,
while Fonzar's eyes grew a little wider, bewildered by her mind-
touch. And yet, he still returned his attention to the guest
dragons.

'I remember the prophecy,' Fonzar stated, unimpressed and
unamused, *'but I don't see what it has to do with me. We have stayed
away from Onis for a long time and leave the elves alone so long as they
stay clear of the water. I believe we have been more than fair. But to
bring elves to my island is an insult to the great mother dragon! Leave
with them now, and I shall overlook your transgression out of respect to
your father Ignisar and to Aeris by sparing her successor.'* Growling
with agitation, Fonzar added, *'It has been a very long time, but I
remember you both, Gothäzer of the Reds and Turathyl of the Silvers.'*

Stepping forward, Turathyl bowed her head in homage to
the Water Dragon monarch and replied, *'Fearsome Fonzar, much
has happened in Onis since you retired to your waters. Life has been
dwindling on land, affecting all of us. Things cannot continue to get any
worse than they already are, or we shall all perish, even the dragons. The
war and plague over the land continue to spread. The land's slow death
is now spilling into the surrounding waters, killing the vegetation that
your sealife—your food—needs to survive.*

*The prophecy predicted a Great Spirit would be sent by the gods
when the land needed it most and the two-leggeds had endured their
suffering. The truth is, we have all been suffering as the land continues
dying. We need to stand united with the two-leggeds against all who*

would challenge the prophecy so that the Omi Méa may fulfill her destiny and restore the land for all creatures of Onis. *I would presume that if she can find a way to clear the land of the plague, that it would affect what is happening in your waters as well.'*

Fonzar thought for a moment and replied, '*I have noticed the sea life has not been what it once was.'* Sighing a heavy growl, he continued, '*What is it that you want me to do with these two-leggeds? You bring them here to ask forgiveness, and they don't even know the damage that they have done! This child isn't any older than a hatchling!'*

With an understanding of the Blue monarch's skepticism, the Red stepped forward, his mighty stature towering over the resting Blue monarch's form as he raised his head regally. '*My father insisted that I protect the elf and her companions and show the other clans that the Omi Méa has the support of Ignisar behind her,'* Gothäzer explained. '*He believes this elf to be the Great Spirit of prophecy and that it is the will of the gods for all the clans to come together if Onis is to heal.'*

Fonzar growled softly at the notion, not sure what to believe. There was no doubt that Ignisar was the eldest and wisest of the remaining dragons, but the Blue just couldn't grasp why he would join league with two-leggeds. At only a few hundred years his junior, and the second eldest remaining dragon, Fonzar liked to give an impression of being just as wise as Ignisar, not to be overshadowed by the Mighty Red Monarch.

'*And I assume Aeris must be in agreement as well if she sent her successor,'* Fonzar mused.

With a respectful bow of her head, Turathyl replied, '*I am Turathyl, former successor to Aeris of Silvers' Mountain, and now Monarch to the Silvers of Lochlann Mountain.'*

Fonzar stared aghast from her statement. He then mightily lifted his mass off the pebbly surface, standing firmly on all fours as he fumed, '*Explain yourself!'*

While she contemplated how to respond tactfully, Turathyl took a deep breath, then began, *'It is no secret that Aeris harbors much hate toward the elves for the belief that they killed our mother, Onis Caelis. That hate has been enduring and has spread beyond the elves to all two-leggeds, blinding the entirety of Onis to the possibility of peace.'*

Turathyl went on to explain in detail the events leading up to her revolt against Aeris, including her promise to the Wolf God who had raised Laila that she would protect the Omi Méa at all costs. She reminded Fonzar of the words of the prophecy and that she, among nineteen of her brethren, defaulted from Aeris's clan, tired of the war and hatred and ready to find peace.

'I regret to say that Aeris was not open to accepting the prophecy as the Mighty Ignisar has. She even refused to acknowledge that we had been waging war against the wrong race the entire time; it was the dark elf elders that killed Onis Caelis and framed the elves, plotting to have the dragons exterminate their enemy.'

The Fearsome Fonzar stomped his front paw angrily, the pebbles spraying out like splashing water from around it while he roared savagely at them. The comrades all trembled, most of them nervously wishing they knew what was going on. *'Do not spout your lies at me, Silver! Everyone knows the elves fear our power and wish to destroy us!'*

"She speaks the truth!" Laila interceded, shaking as she stood up to the Fearsome Fonzar. "The dark elf elders even recorded their misdeeds! The elves were innocent!"

As he glared at the little elf maiden, appalled, Fonzar spread his wings assertively and roared, *'Of course you would say that!'* He then turned back to the dragons. *'How could you fall for such trickery?!'*

Maintaining her stiff posture, Turathyl explained, *'It was the dark elf that revealed the truth to us, and we have been to their territory; his story confirmed.'*

Fonzar glared at the dark elf with skepticism, his lip curling up, revealing his sharp fangs. Nikolean cringed, feeling his body tense under the contemptuous dragon's snarl. He instantly averted his eyes from the black death stare of the monarch while Turathyl continued, *'Just as with the Silvers, the dark elves have also split into two factions: those that hold to the elder's old ways of hate and power, and the Drakka, who wish to eradicate the misdeeds of the past so we may begin to heal this land.'*

The Blue monarch shifted in his spot, the loose rocks crackling beneath him. He was having trouble believing they could have been mistaken for so long.

'Fearsome Fonzar of the Blues,' Turathyl said with benevolence, *'With Aeris already making plans to put a stop to us, we must know; will you join our effort to end this war once and for all?'*

After staring at his guests for a moment, Fonzar tucked his wings back against his side, relaxing his stance and resting his haunches back against the ground. He took a deep breath, and his blue armored chest rose and fell while he glared at them. Then the monarch closed his eyes in contemplation, considering in depth everything he had just learned. With their expansive lifespan, there were very few things that dragons felt rushed to do and a decision of that magnitude warranted more than a hasty response.

The island was disturbingly quiet as the eyes of every creature blinked with anxious anticipation at the monarch. They all waited for an unsettlingly long time, desperate to know his answer but too afraid to press him. At one point, Laila had worried that the monarch had fallen asleep as he sat with eyes closed, completely motionless except for the rise and fall of his chest from his heavy breathing.

The rest of the two-leggeds stayed close to one another, terrified. Glondora, having been able to hear the Blue monarch, decidedly took the opportunity of the long wait to whisper to her companions quietly—for a dwarf—what was going on. While all the dragons waited patiently in complete silence for Fonzar's response, the boisterous whispers of the dwarf were the loudest sound at that end of the island. Fonzar peeked one eye open from his meditation and glared at the tiny two-legged.

Worried that Glondora had annoyed Fonzar by distracting him from his concentration, Hort signaled non-covertly at her with his eyes to Fonzar. He told her to hush incoherently through clenched teeth and tight lips. His attempts became increasingly exaggerated, frustratingly trying to get her to catch his hint. His wife cocked an eyebrow at him, wondering what was wrong with his face while her words trailed off with her thoughts before finally realizing she was being watched. Flustered, Glondora covered her mouth upon seeing the Blue monarch staring at her with one eye and, without thinking, mind-sent, *'I be so sorry, yer royal-dragon-ness! Dunna' mind me.'*

Confused, Fonzar opened his other eye and stared at the dwarf.

'And just how many Omi Méas are there?' Fonzar questioned the Red and Silver, bewildered. *'I thought it was just the elf.'*

Before the dragons could respond, Glondora giggled, flattered and red-faced, then stepped forward to join Laila, eager for the opportunity. Having received advice and tips from both Davion and Nikolean on how to commune with the dragons, she was excited that the Fearsome Fonzar had heard her on her very first try.

With her hands held up non-threateningly, she sent to the dragon, *'Oh my! No, Yer Greatness, not I! I couldna' even imagine!*

No. Only me Lady Laila holds all the powers o' the land. I be Glondora Emberforge, Hydromancer o' Lochlann. We be united by the spirits o' Pynar.'

'*Pynar?*' the monarch repeated, more intrigued, and then asked Turathyl, '*And what about the rest of these creatures?'*

Laila smiled, glad that they finally seemed to have attained the Fearsome Fonzar's interest. Pointing to each of them, she answered in the Ancient tongue, "Nikolean Den Faolin, Rogue of Duep Nordor, can speak with the Silvers. Davion Collins, Human Pyromancer of Lochlann, can speak with the Reds. We suspect that Salyaman Dula'Sintos, Ranger Prince of Má Lyndor, will be able to commune with the Golds when we go before them. Each of them has linked with the dragon clans based on their elemental power."

Nodding understandingly, Fonzar let out another growling sigh. He decided there was much to think on as he stared out over the group. The ancient dragon did not share the sense of urgency that they all felt with the warnings of Aeris's opposition to the insurgents afoot. Instead, he took his time pondering before speaking while they all painstakingly waited yet again.

'*You have intrigued me,'* Fonzar finally said, addressing the dragons as well as Laila and Glondora that time. '*You will stay here tonight. I would like to hear more about this "Pynar" that binds us and learn more about the Omi Méa. If you all survive until tomorrow, perhaps we can discuss an agreement.'*

Nervous about what Fonzar meant by "survive until tomorrow," Laila was hesitant to accept his offer but wasn't certain he was actually giving them a choice in the matter.

"Thank you, Fearsome Fonzar. We would be happy to stay and answer any questions you might have."

The dragon spectators all roared and cawed wildly, filling the skies with their intimidating songs. Laila and the others were chilled to their cores, scanning queasily around at the magnitude of beasts as their daunting chorus resonated over the entire island.

Despite the "invitation," she sensed that the aura from the Blues was not exactly welcoming and could not help but wonder if going there was all a grave mistake.

CHAPTER 29

CHAPTER THIRTY

INTENTIONS

*N*ever in their lifetimes would any of the two-leggeds have ever thought that they would be spending the night surrounded by a myriad of dragons. Even the suggestion of such an idea would have been laughed at atrociously due to its absurdity. And yet, there they were; a high elf, a wood elf, a dark elf, a human, and two dwarves in the heart of the Blue Water Dragons' den. To say they were intimidated or scared would not even begin to cover the extent of their fear at that moment.

Even Laila, who exuded a façade of confidence in the face of the Fearsome Fonzar and his countless dragons, was genuinely shaken to her bones, still unsure of which direction the Blue monarch was going to lean. Try as she might, she could not get a feel for where his thoughts were leading him and couldn't help but see flashbacks of her confrontation with Aeris.

However, as the night crept by, it became apparent that the dragon's interest was still not in Laila, which she found rather peculiar. Instead, Fonzar seemed more interested in her cohorts now, particularly Glondora. The hydromancer did her proud, seemingly at ease with the dragons that approached her as she mind-touched each of them to say "hello" and ask their names or tell them something about herself and their journey.

Of course Glondora was frightened, though she couldn't help but feel exalted being there amidst all the ancient beings, being one of the first two-leggeds to commune with them in possibly forever. A part of her felt that even if she were to die there that night in the grasp of one of these majestic creatures, it would have been worth the experience, and she was determined to make the most of it.

Fonzar primarily stayed to the side in observance of the perplexing tiny creatures with his clan, curious of the strange turn of events, deciding whether he wished to become involved.

Turathyl had headed back to the mainland to keep watch over the mounts, being assured by Fonzar that so long as the two-leggeds did not do anything untoward, then they would be fine. Gothäzer stayed behind with them, keeping watch over Laila and the human that had been growing on him. Laila did not like her dragon's absence in the least, but she hoped that by letting Turathyl leave, it would show her trust in the Blues, helping sway the monarch's decision.

To their relief, the Blues permitted the group to light a fire as a cold breeze swept over the island from the winter evening. They even brought them something to eat; a few fish and weeds of the sea and edible plants from the other side of the island for them to partake in.

As the chill of the wind increased, Nikolean lovingly wrapped his arms around Laila from behind, holding her with a comforting affection for a moment before rubbing his hands up and down her arms for warmth. In a display of trust, they stood with their backs to the Blues as they faced the fire and looked out over the ocean, the evening sun getting close to the horizon.

CHAPTER 30

It was also slightly less terrifying to not look directly at the plethora of dragons baring their eyes into them. She allowed herself to relax a little at his touch, closing her eyes and inhaling the salty sea air. As he gave her a gentle kiss on the temple, she smiled, feeling blessed that he was there with her.

'*You continue to surprise me,*' Laila heard Fonzar tell her in his deep, surly mind-voice, and she turned to look at him whilst still avoiding his onyx eyes. '*This... all of this. It isn't done. Two-leggeds communing with dragons, dragons swearing fealty to protect them, and now a drow and an elf—enemies since the dawn of their existence—together?*'

Fonzar closed his eyes and swayed his massive head back and forth, then looked upon her again. She wasn't quite sure how to respond to him, but he continued, '*It is peculiar enough to see all of the races together, but it seems you have found a way to put aside your hatreds and work toward a common goal.*'

As she took a step apart from Nikolean and toward the monarch, Laila bowed her head to him, responding simply, '*We have.*'

'*What of this "Pynar"? What has bound the others to my kind?*' he asked.

Laila told the old monarch all about their visit to the Ruins of Pynar, sending him mental images of the temple, including the mural of dragons with two-leggeds. She explained the ritual to him and the devastation afterward, then proceeded to tell him how they first discovered the drow rogue's link to the Silver. She revealed that they pieced it together when they went before the Reds and learned the pyromancer had been united with the Fire Dragons.

'*And these ruins that created the united ones, they are completely destroyed?*' he asked.

Nodding, Laila said, disheartened, '*I am afraid so.*'

The dragon remained expressionless, unsure how he felt about that news. *'I see,'* he replied.

'The spirits of Onis brought me to each of my companions,' Laila explained, *'binding us together to fulfill the prophecy, and they had also led me to the ruins. I believe it was the will of the gods for two-leggeds and dragons to commune with one another. From what we saw in the temple, it wasn't the first time.'*

Fonzar lifted his head high, glaring down at her, and asked sternly, *'If I should agree to join you, what is it you intend to do with my clan exactly?'*

To prepare herself, Laila took a deep, anxious breath, then explained, "I am requesting all dragon clans stand down in their tyranny over the two-legged races. I am seeking your support of this goal to ensure our success as we go before the remaining Gold clan.

"Aeris has shown us that not all will be willing to make that change. As I prepare to face the Great Silver Monarch again, I am trying to gain the support of as many dragons and two-legged nations as possible. Once we have all the dragons in agreement, I'm hoping it will help bring peace to the land so all the races can come together without hate and war."

'And how does this restore my waters?' Fonzar asked, remaining skeptical.

Laila averted her sight to the ground, feeling ill at ease. "I am not sure how that part of the prophecy works yet," she admitted. "However, I have been getting stronger in my earth magic and ability to heal nature. I assume when the feuding has stopped, I will find a way to rid the land of its plague so that life can be restored. But first, we must get the feuding to stop."

'I have not been actively involved in the war for a few centuries now, yet you are standing here telling me you intend to confront even more dragons and demand that they step down. And what if they don't?

CHAPTER 30

What will you do then?' he asked her. *'Why would I get back involved and pledge the lives of my clan to you?'*

Not wishing to incite an uproar, Laila said to him in a direct and firm manner, *'I will use the spirits of the land and my allies to ensure the freedom of the two-leggeds however I can, including their ability to return to the water.'*

'So, you would challenge me if I refuse and would kill Aeris?' Fonzar asked bluntly.

With her heart palpitating in her chest, Laila was not liking the direction the conversation was heading, and wasn't sure what he was fishing for. *'I do not wish to kill anyone. I can only pray that it would not come to that, but I will do whatever needs to be done to fulfill the prophecy that has been put on my shoulders.'*

As he strengthened his stance, the monarch shifted his great mass and glared at her. *'You are just a child. You have been given powerful gifts from the spirits and are choosing to use them to go against my kind and take down a great and respected monarch. Why shouldn't I kill you all right now and end this nonsense before it goes any further?'*

Laila suddenly wondered about his real intentions in assuring Turathyl that it was safe to leave them with him, and she wished her dragon were there with her at that moment. With an unconscious step backward, she tried to think fast. A quick glance over at Glondora, who was giggling at one of the dragons, caused the elf maiden to realize that she was alone in knowing they were possibly in imminent danger; the others would be dead before they even knew they were under attack. She had to do something, she had to say something, but she wasn't sure what.

Not having enough time to relay what was happening, she covertly sent to Gothäzer, *'Be ready!'* Then she spoke aloud, still in the Ancient tongue, aware that at least Salyaman and the Red would understand, "I assure you, Fearsome Fonzar, we are only

- 372 -

seeking peace between the races. I humbly request that you not attack us. I do not wish to harm you or any dragons."

With a maniacal laugh, Fonzar roared, *'You really believe you could harm me?! Clearly that didn't work out so well with Aeris, or you wouldn't have need to recruit armies of all races to face her again! Look around you, child!'* The fearsome dragon stepped toward her, his stature broadening in a threatening display. *'There are at least fivefold Blues compared to Silvers!'*

Gothäzer and Davion strode toward Laila and stood firm behind her.

"That is not what I meant; I do not want to fight you!" Laila declared.

While looking downward on the Blue, Gothäzer addressed the monarch, growling, *'And you would attack me as well? Do you not think Ignisar would retaliate if you kill me?'*

'Ignisar isn't here!' Fonzar growled back. *'I aim simply to defend my clan and the future of the Ancients!'*

As the Fearsome Fonzar let out a ferocious roar, rattling the stones surrounding them, several of the Blues launched from their platforms and echoed his call, flying over the comrades' heads.

Glondora, who had still been conversing with the same Blue, immediately began stepping away from it, terrified. Her Blue looked at Fonzar, confused, then back to the frightened little dwarf, holding steady. Everyone immediately grabbed their weapons and prepared for the dragons' attack.

As Fonzar let out another roar, two Blues dove down from the sky toward Laila. Gothäzer heatedly intervened, expelling a scorching flame directly at them, filling the surrounding sky with fire. The Blues screeched, diving frantically away from the flames, and retreated. While the Red's focus was on them, two other Blues darted for the dwarves and another for the high elf.

Glondora promptly began casting, her body revving with the abundant power of the water spirit, as she shot ice shards toward the oncoming dragons, her aim impeccable. Normally—and unbeknownst to her—such an attack would be futile against any dragon, the ice merely shattering against their scaly hides, only able to pierce their vulnerable wings. But despite that, her bolts were powered from being so near the Blues and their water spirit, and they struck firm against the dragons. Although the ice still did not pierce their hides, the beasts reared in the air from the impact. Screeching in pain, they circled above for a moment and then dove at them again more swiftly. Glondora and Hort braced themselves as they neared and Salyaman prepared by protruding thorns from his skin for their encounter, swords ready.

Upon descrying her friends in danger, Laila turned her back to the Fearsome Fonzar and thrust her hands out toward the assailing dragons, casting forth a telekinetic blast, forcing them backwards away from her friends. The dragons flapped their petite wings rapidly and flew away from the blast, back toward the hills.

Fonzar roared again, causing others to descend on the group.

Swirling his staff, Davion joined Gothäzer in fiery assaults on the incoming dragons, casting firebolt after firebolt in the air at the monstrous beasts while more continued to join in the assault on the two-leggeds.

"*Ominus lacassayra!*" he cast, and multiple bolts of fire simultaneously shot out from his staff's gem towards the swarming dragons. Unfortunately, they either evaded or retaliated with icy breath and sprays of water at the flames, dousing them before they could singe any of their hides.

The Blues swooped down at the Fire Dragon and his mage, shrill in their cries. They grazed against their targets, knocking Davion to the ground while Gothäzer snapped at them unsuccessfully, his girth making him much slower than the slim Water Dragons.

As Blues dove at Nikolean, he swiftly darted out of the way, aided by the air spirit, before they could reach him. He tried to slash at them with his daggers, but they never came quite close enough.

Realizing they were too vulnerable, Nikolean and the others quickly made their way to Davion and his Red, knowing they wouldn't stand a chance against the attacks independently. While they all took defensive stances, Glondora cast protections over the group and continued her ice blasts against the beasts, keeping them at bay. Hort swung at each Blue as they approached, but they wouldn't come near enough to be struck by his blade.

With a glimpse at the masses still perched on the rocky hills, Laila panicked, knowing there were just too many dragons to possibly take all of them on. So, she instead turned back to Fonzar, understanding that he was the one that she needed to convince to cease the attacks.

Her entire focus now fixated on the monarch, she let out piercing screams that filled the air as she telepathically demanded him to stop his assaults against them, while her palms shot forth a blazing tunnel of fire. Although she cast it out as a threat toward him, she stopped it short, just before it reached the dragon. Her intent was only to call his attention off of her friends.

With his icy breath, Fonzar easily extinguished the blaze and laughed at the tiny elf. *'You'll have to do better than that!'* he blared at her.

Meanwhile, her friends were doing their best to defend against or evade the assailing dragons, managing to avoid any harm, while Gothäzer snapped and growled at them aggressively.

The Red was confused why they would keep retreating back up into the sky before the group could retaliate, just to dive at them again. He was growing annoyed with their games and thought they might be searching for his weakness or distracting him from the two-leggeds. While spreading his mighty wings, he roared fiercely at them, challenging them to come at him instead of the others.

Laila maintained her focus on Fonzar, who was still issuing commands at his clan to swarm her friends. She pulled from the earth spirit, bringing forth spikes from the rocky terrain around the monarch, but her effort simply made him laugh again as he demolished the jutting earth with his tail.

Discouraged, Laila next called forth the air spirit, summoning storm clouds above. The sky rapidly became dark as thunder rumbled and lightning crashed in the surrounding waters, the waves growing fiercer from the winds. Several of the Blues ceased in swarming the group as they looked warily to the blackening clouds. Her hand flexed and posture firm, Laila reached to the sky and sent a bolt of lightning shooting down right beside Fonzar, scorching the stone at his feet.

'You missed!' he ridiculed.

"I missed on purpose!" she retorted.

The fearsome dragon looked severely upon the young elf. She immediately averted her eyes from his black stare while he emitted a throaty growl and then took a deep, reverberating breath into his chest, puffing it out.

An ominous feeling swept over her and the others as all the Water Dragons went silent and still, looking out to the sea. Their visage was vacant and eerie as they blinked their onyx eyes, staring past them. In their silence, Laila heard a slight roaring sound that reminded her of Onis Falls, which rapidly growing louder as she turned toward the water. Fonzar was calling forth a giant wave from the sea. It was rising high and fierce, well over the height of the mighty Gothäzer, and it was headed for the shore.

Everyone turned, staring in horror at the incoming tidal wave, petrified as it threatened to wipe out the group. Laila thrust her arms out before her, howling a cry at the approaching wave, praying to all the gods for help. Everyone else was frozen in fear as they held their breath, bracing themselves for the force of the sea. As it neared, the wave started to slow from the Omi Méa's power.

Sensing what Laila was doing, Glondora began waving her staff, casting her freeze spell with all the strength she possessed. Little by little, the wave crackled and creaked from their combined effort, freezing in place like a giant ice sculpture. As the last of the giant wave froze in place against the shore, croaking against the struggle of its own weight, the island was left in the immense shadow it cast.

Laila, full of fury and power, screamed at the frozen wall, pushing out with her mind while crossing her arms upward before her. The island and sculpture trembled from her force as the frozen wave shattered in an explosion. The multitude of ice shards sprayed outward in slow motion, soaring like broken reflective glass back to the sea.

When everyone recovered from their shock, the mass of Blues resumed roaring and swooping at the two-leggeds as though nothing had happened, but Laila was exhausted.

"Stop attacking my friends and me! We came here for peace! I only want to stop this war and to heal this land—to heal your ocean! Why do you want me dead?!"

The Blues' roars were muffled out as the loud rumbling of the dragon monarch's laughter overtook the area. His hysterics were irritating Laila to no end. She couldn't fathom what was so funny about any of it and just wanted to scream at him. She partly believed she could kill him if she wanted to, but that wasn't why they had come here. If they couldn't get the other dragons to support their goal, what option did that leave them with?

'Omi Méa,' the Fearsome Fonzar said in an amused voice, standing firmly, his head held high as he glowered at her, 'look around you.'

Hesitantly, Laila did as he said, turning her gaze away from the monarch and over to where her friends were under attack. Except, she didn't see them being attacked. All the Water Dragons were flapping their wings rapidly as they soared in the air over her comrades, who were all staring up at them, terrified. The Blues would dive, swoop down near their heads, then fly back up and hover. Gothäzcr even looked on them in bewilderment, trying to decide if he should take the fight to them.

"I don't understand," Laila said, looking back to Fonzar.

'If I wanted you dead, you would be,' he said smugly. 'I had to see something for myself.'

Her heart still beating hard in her chest, Laila took a deep breath. "If you wanted a demonstration of our abilities, you could have just asked."

Fonzar smirked and shook his head heavily from side to side. 'And what fun would that have been?' he asked snidely. 'Besides, I had to know what you would do; whether you would be quick to try and kill my kind when threatened. So, tell me, why did you hesitate?'

"I told you," she said sternly, "we want peace. I have no desire to kill anyone."

Fonzar eyed the little elf, heaving a long sigh. 'My clan was merely skylarking with your friends. But, Omi Méa, you are going to find that there will be times that slaying your enemies will be your only option if you are to succeed in your war to end the war.'

"Respectfully, I hope you are wrong," Laila responded.

As she inhaled the sea air deeply, Laila's heart fluttered, relieved beyond measure that it had only been a test, and looked back at her friends with a warm smile. Upon perceiving her relief, they all began to gather around her, still trying to figure out what had just happened.

"Are we safe, my lady?" Nikolean asked quietly, his eyes fixed on the Fearsome Fonzar.

Nodding, Laila replied, "I believe so," then turned back to the monarch. "Does this mean that you have made a decision?" she questioned hopefully.

While standing tall and strong before his tiny guests, Fonzar asked her dourly, *'If I decide to join you on this quest for peace...'* The monarch paused with hesitation as though reconsidering before he continued, *'...you promise this will heal my ocean?'*

Laila kneeled before the dragon and bowed her head sincerely. "If you join us in our quest for peace, I promise I will do everything in my power to heal *all* of the surrounding oceans."

The Blues hovering in the sky and those still on the rocky hills all cawed out excitedly, and the two-leggeds and Gothäzer grew more at ease.

With a solemn mien, Fonzar declared, *'The Omi Méa and her followers can count on the Blues as allies in their quest to end the war.'*

As the Water Dragons roared and cawed out again, Laila couldn't help but smile up at the old dragon and bowed respectfully to him. "Thank you, Fearsome Fonzar! May Jayenne and Kyrash be forever on our sides!"

The majestic dragon nodded to the little elf, then asked his clan, *'Who among you will offer to serve and protect the Omi Méa and her hydromancer on their mission?'*

From the base of the hills, a small Water Dragon slowly came forward, hopping toward them. Everyone turned to look, watching as the young Blue peeked around timidly at its clan, who were all surprised by its haste to volunteer.

Glondora was giddy at the sight of the dragon and ran over to meet her. The Blue was much smaller than many of the others and only had a single scarce row of dorsal fins down her neck and back. Seeing the two of them together, Laila realized it was the same dragon that Glondora had been speaking with right before the Blues began their faux assault. She was happy to sense the elation over both of them, clearly a match already.

'I would be happy to go with the Omi Méa and Glondora Emberforge, Hydromancer of Lochlann, on their mission. I am Astryma of the Blues,' she told them, bowing her head to Laila.

'So it shall be,' Fonzar announced. 'Astryma will protect you on your journey. Call for us when the time has come to face any who would oppose the prophecy.'

While she bowed humbly before the Fearsome Fonzar, Laila couldn't stop smiling at their victory of convincing another dragon clan to join them. Now, there was only one more clan remaining, and she couldn't help but experience a boost of confidence from their incredible win with the Blues.

Astryma & Glondora

CHAPTER 30

CHAPTER THIRTY-ONE

HONOR

None of the party slept that night, surrounded by the horde of Water Dragons that were all watching them curiously. Laila cuddled up to Nikolean by the fire to keep warm from the frigid ocean breeze. While laying with her head on his lap facing the fire, she closed her eyes in a futile attempt at a bit of rest. The voices of all the dragons were swirling around in her head, and she was having trouble keeping up the mental block to dim their loud pulsating chatter.

Laila recalled Ignisar's warning that each clan would have aggressors against the prophecy, and she couldn't help but wonder which of the disgruntled voices in her head would brave betraying the Fearsome Fonzar to join Aeris. To her relief, there were a surprising number of Blues that seemed delighted by the idea of the prophecy, particularly the replenishment of their oceans and food supply.

With Glondora chatting up her new dragon pal, Hort found his way over to Davion for most of the night. He patted his back proudly, looking on him keenly with an "attaboy" smile and shoulder-squeeze. The dwarf even thanked Gothäzer for protecting his boy and the rest of them when they thought they were under attack.

Being surrounded by dragons in the middle of the ocean, Hort couldn't believe where their little adventure of helping a damsel in distress had led them to. It warmed his heart that he not only got to take Davion on an adventure after his time at the Magi Academy, as he had always wanted, but that they were sharing in what was undoubtedly the greatest adventure of their lives.

As he looked over the group, Hort fondly imagined them all back in Lochlann, sharing stories with the next generations, his and Glondora's own future children by his feet, intently listening as they would tell tales of battling dragons. He smiled over at his wife, watching in amazement as she talked the ear off of a dragon, who actually seemed to be quite interested.

"Uncle?" Davion said, distracting his thoughts. "Is everything alright?"

"Aye, me boy," he replied, teary-eyed. "Everythin' be just grand. Tis quite the adventure we be on." He turned to face Davion. "And what 'bout ye? Ye been doin' better?"

As he inadvertently glanced at Laila and Nikolean by the fire, Davion couldn't help but frown. "I will be," he told his uncle. "Right now, I'm just doing my best to get us through this quest. Only time will tell what happens after that."

Nodding, Hort replied, "Tis true. And jus' ye wait 'til ye be back in Roco with that Red Dragon o' yers. Why, ye'll have every last lass there pinin' jus' ta touch yer robe and 'ave ye look their way. I guarantees it!"

With an appreciative grin at Hort's efforts, Davion rested his hand on his uncle's shoulder. "Thank you, Uncle."

"Jus' keep that chin up, me boy," Hort added. "Methinks everythin' will 'appen as twas meant ta. We jus' need ta keep in the favor o' the gods."

Salyaman, feeling a little left out with having yet to commune with a dragon, found himself at the fire next to the couple, trying to keep himself warm until sunrise. He was also considerably worried after what they just faced, his mind too abuzz to get any rest himself.

"Do you suppose the mounts are faring well?" he asked Nikolean casually.

Nodding, the drow replied, "I'm sure Tury is keeping them safe."

"That was quite an unorthodox Ranchetal today," Salyaman continued, referring to the undisclosed test of their powers by the monarch. When elves hit puberty, they would perform a display of their powers in a ritual called a Ranchetal, where the elders would then determine their magic class and the best path for their training. "For a moment there, I thought I was never going to meet my unborn child, nor see my love, Shakiera, again."

Perking his head up, Nikolean looked over at Salyaman. "You don't think we would have survived had it been a real attack?"

Salyaman peered back at the drow, somberly shaking his head. "We were not prepared. We had been lulled into a false sense of security, and even Turathyl was not nearby to help."

Nikolean scowled at the fire. "You're right; that should never have happened."

Sighing, Salyaman pointed out, "We should not be so complacent when we face the Golds. I believe we were all still living off the success of having the Reds join us that we forgot there is real danger to be had here. We do not know how much we can trust the dragons—any of them."

Both the elf and drow unintentionally glanced over at Gothäzer.

Laila opened her eyes and looked out past the low flames of the crackling fire. She stared at the calm, rippled water with its tranquil sheen from the lines of light reflecting the two moons, one red, one blue, while she continued to rest her head on Nikolean's leg. They had assumed she'd fallen asleep, but the elf maiden was glad she hadn't. Laila knew they were right. They would have to do things differently when facing the Golds. Luck was on their side that day, and they should not take that for granted.

Surviving the night on Syrpa Island had been quite the experience for the companions, but it was time to say goodbye to the Water Dragons and continue on their quest. As the day broke on the horizon, the calm water of the Blue Sea surrounding them was awe-inspiring. It was smooth as glass, glistening brilliantly in the sunrays, and the group prepared for their leave.

Laila gave a bright smile to Salyaman as she approached him near the raft, ready to hop on board. However, when she saw his face as he shook his head forlornly at her, she realized they had a problem.

"What's going on?" she asked him.

"This raft is not going to make it back across, not without some extensive rework."

Laila's heart sank at the news, but, observing it with her own eyes, she could see what he meant. The vines were dried and torn from the salty water, and it was missing two of the support logs and one from the platform. Even the sail from their sheets had been torn and frayed from the buffeting of fierce winds from Drorzyn and Laila propelling the poor thing across the water. She had already been panicking about all the warnings of running out of time and really hadn't expected to be on the island that long.

While mulling over what they should do and glancing around at the limited supply options offered by the rocky island, the others all began to approach, including Glondora with their new dragon, Astryma.

"What we lookin' at?" Hort asked the group, trying to see.

Laila stepped aside and pointed to their depressing excuse for a boat.

"Well, that's just great," Davion huffed discouraged before heading back over to Gothäzer.

Glondora told them with a mirthless smile, "Astryma wants ta know why we be lookin' at a pile o' logs."

Both aloud and in mind-speak, Laila addressed the dragon. "That was our way back to Onis." She hoped that the young Blue would become comfortable speaking with her as well, not just with Glondora. Laila's relationship with Gothäzer was as rocky as it was with Davion, and she continued to strive to mend those ties. She believed it to be important in part because of how much she cared for Davion and in part because it would be beneficial in a battle if they were all communicating readily.

After looking in confusion at the two-leggeds, the Blue then brought her head close to Glondora and began nudging the backs of her legs with her snout. Glondora kept stepping away, unsure of what the dragon was after. With the third nudge, she nearly knocked the dwarf to the ground.

"Oiy! What ye be doin'?" she asked the dragon.

'I can carry you across,' Astryma replied.

Glondora looked back and forth between Laila and the Blue.

With a polite smile at the petite but well-intentioned dragon, Laila replied, "I think there are too many of us for you."

'I will take Davion,' Gothäzer offered.

'And I can carry the elves and drow,' Drorzyn announced, joining them.

Her spirits lifted as she gleamed at the three ancient beings. She reveled in the idea of making up some of their lost time with the dragons' significantly accelerated speed.

"Are you sure?" Laila asked them, and they confirmed. "Well, it appears the dragons will be taking us across," she told the rest of the group. "Hort, you and Glondora will be with Astryma. Sal, Niko, and I will go with Drorzyn."

"We will meet you at the other side," Davion announced to the group, and Gothäzer spread his massive wings, preparing to take flight.

Laila nodded to him while the Red beat his wings several times and snatched Davion up in his claws on the way into the sky. Then she turned her attention back to the Blues.

"Drorzyn," Laila addressed, "how will you carry all three of us over the water?"

With a shake of his head, the Blue replied, *'Not over, Omi Méa... through. You will need to ride on our backs as we swim. Trust me; it will be much faster for us that way than flying, and we will keep you above the surface.'*

Both Astryma and Drorzyn then laid flat against the ground and looked at the group. Glondora clapped her hands together joyously and rushed over to her dragon, stepping up onto her front leg. She couldn't quite reach Astryma's back and attempted hopping several times to get up, to no avail.

"Hmmm... And methought a horse was bad," Hort grumbled, shaking his head as he went over to assist his wife.

Laila approached Drorzyn with nervous excitement. It was a big moment for all of them, and she was feeling exuberant by how readily the Blues had volunteered to do something so monumental with the two-leggeds. It seemed like there should be a ceremony or something, a big crowd cheering them all on while they ascended onto the dragons' backs.

"After you, my love," Nikolean said, gesturing to the dragon before her with a warm smile on his face.

Even though they weren't going to be flying, it was still incredible how much they had accomplished so far in forming a union with the ancient beings. As she stepped up onto the Blue's arm, she hoped that it would be just the first of many steps of two-leggeds and dragons uniting. The Blue lifted his arm, allowing Laila to hoist herself up onto his back. Drorzyn flattened his fins, creating a safe space for her to sit while Nikolean and Salyaman joined her.

It was a strange sensation to them, not at all like being on their mounts. Laila shifted, trying to find a comfortable position between the fins, testing out adequate ways to grab hold of them. She smiled slyly, remembering King Brakdrath's suggestion of saddles, and really wished she had one at that moment.

Once all were settled on their respective dragons, the Blues squirmed over the beach pebbles, the creatures upon their backs feeling every jerky movement as they made their way awkwardly back to the cool sea. As the dragons splashed down into the icy water, they kept their backs elevated high enough that it gratefully did not affect their passengers. Then, without another word, they were off.

The gang grabbed on the best they could as the Blues swam across the water's surface. The movements of the Water Dragons were smooth and gentle now that they were in the sea. They swam slowly at first as they slithered and stroked the water, but before they knew it, the dragons were torpedoing across to the other side at incredible speed, much faster than the raft had allowed even with Drorzyn's assist.

Laila looked out over the beautiful glistening water, then closed her eyes to feel the wind whooshing over her face, the breeze battering in her ears, her golden hair whipping wildly behind her. Luckily for Nikolean, he had just enough space between them to not be caught in the thrash of her locks as he and the others all enjoyed the moment as well. Even Hort found himself a little excited, albeit scared.

The only negative Laila considered about the ride on the Water Dragons was that it was over barely after it had begun, and she frowned upon seeing the land of Onis coming into view once again. The Blues took them straight up to the shore, back to their mounts, back to her reality of what they must do next.

As they approached, Laila could see that Davion and Gothäzer had barely beaten them back, even with their head start. She watched as the great Red touched down, flapping his wings while settling his hind legs on the rocky surface, with Davion still in his clutches.

Turathyl was resting on the shore with the mounts nearby, and Laila was relieved to see her Merimer alive and well, patiently waiting for her return.

'Now I shall never hear the end of it,' Turathyl groaned, seeing Nikolean upon the back of a Blue.

While Nikolean hopped off of Drorzyn back onto the land, he said wryly, "Tury, you're just jealous that you didn't host me first."

The dragon huffed at the drow, glaring at him and not even dignifying him with a response. The rest of the group dismounted from the Blues and joined them onshore.

"Thank you, Drorzyn. You have been most kind to us," Laila said, bowing before the ancient Blue.

'Omi Méa, it has been my honor,' the Blue replied, bowing back to her.

"The honor has been ours," she insisted.

Then the Blue turned and elegantly headed back out into the water.

Laila watched as the last of Drorzyn's fins vanished beneath the surface and continued to stare for a moment after he was gone, memorizing the beauty of the ocean. She prayed to the gods for a chance to come back one day under more peaceful circumstances.

CHAPTER THIRTY-TWO

CORDIAL

*A*ll mounted back up on Merimer, Orbek, Helna, Midnight, and Friet, the comrades headed east along the coast at a fast gallop, trying to cover as much ground as they could before they would lose another day. With the southern tip of the Du Noir Forest at their left and the Blue Sea at their right, they were able to move swifter by staying along the shoreline. It also made it easier for Astryma, who was following along in the water. Turathyl had assured them that the coastline would lead directly to the Du Noir Hills, where the Golds could be found.

Unfortunately, the Gold territory was still several days away, and Laila was agonizing over how much time they had left, wishing she knew what was going on with Aeris.

Meanwhile, Gothäzer and Turathyl flew above and scouted ahead, making a clear passage to their destination. While they did, they indulged in the occasional wildlife that might have otherwise posed a threat to the two-leggeds. Of course, no one believed that a wimblebuck or two would have posed a threat to anyone, but they let the dragons enjoy their catches of the fat and stoutly cousins of the humans' cattle all the same—so long as they shared a beefy thigh now and then.

When the day was near its end and the mounts had lost their drive, the group decided to stop for the night near the coast. While everyone unburdened their steeds, Astryma came hopping ashore excitedly toward Glondora. The water dripped from her beautiful scales, shining in the setting sun as she pranced around the tiny dwarf. Laila enjoyed the Blue's enthusiasm and how excited Glondora was to have her "very own dragon."

The elf maiden went to join the newcomer and dwarves, hoping to make a better bond with the Blue than she had managed so far with the Red. She still hadn't given up on Gothäzer nor on rebuilding her relationship with Davion, but perceived the spunky young dragon to be much more receptive to the two-leggeds than the mighty Red had been.

Stepping before them, Laila bowed to the young Blue in homage, commanding their attention, but sensed nervousness emanating from Astryma.

'I am honored that you agreed to join our mission, Astryma of the Blues,' Laila told her respectfully. She hoped that mind-speaking with the dragon would help open the Blue up to communicating with her more readily. 'May I ask why you volunteered?'

The beautiful Blue Dragon bowed her head back to the Omi Méa and replied, 'I did not know the mother dragon and only heard stories of the two-leggeds, never actually seeing one for myself. I was expecting you to be evil and attack us, as the stories suggested, but when I connected with Glondora Emberforge, Hydromancer of Lochlann, I sensed a kindred spirit that held not one bit of evil within. It gave me much hope to hear the prophecy of what it is you are trying to accomplish. I have longed to travel beyond our waters and explore the *world of Onis but never believed I could.'* Pausing for a moment, the Blue lowered her head and said, *'I hope you are not too disappointed that a stronger dragon, more well-traveled and battle-ready, did not volunteer for this mission.'*

Laila smiled earnestly at the Blue and told her, *'Astryma, I couldn't be more pleased. The way you and Glondora have bonded is a true testament to our goal of uniting the dragons and other races. I am sure you will do fine with whatever experience you have.'*

Frowning, the Water Dragon looked over at Glondora, and the dwarf stepped forward with a similar look of woe upon her face.

"What is it?" Laila asked.

"Tis alright," Glondora told her dragon, patting her, then added, "She be a bit nervous ta tell ye that she never been in a battle. Astryma 'ere be a very young seventy-six, even younger than meself and me husband."

Laila looked between the two of them, confused. It then dawned on her that if the Blues had all retreated to the waters a few hundred years ago, then Astryma would never have had the need to learn to fight. Upon perceiving the ground rumbling beneath her, Laila turned to find Turathyl approaching them.

The magnificent Silver raised her head regally to the young Blue and told them, *'When we began this journey, even the prophesied elf had much to learn before she was ready, and even then, things did not go as we had hoped. We cannot predict what is to come, but I will do my utmost to help you prepare.'*

Astryma expressed her gratitude, promising she'd do her best not to disappoint. Laila had no notion of what to expect and only prayed that with Turathyl's guidance, the inexperienced Blue's life would not be put in jeopardy when the time came. Even knowing that it was a risk they had all agreed to when they embarked on their quest, it never sat right with Laila. She felt responsible for all of her companions' lives.

After taking her leave, Laila went to rejoin Nikolean while the group began to settle, preparing for the night ahead. Meanwhile, Turathyl took on an almost motherly role to the young dragon, telling her tales of Onis and giving advice that might help her against the different dragon clans.

Despite Astryma's lack of confidence in herself and inexperience, Laila honestly believed that she was precisely the right dragon to have bonded with Glondora. Though, she discerned that the Blue seemed somewhat intimidated by the much grander dragons, actually preferring the company of Glondora and Hort, which she found unexpected and also entertaining at times.

As she stood next to Nikolean, Laila watched on in amusement while the dragon bonded with Glondora. The elf grinned as the spunky dwarf managed to convince her husband to pet the Blue's snout, even though he only agreed to do it so she would never ask him to again. The dragon and Glondora both enjoyed teasing Hort, but he was secretly enjoying it too, especially how happy it made his wife.

With as much enjoyment as the Blue and dwarves were having, Laila was unsettled to espy Davion and Gothäzer continuing to remain set off from the rest of the group. The human was standing near a second firepit he had created solely to practice playing with the flames, honing his skills.

Her success with Astryma gave Laila the encouragement she needed, so she took a deep breath and strode over to the morose duo, determined to be civil with Davion, if nothing else. Albeit, she still desired to reach Gothäzer and build a trust with him as well.

Regally raising his head and eying the approaching Omi Méa, Gothäzer subtly told the pyromancer, 'You may want to focus on calming your fire, young Davion. Your tormentor approaches.'

Turning to face Laila, Davion asked the Red, '*My tormentor?*'

'*Am I wrong?*'

"Hello," Laila said as she neared them.

Davion nodded while Gothäzer continued to stare.

"Isn't it incredible that we only have one more clan to approach?" the elf maiden asked cordially.

"Yes, Lady Laila," Davion replied, maintaining a stoic expression. He watched her keenly, studying her to determine what it was she was after.

"We have been very fortunate so far," Laila continued.

"Yes, Lady Laila," he repeated.

The elf took several steps closer to him. In a softer voice, she added, "We must all be more careful as we approach the Golds. We may not be as lucky with them."

The human continued staring at her, confused. At no point did he feel that either he or Gothäzer had let down their guard with the Blues, as the others had.

"I couldn't bear to lose you," the elf maiden told him. "Any of you."

Gothäzer continued to look on them without a word, and Laila could sense the mighty dragon's resistance to her. Davion's eyes widened slightly, curious of her intent.

"Can I count on you?" she asked with a smile.

Did that mean she had forgiven him? As he gazed into her eyes, Davion felt his heart rate increase while he contemplated her motivation for coming over.

"Of course you can," he replied, smiling back. "Always."

Davion considered stepping closer to her but was painfully aware of the drow watching them closely, and he wasn't interested in another of his friendly chats.

Fighting his urges, he tucked his chin to her in a slight bow instead. "Do not fret, Lady Laila. Gothäzer and I will stay alert and protect you at all costs."

Although smiling appreciatively, Laila was a little disheartened about the formality that had come between them. That being said, she was glad they seemed to at least be getting to a place where they could be cordial with one another.

The elf maiden would be lying if she didn't admit that she missed the human's companionship and closeness, her friend who liked to laugh and would light up whenever she was near. Now, she couldn't recall the last time she had heard him laugh, and it broke her heart to see him so dejected.

"Thank you, Davion," she grinned.

Fidgeting uncomfortably under their gazes for a moment, Laila then made a curtsy gesture before smiling awkwardly and turning to head back to the others. Davion grinned widely, watching as she walked away, clearly nervous.

'I knew it,' he beamed mentally to the Red.

'And what did you know?' he queried.

'She still cares for me. All is not lost.'

Gothäzer glared at the human quizzically. 'I must have been witnessing a different conversation,' he told Davion skeptically. 'The Omi Méa I saw merely seemed concerned about her group all being massacred and failing in her quest.'

Not taking his eyes off the maiden, Davion mind-sent, 'Two-legged women are different. You have to read the subtle things; they never say what they really mean. You watch. You'll see. She and I are connected. We just need to get rid of that drow...' Davion's thoughts trailed off as he grinned darkly back at his firepit, fantasizing a future with the Omi Méa on one side and the Mighty Red Gothäzer on the other.

On their final night before reaching the Golds' territory, Laila stood near the fire, monitoring the others as they slept, while Nikolean walked the perimeter. Turathyl was also awake, keeping an eye out for any possible Gold scouts.

Laila didn't expect to get much sleep that night, dreading what the next day would bring. She feared another battle with the dragons and the possibility that her luck with convincing them to join their cause may have run out.

Closing her eyes to say another prayer to the gods, she smiled when she felt the gentle arms of Nikolean wrap around her in a soothing embrace. She rested her head against his chest, breathing in his familiar scent, and reciprocated his gesture, holding him tightly while he softly kissed the top of her head.

"You should get some sleep, my love," he told her, concerned. "Tury and I have this."

She chuckled a little as though he had told her a joke and picked her head up off his chest to look up into his captivating red eyes. No matter how many times she gazed into them, she still swooned whenever they would lock their sight with one another. "Thank you, Niko, but I don't think that will be possible tonight."

"I understand," he stated.

Laila looked over at the flames dancing in the firepit, finding solace in the dark elf's arms.

Nikolean continued to hold her, wishing he could tell her that everything would work out just fine. "I know that we've been very fortunate with the Reds and Blues, but I am nervous also," he admitted. "Although, I am hopeful that by having members from all three of the other clans, it will help in convincing the Golds to join us as well."

Laila's lips curved into a smile as she released a soft sigh. She prayed he was right, but it didn't change her anxiety over it.

CHAPTER 32

Had the Reds or even the Blues decided that they did *not* wish to join their cause, would any of them even still be standing there? Could they honestly have survived an attack whilst being in the hearts of the dragon lairs? Thankfully, luck had been on their side thus far.

'*I don't believe it is luck,*' Turathyl told her, hearing her thoughts and anxieties. '*You have been blessed by the gods, and they are on your side, Laila. They put you here with a purpose. I can't be certain what the Golds or their monarch, the Powerful Terus, will do tomorrow, but I have faith that you will know what to do when the time comes.*'

Leaning farther into Nikolean's embrace, Laila rested her head back against his chest and thought about Turathyl's words. She recalled that Ignisar had said the same thing to her about knowing what to do when the time comes. Closing her eyes, she finished her prayer to the Goddess Jayenne, asking for her guidance and wisdom. She then prayed to Kyrash for his favor and strength for all of them as they prepared themselves to go before the Golds.

CHAPTER THIRTY-THREE

GOLDS

*T*he day came all too quickly. Laila hadn't obtained a wink of sleep and wasn't even able to enjoy the sunrise as she usually did. Aside from being wrought with worry, it was a sunless sky, completely overcast, with a light fog covering the ground. The air was muggy, with not a breeze to be had, a telling sign that the seasons were readying to change once again.

Laila's stomach was in knots from the anxiety of what the day would bring. It was finally time, the moment they would confront the last of the dragon clans. They could very well have secured support from all four of the clans by that time tomorrow, further increasing their chances of stopping the war.

Or...

They could all die that day. Laila shuddered at the thought. *No*, she told herself, *I will not let that happen.*

'Nor will I,' Turathyl told her.

'Nor I,' Gothäzer chimed in.

The sound of the Red's voice in Laila's mind was startling to her since he still tended to only commune with Davion.

Then, the gentle voice of the young Blue said with pride, '*Nor I!*'

Turathyl came over to the young elf, bowing her head near her, and purred as Laila lovingly grabbed hold of her snout.

'*Thank you,*' she told them all, nuzzling her dragon.

As they started out their day, the group was optimistic, full of hope, and keeping the mounts at a steady trot. After a few hours, their pace grew noticeably slower as they neared the Golds' territory, reality settling in for each of them, and they were down to a wary, languid walk.

An hour had passed since they saw the last of the withering gray trees of the Du Noir Forest, and the terrain had become quite rough, covered in large hills and mounds. Several of them were surprised at the greenery there that flourished more notably the farther they went. Salyaman knew it was due to the dragons' earth spirit keeping the land alive and the plague at bay. But not entirely, for even the Du Noir Hills were not in the same state of lush glory as they had once been; the remaining trees were scarce, and there was nowhere near the diversity of vegetation of before.

The dreariness of the day had the group in low spirits as they crossed into the Golds' territory on high alert, squinting all around them through the haze for any signs of the powerful dragons. They could hear their calls and roars in the distance and knew they were extremely close. Everyone held weapons at the ready, not knowing how their presence would be received.

After covering a few more hills, their accompanying dragons spread their wings slightly and stiffened their stances.

'*They're here,*' their dragons warned them.

"Be ready," Laila relayed to Hort and Salyaman.

A loud roar thundered through the hills, and everyone looked up as three giant dragons materialized in the sky. As they neared, Laila admired their beautiful golden scale armor, imagining how brilliant it must be in the sun. They were beastly in size, grander than the average Silvers, yet not so mighty as the Reds, and were very robust in form. Unlike the Silvers and Blues with their slick and smooth bodies, the Golds covering was jagged and harsh in appearance, like stone.

Instead of coming to face the group, the large masses circled widely around them above, studying their unique guests. Turathyl let out a throaty caw, prompting them to come, but they continued to hover, responding with a monstrous roar.

'They are telling us to leave,' Turathyl relayed.

While reaching her mind out to them, Laila raised her hands into the sky and looked up with a pleading countenance. *'Please, we wish to speak with the Powerful Terus!'* she mind-sent.

The dragons let out a blaring screech in response. *'Leave now!'* one of them sent back to her.

Laila glanced considerately over at Salyaman to see if the mind-voice had harmed him, but he hadn't reacted at all. She was concerned to find him looking up just the same as the others, worried he had not acquired the same gift.

Without warning, all the mounts began to bolt in several directions, everyone holding tight to their reins. Only Merimer stayed steady under the Omi Méa while everyone else hollered, panicking about what was happening while trying desperately to stop their steeds.

'They've taken control of the mounts!' Turathyl roared irately and leaped into the sky, thrashing her wings several times as she gained altitude with haste. *'We must stop them and get them to face us!'*

Laila instinctively stretched out her mind to the mounts, trying to ease them, but felt the resistance from the dragons' control. Gothäzer followed Turathyl's lead, powering his wings toward the ground as he gradually lifted his monstrous form into the air, roaring along with the Silver. After her initial hesitation, Astryma followed the Red into the sky, flapping her delicate wings wildly.

As Turathyl neared the Golds, she sent a gale at them for distraction, causing them to beat heavily against it, breaking their hold on the mounts. Laila's friends struggled to regain control, the steeds rearing, confused and frightened by what had just happened.

The mighty Gothäzer collided into the nearest Gold, his overpowering size dominating the Earth Dragon. He grabbed it with his talons as they twirled in the air, descending toward the ground. All the dragons were shrieking in an uproar as they attacked one another.

A Gold charged at the Blue, who tried her best to evade the much larger dragon as he chased her through the sky, snapping his jaws at her lengthy tail every time he got close. Turathyl aimed her gale at Astryma's pursuer, watching out for the young dragon while the third Gold glared below, focusing on the intruders on the ground.

While they looked on from the surface, the comrades felt both helpless and terrified. The ground beneath them began to quake turbulently, and the steeds pranced over the trembling earth as it cracked and split near them. Merimer leaped with Laila vigorously when the ground crumbled under her, and a large crack opened up. The others all did the same, trying to keep their footing while more fissures appeared and expanded.

When the ground disappeared behind the okullo's hind legs, Glondora screamed as Orbek struggled to scale the ledge with the weight of the two dwarves upon his back. To counter the dragon's power, Laila thrust her hands forward and pulled for part of the earth to rise back up under the okullo's rear hooves, hoisting her friends back to safety. Then she continued to heave mentally at the other cracks with great resistance against the powerful Gold's force, stopping them from spreading any farther.

Above, Turathyl attacked the Earth Dragon, snapping her jaws at it wildly while she grabbed hold of it with her claws, breaking its focus on the cohorts below.

When Astryma could no longer evade her aggressor, she yelped in pain as it caught up with her and clasped its fangs into her long tail.

Glondora hastily waved her staff, shouting, "*Ferétsa ageeran!*" and the dragon on Astryma's tail began to slow slightly from the freeze, but it was not powerful enough to stop it. Regardless, Astryma managed to kick at the dragon, getting it to release her tail, then recovered herself and dove briskly away.

'*Stop this!*' Laila called out desperately to all of them. '*We are here to speak of peace! Please stop!*'

Yet, they didn't stop. The Gold that had been attacking the Blue, angered and confused by Laila's mind-speech, began diving at the tiny companions instead.

Descrying its powerful mass thundering down toward them was a most frightening sight; the dragon's teeth bared aggressively, a loud growl emitting from deep in its chest. As it neared, plunging with its wings tucked, wind billowing around its frame, it aimed for the Omi Méa, ready to crush her into the ground. Laila reached out, sending a telekinetic blast toward the beast, but it didn't even slow it down. Instead, it made the dragon even angrier as it roared horrifically toward her. Laila momentarily froze, shaking, her heart throbbing hard while the blood drained from her face at the sight of the monstrous, murderous form diving for her. The beast brought its feet forward, readying for the impact.

CHAPTER 33

Turathyl slammed into the Gold, forcing it to the ground near Laila with a loud crash, rumbling the surrounding earth. Watching in astonishment, the companions felt the ground vibrations up through their mounts from the collision and rode promptly toward Laila and the brawling dragons. The Silver snapped fiercely at the Gold, grabbing hold of its neck and pinning it down.

Above their heads, the sky was alight with fire from Gothäzer blaring flames at another dragon, while Astryma did her best to distract the third.

'If you're going to kill me, then get it over with!' roared the Gold under Turathyl's grasp.

Laila rode Merimer toward the restrained dragon, raising her hands non-threateningly, as she sent to all of them, *'We do not wish to harm any of you! I am Lady Lailalanthelus Dula'Quoy, the Omi Méa of prophecy that has come to speak with the Powerful Terus to put an end to the war!'*

In an instant, the Golds ceased their attacks, pulling back, and relaxed their stances grudgingly. Although their actions indicated cooperation, the snarls on their lips and faces were unchanged. The Gold pinned under Turathyl stopped fighting against her but maintained its scowl toward the elf, desiring still to crush her.

Laila was honestly surprised they had responded so instantaneously to her request, but then loud booming steps echoed through the hills, commanding everyone's attention. As they all turned nervously toward the thunderous sound of the quaking mounds, a colossal dragon slowly emerged from the fog. Its golden armor was muted in the poor lighting from the muggy day, but it did not appear as withered and worn as the other monarchs had. Even the quills upon its neck and back were not as thick in mass, though they still surpassed Turathyl's, indicating it was much older than she. It held its head regally as it glared out over them, its long horns protruding upward and twisting at the tip, with its wings spread assertively.

'And why would I agree to end the war?' the powerful beast sneered once it came into view.

Turathyl reluctantly released her hold on the Gold under her talons and jaws and turned to face the new arrival before them, lowering her head in homage. Gothäzer and Astryma gracefully flew back down, landing between the rest of the group and the giant Gold protectively. Even though it was the youngest of the monarchs—apart from Turathyl—its presence still surpassed that of Gothäzer.

After dismounting from her steed, Laila bowed before the dragon. "Powerful Terus, we are on a mission of peace!"

'That is not what I have been told,' the dragon declared sternly.

Laila grew more dismayed as she realized that Aeris had probably already reached out to the Golds.

'I am here before you to fulfill the prophecy and restore the land of Onis.'

'The prophecy?' Terus said, cocking his eyebrow and looking over the tiny elf with scrutiny. *'And why now, after all this time? Who are you to claim to be the Great Spirit that Onis has been waiting for?'*

To her surprise, Salyaman dismounted and came up beside her, facing the Gold monarch. He then addressed Terus in the Ancient tongue, "When the land of Onis and its people have endured their suffering, there will be born of an elf a Great Spirit who will unite the races."

Laila looked at Salyaman, smiling, a tear in her eye as she realized he had indeed been hearing the Golds after all; he just hadn't been affected harshly due to his superior elven control. The Ruins of Pynar ceremony had finally completed in joining all the races and elemental magic classes with the dragons.

Gothäzer, taking on a strong stance, stepped forward and joined Salyaman in reminding the Powerful Terus, *'The Great Spirit will engage all of the races and will know no boundaries between them. That spirit will confront the Ancients of the land and ask forgiveness for the two-leggeds' past actions.'*

With a timid step forward, Astryma also raised her head, attempting to show confidence as she added, *'The Omi Méa will be guided by the earth, the air, the fire, the water, and the phantom realm to bring forth peace among all the evolved races.'*

Turathyl joined the others, saying proudly, *'The Omi Méa will bring about a new era and replenishment of life over the land, changing all that was, and all that will be.'* Then she added with conviction, *'I assure you that this young elf is indeed the Great Spirit. She has proven herself to all of us time and time again. Even the Great Wolf God, Lupé Caelis, believed her to be the one of prophecy and raised and trained her since she was a cub. The Great Spirit did not grow up in our world of hate and war. Yet, she has devoted her life to ending it for all of us so that the land may heal simply because she was told that it was her destiny.'*

As the remaining two Golds came down heavily behind their monarch, the powerful dragon heaved a growling sigh and looked around at the other two-leggeds. *'And what of them?'* Terus asked.

Laila explained to the Gold how she was drawn to the others and how they came upon the Ruins of Pynar, uniting them all together. After she introduced each of them, Salyaman knelt on one knee before the monarch, his head bowed, and he mind-sent to Terus, *'It is my honor to have united with the Earth Dragons, Powerful Terus.'*

While the elf maintained his bow, the large Gold contemplated what to do with them now. *'I had heard about an elf attacking the Great Aeris. It sounded rather far-fetched to me. And the thought that the Great Silver Monarch Aeris would be recruiting* other clans for retaliation against a mere elf girl is absurd. It has the aspects of an uproarious tale not to be taken seriously. Even so...' The Gold monarch rumbled a sigh as he paused. 'I have already had several of my children express their desire to join the Silver monarch. So, tell me,' Terus glared at Laila, 'why shouldn't I join the Great Aeris? Do you think you actually stand a chance against her?'

"Powerful Terus," Laila replied, "The dragons and two-leggeds before you are not all that we are. Turathyl has become the new monarch to a band of nineteen other Silvers that readily joined her. Mighty Ignisar has pledged his clan to aid me when the time to face Aeris is upon us, as has Fearsome Fonzar. We are also recruiting the two-legged races and their armies. So far, the dwarves and a faction of the dark elves called the Drakka have pledged their armies to us as well. We are next to see the humans and elves. We believe that by standing united, Aeris will have no choice but to see that the time for change is now.

"You have done well in maintaining life in your hills, but I can sense it dying. Once the dragons agree to stop the tyranny over the two-legged races, I promise you I will find a way to replenish your land again, just as I intend to for all of Onis and its surrounding waters."

'It doesn't matter,' Terus said, sadly groaning while looking at the surrounding hills. He rested his great mass on the ground beneath him, the earth rumbling from his movements. 'None of it.'

"What do you mean?" Laila responded. "Do you not want your hills to be healed?"

As the powerful dragon looked down at her, she could see the pain behind his eyes while he replied, 'It won't bring her back. The two-leggeds killed our mother, and stopping the war still won't bring her back. So what does it matter if the land continues to die around us? There is nothing you can do that will make it right. Perhaps Aeris holds the answer.'

"Ridding the land of two-leggeds won't bring Onis Caelis back either," Laila pointed out.

The dragon growled and snapped his jaws at her. *'You should not even speak her name!'*

The companions shook with the Gold's anger, as did the land beneath their feet, and they feared another seismic quake was coming. With a deep breath, Terus regained some of his composure, the trembling gradually ceasing, then continued, *'It may not bring her back, but perhaps it might just stop the hurting.'*

'Do you truly believe that it will?' Turathyl asked Terus. *'I recall our mother always having a soft spot for the two-leggeds. Do you think she would be happy to see what has become of them by our claws?'*

Astryma perked up as she said, *'What if it was Onis Caelis that sent the Omi Méa?'*

The dragons all looked at the Blue, intrigued by her theory, but the Gold monarch still remained forlorn, swaying his head back and forth. *'Regardless, it matters not to me whether my clan decides to join with you, or with Aeris, or with no one at all. It will change nothing. In the end, the result is the same; more dragons and two-leggeds will be killed. And, unless you manage to put a permanent end to Aeris, I doubt she will ever cease. I believe the only one that could put a true end to the war and stop Aeris would have to be Onis Caelis herself, the reason it all started in the first place. Since that is not an option, I fear we are to be stuck in a never-ending loop. If you kill Aeris to stop her, you will only anger more dragons to rise up in her stead for vengeance.'*

As he stood back up, the ground reacting and shifting with the Earth Dragon's every movement beneath him, Terus continued, *'I will leave it up to my children to decide if they want to involve themselves in your feud with the Great Silver Monarch. Those that wish to join you are free to do so, but I will be staying out of it.'* He turned and looked at the three Golds by him. *'What say you? Would any of you care to join the Omi Méa?'*

None of the dragons moved, nor responded, but continued to stare expressionless at the tiny creatures.

With all his mental strength, Salyaman looked at them pleadingly and mind-sent, *'Powerful Golds, I implore you to help us replenish the land of Onis. I know you must feel its pain, just as Lady Laila and I do.'*

After another moment, the larger of the three Golds walked heavily out before Terus and said, *'The pain of this land and the pain of losing Onis Caelis has weighed heavily on us. We cannot alleviate the latter, but perhaps if we are able to heal the land, we might heal a little ourselves and find some semblance of peace once again.'*

While raising his head high above the group in a proud stance, he continued, *'I am Masonel of the Golds, and I shall join you on this quest. I have been much too long in mourning and am of the same mind that this is likely not what our mother would have wanted for Onis.'*

Terus nodded his head to them in agreement and said, *'I will let my other children know of their options as well.'*

After Laila had relayed the plan to him of where they were to meet before facing Aeris, he spread his gigantic wings, the wind shifting from their magnitude.

'Any others who choose this path will await word from you when the time is nigh,' the Powerful Terus told them. To the Gold, he added earnestly, *'Be well, Masonel. I hope you are right and that your quest will help us to heal as well.'*

Repeatedly plunging his wings, the powerful monarch dragon lifted heavily into the air, the gusts whipping briskly over the group. The other two Golds were quick to follow, the flapping of all their wings resounding through the surrounding hills like the thundering of an imminent squall. Everyone watched as the beautiful dragons flew back the way of which they came, disappearing into the fog beyond.

CHAPTER 33

Salyaman & Masonel

CHAPTER THIRTY-FOUR

STARTLED

*S*tanding in the fog as the Golds disappeared, Laila's eyes began to swell, and her chest tightened. She couldn't believe it; it seemed like a dream. They had survived the final dragon clan encounter and would all live to see another day. Could it really be happening? It hadn't been quite the response that she was hoping to get from Terus, but at least he would not interfere with their plan and was permitting his clan the option of joining them.

As she turned her back to the mist, she gleamed at her group, overwhelmed with pride. Nikolean swiftly scooped her up in his arms, twirling her around in the air for a moment while she laughed in astonishment.

"You did it, my love!" he told her with pride, then lowered her gently back to the ground. He gazed down into her eyes, smiles wide upon both their faces, then he kissed her with elation.

"We all did it!" Glondora hollered to everyone, raising her fist to the sky. "I canna' believe we actually did it!"

While wiping the happy tears from her eyes, Laila watched her group joyously congratulate one another. Turathyl smiled at them, pleased with their excitement, while Astryma hopped around giddily, sharing in her dwarf's delight, even though not fully comprehending what she was so happy about.

To Laila's surprise, she even saw a smile on Davion's lips as he patted his dragon on the foreleg while Gothäzer maintained his majestic stance.

Meanwhile, the newcomer to the group watched them all with curiosity, partially wondering if he had made the right decision.

'It is getting late,' Masonel pointed out. 'After your comrades have settled and are safe, I will use the remainder of the night to speak with my clan about the prophecy. Perhaps I can convince others to join you as well.'

Laila gave an appreciative nod to the golden dragon. 'Thank you,' she told him earnestly. 'And I hope that, with time, you will consider them to be your comrades as well.'

As the Gold continued to look on her without expression, she noticed that Salyaman had been standing back, observing them from a distance, arms crossed over his chest. After excusing herself for a moment, she walked over to the high elf and took his hand in hers. Salyaman stared at her, confused, as her lips curved in a warm smile.

"Come with me," Laila told him.

Slowly, they approached Masonel, and the Gold stared down at them apprehensively. His monstrous form was stiffly posed, and his wings were still spread assertively. Laila and Salyaman bowed before him.

"Powerful Masonel, this is the elf prince of Má Lyndor. He is a ranger united with you through the spirits of Pynar."

The Gold stared at the elves, unimpressed, not understanding the relevance.

'*You were the dragon that created the cracks in the earth,*' Salyaman mind-sent to the Gold with a reverent demeanor.

Masonel responded with a slight nod.

As the elf and dragon conversed silently, Laila grinned and took her leave, giving them a chance to get to know one another better.

"Well, lass," Hort called to her as she approached the rest of the group. "I be sorry I ever doubted ye. Ye jus' might not be crazy after all!"

The elf maiden gave a half-smile to the dwarf, appreciating his gesture.

"We will rest here for tonight," she announced to the group, and everyone agreed.

Settling in for the night had suddenly become much more crowded with another giant dragon in their midst. It was quite the entourage Laila had gathered for herself.

While she observed Davion light a fire and the others prepare for the night, Laila couldn't help but think back to her Wolf God mother. She wondered if Lupé Caelis had any way of knowing what she had been up to the entire time, and if she'd be proud of her. Laila prayed for the day that she would get to return to her quiet little den in the Sacred Forest and tell Lupé Caelis all about her wild adventure with the dragons. The thought of introducing her to Nikolean made her nervously excited, fearful of whether the Great Wolf God would approve.

'*If I survive this, I promise I will see you again, Mother,*' she thought aimlessly into the darkening sky.

Laila then walked with Merimer toward the outskirt of the campsite, joining the other mounts. The beautiful unicorn-elkah followed her loyally while she led her to the water Glondora had set out for them. While the mystical creature took a drink of the cool refreshment, Laila stroked her neck fondly, lost in her thoughts of the day's events. She was startled when she suddenly heard a voice behind her.

"What's the plan for tomorrow?" Davion asked her, approaching.

Laila jerked her body around to face him with a nervous gulp, her heart racing from the surprise. She instantly noticed they were alone and reflexively crossed her arms over her chest. It was such a strange feeling to be startled by Davion, but they had grown so distant from each other that she wasn't sure what to expect from him. As he stood there staring at her with a slight smile brushed across his lips, she cleared her throat.

"I suppose we leave for the next closest city," she told him. "We still need to go before the humans and the elves again, now that we have much more influence."

"The next closest city would be Mira, a human town," he told her. "It would be good to stop there for supplies. The king isn't there, but I know some powerful mages that are. Perhaps they might agree to help us."

As she smiled warmly at him, she said, "That would be wonderful! Then, I suppose tomorrow we are off to Mira."

Laila was about to return her attention to Merimer, but realized that Davion wasn't leaving. He took two more steps toward her, bringing himself uncomfortably close, and she started growing a little antsy. The smile faded from her face as he then drew even nearer. She couldn't help but remember the last time they were that close, flinching at the remembrance of the pain on her arms from his flames.

Upon perceiving her discomfort, Davion raised his hands in acquiescence while he took a step back, offended that she seemed almost afraid of him. With her attempts at being civil toward him, he believed they were moving past what had happened, hopeful of rekindling some fraction of what they had before.

THE DRAGONS

"I only wanted to congratulate you, Lady Laila. You have managed to do the impossible." Pausing for a moment, he discerned her relax a little, then added, "And, the gift you have given me..." He hesitated to continue, reconsidering what he was about to say.

Even though he had been referring to his secret fire spirit that she had forced into him with who-knows-what-else, he glanced briefly at the Red. The dragon was holding a statuesque pose while glaring annoyedly at the happy peppy dwarves and Blue around him.

Looking back to the elf maiden, Davion continued, "...Gothäzer, I mean. To be linked with a dragon has been incredible. To feel my power increase through our connection has been even more so."

"I have noticed the two of you have been growing closer," Laila told him encouragingly. "I am glad you have each other."

"Well... It wasn't love at first sight," Davion attested with a sly grin. "But, it's a start. Although, in time, I hope to grow even closer with someone else."

When he witnessed Laila's anxious expression return from his implication, he added, "Rest well, Lady Laila."

Then, the human gave her an exaggerated bow and a mischievous smirk before turning and leaving her in her thoughts.

Try as she might to understand him, Davion had become a mystery to Laila. She couldn't quite get a sense for what was going on with him anymore, and, after the hostility from Gothäzer last time, she didn't dare eavesdrop into his mind again to find out.

"Are ye alright, me boy?" Hort asked, catching Davion as he strode heatedly back toward his dragon.

Stopping, Davion turned to Hort but couldn't look him in the eye as he heaved a heavy sigh and crossed his arms. "I'm not sure, Uncle," he replied, looking beyond him into the barren hills. "I thought we were getting past what happened, but now I just don't know."

"Come sit," Hort told him, putting his arm around Davion's back and leading him to the fire.

Once they were settled, Davion stared into the flames while Hort told him sympathetically, "I canna' say what be goin' through the lass's mind, but I knows yer a good man. She jus' wasna' the right lass fer ye tis all, but I believe ye'll find the one yer meant ta one day, hopefully when this all be over wit'."

Davion finally looked at his uncle, the human's eyes glistening as he told him, "I'm not sure I agree with you, Uncle. Either way, you're all I have left in the world. I am really grateful you're here with me right now. Otherwise, I don't know if I could bear to watch her be with him another day."

Handing him some dried meat to munch on, Hort added, "Well, ye'll always 'ave me, lad. But, hey! Ye got yerself a dragon now, too!"

With a brief glance at the Red, Davion sighed. "I'm not even sure he likes me."

"Hmmm..." Hort grumbled, looking toward the pit. "He isna' exacitally the warmest dragon considerin' he breathes fire. But, me boy, ye can also be rest assured that yer mum and paw be watchin' over ye as well. They'd be so proud o' who ye are and all that ye've done so far. They'll always be wit' ye, me boy. Dunna' forget that. And jus' wait and see, ye'll find someone real special when tis the right time."

Davion sniffled, wiping a tear from his eye as he watched the fire with Hort. "Thanks, Uncle, but I know there's no one that could ever take her place. I still believe there's hope for us. I just don't know how to get back what we had before. She and

I are still tied somehow, and I have to trust that it is the gods telling us we're supposed to be together. She is just blinded by that drow."

"Well," Hort sighed, "I 'ope ye be right. But if not, jus' remember that there be plenty o' laidens that would be more than lucky ta 'ave ye."

Hort remained with Davion, sitting quietly as they viewed the fire together. He wished he had some magic of his own to cast over the boy to help him move past his feelings for the Omi Méa. The dwarf was not as convinced as the human about them being destined to be together and hated to see him clinging to that hope.

Drowsily blinking her eyes open, wrapped up in the arms of her love, Laila smiled as she saw her exquisite Silver friend soaring by above them, heading away as she did her morning rounds. She took a deep breath, letting the sunshine kiss her awake, not ready to disturb Nikolean, who was still asleep. The land had been growing warmer, and she sensed she was once again near to her Sacred Forest, feeling it through the earth. It made her nostalgic and hopeful.

The group was on their final day of traveling to their next destination, the human town of Mira, and the two-legged companions were eager to have a chance to sleep in a real bed again, even if for only one night. On the other hand, the dragons were less than eager to see the human town, knowing they would not be a welcomed sight by the two-leggeds. It was astounding to Laila how close Mira had been to where she grew up and yet so far away, never having known any of it.

As she detected Nikolean beginning to stir, Laila decided it was time to begin their day and sat herself up. While stretching out her limbs, she glanced around and her face turned red as she realized that she and Nikolean were the last ones to wake, the sounds of morning chatter already filling the air. She couldn't believe how tired she had been after having lost so much sleep in anticipation of confronting each of the dragon clans. Now that they had faced all four and had an Ancient from each clan by their sides, Laila felt significantly more at ease. Even her cohorts would never have predicted how comforting it would be to have dragons so near.

While munching on her rations, Laila grinned delightedly in her surveillance of the others. Salyaman had a slow start with Masonel, but once they broke the ice, they found they got along rather well. The elf was currently sprouting vines from the ground to ensnare the powerful dragon's feet. It was impressive but by no means a match for a Gold yet. Masonel chuckled as he effortlessly broke his paw free, but pushed the elf to keep trying. Salyaman relentlessly practiced all his spells, testing their new limits and powers with Masonel's help, and wondered what new abilities he might have gained that he hadn't even discovered yet.

Before they left the Golds' territory, Masonel managed to recruit another seven of his clan, and more were still considering. Unfortunately, several did not believe in the prophecy or believe it possible to forgive the two-leggeds, and left to seek out Aeris. They learned that the Gold clan did not share the large numbers of the other clans with only a couple dozen. There had been only two new hatches since Onis Caelis had been killed, and the group was beyond grateful to have gained any Gold followers at all.

The most surprising of her companions to Laila was Hort. She discreetly observed him with amusement after she caught him talking to Astryma once again, assuming that no one was looking. It had happened several times now, the dragon clearly growing on the dwarf, but she knew better than to mention it to him or anyone, knowing he was too proud and would deny any such accusations. Laila didn't think she would ever see him appreciate a dragon the way he did Astryma, and she couldn't help but snicker quietly to herself while watching them.

Davion had finished his breakfast and was toying with flames in his palms, creating and extinguishing the small fires repeatedly and wordlessly while he ignored the rest of the group. Laila wondered if she and the human could ever converse without turmoil again but refused to let it bring her down.

While handing her a flask of water, Nikolean sat down beside Laila, asking, "And what has made my lady so cheerful this morning?"

"All of this," she replied, turning her attention back to the rest of the group. "We have come such a long way from where we all started, and it is more than I had ever dreamed possible when I left my home. Hopefully, over the next few days, we will gain the support of the humans, and perhaps, in our traveling to the elven capital, I will finally get to see my elven mother's home, Othsuda Theora."

Nikolean stared at her attentively, forcing a smile for her benefit. He was happy to see her optimism about what lay ahead and did not want to ruin her euphoria. That being said, aside from not looking forward to the hatred from the two races yet to approach, he hadn't forgotten that they're not on an excursion to explore Onis and make new friends; there was a war going on. "All of this" was them trying to build an army because they were about to make history in an attempt to confront the most significant threat the land had ever faced. But, no, he would not take her moment from her. Instead, he wrapped his arm around his love and sat meekly with her while she finished her meal.

Handing Nikolean back the flask, Laila stood up and started dusting herself off. Suddenly, the smile waned from her

CHAPTER 34

face as a feeling of nausea swept over her, and she began to feel very lightheaded. Something was wrong. She knew it. But she didn't know what. Frantically looking around at the group, she searched for anything alarming, but everyone was going about their morning routines, just like any other day, with smiles upon nearly all their faces.

"My lady?" Nikolean stood, concerned by her demeanor.

As she searched the skies, Laila saw Turathyl coming back into view from the clouds to the north, and she heaved a sigh of relief. She reached out her mind to her Silver to welcome her back, but was startled to be met with resistance, and her heart instantly stopped. It wasn't her Silver at all.

Struggling to discover who it was, Laila squinted her eyes against the sky and focused her gaze on the approaching dragon. The elf maiden's body went heavy and numb, her eyes grew wide with dread, the back of her neck beaded in a cold sweat as her jaw dropped, and she froze in shock while time slowed down. The Silver was not alone.

More and more dragons were materializing out from the clouds. There were well over a dozen of them heading straight towards the group, and she could sense with certainty that they were most definitely *not* friends.

In an all-out panic, Laila screamed to everyone, her voice piercing through the clamor as time caught back up with her, "THE DRAGONS ARE COMING!!"

CHAPTER THIRTY-FIVE

DRAGONS

A fierce wind billowed through the camp as the gargantuan Red and Gold Dragons powered their wings with force to take flight. While blocking their faces from the stirring gale, the tiny beings grabbed firm to their weapons. Astryma stayed on the ground with the others, protectively close to the dwarves.

Sensing the energy shifting on the winds, all the mounts, except for Merimer, pranced nervously before darting south, away from the incoming horde. The hybrid stayed near Laila, out of the way, snorting to let her know she would not leave should she need her.

It was a deadly storm of killing machines heading their way, and thunder drummed like a battle song through the ominous skies. Laila stared at the terrifying clouds with thrashing wings, waveringly flush as they approached, as though her blood were pooling in her feet.

As the warnings of the dragons coming took form before her, she was agitated by Dragonsbane vibrating in her shaking grasp. Her bottom lip trembled in fear. Laila took a deep breath, closing her eyes, and then let the breath out slowly, trying to control her nerves and steady her body. She didn't have the luxury of being weak, not now. The dragons were coming fast and full of wrath, their calls cutting through the sky threateningly.

'*Where are you, Tury?*' Laila questioned, searching the skies desperately with her thoughts.

Someone's unexpected grip on her hand startled her, prompting her to swiftly open her eyes. She felt a wave of comfort wash over her when she saw Nikolean by her side.

'*I'm coming!*' they both heard Turathyl call back from the opposite direction of the incoming army, and were relieved she was okay.

Laila gripped tightly on her Dragonsbane spear, her focus sharp and heated as she glared upon the incoming score of dragons, quickly counting twenty of them. The majority of the flock was comprised of Silvers, but five Reds were amongst them as well.

Overhead, Gothäzer roared ferociously. The ground beneath the comrades' feet shook, and they were chilled to their bones from the resounding thunder of his anger, a tingling sensation crawling up their legs and spines. As they beheld the mighty dragon, the largest of all those present, with a muzzle glowing like a burning oven, they were grateful that the Red was on their side.

'*Kainüs is with them! My traitorous brother!*' Gothäzer growled before roaring out again.

As the dragons neared, Laila recognized the Silver leading them, and her mind flashed back to the place of her nightmares. The lead dragon had the same arrogance and animosity as when she first encountered the spiteful Silver scout.

Griton, she fumed inwardly, her eyes glaring at him with disdain. It was the same Griton who had attacked her on the side of Silvers' Mountain, the same Griton who had lifted her up to the Great Aeris, where she was nearly killed. It appeared he had been promoted by the Silver monarch since last they met for their shared contempt of the two-leggeds.

Laila quivered at the memories flashing through her mind. She had believed she had overcome that moment, that feeling of failure and dread. Yet, in the presence of all the hostile dragons, cognizant of the hatred radiating off of them as before, she felt like that same scared young elf all over again.

No, she told herself adamantly, *I can do this. I have to. I cannot fail again!*

The heat boiled up inside Laila while she stared at the Silver. She remembered the hatred she felt from him back then, and sensed now that it had only grown.

With a glance over at her group, she saw that everyone was readying themselves for the dragons' attack as the monsters grew close. She perceived her comrades' fear and trepidation, but she would have to count on them to be ready for what was about to come.

Once within range, the flock of dragons slowed and hovered apart from them, glaring at the group and the two airborne dragons. Anticipating their attack, Laila's heart was palpitating and her breathing heavy as she waited to see what they would do. She didn't feel prepared, but recognized it was a relatively small force to be considered a full-scale attack. Sadly, that offered her very little relief.

'Elf girl!' Griton hailed. *'We come with a message! End this blasphemy now, admit you are no match for the Great Aeris, and we will spare the lives of your dragon followers and two-leggeds. Only one two-legged need die today! You will not receive this offer again!'*

Before Laila could respond, Gothäzer called back to him, 'And if we refuse?'

Laila could discern the smugness in Griton's mind-voice, sense the smile on his lips, the enmity in his heart, as he replied, 'Then Aeris has declared that no one will be spared! We will wipe all of Onis of the two-legged races, and we are to start with the elf girl and her cohorts!'

Gripping her spear tight, she peered at him and sternly sent for all dragons to hear, 'I am no longer the elf girl on your mountain, Griton! I am the Omi Méa of prophecy, and I have a message as well! Tell Aeris to end her tyranny over the two-leggeds, and ALL can be spared! We only want peace for the land of Onis!'

'So be it!' the Silver replied solemnly before shutting off his mind to the Omi Méa.

Griton began cawing out, and all his followers reacted to his call. Determining the opposing dragons as the more significant threat, Griton's band roared while several charged toward Gothäzer and Masonel.

A cool breeze wafted over the group on the surface below, tingling their spines and prompting goosebumps on their necks and arms as the skies above grew dark and foreboding. Clouds thickened in masses as the Silvers called forth a raging tempest, and rain torrented down over the field. The winds rapidly picked up strength, whipping with fierceness over the expanse above and below.

Laila raised her hands to the sky, pulling the air spirit from within her while strenuously compelling the storm to dissipate, but the force of so many Silvers was simply too much, even for her. She could feel the energy building in the air, see the flashes of light and rumblings in the clouds, and knew what was coming.

Unable to stop it, a lightning bolt broke through the Omi Méa's resistance and shot down toward her. Laila's eyes grew wide in alarm. It was as though time slowed just enough for her to see the tip of the bolt descending toward her. She winced, pushing out energy from within, forcing the bolt to veer slightly and land a few feet from her instead.

Unlike the Blues, those monsters were unmistakably not toying with them. Laila knew she would have to be more aggressive than when they had faced the dragon clans to speak of peace. These dragons clearly had no interest in speaking of peace with them. They were happy with the Reign of the Ancients and would not give it up without a fight.

Without further delay, Gothäzer and Masonel charged through the air toward the inbound dragons. The rain pelted across their faces and backs as the beasts collided, the skies roaring with a thunderous clamor from the clash while multiple aggressors clasped on to the two ally dragons.

While the Red and Gold battled the horde above, two Silvers dove out of the scuffle toward Astryma, still on the ground. The young dragon flailed out her fins aggressively. She was shaken to her core as the much larger beasts soared down at her, teeth bared and claws ready. Laila knew the young dragon was not prepared for that challenge, feeling the fear emanating from her just as the rival dragons could.

Laila tapped into the storm's energy, unleashing bolts of lightning that surged towards the descending Silvers, striking them both. Unfortunately, the lightning barely affected the Air Dragons, their powers stemming from the same spirit, leaving Laila dismayed.

In fear for his uncle, who was next to Astryma, Davion cast large flaming spheres at the advancing beasts. The fireballs slammed into the Silvers' sides, sending them both plowing to the ground nearby. The dragons were flummoxed by the beyond-human power behind the pyromancer's assault, crying out and hissing at the puny pests. While snapping their jaws angrily in the air and rumbling cautionary roars, they limped toward Astryma and the dwarves, not yet ready to give up the fight.

"*Ominus unasceiry!*" Davion shouted with a combination of maneuvers and thrusting his staff tip forward in the direction of the Silver monsters. His most powerful ball of blue burning flames shot forth from his staff's garnet gem, darting across the field at the beasts, appearing as a shimmering blue bolt of light from its haste.

Blocking Davion's attack, the closest Silver swatted nonchalantly at the human's feeble attempt, aiming to knock the fireball away, but it exploded against the dragon's palm. The strike continued to sear the dragon as it shrieked in agony while its forepaw burned away, through to the other side, smoke wisping from the smoldering flesh. Then the Silver launched itself into the sky, thrashing its wings fiercely as it ascended, leaving its comrade behind. The retreating dragon gnawed on its limb frantically as the burning continued up toward its body.

Davion gleamed with pride; his most potent spell evidently stronger now. Unfortunately, it still drained him as before, leaving him temporarily hazy and weakened.

Glondora and her young Blue cast ice shards in unison at the remaining dragon on the ground, striking and battering it excessively. Hort could feel the adrenaline coursing through his veins as he prepared for the imminent foe, readying his axe and shield for combat.

Upon spotting the beast coming at the dwarves and Blue too quickly, Laila reached out and brought forth vines and roots from the ground, wrapping them tightly around its legs. But, alas, the dragon was still too strong to be stopped by such measures.

Glondora was inspired by the Omi Méa, forming a similar idea, and she waved her staff, bellowing out her freeze spell, "*Ferétsa ageeran!*"

By itself, the dwarf's spell barely affected the giant dragon, but Astryma followed her lead by wafting an icy breath from her jaws toward the Silver. Through their collaboration, their opponent gradually slowed down as its joints and limbs became stiff and hardened. Laila continued her efforts with the roots, further restraining their opponent. As it fought against the cold taking over its body, the bound dragon tried to call out but could only release a frigid puff.

With the dragon immobilized, the other comrades leapt forward in attack at the opportunity. With a loud battle cry, Hort charged towards it, his axe raised high above his head. Salyaman and Nikolean joined him. The high elf and ashen elf darted around the dragon, slashing the beast with their blades to distract it. With its glare averted, Hort leapt at the towering Silver while it snapped in annoyance at the two elves flitting about it. His hollering pierced the air, his face red and wrinkled with fury, as the dwarf firmly drove his axe down into the beast. Even though he had missed its neck, his target, he managed to land a blow into its tough shoulder.

Planted on the monster's scaly hide, the dwarf heaved as he withdrew his weapon to strike again, and the dragon shrieked in agony, jerking its head toward him. Hort fell away onto his back from the dragon's jolt, and his shield rattled to the ground an elkah's leap away from him as he smacked into the hard terrain.

While Hort moaned in pain from the impact, Nikolean planted himself between the dwarf and the dragon, holding his sword firmly before him as he faced the beast. Hort rocked on the ground, trying desperately to get back to his feet as they heard a roar from close above them.

With a look of panic up towards the sky, the comrades braced themselves for another dragon. An additional Silver swooped down to the group, batting Nikolean away with its tail as it neared, sending him soaring through the air. The dark elf crashed into the dirt, scraping along his arm and side, bleeding also from where the tail quills had grazed his skin.

Once alongside its ally, the Silver freed the two-leggeds' captive from its roots, ripping them away with its teeth and claws, then forcefully nudged the other dragon back to its feet. The newcomer roared threateningly at its surrounding adversaries as it guarded its friend. While under the protection of its comrade, the injured Dragon fought to overcome the dwindling freeze spell, stretching its limbs and waveringly expanding its wings. As the dragon recovered, the Silvers roared viciously at their surrounding foes, eager to crush them and rip them apart.

Intent on distracting them away from his uncle, Davion hurriedly cast more flames at the grounded dragons, scorching their armored hides. Laila joined him with fiery blasts, witnessing how vulnerable they seemed to the fire. In distress and covered in blackened scorches from the burns, the Silvers snarled at them as they turbulently beat their wings, returning to the skies.

With the massive creatures soaring away, Hort and Glondora bellowed a triumphant cheer. Nikolean and Salyaman congratulatory braced forearms while Laila howled proudly after the retreating dragons.

His confidence heightened from his growing powers, Davion grinned egotistically from driving away not one but three dragons. It was a small victory, for the battle was far from over, but it instilled the courage they would need in the moments to follow.

While basking in their success, the sky above them lit with red and orange light, filling with fire. Gothäzer was blazing his unholy flames, attempting to torch the dragons encircling him. The mighty Red kicked and clawed at those clamped on his hide like a pack of wolves bringing down a large buck, their teeth holding tightly to him.

Infuriated from watching the Red being swarmed, Davion screamed brazenly at the top of his lungs, "Come on, you worthless lizards! Come down here if you dare!" He raised his staff in a taunt, begging for their attention.

"Shut yer pie hole, boy!" Hort yelled at him, but the human kept goading them, overly confident, still on a high from the last three wins.

Provoked by the taunt, two Reds refocused their attention and swooped down at him. Their sneers displayed sharp teeth and a red glow past their slithery tongues as they readied to ignite him.

None of the Reds dared attack the Mighty Gothäzer, perceiving that act to be as egregious as attacking their monarch Ignisar himself. They may not have agreed with Ignisar's declaration, but would always hold too much respect to attack the monarch or his sons. Despite that, they were more than willing to go after the other dragon and two-legged adversaries.

While utilizing his enhanced fire spirit, the young pyromancer hurled fireballs with great skill at the incoming Reds, striking them securely against their hides. Regardless, the beasts continued their descent, a villainous grin across their faces at his pathetic attempts. The fire had not affected them at all. It was becoming apparent that the different dragon clans were more susceptible to elements other than their own.

Davion's confidence sank as he realized his fire magic would prove almost useless against the Fire Dragons, and his smugness fell instantly away.

Salyaman muttered his cast for his rapid shots and sent arrows flying at the two dragons. Under normal circumstances, shooting arrows at dragons had proven to be a relatively futile attempt, awarding only a distraction. However, it was not his

CHAPTER 35

usual magic. Instead of the arrows pinging off of the Red Dragons' scaly hides, they hit with an explosive force, jolting the beasts. Both the dragons and Salyaman alike were surprised as the arrowheads pierced through the thick, scale-armored hides.

The scarlet beasts emitted shrill shrieks at the high elf. A surge of adrenaline coursed through Salyaman as he witnessed the hits and continued shooting the explosive arrows rapidly. He could feel his increased power from his connection with the Gold filling his entire body.

Furious from the piercing arrows and irritating fireball attacks, the Red Dragons veered toward their assailants. One aimed for Davion, and the other targeted Salyaman.

Astryma and Glondora united in casting freezing spells toward the Red nearest them, Davion's attacker. Their spells cooled the dragon's internal fire, sizzling out the flame from its mouth. Unfortunately, it was too late; a fiery sphere had already escaped. Seconds later, the other dragon shot an additional ball of fire at Salyaman.

With bated breath, tension swept over the group as they watched the first fireball head straight toward the human. The comrades were astounded when Davion didn't dodge out of the way. Instead, he stood firm and reached out his hands. The flaming sphere stopped abruptly in midair, only a foot away from the human, as he strained to take control of it. Davion heaved with all his might, hollering out with intensity while he flung the dragon's fireball outward. The flaming sphere shot through the sky, forcedly crashing into the other fireball heading for Salyaman, and directed it off course—saving the elf.

When they recovered from their shock, Glondora and Astryma resumed casting ice spells, cooling the second dragon's heartfire before it could manage another flaming attack.

With the imminent dragons weakened and their fires vanquished, Laila directed a fierce gale at the two Reds, hindering further advancement toward her friends. The beasts beat their wings frantically against the forces, resisting her, but the Omi Méa strengthened her focus, pulling at the surrounding winds. From the Omi Méa's power, the air began to twist fiercely, circulating around the two dragons and catching them in a developing funnel. As the wind force grew, a powerful twister began to form. Everyone on the surface backed away from Laila's storm, watching, afraid of being swept up in the perilous winds, while Hort clung tight to his helmet.

As they beat their wings hard against the air currents, the dragons felt themselves losing to it. The Reds decidedly withdrew from the twister before it could manage to take complete control of them. Furious and chagrined, they ascended with haste back toward the other dragons in the clouds, back to Griton, full of shame.

With them gone, Laila released her hold on the developing tornado, and the winds dispersed before its formation was complete.

Meanwhile, in the skies above, the horde of dragons continued their assaults on Gothäzer and Masonel. As dragon attacked dragon, the powerful Gold and mighty Red were finding it increasingly difficult to fend off the several Silvers from their pierced and battered hides.

Becoming overwhelmed, Gothäzer came falling from the sky while three of the Silvers remained attached to him by their claws and teeth. As he neared the hard surface, the mighty Red Dragon twisted at the last moment and crushed one of the Silvers under his extreme mass. The earth quaked fiercely from the impact as Gothäzer pulverized the Silver into the terrain, breaking its bones and rendering it useless. The Red then continued tearing at the other two that were still on top of him.

Davion feared for his dragon upon seeing the extensive slashes covering his immense body and wings, his blue blood trickling down and painting the rocky surface. He ran toward the feuding jumble of dragons, his hands aflame, and forced a powerful column of fire at his targets. The two Silvers atop Gothäzer yelped and reared from being roasted by the human's attack. One Silver limped away, its leg brutally mauled by Gothäzer, retreating like a coward before Davion's fiery assault died out. Unfortunately, the other continued its ruthless attack on the Red, its beautiful silver scales sooted black from the fire.

With a mighty snap of his jaws, Gothäzer bit into the remaining foe's neck, penetrating through its tough scales. Then, in one savage motion, he yanked his head sideways and ripped out the Silver Dragon's jugular. A spray of dark-blue blood streamed out from the Silver, splashing over the surface. The dragon's screams died out quickly as it fell limp to the ground, its eyes wide and frozen in shock, and its slithery tongue flopped out past its sharp-toothed jaws onto the dirt.

Laila gasped in shock at the dead dragon on the ground and the crushed one too mangled and broken to move. The sight had her heart panging in her chest, making it hard to breathe or focus.

As she gawked at the charred silver-scaled corpse covered in blue blood, the words of the Fearsome Fonzar echoed tormentingly through her mind, 'There will be times that slaying your enemies will be your only option if you are to succeed.' Was that really how it was meant to be?

The elf maiden's body trembled and shook at the horrific sight before her, wishing it were all just a horrible dream. In spite of that, a mighty roar from Gothäzer snapped her attention back to what was happening around her. The Red heaved out a victorious column of fire, blaring it into the air toward the enemy dragons, his eyes fixed on Kainüs.

'Face me!' he belted challengingly to his brother.

But Kainüs held steady, glowering down at him. The eldest brother was no fool; he knew he stood little chance against his much mightier younger sibling, Gothäzer, the prized champion son of Ignisar.

Laila sensed that the Silvers high above were strengthening the storm again, screeching and beating their wings heavily, readying the lightning. She focused all her attention and powers on stopping them before they could send any more bolts at the companions, and countered their efforts with her own in a desperate attempt to calm the storm. To her dismay, Laila was still having very little success against the air spirit of so many Silvers. As she filled with vexation against the relentless dragons, the Omi Méa decided it was time to call upon a different spirit—a darker spirit.

CHAPTER THIRTY-SIX

RAGE

Taking a deep breath, Laila glared at the Silvers hovering above, her rage building up within her. The sky grew even darker than from the storm, as though night were approaching prematurely. Everyone on both sides looked around, frantic, unaware of what was happening. Laila's dampened hair whipped wildly in the increasing winds as she called forth the spirit of the phantom realm with more intensity than ever before. Gloom hauntingly shrouded over the Omi Méa's eyes until they were shadowed in their entirety, like two gaping holes. The blackness of her glare spread outward through her veins, visibly darkening and throbbing while the phantom spirit spread consumingly throughout her.

Suddenly, a loud crack echoed through the hills as black lightning unnaturally parted the sky. Except, it wasn't lightning, and it remained even after its thunder had ceased. The black parting was hazed by an otherworldly cloud, with smaller ripples of lightning flashes crackling within the fog.

In the Omi Méa's demonic guise, she raised her hands, and a harrowing sound of wailing spirits flooded the area, sending chills up everyone's spines. A vast black mist emerged from the crack in the veil, full of glowing red eyes, as countless wraiths escaped their phantom realm. The menacing spirits aimed straight for the enemy dragons at Laila's command. The Ancients screeched as the wraiths surrounded and swarmed the beasts.

Masonel the Gold used the distraction to dive to the comrades below, eager to be away from the tormenting wraiths and free of the adversary dragons' assaults.

The spirits scathed the skins of their prey with a cold burn as though brushing against liquid nitrogen and the dragons' cries from the assailing specters were nerve-wrenching. In an attempt at blocking the piercing pain of the horrifying sounds flooding the expanse, the two-legged companions agonizingly covered their ears. Their hearts pounded hard in their chests, tears filled their eyes as they tried to look away but couldn't, and their hairs stood on ends while the phantoms ruthlessly ambushed the dragons and overtook the battlefield.

As the spirits continued to be released from the tear in the veil, Laila was finding it increasingly harder to hold control over them. In her losing battle against the wills of the ever-increasing specters, they began to scatter. Several of them immediately headed for the two-leggeds and united dragons below, a black mist trailing behind as they screeched a high-pitched ghostly scream.

Panicking, Laila turned her focus to her friends, promptly grabbing hold of as many spirit essences as she could with her mind.

Upon descrying the phantoms approaching, the companions quickly became terrified. Heightening their dread was a chilling, other-worldly presence wafting over them, making it harder to breathe. The targeted two-leggeds ran away hysterically, screaming as they evaded the wailing phantoms.

In their retreat, Glondora tripped and fell to her knees, and a specter's deathly chill grazed across her. Hort swung at it, trying to scatter it with his shield, while Salyaman grabbed Glondora's arm, dragging her to her feet, and they continued running to escape more attacks.

With Laila's attention off of the dragons above, the wraiths began easing away from them. The enemy Reds blared flames at the regressing red-eyed mist, and the spirits screamed with their ghastly voices before going up in smoke, disappearing into nothingness. The Silvers beat their great wings, forcing some of the spirits back away from them, and the rival dragons started to recover themselves.

As she realized there were just too many for her to control, Laila became discouraged and began expelling the phantoms forcefully back through the portal she'd created, a handful at a time. As she continued driving the resistant wraiths into the tear, she was finding it ever more challenging to keep them from breaching back through.

When she could grab no more, Laila immediately blared a stream of black fire at the tear, forcing the edges of it back together, and she screamed with the force being pulled from within her. While the unholy flames prevented any from escaping, she promptly tethered it closed with tendrils from her mind. To her relief, pulling the tethers closed proved to be somewhat more receptive than the veil in the Faolin home, having been freshly created by her own powers. Still, with great strain, she managed to seal the last of it, and the screeching from the wraiths subsided as the black fire dissipated.

Although her attempt had not won the battle, the enemy dragons were wounded, their hides still stinging from the deathly burns.

While trying to recover from the wraith attack, the Silvers' focus was thankfully no longer on the squall, which had now dried up, the clouds dissipating, and light returned to the battlefield.

Once the fear and pain of the phantom menaces were at rest, the assailing dragons were quick to return to their mission. Unfortunately, they were even more outraged than before as they came at the two-leggeds and their united dragons again.

Weakened from the exertion of her ploy, Laila dropped to her knees. As she placed her hands against the soil, pulling energy from the earth spirit to replenish herself, the grassy hills surrounding her became carpeted with dried brown blades.

Gothäzer glowered up at Kainüs still lurking in the skies and screamed again to his brother, 'Why won't you face me, you coward?!'

Kainüs roared in retaliation and anger, then dove toward him, along with several Silvers at his side. But, even with the aid of the others, he was still not willing to take the risk of confronting Gothäzer head-on. Instead, he held back as he neared, sending the Silvers onward ahead of him to tackle the Mighty Gothäzer.

At the same time, another Red dove toward Laila with Nikolean again by her side. It opened its monstrous jaws, hatred seeping from its glare, as it sent a flaming stream shooting down toward them. Laila screamed, raising her hands to it as she shot out her own column of fire from her palms. Their flames collided in the middle in a brilliant light, and Laila struggled against the dragon's power as it hovered, maintaining a steady flux of the heated attack.

With the Red distracting Laila, a limping Silver came stealthily at them from the side. Nikolean turned to face it, sword ready, but, to his detriment, looked the Ancient directly into the deathly blackness of its eyes. The moment he did, his arms fell feebly to his sides, his sword tip resting in the dirt, and he stood there swaying helplessly, trapped in his own mind as the dragon entranced him. The Silver donned a wicked grin as it continued to approach.

Filled with dread at his impending death, Nikolean was astonished when a fierce roar vibrated both through his cerebrum and all around them. The Silver went flying sideways from his sight as the Great Turathyl slammed into the assailant, snapping her jaws on its wing while trying to get a hold of it. The dragon's enchantment on the drow was broken, and he grinned, pleased with her fortuitous return. But the rival Silver growled back at Turathyl before clamping down on her tail, causing her to shriek and lose hold of the menace's wing.

Nikolean darted toward their foe, quick like the wind and light as a feather, and flitted up its tail onto its back. Then, taking his sword firmly in both hands, he thrust it down hard and deep through the scales and flesh beneath him. The dragon released Turathyl's tail, crying out as it turned its long neck to face the drow upon its back.

With the dragon's head nearing him rapidly, Nikolean withdrew his sword, facing the beastly head as it opened its mouth wide to snatch him up. He propelled from the dragon's back, jumping high into the air above while the beast veered its gaze to follow him. However, he had leapt much higher than he had intended due to his increased air magic from Turathyl being so near him. Nikolean flailed his arms and legs, trying desperately to get a hold of himself as he flew through the air. To his horror, he began to descend right toward the dragon's open, waiting jaws.

Laila's assailing Red was cast aside by Masonel the Gold as he collided with the larger dragon, bringing it circling toward the ground. Freed from the distracting Red, the elf maiden then gasped as she witnessed Nikolean about to get snapped up by the Silver.

"NIKO!!!" Laila screamed, instantly thrusting her clawed hands outward in the air toward them. She grabbed hold of the dragon's head with her mind, entwining her thoughts with the blood flowing through its veins. With control over the beast, she forced it to turn its jaw away from Nikolean while the drow rapidly descended toward it. Nikolean swiftly took his sword, pointing it downward, and rammed the blade into the dragon's immobilized skull as he landed atop it, killing the hostile Silver.

Upon feeling the blood flow stop, Laila released her hold on the dragon and again felt the pang in her chest, watching as another lifeless dragon toppled over before her. She was not angry at Nikolean for killing it, nor Gothäzer for killing the other. She was angry that they had been put in the position to feel the need to do so.

Meanwhile, Gothäzer had been bombarded with the Silvers from Kainüs's craven attack. Davion was quick to aid his Red, casting flames at the dragons on his companion. Salyaman joined the human, shooting rapid shots at the scaly hides.

Masonel, having crippled the Fire Dragon he had brought down earlier, roared ferociously alongside his elf companion. Roots then sprouted from the ground, wrapping themselves around one of the Silvers, prying it off the mighty Red. As the Silver resisted the roots, managing to snap free of them, Salyaman joined his dragon by casting his own ensnaring roots spell upon the beast. More of the wriggling plants broke through the ground, entrapping the enemy Silver. The elf was surprised by the strength of his union with Masonel and that their attempt was actually working. The roots streamed around the Silver Dragon like powerful ropes, forcing it to the ground, helpless, as they continued to encase it in a cocoon of rootstock.

Hort raised his axe high over his head, ready to dart toward the entangled Silver, but then heard an ominous roar above them. He looked to espy a colossal Red diving toward Davion, distressed to discover that he and Gothäzer were too engrossed with combating the Silvers to notice. The dwarf promptly let out a bellowing cry as he instead raced toward the boy as fast as his short legs would allow him.

"DAVION! ME BOY!" Hort screamed. "LOOK OUT!"

Davion turned, alarmed, just in time to see the Red Dragon plummeting toward him and was instantly shoved backward to the ground by his uncle. Within a blink, the dwarf was hoicked off his feet instead of Davion, ascending quickly away from the ground, snatched up in the mighty Red's claws. It was Kainüs.

Hort screamed and cursed wildly in the dragon's clutch, and Davion instantly jumped back to his feet, casting a bolt of fire at the beast. However, when the fire slammed into the Red Dragon, it was unaffected by the flame. Not knowing what else to do, the pyromancer continued to blast fire at Kainüs, careful not to hit his uncle, while yelling to the others for help.

Gothäzer roared fiercely and pushed with all his might off the ground, knocking away the Silvers still attacking him as he leapt for his brother, rage and fire in his eyes. As Gothäzer reached Kainüs, he bit down viciously on the traitor's leg. Yelping in pain, the Red lost hold of the dwarf, sending Hort falling through the sky, his loose helm flying from his head away from him.

"UNCLE! NO!!!" Davion screamed as Hort flailed in the air. He wanted to run to him, but a threatening growl from one of the Silvers he'd been battling tore his attention away. With Gothäzer gone, Salyaman, Nikolean, and the Gold expeditiously came to Davion's aid to keep the remaining Silvers at bay.

Hearing Davion's screams, Laila turned and saw from the corner of her eye Hort falling rapidly. Immediately, she reached out to the air spirit in an attempt at softening his landing, but wasn't able to stop his fall. She wasn't even sure if she had done enough in time, watching mortified as Hort slammed against the hard ground.

Gothäzer tackled his brother, crashing him into the terrain below, sending mighty quakes throughout the battlefield. He skillfully pinned Kainüs on his back with his head beneath his claws as he scowled down at him.

'*Why have you turned against our father?*' Gothäzer asked his brother, hoping for him to redeem himself.

'*Father is a fool!*' Kainüs blared, snarling up at him from beneath his claws. '*All the two-leggeds must die, even if the Mighty Ignisar gets in the way! They are nothing but vermin plaguing and killing our land!*'

Disgusted by his betrayal to their father, Gothäzer knew there would be no redemption for his brother, and—for their mission and for the honor of the Mighty Ignisar—Gothäzer feared what he must do. As he paused, trying to work up his courage for such an act against his own kin, Kainüs wriggled and writhed, managing to free himself from Gothäzer's grasp. The smaller Red pounced away out of his reach and thrashed his wings, escaping back into the sky. Gothäzer roared threateningly as his brother fled, but did not pursue him.

Laila witnessed Glondora running to aid her husband and planned to do the same. Even so, before she could join the dwarves, she was distracted when the wind whipped violently around her. It immediately became hard for her to breathe as she felt the air being stolen from her lungs. Grasping on to her neck, Laila's eyes grew wide and terrified, her mouth agape, as she struggled unsuccessfully for breath. She looked to the sky in panic, finding Griton above her, smiling smugly as he beat his wings, pulling the air from her. Her vision grew blurry as she labored to breathe, and she no longer saw Griton above her. Instead, with her altered sight from her deteriorating state, she beheld the Great Silver Monarch Aeris smiling and chortling her sinister dragon laughter down on her.

Laila gasped and wheezed helplessly, her nightmare transpiring before her. Unable to catch her breath, she fell to her knees as her world grew dark.

CHAPTER THIRTY-SEVEN

PAIN

With a ferocious roar, Turathyl promptly launched above and charged for Griton, colliding with him and breaking his spell on the Omi Méa. They swirled in the air, clawing and snapping at one another as Griton tried to escape the greater dragon's assault.

As the air returned to her lungs, Laila collapsed forward on her hands and knees, panting and wheezing heavily to catch her breath. Her head was throbbing and body shaking from the lack of oxygen while she forcedly blinked her eyes, trying to focus on the silver scale dangling from her neck as it swayed back and forth between her and the dirt. Her vision gradually became more clear, but then Laila shuddered upon hearing even more dragon roars and caws coming from behind them.

Still hunched over, propped against the ground, Laila turned her head sideways just enough to see a flock of nine Golds heading for the field. She gasped out a cry, her body still shaking, feeling defeated and too weakened to fight even more dragons.

As the Golds neared, Laila forced herself to stand, quickly pulling what strength she could from the earth to rejuvenate her for another round of dragons. She raised her quivering hands, preparing to counter their assaults on her and her friends, but then watched in shock as the golden beasts soared past them. The powerful Golds emitted a trembling roar as they charged at the attacking Silvers and Reds. The ground shook beneath the comrades as an earthquake rumbled and vibrated through the hills from the dragons' fury and spirit. The group braced themselves, their balance faltering from the tremor.

Intimidated by the incoming Golds, the remaining combatants on the surface viciously beat their wings, lifting off away from the comrades and their united dragons, hastily gaining altitude back up to the sky. With the wind rushing through the battlefield as they departed, Laila realized that their foes were actually withdrawing.

'This is not over, elf girl!' she heard Griton call to her as he evaded Turathyl's grasp and joined the others in retreat. 'This is only the beginning!'

The beautiful golden dragons went chasing after them, growling and shrieking combatively, but the Silvers were much too swift and flew speedily out of their range. Two Golds managed to grab hold of a straggling Red, but it blasted fire at them, scorching their hides. They were forced to let go of the straggler, and it, too, managed to get away.

Gothäzer blasted his flames in the direction of their retreating adversaries while the other United Ancients let out victorious roars into the sky. The cohorts joined them in their triumphant celebration, cheering and yelling after the departing dragons. Except for two.

As the roaring waned, everyone's attention was drawn to another alarming sound overtaking the battlefield; Glondora crying hysterically. The dwarf was holding her husband limply in her arms, rocking back and forth, pouring her tears over him as Astryma stood nearby, her head hanging low.

"UNCLE!" Davion shouted, running toward them.

Laila immediately joined him, hurtling through the air, her feet barely touching the ground until she collapsed at the dwarf's side. Without a second thought, she dug her fingers into the soil at her knees and placed her other hand on the dwarf's arm where his skin was exposed.

"M'lady, methinks tis too late fer 'im," Glondora said, sniffling. "He didna' stand a chance. Smacked 'is 'ead as he'd come down and was nothin' I could do." She tried to calm herself while observing the Omi Méa at work, a glimmer of hope in her eyes despite her doubts. Then she rested her husband on the ground, giving Laila space.

"Let me get his armor out of the way," Davion offered, removing his uncle's chest plate for Laila.

Still clinging to Hort's arm while Davion undressed his armor, Laila pulled energy from the earth, forcing it up through her body and out into the dwarf. But she was being met with much resistance. She could not detect any heartbeat; she could feel nothing. With her own heart stopping, she glanced up at Davion's hopeful face with sad eyes, and slowly shook her head.

"Help him!" he hollered at her, not understanding why she was just sitting there looking at him like that.

Salyaman and Nikolean had joined them but were keeping a respectful distance in observance, the elf saying prayers to Jayenne for the dwarf to recover.

Laila moved her hands over to Hort's chest and closed her eyes again, concentrating her thoughts to his body, searching for anything that might help her to heal him. As she recalled when she had nearly lost Davion, the Omi Méa pulled from the air spirit, perceiving its energy surging through her body as she directed it toward the dwarf's silent heart.

Hort's body jolted from the energy surge, then went limp as before. Laila sent the surge again. And again. And again.

"Lady Laila, I fear Glondora might be right," Salyaman stated, keeping his distance from the shocks.

But Davion would have no part in that, pleading to her, "Keep trying! You did it with Tury and me. You can save him too!"

With the jolts not working, Laila searched for the damage to his head, applying her energy to pulling the wound together. But nothing would happen; it wasn't working either. There was no energy or life left in the flesh, and it was refusing to heal. His body would not absorb any further attempts she made to give him energy from the earth, either. Laila's tears mingled with her determination as she continued to search for a solution, feeling defeated and powerless to save him. Glondora started weeping again as well, seeing the Omi Méa losing hope, both of them angering Davion.

"Don't you dare give up on him!" he shouted furiously at Laila. "Keep trying!"

In a desperate attempt, Laila pulled simultaneously from the earth spirit again for energy and the water spirit as she forced the blood to flow, forcing his heart to beat. Everyone was on the balls of their feet in anticipation while she continued straining to maintain the flow.

"You're doing it!" Davion blurted excitedly, seeing his uncle's flesh becoming more flush again. "You're saving him!"

But Laila was draining quickly, her hands shaking as sweat beaded on her neck and forehead, and she was unable to sustain it. Even with pumping his heart, she still couldn't force his lungs to breathe, nor his brain to heal.

As Laila cried out in defeat over Hort's motionless body, she let go of the spirits and buckled, falling backward.

"NO!" Davion cried out. "You had him! You can't stop now!" Tears flowed from his eyes as he raved at her, his heart breaking apart. "What about the phantom realm? You took life from orcs to help Tury. Use me, take from me! It should have been me!! Or raise him like the drow necromancers! Just do something! Anything!!"

Glondora stood to face Davion, smearing the tears on her cheeks. "Lad, I dunna' want ta accept this neither, but bringin' 'im back from the dead isna' the answer. Twould not be 'im that comes back."

"She is right," Salyaman added. "Neither you nor the Silver was already gone. I fear there is nothing even the Omi Méa can do for him now."

"No!" Davion shouted at them all, then bent down beside his uncle, beating on his chest. "Wake up, Uncle! Right now! You can't do this to me too! Wake up!"

The human continued beating on the dwarf's chest, tears streaming down his face and over his uncle's body, until he finally collapsed over him. Davion shook as he brokenly wailed, refusing to accept his Uncle Hort's death, but there was nothing more Laila could do.

Anger, resentment, wrath, vengeance. They were not just feelings that were cycling through Davion's entire being, but Laila's as well. She was angry at herself and aching with guilt that she wasn't able to save Hort like she had saved Davion and Turathyl. She resented the dragons so stubborn in their hate that so many people had to die by their talons and that they would not stop in their tyrannical rule. She was full of wrath for the beasts that caused it and for the gods who allowed it. She was full of vengeance, ready more than ever to put a stop to their killing, particularly of her friends whom she loved dearly.

Following the battle and the honorable Hort's demise, they learned that Masonel had summoned the Golds to their defense. They assured Laila of their allegiance to the prophecy before heading back to their territory until such time that they would be needed again.

Gothäzer had ruthlessly finished off the crippled Silver Dragon that was left behind before Laila had a chance to protest. She chastised him for doing so, but wasn't convinced she had got through to him. Angry with the Red Dragon, Laila wished they had at least attempted to get some information from the Silver about Aeris's plans, or even possibly convert the dragon to their side. Regardless, the Red held no regrets for his actions, and it was becoming apparent that there would be many more losses before the completion of their quest. It made her sick to her stomach, and she knew that she would have to grow a thicker skin, but was also determined not to give up hope of ending the bloodshed wherever possible.

The healers mended those harmed in the battle. The dragons had taken the brunt of the attacks, particularly Gothäzer and Masonel, but Turathyl had her share of wounds as well. After Nikolean's injuries were remedied, he helped by gathering the scattered mounts. Merimer had never gone far and returned to Laila's side on her own. The mystical creature shared in the elf's pain and tried her best to comfort her by nuzzling her with her muzzle.

Davion had shut himself off from everyone, even shutting out Gothäzer from his mind. The dragon didn't understand human attachments, but was respecting his need for space. They all sensed the brokenness Davion was experiencing, as he lost the last person he believed had loved him; the man who had saved his life more times than he could remember; the man who had died saving his life one final time. He felt utterly alone and consumed with pain from the loss—and from the guilt.

Not knowing what to do for Davion, Laila tried to make herself useful by assisting Glondora with wrapping up her husband in leather bindings, preparing to send him to the Beyond. The dwarf laiden appreciated everyone's aid but wished she knew how to help the boy. Out of them all, Glondora had known him the longest, but she believed everyone had their way of coping and that that was his. In the meantime, she had her own way of processing the loss by preparing her husband for the afterlife, readying to send him off well in the way any respected dwarf warrior should go.

While sitting on a nearby hilltop deep in thought, Davion faced away from the group, staring blankly over the empty range before him. He felt numb inside. He could cry no more. He had lost everything. It was unbearable to think that his Uncle Hort was truly gone. Who was going to pull him out of the hole in the floor and lift him to safety now? Who would care enough to? The only other person he cared for—loved—seemed to be able to save everything and everyone except for the one person he had left in the world, the one who had sacrificed everything for him. He was once again wishing he could hate her, but now for her failure to revive his uncle. It didn't matter, though; he knew that wishing it was a fruitless effort, which only frustrated him more. The only person he hated was himself for being the reason Hort was gone at all.

As he sat there stewing in his thoughts, heartbroken, he didn't even hear Glondora approaching.

"Lad," the dwarf laiden said softly to get his attention. "We be nearly ready ta begin."

Without averting his gaze from the scenery, Davion drew in a long, deep breath. His head throbbed while he held it for a moment before slowly releasing the air back out. Unable to look her in the eyes, he instead gave her a simple chin tuck, tears beginning to well in the corners of his eyes again. He had been sure that they had all dried up, but his chin started to quiver as he discovered that he had been wrong.

The dwarf turned and left, and he heard the grass scuffle as she dragged her feet mournfully over the hill's surface, back to her eternally sleeping husband.

After several more minutes of trying to collect himself, Davion braced to stand, his knees being defiant under him, but he managed nonetheless. Turning toward the group, he saw through blurry eyes all of them gathered together around a wooden funeral pyre with his uncle's corpse wrapped tightly in leathers. Hort's shield and dented helm were resting upon his chest. Trekking somberly over to them, he could feel all of their eyes watching him as he stared at the ground, trying to keep his inner fire at bay. When he neared, he knelt before the pyre and bowed his head.

"Welcome him with open arms, Goddess Jayenne," Davion prayed. "He died honorably and was a truly good man. Kyrash, Hort Strongarm died in battle fighting for peace for all of Onis. He deserves whatever honors you can bestow on him in the Beyond. Please accept his sacrifice for our quest."

As Davion finished the prayers for his uncle, Laila glanced over at the dragons lying dead on the battlefield. Ignisar's warning was revived within her mind from Davion's words; *Sacrifices will be made by all.* Pressing her hand over her aching heart as she looked back upon the pyre, tears rolled down her cheeks, and Laila agonized over how many more sacrifices must be made before it would all be over.

Davion stood back up and pressed his hands together before him, bowing respectfully to the man that had raised him since he was a child. "Although you may have been my 'Uncle

Hort,' you were always more of a father to me. You have been there for me from the first day we met and through my whole life ever since, right until the very end." Wiping tears from his eyes, he continued, "I can never tell you how much that meant to me. You will be severely missed by many, but especially by myself. I love you, Uncle. I only hope that I can make you proud and be greeted by you when my time has come as well. May the Goddess Mother keep safe your soul. Goodbye, Uncle Hort."

While clenching his quivering jaw and blinking more tears from his eyes, Davion took several steps back and stared mournfully at the helmet on Hort's chest. Everyone was a blur to him as they each paid their respects and said their prayers for his uncle. In his pain and suffering, Davion saw only the dented metal helm, his insides burning hotter the longer he glared at it. He could see the details around its plate rim that had been etched by the Lochlann smiths for Hort's father. He could see how the sun gleamed particularly brighter against the edge where it dented inward along the upper left side. And he could make out several scrapes in various locations from battles past—and present. Davion had never before noticed there was a subtle bronze tone to the crevices of the slashes against the gray metal, and he continued to stare and study it, fuming as he boiled inside.

After everyone had finished and lined up beside him, Davion reached his breaking point. He strode rapidly back to his uncle's corpse and snatched up the helmet. With it tight in his grasp, he stormed several paces away, raised his uncle's dented metal wobbly helm with a recessed arm, then whipped it wildly through the air with all his might.

Davion released his inner fire in a rage of flames, blazing them against the helmet still flying through the air as he yowled.

"I told you to replace that blastit old helmet! You stubborn dwarf!"

Once the helmet flared out of sight, Davion fell to his knees, wailing angrily, his cries carrying through the hills. He stayed on the ground for a long while, sobbing and staring off in the direction of the catapulted helmet.

Everyone watched him silently, giving him a moment to grieve.

When Davion could once again see through his dampened eyes, the human swallowed his anger and managed to stand back to his feet, his expression still displaying the pain within.

He could hear his aunt's scuffle as she approached, but remained looking off into the distance as she gently placed her hand on his arm.

"I'm so sorry, lad," Glondora told him, commiserating with his heartache. Wrapping her arm in his, she led him slowly back to the others, brooding with him over Hort.

Everyone stayed quiet while the two of them settled back at the pyre, allowing them a moment.

When Davion's breathing had steadied, Glondora asked him softly, "Would ye like the honors?"

As he realized what she was asking of him, his body shuddered, holding back his pain to keep from losing control, and he shook his head adamantly. "I can't," he told her, his voice cracking.

The ground shook from each thunderous step as the Mighty Gothäzer came forward, placing himself on the other side of Davion.

'I would be honored if you would allow me,' the Red told him.

After a moment of hesitation, Davion finally nodded his head in small jerks, indicating his approval, even though still not ready.

Stretching his long neck out, the scarlet dragon wafted a cone of fire out from his jaws, blaring it back and forth over the pyre and the wrapped body upon it until all was aflame.

Glondora tenderly squeezed Davion's arm, as much for him as for herself, then began to sing while they all watched the roaring fire, her voice soft but strong, her heart aching.

To hear this song online, go to
https://youtu.be/RX0SvcFEzwk

Ye are away, away on a journey
On a road that's paved in gold
Where troubled waters have all been tamed
Mountain winds whisper out yer name

Ye are away, away on a journey
To a place with no more pain
Lay down yer blade, tis all been done
All yer battles have now been won

Ye're headin' home
Ye're headin' home
For all of us, ye'll clear the way
Ye're headin' home
Ye're headin' home
We'll reunite one glorious day

Ye are away, away on a journey
Where the fields be lush and green
The flowers bloom, the skies are clear
Tis alright, love, have no fear

CHAPTER 37

Ye're headin' home
Ye're headin' home
Follow the light up to the moons
Ye're headin' home
Ye're headin' home
Trust, my darlin', I'll be there soon
Trust, my darlin', I'll be there soon

The Mighty Gothäzer

CHAPTER 37

CHAPTER THIRTY-EIGHT

BEWILDERED

"*I* still canna' believe he be gone." In a daze, Glondora stroked Orbek's snout under the early morning sun, her eyes fixed on the sad okullo eyes. Laila stood near her friend, unsure if there was anything she could say in that moment that would offer any comfort at all. "We was jus' gettin' started," she added mournfully, then stared over at the young elf with a look of confusion on her face.

"I'm so sorry," Laila told her earnestly. "I wish there was something I could have done."

While taking a few steps toward her, the dwarf let her arms fall to her sides, twinging the corner of her mouth. "I knows ye does, m'lady. Me too."

Closing the rest of the gap, Laila wrapped her arms around Glondora in a compassionate embrace while the dwarf heaved a heavy sigh. Then, patting the elf's back, Glondora said, "Twill take some time, but I'll be fine. Tis the boy me be worried 'bout." She pulled away and looked over at the human.

Davion had remained on a hill in the distance throughout the night, lost in his misery, unable to rest his eyes. He was sitting, facing away from them, as he fiddled with the scorched helmet he had managed to recover. The elf's heart sank as she joined Glondora's gaze.

"My lady," Nikolean said, distracting her attention as he approached, "they are waiting to speak with you." He gestured over to Salyaman and the four poised dragons, all focused on the Omi Méa.

Discomfited, Laila nodded to him as she cleared her throat, unsure of what to do next. Things had undoubtedly taken a sharp turn with the dragons' attack.

With every step, Laila mustered as much confidence as she could while she approached the group of awaiting dragons, Nikolean's firm grip on her hand giving her strength as he accompanied her. He gave it a gentle, supportive squeeze when they neared the group, and then he broke away to stand dutifully with Salyaman. Glondora had followed them back and joined the others as well, staying close to Astryma.

'Are you alright?' Turathyl asked, sensing her pain.

Laila simply nodded. Her pain over the sacrifices on both sides seemed to pale in comparison to what the human was experiencing at that moment.

"Shouldn't we wait for Davion?" Laila asked the others, glancing over at the grieving human lost in his own thoughts. She silently agonized to see him so lamented over his uncle's death.

Gothäzer emitted a low rumble in the back of his throat, lowering his head as he told her, 'We may continue. He is in no right mind for this.'

"Okay," Laila said understandingly. "I suppose we need to decide what to do next." She peered around at the group, unsure of how to continue, unsure of anything. They had been so encouraged after having acquired assistance from each of the dragon clans, but now...

"Aeris feels threatened by us, or she would not have issued a preemptive strike," Salyaman surmised. "That being said, we do not know how long we have until the next attack or even where it will be. I would not be surprised if she increases her attacks on the cities instead of coming straight for us again."

"I agree," Nikolean added. "We still have yet to meet with the humans and elves again, and Aeris is building an even greater army. We are running out of time."

"And what of me people and the drow?" Glondora asked. "Twill take them time ta move their men across such a distance. If we intend ta stick ta the plan, we best be hailin' them now."

"You're right," Laila declared. "All of you. Things have just become much worse, and I'm not sure if we can stick to the plan." She sighed, exasperated. "At the rate we're going, Aeris is likely to have destroyed all of Onis by the time we are even ready to face her."

"We need to move with more haste if we are to defeat Aeris," Salyaman stated. "We are already near the human town, so I suggest we start there."

"And then what?" Nikolean asked. "It will take too long to travel to both the human and elven capitals from there. Do we honestly think Aeris is just going to wait for us while we gallivant around the rest of Onis?"

'Sorry to interrupt,' the Blue sent meekly to Laila.

"Astryma? Go ahead," Laila told her, and the Ancients relayed the dragon-speak to their two-leggeds.

With a nervous look around at the other dragons looming over her, she said humbly, 'Why don't we just fly?' Upon seeing a look of bewilderment over her audience, she continued, 'I know that I'm not the fastest, but it would still be much faster than we have been going if Glondora were to ride upon my back.'

Gothäzer chuckled, his laughter disturbingly frightful. *'You want us to be their mounts?!'* He laughed again, rumbling the ground. *'Yes,'* Turathyl responded candidly in the Blue's stead. *'I, more than any, am not fond of the idea either, but I am not certain we have a choice anymore if we are to accomplish our goals before Aeris attacks again. Even with our flight, it may not be fast enough, but at least we would stand a much better chance.'*

As he stared with a critical eye at Turathyl, Gothäzer heaved a disgruntled rumbling sigh, and Masonel joined him in his animosity of the suggestion. Meanwhile, Astryma perked up cheerily at the idea, and Nikolean did his best to withhold his snide remarks from his dragon in fear of changing her mind.

'It is just not natural,' Masonel huffed after a long moment of contemplation.

'And yet,' Turathyl said, *'it has been done before. We saw proof of it in the Ruins of Pynar.'*

Laila shared with them the memory of the mural and the flashes of an elf riding a dragon from when she had touched the cross table, confirming the Silver's statement.

"Allowing my comrades the honor of soaring with you as riders would most definitely increase our chances, but I would never insist on it if you are not comfortable with doing so." Laila looked with anticipation at the dragons, giving Astryma a side-smile at her excitement.

'And what of you and the mounts?' Gothäzer asked.

'I will take Laila and Niko, and the mounts will have to be carried,' Turathyl replied.

'We can carry the mounts as far as Mira,' Masonel added gruffly. *'They will be safe there. I won't carry an elkah all over Onis. It is enough to ask me to carry an elf.'*

CHAPTER 38

The other dragons nodded their agreement, then everyone stood in silence for a moment, and Turathyl noticed an unusually large grin on Nikolean's face.

'Don't make me regret this, drow,' the Silver told him sternly, annoyed.

"Of course not, Tury," he replied humorlessly, trying to wipe the smirk from his face.

Salyaman was unsure how he felt about riding on the back of a dragon. His whole life had been spent despising the creatures and hunting or evading them as their mortal enemies. Then again, he could say the same about the dark elves, and yet Nikolean had grown on him rather irritatingly and against his better judgment. Perhaps the new world they were fighting for was worth him further setting aside his hatred for the beasts and trusting one of them with his life. He only wished that he had been awarded more time to get better acquainted with Masonel as Nikolean had with Turathyl. Unfortunately, since time was a luxury they didn't have, he supposed it would be best to get the first flight over with and hope a more substantial bond would come.

"When shall we depart?" Salyaman asked.

As she scanned over the group, Laila saw no reason to wait any longer and bared a nervous smile. All of them were eager to move on and anxious about what was to come now that an even greater war had been declared. Turning her focus to Davion, she took a deep breath and sighed out heavily.

Glondora followed Laila's gaze, then suggested in a somber tone, "Methinks we should let the lad know what be goin' on."

When Glondora took a step in his direction, Laila nodded and held up her hand to the dwarf. "Prepare to leave. I will speak with Davion."

In a brisk walk, Laila crossed over a few mounds and scaled the hill up to the lone human. She paused just before reaching him, staring at his back as he sat on the ground, hunched over. Not entirely sure how to approach him, the elf maiden suddenly grew nervous, second-guessing herself. She considered that perhaps Glondora should have been the one after all. But it was too late now, for he knew she was there.

"What is it?" he asked her without turning around.

Laila stood there for a moment, contemplating what to say, unsure if she should jump to the point or ask how he's doing first. Anyone could see he wasn't doing well, and she realized what an absurd question it would be, but what could she say that would be appropriate? It was a very unfamiliar situation, and she wished she could go back in time and stop it from ever having happened—for multiple reasons beyond her own current discomfort.

"Well?" Davion spat, turning his head sideways to where she could see the side of his face while refraining from looking directly at her.

"I'm sorry, Davion." Was all she could think to say.

While heaving a heavy sigh, Davion stood up and decidedly faced her. "I thought I told you to stop apologizing when you have done nothing wrong."

Laila couldn't meet his gaze and stared at the dirt at his feet instead, her face partially hidden by her tangled hair. In her heart, she did feel she had done something wrong by not more effectively stopping Hort from falling, or by not getting to him in time to heal him.

As she forced herself to look up at Davion, gradually raising her eyes upward over his robes until she locked her sight with his, she held her breath for a moment while she observed him. The pain she detected radiating off of him, which was also

CHAPTER 38

plain as day upon his face, was excruciating, and she wished she knew how to comfort him.

"We are preparing to leave for Mira shortly," she told him stoically, stifling her feelings.

He fidgeted with the helm in his hands, averting his gaze from her for a moment, and replied, "I see. I suppose I better go ready Helna then."

"That won't be necessary," Laila said.

Peering back up at her with a raised eyebrow, he asked, "And why's that?"

Laila gave him a skewed smile as she told him, "Because you will not be riding Helna. You will be riding Gothäzer."

The human's mouth gaped open in disbelief as he glanced over to his Red in the distance by the rest of the group. His heart jumped a little in his chest as the dragon nodded at him, sending him thoughts of confirmation. Despite that, he suddenly appeared sullen again and shook his head. "And what about Orbek and Helna? I can't leave Helna. He gave her to me. I can't leave either of them."

Upon seeing tears welling again in Davion's tired eyes, she swiftly stepped toward him to grab his hands that were still fondling the helmet. Misreading, Davion opened his arms, stepping forward, and wrapped her in an embrace. At first, the elf maiden was taken aback, but then reciprocated, closing her arms back around him comfortingly.

"You don't have to," Laila told him.

Overcome with a feeling of loneliness, Davion held on tightly to Laila, seeking solace as he buried his face in the softness of her hair. He was no longer concerned with the watchful eyes of the dark elf, wishing he never had to let her go.

While rubbing her hands soothingly up and down his back, Laila no longer felt the wedge and distrust that had been between them. She only felt her caring and love for him as she explained, "The dragons will take the mounts as far as Mira to stable until we complete the quest. But with Aeris preparing her army, we will need the speed of the dragons."

Relieved about Helna and Orbek, he nodded while hesitantly releasing her and wiping his face with the back of his sleeve. He stared at her for a moment, searching her eyes for their shared connection, needing to reignite that spark of hope he continued to cling to.

As her crystal-blue eyes sparkled back at him, he said simply, "Okay."

He forced a pained smile, looking upon her with fond, glistening eyes. As he tenderly brushed a lock of her golden hair from her cheek, he continued, "So, what are we waiting for?"

Davion wasn't ready to be moving on so quickly, but he was aware that they had little choice anymore.

Laila smiled back warmly and replied, "Not a thing."

CHAPTER THIRTY-NINE

UNITED

*T*here was an eager anticipation resonating throughout the group of two-leggeds. Laila knew how much the dragons—aside from Astryma— were not keen on the idea of having the two-leggeds ride atop their backs, but they were all in agreement that it was the only logical solution to their predicament, and that would just have to do for now. Only with the speed of the dragons would they even stand a chance to cover the rest of Onis before Aeris could thwart their plans and cause them to fail in their quest.

With everyone ready, the dragons lowered themselves against the terrain as much as they were able, flexing out a leg for their companions so they could hoist them up.

Laila noticed that Glondora's excitement had waned, and the dwarf was standing forlornly by her dragon. She recalled the last time Glondora had scaled onto the Blue's back, and her husband had to help her up. As she reached out her concern to Astryma, the Blue Dragon looked at Laila and sent back a mental nod.

The elf maiden rushed over to the dwarf and reached out to her. "Would you like a hand?" she asked.

With an appreciative nod, Glondora took Laila's outreached hand and walked with her over to Astryma's paw. From there, she climbed up onto the creature's foreleg and reached up her side. Laila clasped her hands together and crouched for the dwarf to step onto them, then, with her elven strength, lifted her up toward the dragon's back.

Huffing and hawing, Glondora crawled her way up and placed herself squarely atop the beautiful sapphire dragon, its backfins flattened for her comfort. "Well now," she said once settled, "this isna' so bad."

Then the dragon raised herself from the ground until she was standing solid on all fours, and Glondora held on for dear life, hollering as they moved. Once Astryma was still again, the dwarf chuckled, embarrassed, and pat her dragon, wondering why she had agreed to do it so readily. Without Hort there to give her strength, and the knowledge that they were about to be airborne, she was much more unnerved by the experience than when they had merely been preparing to swim across the sea.

Content to see Glondora established, Laila strode off to check on the others to see how they were managing. Nearing the high elf, she caught him looking at her oddly. "Is there something wrong, Salyaman?" she asked while approaching him.

The elf smiled at her, and Laila found it a little strange. It wasn't that his smile appeared more strange than any other smile. It was actually quite nice, happy even. The oddity was that it was on the lips of the stern elf prince, even though standing next to a dragon, which was truly a momentous event to see.

"Before we leave, I wanted to thank you, Lady Lailalanthelus Dula'Quoy," he told her wholeheartedly. "Serving you on this quest has been my greatest honor. To make history now as an elf and dragon come together to form a united pair is an unprecedented miracle and would never have been possible without you. Whatever is yet to come, I believe that you have already created change in this world for the better."

Falling to old habits, Laila wrapped her arms around Salyaman in a friendly embrace and said, "Thank you." To her surprise, he wrapped his arms back around her, holding her tightly for a moment before letting go.

The elf prince then gave a regal bow to the Omi Méa before turning to the powerful golden Earth Dragon. With cat-like reflexes, he effortlessly scaled the mountain before him and positioned himself almost naturally on the dragon's back.

Upon descrying her friend Davion experiencing a similar dilemma with his gigantic Red Fire Dragon as the dwarf had with Astryma, Laila strode over and joined the two of them next. "Would you like some help?" she asked as she approached.

The human was reaching up the side of Gothäzer rather lamely, and he huffed, turning to face her. "Do you have a ladder?" he asked her, smirking.

Laila was encouraged at his attempt at humor, seeing his spirits slightly lifted, even though she knew he was still full of pain from losing his uncle. With a playful smirk back at him, she replied, "Sort of." Then she raised her hand in his direction.

As his feet lifted off the ground, Davion began screaming at her, disliking the lack of control over his own body. His heart pounded in a panic as he floated up overtop of the dragon, flailing his arms and legs about.

"I still don't like this!" he exclaimed.

After she lowered him down gently and safely atop Gothäzer's back, he took a deep breath and clung to the dragon, contented to be back on something solid.

'You do realize that you are about to fly much higher and faster than that?' Gothäzer snidely pointed out.

'No, dragon,' he replied. 'You *will be flying much higher. I will be holding on with my eyes closed and imagining I am somewhere else completely.'*

The mighty Red rumbled a chortle at his human and replied, *'We shall see.'*

With Davion settled, Laila headed back to Turathyl and Nikolean, who were patiently waiting for her to join them.

"Ready, my love?" Nikolean asked her, greeting her return with a warm smile.

She smiled back at the dark elf while she approached the Silver Air Dragon. Before she could reach them, Laila was startled as her unicorn-elkah thrust herself between her and the others, neighing and rearing wildly. The mystical creature kicked her hooves dangerously close to the elf maiden's head, causing her to jump back in alarm.

"Anaksula!" *Whoa!* Nikolean yelled in Drow while rushing forward, ready to challenge the beast.

Raising her hand to halt Nikolean, Laila looked into the beautiful hybrid's eyes, perceiving a feeling of great distress emanating from her. "It's okay," she told Merimer, sending a mental reassurance to calm her. "They won't carry you. You are free now. You can go."

The elf maiden reached out to take her snout lovingly and say goodbye, her heart aching. She felt as though she were parting with a piece of herself. Yet, before she could touch her, Merimer abruptly yanked her head away from Laila's hands. The hybrid screeched as she reared again, sending the elf falling backward to the ground.

Instinctively grabbing his dagger, Nikolean headed for Merimer, but Laila raised her hand again, forcing him back with her mind.

"Send her away then, before she hurts you!" he called at her, frustrated.

CHAPTER 39

'Laila,' Turathyl said softly. 'Just force her aside while you hop on my back, and we shall leave. Merimer will be alright.'

As she got back to her feet, Laila sent the hybrid more calming thoughts and commands for her to settle. But when she went to take a step toward Turathyl, Merimer squealed, placing herself as a barrier between them again. Laila could sense in Merimer's mind that she was adamant not to let her pass and knew something was severely upsetting her that surpassed the thought of being parted from the elf maiden.

Despite the hybrid's disobedience, Laila wouldn't harm the creature in order to force her away. Instead, she raised her hands passively, sending a mental adherence to the unicorn-elkah's wishes, along with her warm affections. With a soft nicker, Merimer stopped her misbehavior and stepped toward the elf maiden. She lowered her head low for her to pat, and Laila stroked her friend's muzzle.

"My lady, just leave her," Nikolean urged.

"No." Laila shook her head. "I will ride with Merimer. She has already shown that she can match the Red's speed and likely won't be carried, and she has no intention of letting me leave her behind."

"Are you sure, my lady?" Nikolean asked trepidatiously. "Wouldn't it be safer if you were with us?"

After sending reassuring thoughts to Merimer, Laila stepped around her toward Nikolean and took his hands in hers. "I'm sorry, Niko, but it appears you will be making this flight without me. We will follow on land." Upon seeing the worry in his eyes, she added, "At least it isn't far to Mira. It will be over in a moment."

"I don't like this. This should be your flight if anyone's," he told her sincerely.

She stared up into his eyes and smiled. "I will be close, I promise. But this is how it must be."

He brushed some hair from her face, then leaned in and kissed her lovingly while holding her in an amorous embrace. As he looked back into her eyes, wishing he didn't have to go without her, he knew there would be no changing her mind. Sighing with disappointment, Nikolean nodded and gave her a tender kiss on her forehead. "As you wish."

After exchanging a last soft peck, Laila grinned while she watched him turn and flit facilely up onto Turathyl's back. Then, grabbing hold of Merimer, she mounted up and gave her a comforting pat.

It was a strange feeling seeing them all atop the dragons, the early afternoon sun warmly gleaming down on them. It had always been her dream to fly through the skies as one of the Ancients, observing the world below. Yet, she was strangely content nonetheless as she sat on the mystical unicorn-elkah, believing that was where she was meant to be.

"Canna' we jus' 'ave a quick practice flight first, get a feel fer each other?" Glondora hollered nervously to the others.

Laila could sense they were all experiencing the same nervousness being atop the mighty beasts and thought it was a great idea.

"Who'd like to take the first flight?" Laila asked the group.

Turathyl raised her wings while Nikolean smiled down at Laila. But Davion would not let him steal that from him as well.

Gothäzer immediately spread his mighty wings, sharing Davion's desires, and plunged them with haste towards the ground. While they lifted off into the air, Davion took deep breaths, trying to let go of his fears.

Turathyl and Nikolean stood down with good grace, and everyone squinted against the sun as their eyes fixed on the heightening Red and his rider.

CHAPTER 39

Davion's heart was throbbing intensely with fear and excitement as he watched the ground drift away from him and felt the wind whipping fiercely across his face. He held tight to the quills on the dragon's back, tensing every time the dragon's weight shifted. Albeit, after only a brief moment, Davion smiled with elation as he began to experience a strange new connection to the beast beneath him, feeling the immense strength and power of the mighty dragon like an extension of himself. It wasn't long before he could predict his movements, adjusting his posture, moving in unison with the dragon as a single entity soaring through the sky.

Even though he held no anger in that pivotal moment, and all his feelings of despair had temporarily floated away on the wind striking across his face, he could sense his inner fire boiling up forcedly within, threatening to erupt. He tried desperately to take deep breaths, but was unable to quell the internal flames.

Gothäzer sensed the human's distress, but he was also experiencing a similar problem himself, and veered back toward the group so they could land. They both knew that something was seriously awry.

As they were coming back into view of the group, Davion abruptly screamed, unable to hold it in anymore, and his whole body expelled fire all around him. He watched frantically as the flames spread beyond him, and then he gasped when more fire seeped out from the dragon's very pores as well. The blaring fire was encompassing Gothäzer and Davion in their entirety, all the way to the tips of the dragon's wings and tail.

Below the glowing display, the group all held their breath as they looked in terror upon the monstrous flame-engulfed dragon and rider in the sky, unsure of what they should do or if Davion and Gothäzer were even alright. Laila knew Davion's powers had been growing, but she had no idea to what extent and wondered if he had caused it. She tried reaching out to Gothäzer, as did the three other dragons, but they were all being blocked by whatever was happening to the Red and the human.

The pyromancer gaped at the flames, confused, then closed his eyes as he threw back his head and screamed boisterously into the sky while the dragon echoed him. The human and dragon alike were completely aflame. Yet, they did not scream out in pain, but in excitement, for the flames were cool against their skin, and Davion was ecstatic with the power that was surging through his veins.

As he stretched his arms out wide, he opened his eyes and looked around. He was in shock again when nothing looked as it should. Everything appeared blurry and peculiar at first as he tried to adjust his sight with extreme vertigo. Then he realized his joining was even more significant with the dragon below him as he was no longer seeing with his human eyes. He could perceive the dragon's thoughts coalescing with his own, their sight shared, their bodies moving as one. Their very souls had merged, and their bonding was now complete.

Feeling as powerful as the dragon he was mounted upon, Davion wailed his excitement out in disbelief of what was happening to them. But, as he opened his mouth, he discovered that even their voices were as one when a dragon's elated roar bellowed out from between his human lips instead.

With the transformation completed, Davion's and Gothäzer's minds opened back up to what was going on around them, and they could hear all the concerned roars from below as Turathyl penetrated back into the Red's mind.

'What's happening?!' she finally broke through, Laila echoing her concern.

'It is the ritual of Pynar that united the two-leggeds with us. Come! Join us!' The Red boasted back to all the dragons, 'It did *not just make them stronger. I can feel it has given me greater power as well!'*

In unison, the great, powerful, fearsome ancient creatures raised their wings with eager excitement and began thrashing them forcefully, lifting as gracefully as feasibly possible in consideration of their passengers.

Laila watched in awe and fear as they ascended into the sky, ecstatic at the sight of the dragons and their riders. As they reached the pinnacle moment, a sudden storm began to materialize, lightning flashing and thunder crackling in the skies. Then, out from the storm, a bolt of lightning shot down and hit Turathyl directly.

Laila stopped breathing, and her heart pained in her chest, terrified for Nikolean. She watched as the energy from the bolt charged and flickered along Turathyl's scales, continuing to increase and expand.

'*Tury!*' she pressed. '*Are you both alright?!*' But just as they could not reach Gothäzer, she was blocked from the other dragons' minds as well.

Turathyl's scales glistened as the energy source stormed over her entire body, but Laila caught a glimpse of Nikolean's head, and he appeared to be unharmed. Even so, the same sparks of lightning were jolting around him as well. As the fire had engulfed Davion and the Red, Nikolean and Turathyl were equivalently filled with and covered in an electrical charge, sparking dangerously along their bodies.

When she glanced over at the other dragons, she recognized they were being affected in a similar fashion by the bonding. Masonel's and Salayaman's skin were as stone, flying with force through the sky, like a colossal animated statue. Astryma and Glondora seemed to have a layer of water covering their entire exterior like a thick lacquer finish but fluid in motion.

As their bondings completed, their essences joining as one, it dawned on Laila why Merimer would not let her ride with Nikolean and Turathyl. The ritual from the Ruins of Pynar had not yet been completed, not until they took their first flights. Now, they truly were "The United."

Upon completion of the ritual, the dragons' and riders' skins returned to normal, but they were still tied in their thoughts and sights. All were eager to discover what new possibilities awaited them with their new United Powers. The four Ancients then swooped down in turn, grabbing the mounts in their clutches before returning to the skies and veering north.

Without the need for a command, Merimer bolted into action, charging forward in the direction of the dragons. Laila was astounded by her ability to keep speed with those above, the wind whipping forcefully across their faces. The unicorn-elkah flew over the stony surface, her hooves barely making a sound as they scarcely grazed the terrain.

Watching her friends above in wonderment, Laila powered forward while the dragons with their United Riders filled the skies above her with exultant roars. She tilted her head back, raised both arms in the air, fists balled tight, and triumphantly belted out, "Ahh-wooooooo!"

Feeling more powerful than ever, the companions were primed for the rise against the Ancients.

R.E. DAVIES

To Be Continued...

THE DRAGONS

HERE ENDS PART TWO

OF

REIGN OF THE ANCIENTS

Thank You for Reading!
Please take a moment to leave a review online.
To continue the adventure, see below for the next book in the series.

THE ONIS CHRONICLES

R.E. DAVIES

REIGN OF THE ANCIENTS:

Part 1: The Prophecy
Part 2: The Dragons
Part 3: The Rising

A NEW ERA:

Veiled In Grace
Raised In Ruins

Visit
www.redaviesauthor.com
or scan QR Code
for current information

GLOSSARY

PRONUNCIATIONS

Aeris [AIR-iss]
Akayra [ah-KAY-rah]
Amillia [ah-MILL-ee-ah]
Annallee [ah-NAW-lee]
Astryma [ah-STREEM-ah]
Brakdrath [BRAK-drath]
Brilldessah [bril-DEH-sah]
Coryln [cor-ILLN]
Dailan [DAY-lin]
Davion [DAYV-ee-uhn]
Drakka [DRAH-kah]
Drorzyn [DROR-zin]
Duep Nordor [doo-EP nor-DOR]
Elkah [ELK-ah]
Fonzar [FON-zar]
Glondora [glon-DOR-ah]
Gortax [GOR-taks]
Gothäzer [GOTH-ah-zer]
Griton [GRYE-tin] (GRYE rhymes with try)

Haddilydd [HAD-ih-lid]
Handul [HAN-dul]
Helna [HEL-nah]
Hort [HORT]
Ignisar [IG-nih-sar]
Jayenne [jay-EN]
Kainüs [KAIN-us]
Kilgar [KILL-gar]
Kull Merzumar Den Fraül [KUL mer-zuh-MAR den FROWL]
Kyrash [KEE-rash]
Lailalanthelus (Laila) Dula'Quoy [lay-lah-LAN-thuh-luss (LAY-lah) doo-lah'COY]
Leonallan Dula'Quoy [lee-OH-nah-lan doo-lah'COY]
Lochlann [LOK-len]
Lupé Caelis [LOO-pay KAY-lis]
Má Lyndor [maw lin-DOR]
Masonel [MASS-on-el]
Merimer [MAIR-ih-mer]
Merla [MER-lah]
Mira [MEER-ah]
Nelgour Frostspine [NELL-gor FROST-spine]
Nikolean Den Faolin [nik-OH-lee-en den FAY-oh-lin]
Nikososo Den Faolin [nik-oh-SOH-zoh den FAY-oh-lin]
Notdras [NOT-drahss]
Okom [OHK-uhm]
Onis Caelis [OH-nis KAY-lis]
Orbek [OR-bek]
Othsuda Theora [oth-SOO-dah thee-OR-ah]
Rathca Saelethil Dula'Sintos [RATH-cah SAY-luh-thill doo-lah'SIN-tohs]
Roco [ROH-koh]
Rogg [ROG]
Salyaman Dula'Sintos [sal-YAM-in doo-lah'SIN-tohs]

Shakiera Nesu [shah-KEER-ah NEE-soo]
Silex [SYE-leks] (SYE rhymes with my)
Terus [TAIR-us]
Thas Duar Moran [thas dew-AR mor-AN]
Thornton [THORN-tin]
Turathyl [tur-AH-thul]

ANCIENT LANGUAGE

caelis [KAY-lis] — mother
halvah [HAL-vah] — hello
lupé [LOO-pay] — wolf
méa [MEE-ah] — spirit
mow [MOW] — must
nied [nee-EHD] — heal
omi [OH-mee] — great
onis [OH-nis] — the one
pavula [pa-VOO-la] — child
pynar [PEYE-nar] — united

DROW LANGUAGE

anaksula [a-NAK-soo-la] — whoa-there/settle down
akahn [ah-CAHN] — hand
att [AT] — the
chürra [CHEW-rah] — flows within
den [DEN] — of / high ranking or honored family title
edüner(z) [ED-oo-ner(z)] — friend(s)
eis [EES] — they
ëit [EET] — he
ëita [EET-ah] — father
ëlla [ELL-ah] — all

gah [GAH] — think/believe
gaht [GAT] — thought/believed
hiym [HEYE-em] — I/me
hunna [HUH-nah] — hello
ir [EER] — we
ise [ICE] — you
jernam [JAIR-num] — each other
ket/ketta [KET]/[KET-ah] — no/not
kon [KON] — that
lafett [lah-FET] — fear
liet [LEE-et] — (a) part
moén [MOH-en] — like
myvern [MY-vern] — dead
naëm [NAY-em] — do
ni [NEE] — is
nid [NID] — are
niyalum [NEYE-yah-lum] — lightning
ra [RAH] — with
rashukk [RAH-shuk] — a curse when being caught off guard
revvük [rev-VUHK] — crazy (mad with insanity)
taggürrah [tah-GOO-rah] — commander
tös [TAWSS] — stop
vintay [VIN-tay] — charge
waras [WAIR-ass] — water

DWARVEN LANGUAGE

aise [AYSS] — in
baccat [BAH-cat] — a curse
barden cake [BAR-din cayk] — a very sweet dwarven cake
blastit [BLAST-it] — damned/darn it
borghyn (ghyn) [BOR-ghine] — goodbye (bye)
cabi [CAB-ee] — cave

draikuhn (draiky) [DRAKE-uhn] — dragon (draggy)
dumbest thing I 'ad tickle me ears — slang, dumbest thing I've heard
geil [GAIL] — let
Ignisar's lair — as slang, means the equivalent of "Hell"
laiden [LAY-den] — lady
muk [MUK] — false
narda [NAR-dah] — crystal
nuhd [NUD] — us
okullo dung — slang, bull crap
shut yer pie hole — slang, be quiet
tardub [TAR-dub] — scoundrel
tickled under one's beard — slang, very happy
what a load o' okullo dung — slang, what a load of crap
ye got dragon's fire in yer britches? — slang, you mad about something?
ye look lower than a basalure's belly — slang, you look glum

ELVEN LANGUAGE

Note: "r" before any vowel is pronounced similar to a rolled "r" but sounds more like an "rd" by tapping the tongue to the roof of the mouth.

ageeran [AH-gee-ran] — water source object
diascing [di-ah-SING] — splash
Dula' [DOO-la] — Lord/Lady/Royal
énaht [EE-naht] — wave
énim [EE-nim] — water
ferétsa [fair-EE-tzah] — freeze
ferostya [fair-AWSS-tya] — ice
helna [HEL-na] — horse

illioso [ill-ee-OH-soh] — ignite
lacarté [la-CAR-tay] — bolt
lacassayra [lah-kah-SAY-rah] — multi-bolt
luminas [LOOM-ih-nas] — illuminate
mornder [MORN-der] — death
norn [nORn] — black
Norn Mornder [nORn MORN-der] — Black Death (a spirit
    stone)
ominus [OM-ih-nus] — fire
Ranchetal [RAN-cheh-tal] — Elven ritual display of powers
Rathca [RATH-ca] — Ruler/Prince
unasceiry [OO-na-sair-ee] — orb of death

BESTIARY

elkah [EL-kah]
> A beautiful hoofed creature, slightly taller than a horse, with long slender legs and silky-white fur with brown speckles. They have long, thick red antlers protruding up high from strong but dainty heads, big doe-brown eyes, brown nose and lips. They are used as mounts by the elves.

okullo [OH-kul-oh]
> A favorite mount among the dwarves due to their short and sturdy stature. They are about half the height of a typical horse with buffalo-style horns lying on their heads, a long-bearded chin, and furry hind legs. Their front legs and all four feet are striped black and white like a zebra, and they have white patches around their eyes, while the rest of their head and body is a deep, dark brown. They aren't quite as fast as a horse but are stronger and superior in battles.

orc [ORK]

Large monstrous humanoid creatures over eight feet tall, bulging with a combination of fat and muscle. They have rounded heads with small beady yellow eyes, and tusks that jutt out from their muzzles. Their skin is grayish-brown, and they wear tattered animal-skin loincloths. There are no orc caster classes like with their troll cousins. Very vicious, ruthless, and strong, but also dimwitted. Cannibals.

pex [PEKS]

A small fairy-type creature tied to the earth spirit. They have large and solid cobalt-blue eyes, a long tail, translucent blue and gold wings, sharp-fanged teeth, and aqua-blue skin with decorative pink lines over its body. Instead of clothes, they are concealed modestly with white, pink-streaked fur. Atop both their heads and at the tips of their tails are white and pink tufts of fur shaped like raindrops.

rock fiend [ROK feend]

An aggressive creature found primarily in Silex Valley. They are muddy beige color with glassy-yellow eyes, have razor-sharp claws, teeth, and long tails with spiked clubs at the tips. A flexed razor mane cascades down their firm backs.

sorechon [SORE-kon]

Robust beasts with gray, thick-armored hides that live in the northern territory near the Gorén Mountains. They have horns protruding tandemly from their muzzles to their scalps, a large upper torso, razor-sharp claws, and a loose jaw hanging with jagged teeth and long slobbery tongues. Their hind end is less robust and more exposed, sporting a stubbed-tail with a tuft of hair at the tip.

treant [TRENT]

Spiritual beings resembling the trees of the forests where they live. Treants are strong and powerful and can move over the earth by separating their trunks into perceived legs. They have roots that come out of the ground as they move across it and can use those roots as weapons as well as their branches. Their faces are camouflaged in their bark, only appearing when they wish.

troll [TROHL]

Tall and lanky humanoids with a broad upper torso and green skin. Intelligence to create weapons from tree branches and wear animal skins to protect their flesh. Possess a few magic classes, such as shamans. Hide mainly in the forests, emerging primarily to plunder cities or loot travelers.

wimblebuck [WIM-bul-buk]

Fat and stoutly cousins to the humans' cattle, similar to a small bison. Found in the Southeast Region.

wurryn [WUR-in]

A dark-blue creature approximately half the size of an okullo with matted fur and pointed ears. Hunted for food.

To hear Away on a Journey on youtube.com go to:
https://youtu.be/RX0SvcFEzwk

AWAY ON A JOURNEY

Written for the novel "The Onis Chronicles, Reign of the Ancients: Part 2"

RE DAVIES

2

one glor-ious day. Ye are a——way, away on a jour-ney, where the

fields be lush and green. The flo-wers bloom, the skies are clear. Tis al-right,

love, have no fear. Ye're hea-din' home. Ye're hea——din' home.

Fol-low the light up to the moons. Ye're hea-din' home. Ye're hea-

-din' home. Trust, my dar-lin', I'll be there soon. Trust, my dar-lin', I'll be

there soon.

THE DRAGONS

ABOUT THE AUTHOR

R.E. Davies is the Best Selling Author of The Onis Chronicles. After embarking on her own journey in 2001, she left her home in Canada to follow her heart and is now a Canadian-American living in Florida. Since then, she has completed her Bachelor's Degree, found and married her other half, and had five incredible children. In 2012, all her plans changed with the birth of her first son. He was born with a rare genetic disorder called Cornelia de Lange Syndrome (CdLS,) severely affecting both his mind and body. In addition to her adventures of learning how to be a special needs mom, she has also battled and won against both thyroid and skin cancer, motivating her to cherish every day she has with her family. No matter where fate took her throughout life's adventures, there has always been one thing that she could never move past; writing. She began writing as early as elementary school when she wrote and directed her first play to perform for her classmates. Whether it was plays, poems, short stories, novels, or songs, she has always loved sharing her stories and fantastical lands with those she loved and is now even more excited to share those tales with others.

Connect with R.E. Davies (@REDaviesAuthor) on Facebook or via her website (www.redaviesauthor.com) for news about upcoming books, links to songs, maps, and other great information!

ACKNOWLEDGEMENTS

Without the love, support, and patience (mostly) of my husband, this installment of Reign of the Ancients could have taken another 25 years to achieve—should I be so lucky to see that many more! So I am very thankful for all he has done to help give me the ability to trek forward on this quest. My children have encouraged and inspired me through this journey so far, and I can only pray that they feel the same about me, watching as I pursue my passion.

To my parents, you have continued to support my dreams, and your love and encouragement have not gone without notice. This has been such an exciting opportunity and learning experience for me and continues to be so! I'm proud to have such great parents to share this journey of mine with.

To my proofers, I think those of you that also proofed "Part 1: The Prophecy" can agree that I'm getting better at this writing thing! I'm glad you didn't find it quite as painful to read the first draft this time around. A special 'cheers' to my step-dad, Richard; your help has once again been priceless during this process, and I can't thank you enough. To Patricia Hausner, your aid and keen eye have been very much appreciated, and I have found your input and confidence in my tales to be delightfully uplifting! To my new friend from Ireland, Eylene Kissane, it has been so wonderful getting to know my first "fan"—

the first reader to reach out to me. I am truly grateful for your friendship, for your feedback on proofing this installment, and for opening my eyes to a whole new audience in the UK that hadn't yet occurred to me. I may just have to plan a book signing tour overseas!

Thank you, of course, to all my readers! I have been so thrilled by the positive feedback, and it has helped to push me forward so that I can keep pulling you back into the land of Onis with me! I hope to see you there again soon with "Reign of the Ancients - Part 3: The Rising"!

Thank you all SO much, from the bottom of my heart!

Printed in Great Britain
by Amazon